D-NOTICE

D-NOTICE

BILL WALKER

DeLarge books

2021

*To my late friend, Sean Barry Weske,
whose marvelous tale fired my imagination...*

THE SON: 1951

1

The boy stared at his father's effects, his eyes wide with fascination, his nose wrinkling at the pungent odor of naphtha. He'd been told a hundred times to stay out of the attic, could hear his mother's admonishments that it "...was not the proper place for a boy to play...." But her stern words could not overcome the boy's innate curiosity.

And now the dusty old steamer trunk lay open, its sand-colored exterior battle-scarred and dented, the stenciled name barely visible on its lid:

WD

MAJ. MICHAEL THORLEY

He knew the contents of the trunk by heart: On top lay the khaki blouse of his father's uniform, the single crown on each epaulet denoting his rank. It was devoid of any other markings. Below the blouse lay the pants, leggings, and boots. At the bottom of the trunk sat his "Tommy" helmet, leather "Sam Brown belt," and a small automatic pistol, its blue-black finish gleaming dully. Instinctively, the boy reached for it and held it in his small hand, marveling at its weight. Looking closer, he spied the name, *Carl Walther*, etched into the barrel slide.

Curling his hand around the gun's Bakelite grip, he aimed it toward the rough-hewn beams overhead and squeezed the trigger. It stuck. A sudden chill slid up his spine then, as if the temperature had plunged, and he quickly replaced the pistol next to a shiny German Pilot/Observer's badge.

He turned his attention to a beloved relic, a leather-covered box with "Military Cross" stamped in gold on the lid.

Smiling, the boy reached for the medal, swung open the lid and stared in awe at the silver cross with its four crowns at each tip, the royal cipher—*GR*—in the center. The ribbon felt silky smooth under his ten-year-old fingers, its alternating stripes of white/mauve/white, the one splash of color.

The boy replaced the medal with a reverence that belied his years and reached for the helmet and the Sam Brown belt. He put them on, as he'd done countless times before, then stood. He turned to a tailor's dummy enshrouded in a lacy wedding gown, the fabric yellowed with age.

The sun came out from behind a cloud, shooting shafts of golden afternoon light through the one oval window, making the dusty room glow like Aladdin's cave.

Snapping his heels together, the boy brought his hand up in a salute, his palm facing outwards, his hand bouncing slightly as it hovered over his brow. He stared at the dummy. "Lieutenant Michael Thorley, Jr., reporting as ordered, SIR!"

The dummy remained silent.

The boy dropped the salute sharply to his side and nodded. "Very good, sir, at once."

Hefting an imaginary rifle, he began to march around the attic, executing a Manual of Arms. He threaded his way through boxes of old books and newspapers with headlines that screamed: "MONTY TROUNCES THE DESERT FOX!" and "HITLER IS KAPUT!" He marched past a crate filled with his old toys, ignoring his once treasured clown doll, watching him now with its one remaining eye. The boy did an about turn and pretended to thrust a bayonet at an ancient Victrola, its brass horn now dulled and flecked with spots of corrosion.

"Die, Nazi bastard!"

Suddenly somber, he returned to the trunk and replaced the belt and the helmet exactly as he found them, and then lifted out an old photograph, browned and ragged at the edges. It showed a young man seated in the passenger side of a Jeep, his eyes staring out past the camera, his expression one of sadness.

"What happened, Dad?" the boy whispered, his index finger tracing the shape of the face in the photograph. "What bloody happened?"

Sighing, the boy returned the photo to its rightful place and reached for the trunk's lid. It was time to go; his mother would be returning from her daily shopping any moment, and he wanted to be safely downstairs engrossed in his homework.

It was then that he noticed the slight bulge in the gaily colored paper lining the lid. Was something under there, or was it just a fault in the glue allowing the paper to bubble up in one spot?

Now more curious than ever, the boy reached forward, his slender fingers only inches away from the tell-tale bulge.

A door slammed downstairs.

"Michael? Where are you, dear?"

He slapped the lid closed, snapped the clasps, and heaved it off the floor with a grunt, his muscles straining.

"Michael?" his mother called out, closer now. "Are you up in the attic? You know how I feel about that. I'd better not find you into your father's things again, or I shall put them under lock and key!"

With one last look to see that everything was back in its proper place, the boy scampered down the stairs, leaving the ghost of his father and his unanswered questions behind.

THE FATHER:
1941

2

Michael Thorley slipped the heavy Bakelite headphones from his ears, feeling the rush of cooler air play across his lobes, making them tingle like the jab of a thousand tiny needles. He sighed, rubbed his tired, burning eyes with the thumb and forefinger of one hand while the other, holding a pencil, completed the translation in swift short strokes.

He'd just spent the last eight hours glued to an obscure radio station in Upper Silesia listening to farm reports droned in a stentorian monotone extolling the latest wheat and potato harvests. And it was up to him to take down every blasted word. Now that the farm reports had ended, the station would play Wagner's Ring Cycle opera for the rest of the evening—all eight hours of it. It was time to pack it in.

Disgusted, Thorley threw the pencil onto the table next to the receiver and scanned the room through the omnipresent haze of tobacco smoke, wondering just what he'd done to deserve this stygian fate.

Barely ten by ten, with cracked, yellowed plaster and mahogany wainscoting scarred by years of neglect, the "Radio Room" was a rabbit warren squirreled away in the northeast corner of the Foreign Office building. It was home to five other men, each with his own receiver and headphones, listening intently while scribbling away on a pad of what they laughingly called paper: unlined straw-colored foolscap, hole-punched on one edge.

The irony was that no more than five stories below him lay the busiest address in London. At all hours of the day, one could get a bird's-eye view of history being made down there at Number 10 Downing Street, where Churchill and his cabinet constantly came and went, busily conducting the war.

And here he was listening to blather. What he wouldn't give to sit in just one of those meetings.

Snapping out of his reverie, Thorley mentally transformed the loops and whorls of the Pitman shorthand into the King's English.

Boring. It was all so bloody boring he wanted to scream. And yet it was vital. His superiors—the old men who dressed in tweeds or expensive Savile Row suits and spoke of gardens and pheasant hunting in the measured tones of Oxford and Cambridge—wanted to know every detail of the German harvest. How better to know the state of the enemy's fighting man, than to know if he was going to have a full belly the following winter. And there was the rub.

It was vitally important, yet utterly without challenge. A second-year language student could have done the work, but not without the airtight security clearance Thorley possessed. And then again, someone had to listen to all the minutiae, the drivel that came out of Hitler's Third Reich, for amongst the dross might lay that inestimable pearl of truth that would mean the difference between victory...or utter disaster.

Shaking his head, Thorley gathered up the last of his translations. "You all right, Michael?"

Thorley looked up and saw that the man next to him had his headphones off and was gazing at him with an expression consisting of equal parts concern and curiosity.

Cursed with a head of blazing red hair and a mass of freckles that covered every inch of his gangling six-foot frame, Roger Hornsby had the look of an innocent schoolboy. It was a look that engendered immediate trust, and had, on more than one occasion, engendered members of the opposite sex right into bed.

"I'm sorry, did you say something?" Michael asked, frowning at something on his pad. He erased one of the characters and replaced it with one very similar, then glanced at Roger.

Roger lifted a ginger eyebrow, his face splitting into a wry grin. "I asked you if you were all right. You look a bit knackered."

Thorley nodded and stood, grabbing up his foolscap. "That's the word for it," he said, placing the headphones on the chair for the next listener. "I've bloody well had it."

"Then Dr. Roger suggests that we raise a pint or two across the way. My treat."

"Now *that* is an occasion," Michael said, smiling for the first time. "Unfortunately, I must miss that epochal moment. Lillian's making a bit of tinned beef this evening."

"Good Lord, where on earth did she scare that up?"

Michael shrugged his narrow shoulders, the glint of humor still in his eyes. "She won't say. Claims it's a state secret."

"My missus is always prattling on about such things, too. Ah, well, to wives and secrets, then," Roger said, hoisting an imaginary glass. "I suppose now I'll have to find some female companionship, instead of your sterling company."

Michael laughed. "You're a rotter, Hornsby, a real rotter."

"Count on it, old boy," Roger said, a sly grin crinkling the corners of his eyes.

Michael nodded to the others, grabbed his Trilby hat and gas mask box off the coat stand, and walked down the narrow hall until he reached the typists' room, where he handed off his sheaf of papers to an owlish girl with milk-bottle glasses. "Just the usual," he said.

The girl shrugged, placed the papers on the table next to her and immediately began clacking away on her Underwood, her expression one of grim determination.

From the typists' room, Thorley took the stairs to the ground floor and was almost out the door when one of the Wrens came running. "Mr. Thorley, sir, please wait!"

Thorley turned, reluctantly. "Yes?"

The girl, a young slip of a thing with a mousy brown pageboy and bright red lipstick, thrust an envelope into his hands. Thorley started to shove it into his coat pocket.

"I'm sorry, sir, but you're to read it straightaway."

Sighing again, Thorley tore open the plain buff envelope and unfolded a single sheet of thick, creamy vellum. The name engraved at the top that brought him up short, as well as the twenty terse words written in a hasty angular script:

Your presence is required in the office of the Director at 54 Broadway Buildings, St. James's, at precisely 1900 hours, Sir Basil.

Thorley's pulse quickened, and a lone trickle of sweat began the long slow journey down his spine. He was being asked, no—*ordered* to appear at the headquarters of MI6, the arm of Britain's Secret Service responsible for intelligence gathering outside Britain's borders. And while his work as a translator for the Foreign Office touched upon MI6's territory, there was no reason for them to be calling him in. Unless, somehow, he'd failed them, botched up a translation. Sometimes one word could change the whole meaning of a sentence, cast a more ominous light on something one would at first think to be an innocent statement. Or, as with troop movements, that one word could mean the difference between knowing the true whereabouts of a certain Panzer division, or where a *Luftwaffe* squadron was based. The German language could be capricious in that way. Something was wrong and they were probably going to pack him off to the Outer Hebrides, Scapa Flow, or some other godforsaken place where he could do little harm, and less good. The thought of that possibility drove his spirits into the depths of despair, for as much as the work bored him at times, it made him feel vital—needed.

But as quickly as the depression descended on him, it lifted when he realized that a transfer would come in the form of a personal visit by his superior, Sir Basil Ravenhurst, during regular hours. Sir Basil, as fair-minded a man as any he had ever worked for, would take him aside and, with solemn regret, tell him that his services were needed elsewhere. Thorley had seen it happen more than once. And even if that were the case, he could always resign and go back to his old post as a Professor of European Languages at Balliol College. Would that be such a bad thing? And suddenly he knew that it would, for he'd spent far too much time there to go back to the cobwebbed halls of Oxford.

"Sir?"

Thorley tore his eyes from the note and glanced up at the Wren. She had an expectant look on her round unlined face.

He started to speak, to ask her what it was all about, but he swallowed the words, knowing it was useless. Everyone tended his own garden; it was an unwritten and unspoken law every bit as sacred as those debated in the Houses of Parliament. It was the reason Thorley had not asked Roger what station he'd been listening to—it wasn't cricket, as some would say. Thorley handed back the note.

"Tell Sir Basil I'll be there," he said.

"Very good, sir." The Wren spun around and headed back the

way she'd come, the heels of her sensible shoes clacking across the parquet flooring.

It never ends, Thorley thought, taking off his hat. The meeting would convene in exactly one hour, which meant he had no time to go home, and the special dinner Lillian was preparing would now go to waste.

Tramping back up the stairs, he walked into an empty office, picked up the phone, and dialed: BRIxton-1631.

"Hello?"

Her voice caressed his ear like warm velvet, in a way that always made his mouth go dry. This time it only made him feel guilty.

He and Lillian had only been married a year. She'd swept into the room at a Foreign Office party on the arm of a Flight Lieutenant and had abandoned the poor sod the instant their eyes met across that smoke-filled room. Until that singular blinding moment, Thorley had always pooh-poohed the idea of love at first sight, thought it the stuff of Hollywood claptrap. And, yet, one look into Lillian Dudley's hazel eyes and Thorley was lost.

They'd spent the entire evening together pouring out their life stories: his in sheltered academia, hers spent in orphanages and foster homes, and not even the air raid that drove the party into the basement shelter could stanch the tide of romance. He noted, with no small irony, that it now seemed as if they spent more time apart than together.

"It's me, love."

He heard her sharp intake of breath. "Dear God, Michael, where are you? Dinner's almost on."

"I'm still here, something's come up. Sir Basil's ordered me to a meeting at MI6 in about an hour. Knowing those chaps, it could last quite a while."

"That sounds serious," she said, her voice edged with concern.

"It's always serious. I just wish I'd left thirty seconds earlier. Are you cross with me?"

"No," she said. "Just disappointed. I wanted this evening to be special."

"Every evening's special with you."

"You always know how to make it all right," she said.

"And you're always the trooper."

"Oh, Michael," she said, the disappointment in her voice becoming palpable. "Will you at least have a sandwich while you're out?"

"I will, sweetheart. Got to go. Love you. And sorry about dinner."

He replaced the phone in its cradle and glanced at the large clock hanging on the far wall. Half past six.

He'd have just enough time to walk it.

Returning to the ground floor, he put on his hat, grabbed his cardboard box and rushed out the door.

Outside, the sun hung just above the spires of Westminster Abbey, that venerable sepulcher of Kings and Queens, sparking off red-gold reflections that dazzled the eye and stirred the soul. Thorley shivered, feeling the cool breeze that blew in off the Thames. It was early August, and yet it still felt as if winter lurked in the shadows.

Turning up his collar, Thorley turned south on Whitehall, heading toward Parliament Square a block away.

The early evening crowds thickened as he crossed King Charles Street and passed in front of the Treasury. On his left, looking like some giant medieval toad, sat the red-bricked, turreted building that was Scotland Yard, headquarters of London's world-famous police force.

D-NOTICE

Normally, Thorley felt a certain irrational sense of security seeing it there as he passed it day after day. Now, he found himself growing more anxious, turning the summons over in his mind as a cat would play with a dead mouse.

Reaching the square, Thorley turned west into Great George Street, fighting through a phalanx of grim-faced clerks determined to reach the tube station on the Embankment.

And everywhere he looked Thorley saw uniforms.

Army. Navy. RAF.

Proud men, vitally committed to their nation's survival, men whose eyes gleamed with danger and purpose, their girlfriends clinging tight to their arms, breathless and heady with romance.

These men exuded a decisive power and it made Thorley self-conscious. For even though he was every bit as committed to England's survival—a commitment that no one who knew him would ever question—he nevertheless felt inadequate, as if he were still an outsider.

Moments later, he passed into Storey's Gate and then right into Old Queen Street. Here the crowds dwindled to the occasional passerby.

Sensing that time was growing short, he quickened his pace, turned onto a narrow carriageway that widened into Dartmouth Street, then doglegged into Broadway.

Moments later he stood in front of number 54.

It was an unprepossessing group of terraced houses in the ubiquitous Georgian style so common in the mid-to-late-eighteenth century when most of the Westminster area was built, and it was for precisely this reason, as well as its proximity to the center of power that made it the perfect choice for the Secret Intelligence Service, better known as MI6.

BILL WALKER

Organized in 1909 as the Foreign Section of the Secret Service Bureau, its main purpose was to neutralize the effectiveness of foreign agents working on British soil, primarily German agents sent in by Kaiser Wilhelm II. In those days it was run with a benevolent iron hand by Sir Mansfield Cumming, a former Captain in His Majesty's Navy. By 1922, it had become the SIS, or Secret Intelligence Service, and operated under its own mandate to ferret out and destroy threats to British interests *wherever* they might be found. Cumming himself had recently retired, yet his presence remained tangible. His successor signed all documents as Cumming did: with the moniker "C".

Glancing once more at his wristwatch, Thorley steeled his nerves and walked into number 54 through the massive glass and wrought iron door, the glass now crisscrossed by adhesive paper strips to reduce the dangers of flying glass in case of bomb blasts. It was one more reminder that life in Britain had changed for the duration.

Inside, Thorley found himself in a tiny dimly lit foyer of dark paneled wood that smelled of oil soap and furniture polish. It was devoid of any ornamentation, save for the portraits of several nameless seventeenth century nobles lining the walls, their catlike eyes gazing out of faces draped with long powdered wigs and haughty disdain.

Beyond the portraits and the sumptuous Persian throw rug that covered the walkway sat a plain utilitarian desk that belied the old-world look of the building, as did the straitlaced naval officer perched behind it. The boy, for that is what he appeared to be in his tidy Lieutenant's uniform, had the well-scrubbed look that one saw so often on the children of the privileged. Thorley approached, and was about to speak when the young officer opened a fat ledger bound in red Morocco leather and pushed it toward him. He then handed Thorley a heavy Monte Blanc fountain pen.

"Please sign in, sir."

Thorley scrawled his name on the next empty line and handed back the pen, noting that his name lay directly under that of Sir Basil's. The officer glanced at the ledger and nodded. Thorley could almost hear the boy's mind counting off a mental checklist.

"Yes, sir, Mr. Thorley. You're expected."

He motioned to a Military Policeman Thorley hadn't noticed before. The man moved forward and took a position that placed him squarely between Thorley and the stairs. He watched Thorley with a flat beady-eyed stare that betrayed not the slightest emotion. It made Thorley even more nervous.

"The Director's office is on the fourth floor on the Broadway side," the Lieutenant said, breaking into Thorley's thoughts, "Sergeant Hutchins will escort you. Please do not venture onto any of the other floors, and do not speak to anyone you may meet in passing. Is that clear?"

Thorley noticed a tiny smirk on the Lieutenant's face. Was it mockery, contempt? He couldn't be sure, but it was enough to make him forget his fear for the moment.

"Quite clear," Thorley said, his voice tight with annoyance.

"You may proceed. And please be so good as to hang your hat and gas mask over there." He pointed to a coat stand by the stairs.

Keeping his face neutral, Thorley mumbled his thanks and moved toward the stairs, placing his things on the coat stand as he passed. The military policeman dogged his heels. He knew the lieutenant was still watching him, could feel his eyes probing; and he realized that even though the boy had been the essence of courtesy, his eyes had been the same as those he'd seen in the ancient portraits: cold...suspicious...dead....

Grabbing the carved oak railing, Thorley mounted the stairs, his mind turning uneasy somersaults.

3

Lillian tried very hard not to cry. It was a losing battle. The tears came, lapping out of her eyes like too much tea poured into a cup too small. They ran down her face and soaked into the bodice of her special dress, the one she'd purchased just for this evening. It was silk and would probably be ruined.

She had it all planned: the dinner of tinned beef prepared as Beef Wellington, along with the few fresh vegetables she'd managed to coax out of their meager garden, a pat of precious butter, candles, wine, the lace tablecloth. The perfect atmosphere for letting Michael know that he was to be a father. But instead of feeling joy, all she felt was dread, and the bitter taste of bile in her mouth.

She'd known about the baby for several weeks. And at first, Lillian wanted to die. Swearing the doctor to secrecy, she went home and said nothing to Michael, planning to go to a discreet doctor that Paul knew. Michael noticed something, of course, the dear man would, but she put it all down to a lack of sleep and a persistent case of anemia. But as the days turned into weeks, Lillian realized she wanted the child very much, could feel it growing day by day, along with her love for this unborn being. She resolved to tell Michael at the first opportunity. But she didn't want to just spring it on him, he deserved better than that. Thus, she had concocted this special meal, telling him that it was just something she wanted to do. And she loved him all the more for not questioning her further.

And that left Paul.

They'd been lovers before she'd met Michael, and she'd kept the affair going even after it was clear that Michael meant far more to her. Yet, she couldn't break away from Paul. Could not cut ties that bound her to him body and soul, for if it were not for Paul her life would be far different and far darker.

Crying anew, she went to the phone with the intention of telling Paul the truth, that she wanted her life back and that it was Michael's child, not his, but she couldn't bring herself to do it.

God might forgive her for loving two men, but she could never bring herself to kill her child. She'd sooner kill herself along with it. It would amount to the same thing.

Wiping her tears, Lillian blew out the candles and finished rinsing the dishes. Afterward, she sat by the fire and tried to read the latest Agatha Christie, finding that she was reading the same words over and over. She glanced at the clock and saw that it was a quarter past seven. Michael would be at his meeting, now, she thought. And might not be home for hours.

Almost as if someone threw a switch inside her body, images of Paul began to flood her mind. Her heart pounded and a warmth spread through her loins that made her gasp, as Paul's strong arms seemed to grip her in one of his all-encompassing embraces.

"God help me," she pleaded.

Lillian marched toward the phone, feeling much like a condemned man on his way to the gallows, picked up the receiver and dialed. She listened to it ring several times, praying that he would be out, yet hoping that he would answer. A moment later he did.

"I knew it would be you," he said, his mellifluous accent making his rich baritone sound all the more exotic and thrilling.

HANG UP! her mind screamed.

"P—Paul, I—"

"Ssssh, quiet, my love. Everything will be all right. Now tell me what's wrong."

"Michael's been called to a late meeting, and I guess I was feeling lonely."

"Will he be long?"

"Yes, he said he would."

"Come to me, then. I want to see you."

"You know I can't—"

"You must come."

It was useless to argue with him. In the end she would succumb, as she always had.

"Where?" she said, resigned.

"I'll send my car. Wear something nice."

"I already am," she said, choking back the tears again.

"That's my Ninot—my girl. I can't wait to see you."

They hung up and Lillian went into the bedroom to freshen up her makeup. Unfortunately, nothing she could do with her dwindling supply of Max Factor could hide the guilt and self-loathing etched into the planes of her aristocratic face. Later, she stood watching out the front window until the long black Daimler with its CD plate pulled up in front of the house. With one last look at the table with its lace tablecloth, she walked out into the night and into the arms of a man to whom she was inextricably bound, a bond that would only end when one of them was dead.

4

With each step up those winding stairs, Thorley's frayed nerves tightened an invisible band around his chest, making him more and more anxious. His throat had a dry coppery taste, as if he'd been running for miles and his head throbbed with every heartbeat.

Reaching the fourth floor, Thorley noted it was much the same as the other three, only here the old portraits alternated with framed prints of foxhunting scenes and brass sconces that sprouted from the walls every few feet, casting a weak amber light that did nothing to dispel the gloom. As for the Lieutenant's warning, he needn't have bothered. There was no one about, the only noise being the incessant chatter of a lone Teletype somewhere nearby.

The Director's office lay at the very end of the hall, the door leading into it resembling something out of a medieval castle: stout, secretive, impregnable. All it said was: Private.

Typical MI6.

No secrets would ever escape from behind a door like that, and once more Thorley had to fight an irrational impulse to turn and flee, as if he instinctively knew, somehow, there would be no turning back once he crossed that threshold.

He raised his hand and knocked. It was answered almost immediately by a callow-faced youth dressed in a somber pinstriped suit. The young man's lips creased into a chilly smile. "Come right in, Mr.

Thorley," he said, with the proper air of condescension. "They're waiting."

"Thank you."

Thorley walked past the young man and into the room. Spacious by anyone's standard and paneled in the same dark wood as the foyer and the hallway, it boasted floor to ceiling bookshelves rimming the entire room. The only parts of the room excepted were the bank of sash windows facing out onto Broadway, its heavy blackout curtains pulled back to let in the last rays of the dying sun, and the ornate mantled and grated fireplace. A fire blazed there now, casting its saffron glow onto the mahogany desk that dominated the room. The fire was wholly inappropriate, at least for Thorley, who'd begun to sweat.

Aside from the young man who'd answered the door, three other men occupied the office. Thorley recognized his superior, Sir Basil Ravenhurst standing by the mantel examining a petite Ming vase with all the intensity of an entomologist about to spear a prized specimen with a pin. Tall and razor thin, he boasted a full head of shocking white hair and a handlebar mustache to match under a sharp aquiline nose. Smoke swirled about his head emanating from his trademark Meerschaum, and he was dressed—as always—in crisply pressed trousers and navy-blue cardigan. He turned to face Thorley.

"Ahh, Thorley, good show. On time, as always. Please, sit down." He indicated a leather wingback chair. It was entirely too close to the fire, but Thorley took it, feeling the soft leather molding to his form with a whispered groan. He had to make an effort not to appear that he was slouching, adding to the litany of his discomforts.

Sir Basil turned to the two men sitting next to each other on the matching leather divan. "Allow me to introduce William Atwater, Director of MI6, and Peter MacIlvey of SOE."

Atwater, a florid faced man with sand-colored hair and a nervous twitch in his left eye, smiled and nodded. "Pleased I'm sure."

MacIlvey only nodded, his gray eyes boring holes through Thorley's head. Bald and pasty complexioned, and dressed in a dark blue double-breasted suit, he seemed more like a funeral director than an intelligence operative.

"Michael," Sir Basil continued, "we invited you here because we have a problem of a very delicate nature—"

"Sir, I haven't done anything wrong, have I?"

Sir Basil looked puzzled for a moment. "Good Lord, no! Why on earth would you think that?"

Thorley felt foolish. "Your note, it didn't really say anything. I—I assumed that one of my translations was faulty in some way...."

"Nonsense, old boy," Sir Basil said, "Your work is exemplary, absolutely top-notch."

"What Sir Basil is trying to say," Atwater interrupted, "is that we need your help."

"I'm still not convinced he's the man for the job," MacIlvey cut in, his dour expression deepening. "He's got no bloody field experience at all. Nothing."

Thorley glanced around the room. "Field experience?"

Sir Basil threw MacIlvey a dark glare and then turned to Thorley, his expression softening. "Michael, we've recently had a communication from the German forces in Finland. They're requesting that we send in an agent, someone who speaks fluent German. Apparently, they want no misunderstandings."

Thorley sat up straighter in his chair and leaned forward. "Are you telling me that you want to send me behind enemy lines? To Finland? Me?"

Atwater nodded. "That's exactly correct, Mr. Thorley."

"I don't like it," MacIlvey spat.

This man's sour attitude and his obvious antagonism made Thorley angry, enough to overcome his natural reticence in front of superiors. "And who are you, sir, if I may ask? I don't believe I've ever heard of SOE."

MacIlvey glared back at Thorley. "That's none of your business."

"You men asked me here, I believe it is."

Sir Basil chuckled and clapped MacIlvey on the knee. "Easy now, Pete. Thorley's right. The least we can do is tell him the truth." He turned to Michael. "SOE stands for Special Operations Executive and is charged with training and sending agents behind enemy lines, the purposes of which are manifold. The mission we wish you to undertake falls under Pete's jurisdiction, and he has the final authority on whomever we choose."

Thorley saw MacIlvey studying him with newfound interest and nodded. "Why me? Like Mr. MacIlvey said, I have no field experience. Why not use one of your own agents? Surely some of them can speak German as well as I."

"Quite so, Michael," Atwater replied. "The truth is the Germans specifically asked for someone who was, as they put it, clean, someone outside of our network. And as far as we're concerned, anyone we send will have his cover blown, anyway. His field career will be over."

"So, you might as well send in someone who's never had one to begin with."

"Exactly."

"Why should we trust them? They're the enemy!"

"Because, Mr. Thorley," MacIlvey interjected, "it is in our best interest in this case to honor their request."

"Still doesn't answer my question. Why me?"

Atwater rose to his feet and began to pace the length of the room. "Because you went to school in Germany, Michael. You know the culture. You know how they act—how they think. And because you speak the language without an accent, you'll be able to pass as a German if the need arises."

Thorley's eyes flicked over to Sir Basil, who watched him now as intently as MacIlvey. "If they know I'm British, why *would* I need to pass for German?"

"That's not important right now, Michael," Sir Basil said, re-lighting his Meerschaum. "What *is* important is that we have a man whom we can trust, a man who can see past any attempt to lie to us. Can you understand that?"

Thorley nodded.

"Of course," MacIlvey said, "you'll have to be commissioned as a formality. None of my operatives are civilians."

"You'll become a Major in the Royal Guards with a significant increase in your current pay. Is that agreeable?" Atwater smiled, his face taking on a paternal glow.

"Before I say anything one way or the other," Thorley replied, leveling his gaze at the others, "I want to know what you're holding back."

The three older men glanced at one another, their expressions guarded, then Sir Basil nodded, his sober countenance softening with a smile. "I knew you were the right man," he said, "even if old Pete here still has his doubts. You've always looked beyond the obvious.   "Unfortunately, we *can't* tell you anything more. We don't know what it is they want to show us, and they won't say. All they *will* say is that it's a matter of the utmost importance. That the entire course of the war will be affected by it."

Michael raised an eyebrow. "A surrender, perhaps."

"We thought of that, and we aren't ruling it out, but this doesn't have the same ring to it as their entreaties in the past. It's something else, something altogether bad, I'm afraid." The older man approached Thorley and laid a fatherly hand on his shoulder. "Michael, I've known for some time that you've been dissatisfied with your job. I would have to be a doddering old fool not to have seen it. And while your work has always been impeccable, even a doddering old fool can see that sitting out this war's killing you from the inside out."

Thorley glanced up at Sir Basil, noting the older man's impassioned gaze.

"I know it's risky," Sir Basil continued, "but we need to find out what's behind all this. If what they're saying is true, we might shorten this bloody war. I think we all want that."

"Yes, sir," Michael said.

"The Germans have assured us that you'll be protected at all times. And you won't be alone; the Swiss will be there, as well." He paused again, his emotions welling. "I don't want to see you consume yourself, Michael. You're too bloody valuable to waste. That's why we're giving you this chance. And I hope you'll take it, but if you don't, I'll certainly understand."

Thorley found his mind a raging torrent of conflicting emotions. Here was the chance to take a stand, to really contribute to the war in a way that no one could ever dispute. On the other hand, it was very likely a contribution he would never be able to talk about, and worse, one from which he might never return. Still, there were thousands of men taking the same risks every day, and dying. What right did he have to refuse?

And then there was Sir Basil. That the old man had thought highly enough of him to trust him with this mission touched him deeply. He only hoped he could live up to the other man's image of him.

Thorley let out a breath, feeling the tensions of the day leave him in a rush. "All right then," he said finally, "I'll do it, if you'll have me."

Sir Basil nodded, his proud expression turning serious. "There's just one other thing," he added, returning to his place beside the hearth. "You must leave tonight, now in fact."

Thorley's eyes widened. "Now? But my wife, I'll need to tell her."

MacIlvey was shaking his head vigorously. "Not possible. You accept the assignment—it must be on *our* terms."

They had him. They'd played him like a prized fiddle, as the Americans were so fond of saying—knew exactly what it would take to win him over. The odd thing was, he didn't even mind so much.

Thorley went to the window and gazed onto the London skyline. In years past, the lights would have made the city glow like a magical place, a place of myriad possibilities. Now, the grand old town was dark, a place of shadows and furtive machinations. Now, he was being asked to be a part of those machinations.

Looking southeast past the houses of Parliament, he imagined he could see all the way to Brixton, to his house on Benedict Road with its fenced-in yard and the cast iron bird bath adjacent to the narrow flagstone walk.

I'm sorry, sweetheart, but it's something that I need to do. I hope you'll understand.

He turned from the window and faced the three older men. "All right, then, let's have it."

Then they told him.

As he listened to them quietly and calmly outlining the mission, he wondered if perhaps he wasn't making the biggest mistake of his life.

5

While Paul lay sleeping, his bearlike form curled into a fetal ball, Lillian slipped out from under the cool silk sheets, and began putting on her clothes. She dressed quickly, not wanting him to awaken and find her still there.

God forgive her for it, but she'd let Paul continue to believe that he was the baby's father. And now, there was no turning back. She would always have a link with him, and a power over him, where before the power had all been his. Now, he would not be able to force her into any more compromising situations. She was retired, Paul had insisted on it. She found it strange that he would allow the child to be raised by another man, but his position was too important to be jeopardized by any hints of scandal. He would keep tabs on her and the child, he'd said, and make sure they had everything they needed. But Lillian had refused, and their evening of love had almost turned into a row.

After their passions had been spent, all she wanted was to flee, run home to her husband and hope that she could put it all behind her.

Slipping on her shoes, Lillian checked the clock on the bedside table, its radium dial glowing faintly. 8:45.

Michael's meeting had started an hour and forty-five minutes ago, and would no doubt go on for a while. She had plenty of time to make it home before him, so why did she feel so anxious?

Perhaps, it was that ominous tone in his voice when he'd called her, that certain hesitation that signaled that something was amiss. Then again, why was she trying to fool herself? It was guilt, plain old guilt that made her feel this way. And time would be the only purgative that would rid her of it. Time...and Michael's love. She'd betrayed him in body and soul, but now she would stick by him, no matter what happened. Paul had promised to stay out of her life unless absolutely necessary. Lillian said a small prayer that he was as good as his word. She wanted no more of his secretive ways.

Retrieving her coat from the chaise lounge, she took one last look at her lover, her eyes tracing the heavy line of his jaw and the soft pout of his lips. Then she left the room, taking the back stairs and exiting the hotel through a fire door leading into the alley.

She hailed a cab on the Strand, taking it to Charing Cross station, where she boarded the 8:55 train to East Brixton. It was blessedly empty, allowing her to sit and compose the thoughts that raged through her jumbled mind. She wanted to be home before Michael, she wanted to feel his arms around her and know that everything would be all right. And when he walked in that door, she would have the candles lit and the news of his child on her lips.

When the cab pulled up in front of 28 Benedict Road at 9:23, Lillian paid the driver and then rushed inside, slamming the door behind her, a sigh of relief escaping her lips. She left the lights out, preferring the dark, and padded into the kitchen where she brewed up a pot of Darjeeling. The odor of the warm, fragrant tea filled the tiny kitchen, reminding her of her youth and bringing unwanted tears to her eyes. It was a childhood far different than the one she'd told Michael when they first met, one that would horrify him for a vastly different reason. It was one more lie, one more secret between them, and she wanted it all to stop—here and now. She vowed that someday, when this ghastly war was over, and their futures were more secure, she would risk the loss of his love and tell him the truth.

For now, however, the truth must remain where she had always lived...in the shadows.

6

The sleek black Humber staff car shot northward on the A113, its eight-cylinder engine thrumming with unchecked power. At this late hour, the road was all but deserted, a narrow winding black ribbon pelted by a driving rain. The tires swished through puddles and the wipers marked cadence in time with the dull throbbing in Thorley's temple.

Slouched on the butter-soft maroon leather seat directly behind the uniformed driver, Thorley listened as Peter MacIlvey continued briefing him on his mission. The older man's voice was a heated whisper, as he hammered home the facts over and over again. For a brief moment all the sounds he heard blended into a soft roar and his vision blurred.

It was hard to believe that scant hours before, he'd been sitting comfortably in his little rabbit hole listening to the radio. Now, he sat in an overheated staff car headed north toward an airfield outside Chipping Ongar, where a plane waited expressly for him. Thorley found it odd they were heading away from the coast and asked MacIlvey why he wasn't flying out of Croydon or Lympne. He was told that his mission was so secret, they couldn't risk even the slightest attention by civilian or other military personnel.

Watching as the dense, crowded city turned to soot-stained suburbia, Thorley found he couldn't keep Lillian from intruding into his thoughts. It was now just after 10:00 p.m. and he knew she would be frantic with worry, wondering if something had happened to him. Sir Basil had promised him he would personally inform her as to Thorley's circumstances, all within the limitations of the Official Secrets Act, of course. But that promise was little comfort.

Feeling dizzy, Thorley cracked open the window next to him, letting the frigid night air and the cool rain blow into his face. It felt wonderful.

"Thorley, be a good man and close the window," MacIlvey said, his lips pursed with disapproval. "It's bloody freezing."

He shot the older man what he hoped was a hateful glare, and cranked up the window, instantly raising the temperature in the car back to its former oven like state.

"How much further is it?" Thorley asked.

MacIlvey squinted into the dark, as if trying to spy a familiar landmark by the two tiny pinpoints of light emanating from the Humber's masked headlights. "About five miles. Are you clear on everything? Do you want to go over it again?"

"No thank you. I think if I have to hear it all one more time, I'll go mad. How could something like this have happened?"

MacIlvey's eyes narrowed and he focused his attentions somewhere out in the dark. "I won't insult your intelligence by telling you that it's the fortunes of war, and all that rot." He paused, letting that thought sink in. "Let us just say that sometimes politics and expediency are more important than people."

"If that's true, then we really don't deserve to beat that bloody corporal."

MacIlvey's laugh sounded dry and humorless. "You have a lot to learn, my boy, a lot to learn."

Thorley was about to rejoin with something pithy, when the Humber turned off the narrow two-lane road onto a dirt track hemmed on either side by tall fir trees. The heavy boughs scraped the roof of the car as they bumped and jounced their way along the deeply rutted road. A moment later the car broke out of the trees and Thorley spotted the airfield.

Little more than a large pasture pounded flat by steamrollers, it consisted of a single concrete runway with several aircraft parking areas branching off it along its length and a Nissen hut. A windsock hung limply from a pole standing several yards from the control tower: a two-story concrete blockhouse with its control nest and observation deck atop the roof. The windows on the ground floor glowed with a golden light, and Thorley saw a shadow cross in front of one them. Someone awaited them.

The Humber made for the blockhouse, and a moment later the car screeched to a halt and the driver scurried to open the door. MacIlvey climbed out and marched into the blockhouse. Thorley followed, feeling queasy. The throbbing in his temple had worsened.

Inside, Thorley saw a sea of empty wooden desks, their scarred surfaces littered with papers and other debris left over from a day's work. The walls were covered with various maps stuck with pins, and a Teletype clattered lazily somewhere off to his right. But straight ahead, inside one of the enclosed offices, Thorley spotted MacIlvey arguing with an RAF officer.

"...I don't give two bloody shits about priorities, mate. I want that plane here within the hour, fully fueled and ready to go with the crew I ordered. Is that clear?"

As Thorley approached, the conversation died. The officer stalked past him, muttering, his face flushed and his gaze focused on the floor.

"Close the door, Thorley," MacIlvey ordered. He then pointed to a document on the otherwise immaculate desk. "These are your commission papers, please sign and date all three copies. I'm sure I don't have to remind you that you are still bound by the Official Secrets Act, or the penalties for divulging any particulars of your mission...."

Thorley sat down in the wooden swivel chair and took up the fountain pen lying next to the commission papers. He stared at them a moment, the official-looking language swimming before his eyes like a cloud of black flies.

He almost put the pen down then, almost told MacIlvey where to shove his bloody papers and his tawdry secrets. But then, as if in a dream, he found himself signing the papers, first one copy, then the next, and finally the last—everything in triplicate.

"Welcome to His Majesty's Armed Forces," MacIlvey said without a trace of irony.

Thorley looked up at the man and thought he saw something in those steel-colored eyes, something akin to envy; and he realized that, given the choice, MacIlvey would take his place in a heartbeat, had probably been a topnotch operative before age and infirmity had taken its inevitable toll. For the briefest of moments, Thorley and MacIlvey connected.

"You'll find your uniform in the cabinet behind you," MacIlvey said, breaking the mood. "I'll wait outside while you change."

And then he was gone, leaving Thorley alone with his thoughts again. Standing, he turned and opened the gun-metal gray cabinet. He found the uniform arrayed on the middle shelf: Cap, socks, underwear, tunic, and trousers, all neatly folded and arranged pyramidally. Next to the pile sat a pair of brown brogans polished to a mirror shine.

The uniform draped his body as if it had been tailored for him, and that made him uneasy. To have known all his measurements so thoroughly meant that they knew him far better than he would have liked. The inside of the metal cabinet held a full-length mirror, and Thorley gazed at his reflection. To everyone but himself he would appear to be the essence of a Major in the Royal Guards, replete with the proper medal ribbons for a man of his age and rank, decorations he did not deserve.

Suddenly depressed, he shut the cabinet and left the room. He found MacIlvey waiting just outside the blockhouse staring up at the night sky. He turned and gave Thorley an appraising glance, then returned his attention to the stars. The sight was awe-inspiring. Unlike the skies over London, where one was lucky to see the odd star through the smog, here the air was cool, clear as crystal, and smelled of pine tar and wildflowers, laced with a hint of cow manure.

MacIlvey broke the silence. "My father gave me a telescope when I was twelve. Since that time, I've never gotten tired of looking up. When you understand what's out there, and the obscene distances involved, you realize how small and insignificant man is."

"Heavy stuff for—"

"—an old coot?"

Thorley nodded, embarrassed.

MacIlvey chuckled. "Well, I wasn't always so philosophical, or so old, for that matter. What I said about politics being more important than people.... It's the way the world is, Thorley. I wish to Christ it wasn't, but there it is. I learned long ago that I had to play the game *their* way or I'd be out of it."

"And that was important to you, to be in 'the game'?"

"Bloody right on that one. I wanted in because I thought I could change it from the inside. Instead—"

"—It changed you."

MacIlvey nodded. "Someone once said, I forget who it was, that all cynics are disillusioned romantics. That's me, to a tee."

Thorley was about to offer a comeback when the sound of engines floated in on the wind. MacIlvey gave a curt nod. "Well done, Gormley, well done."

Thorley looked toward the source of the sound and saw, off to the west, the landing lights of a lone plane flying toward the field. When it drew closer, he saw that it was a Vickers-Wellington, a dual-engine medium bomber. It was painted a drab brown, and had the RAF bull's-eye painted on both wings and the rear fuselage, along with a series of numbers in a pale yellow. Wagging its wings, the Wellington made a sweeping pass around the field, then landed, coming to a stop about fifty yards away from where Thorley and MacIlvey stood. From off to their left the fuel truck drove up and two ground crewmen uncoiled a hose, connected it to a spot on the wing and the refueling process began.

"Let's go," MacIlvey said, motioning for Thorley to follow him. He found he had to trot to keep up with the older man, who marched across the runway with long impatient strides, barking orders at the ground crew to hurry it up. When they closed in on the plane, Thorley noticed more details about the aircraft: the drab brown was really an intricate camouflage pattern. Conversely, the underbelly was painted a light sky blue, an odd-looking combination until one realized that, from the ground, the plane would be less easy to spot by trigger-happy German anti-aircraft gunners. The other thing he noticed about the Wellington made him uneasy. It bristled with .303 calibre machine guns.

Thorley caught up with MacIlvey as a hatch under the plane's belly, just to the rear of the cockpit, swung open and the pilot dropped out onto the runway. Exuding the natural confidence of men who daily risked their lives, the pilot strode toward them, the buckles and zippers of his flight gear clacking together. He was tall, recruiting-poster handsome, with a pencil mustache, and cleft chin. The pilot stopped in front of MacIlvey and nodded. "Right. This the package?"

Thorley felt a hot flash of anger at the man's impersonal reference, but forced himself to calm down. He was past the personal at this point. Only the mission and its successful outcome mattered now.

"Quite," MacIlvey replied. "You have the flight plan?"

The pilot looked off into the distance, as if gauging some unseen menace. "Bloody Göring's got twice as many 110's up tonight. From the reports we've heard over the radio, it'll be the deuce getting over the Bay of Biscay."

MacIlvey stared at the man, a vein in his temple throbbing. "Sounds like you'll be earning your pay, then."

The pilot sighed, a world-weary expression passing over his face. "No rest for the wicked, eh what?"

"Just make sure you get him there in one piece."

"We always do."

MacIlvey turned to Thorley and thrust out his meaty hand. Thorley took it, feeling the small bones of his hand grind against each other. "You're in good hands with Flight Lieutenant Mullins," MacIlvey said, nodding toward the pilot. "Just make sure you bring back the truth. I don't trust the bloody Hun, not since the last war."

"I'll do my best, sir," Thorley said, feeling silly, as if he were being packed off to boarding school. But the look in the older man's eyes snapped him back to reality.

"Whatever the truth is, I'll find it."

MacIlvey smiled. "Good show."

The copilot leaned out the side window. "We've got to leave now, Flight, there's a front moving in."

The pilot nodded, then twirled his hand. The copilot disappeared back inside the cockpit and a moment later the plane's two Bristol-Hercules engines fired up with a gut-shaking rumble. Prop wash buffeted them, making it difficult for Thorley to stand. MacIlvey mouthed something that was lost in the clamor, then tried repeating it. He gave up with a shrug, saluted, and walked back to the Humber, which had discreetly moved from its spot by the blockhouse. A moment later, it accelerated away, retracing its route back toward the trees and the city.

Thorley suddenly felt very alone, as if he'd been abandoned by his last friend. He spotted the pilot standing by the open hatch, beckoning him with an impatient wave.

There was no turning back now, nowhere else to go.

Holding his cap to his head, Thorley ran to the hatchway and stopped. The pilot thrust his face next to Thorley's ear and shouted. "You've got to pull yourself inside, sir!"

Thorley nodded, reached up and grabbed the rim of the hatch with both hands, then jumped to give himself the necessary momentum to carry him up into the plane. He made it halfway, and instantly two pairs of hands grabbed him under the arms and hauled him inside.

The two men belonging to those hands, both pilot officers, dressed in flight gear and wearing parachutes, smiled at him. "Welcome aboard, sir," they said, saluting.

Thorley returned the salute, feeling foolish.

The pilot followed him in, closed and battened the hatch, then turned to the two other officers. "Gibby, you take the tail tonight, and bloody well keep your eyes peeled. We're carrying enough extra fuel to roast us to cinders."

Gibby nodded. "Yes, sir," he said, turning and running off down the narrow catwalk, the rubber soles of his sheepskin-lined boots silent on the latticed steel. He disappeared behind the bomb bay, now occupied by a special long-range fuel tank instead of the usual complement of five-hundred-pound explosives. The pilot faced the other pilot officer, a fresh-faced boy with tousled blond hair and mischievous grin. "Once we're aloft, Hildy, you're to lay in a course for Lisbon, and keep us over water this time." He then turned and climbed into the cockpit, which was separated from the rest of the cabin by steel meshing. The copilot nodded to Thorley, then turned his attention back to his gauges.

Hildy pointed to a spot next to the navigator/radioman's chair, where a spare parachute lay. "I'm sorry we don't have a seat for you, sir," he said. "But the lady here wasn't designed for comfort."

"Quite all right...."

"Sims, Major, Pilot Officer Hildy Sims."

"Carry on, Sims."

Thorley sat on the parachute, deciding that if he really needed it he'd put it on at the appropriate time. Chances were good, however, that the pilot was correct. With all the extra fuel in that large tank in the bomb bay, they'd never have the chance to get out. Pushing that unpleasant thought from his mind, he leaned his back against the bulkhead, feeling the vibration of the engines. Hildy sat down in the fold-down jump seat, turned on the radio and put on his headset, then pulled out his charts and began plotting the course that would take them out over the Atlantic and then south over the Bay of Biscay to neutral Portugal.

A moment later, the engines throttled up and the rumbling idle became a full-throated roar. He felt the brakes ease off and the Wellington move forward, rapidly picking up speed. As they approached take-off speed, wind howled through the open gun ports adding to the cacophony and further jangling his nerves. He felt the wheels jounce once as the plane lifted off the earth. He was thirty-five years old, heading off into God only knew what, and this was his first time in the air. Turning his eyes heavenward, he beseeched whatever deity might be listening that he sincerely hoped it wouldn't be his last.

❈ ❈ ❈

The plane banked sharply, turned south first, then due west. A few downdrafts jolted the plane, making Thorley's stomach twist and his knuckles turn white. His hands ached as he gripped a piece of the plane's superstructure. Looking toward the cockpit, he saw the copilot pointing at one of the Perspex windows. "Our escort has arrived," he said.

It was too dark to see from where he was sitting, but Thorley knew the copilot referred to a fighter escort, no doubt two of the highly maneuverable Spitfires. Instead of making him feel better, this only increased his anxiety.

"Good show," the pilot replied, his eyes on the altimeter. "Leveling off at fifteen thousand feet." He put his hands to his throat mike. "This is Red Leader…do you copy Little Friends? Over."

A crackling of static.

"We copy loud and clear, Red Leader. What are your orders? Over."

"Stay with us until the far beacon. We should be all right after that, over."

"Roger, Red Leader, we're with you all the way to Tipperary. Over and out."

The pilot smiled at the fighter escort's joke, and was about to offer a comment to the copilot when the plane dropped two hundred feet and began to vibrate as if shaken in a giant paint mixer. Alarmed and thinking the worst, Thorley grabbed onto a stanchion and grit

44

his teeth. And then, as quickly as it all began, the shaking ceased and the plane flew on, steady as a watchmaker's hand. Thorley uncoiled himself from the stanchion and sank back against the bulkhead. The pilots grinned at each other.

"Your first time up, Major?" the copilot asked, a devilish gleam in his eye.

Thorley ignored the man.

"Don't worry, sir," the pilot offered, "we've never lost one to turbulence yet. It's only Göring's goons you have to worry about."

Thorley stared back at the man, his gaze level and calm. "How long is the flight, Flight Lieutenant?"

"About six hours, sir."

"Good, then keep it buttoned until then."

The pilot's eyebrows shot up. He gave the copilot a nervous shrug, then returned his attention to the plane.

Nothing happened until they passed near the French coast. Out of nowhere, two Messerschmitt Bf 110s dove from the clouds, their 20mm cannons and 7.92mm machine guns blazing. One moment it was quiet, the next it was pandemonium with tracer bullet accompaniment.

The pilot wrenched the yoke and the Wellington dove to the left. The radio blared: "Red Leader, Red Leader, Messerschmitt on your tail! Bank right!"

Immediately, the Wellington rolled over to the right. Thorley heard the chatter of the Wellington's nose guns and saw the red streaks of tracers arcing out into the night.

The radio blared again: "Red Leader, Dive, dive, dive!"

But before the pilot could react, a fusillade of bullets ripped through the side of the plane, tearing up the instrument panel and nailing the copilot in the head. It exploded like a ripe melon, spattering blood against Thorley's face. As horrified as he was, what really scared him was that the nose guns had fallen silent.

Next to him, Hildy threw off his headset and grabbed Thorley by the arm. "Do you know how to operate a three-o-three?"

"N—no."

Hildy pulled him to his feet. "No time like the present. Come on."

Thorley tried to stay on his feet while the Wellington maneuvered to avoid the Messerschmitt's relentless cannon fire, which thwacked against the fuselage with sickening regularity. Passing the bomb bay, they came upon two flexible .303 calibre belt-fed machine guns on swivels mounted to the deck, each aiming out one side of the plane. Farther aft, Thorley heard the rear-gunner's .303 clattering in staccato bursts, punctuated by Gibby's gleeful cursing.

"You hear that?" Hildy shouted, pointing to the tail. "Fire it only when you've got them in your sights. You've only got five thousand rounds, and these babies will chew them up faster than you can imagine."

A Spitfire streaked by the open port chasing one of the Messerschmitts, dark blurs against a darker sky. The Wellington rolled, forcing Thorley and Hildy to brace themselves until it leveled out. "How the hell can I *see* them, much less get them in my bleeding sights?"

"Watch the tracers. Then aim a little farther back from the source of the fire. *That's* your target."

Hildy pushed him toward the .303 on the starboard side and Thorley grabbed the handles and pushed the trigger.

Nothing.

The bolt, you idiot, pull the bloody bolt back.

Hildy's gun began firing behind him, the horrendous chattering adding to the already deafening clamor. Thorley searched frantically for the bolt, his fingers fumbling over unfamiliar territory. He found it to the side, grabbed it and yanked it back, feeling it slide smoothly along its oiled track. Focusing on the sky outside the plane, he squinted, trying to distinguish one of the Messerschmitts from out of the gloom. A dark shape whooshed by, making him jump, which was just as well as the bullets that slammed through the skin of the Wellington missed him by fractions.

"Shoot the bloody bastards, damn you!" Hildy screamed.

And that was all it took. He grabbed for the handles, his untrained fingers accidentally pressing the trigger. The gun spat out five bullets in the blink of an eye, and he watched them fly away from the Wellington, the phosphorus in their tails burning bright red arcs into the sky. Suddenly, tracers of a different color, a blazing yellow streamed back toward him, as if out of nowhere. A Messerschmitt.

Resisting the urge to duck his head, he placed the source of the tracers right in the crosshairs of the sight and fired. Empty shell casings clattered about his feet as the .303 spat tracers at the German plane. Thorley tried to follow it as it flew by but the swivel had a very short arc.

A split second later, the Messerschmitt streaked back around for another pass. This time, Thorley remembered what Hildy said and aimed the .303 slightly aft of the source of the fire, then pressed the trigger. The gun rattled and he saw some of his tracers hit home, sending up a shower of debris from the German plane.

And then the Messerschmitt exploded in a ball of orange flame that lit up the inside of the Wellington. He watched the fiery wreckage spiral down in lazy circles until it was lost from sight.

"Bloody good show!" Hildy screamed over his shoulder, still firing.

But Thorley saw very little good in it. In spite of the fact that the pilot of the Messerschmitt had been shooting at him—had tried to kill him—he was just doing his duty, like Thorley. No, there was no good in that; just a dirty job that left one feeling turned inside out. And that was nothing to celebrate. Except for the fact that he was still alive.

Returning his attention to the night sky, Thorley saw the remaining Messerschmitt make one last pass, its tracers missing the Wellington by a wide margin. Then, as if sensing that its moment had passed, it turned tail and headed back toward the French coast, its nose bloodied.

Drained, Thorley let go of the .303 and collapsed against the bulkhead, his head throbbing and his ears ringing.

"You all right, mate—sir?" Hildy asked.

"I suppose, but I never thought it could be...."

His voice trailed off when he saw the blood on Hildy's arm.

"Christ, you're hit!" he said, scrambling to his feet.

"It's nothing, passed right though. Just a nick, really."

"To hell with that. Let me look."

"It'll wait. We've got to check on Gibby."

Thorley nodded and the two of them headed to the tail. Hildy crouched down and banged on the door leading into the tiny cramped quarters of the rear gunner.

"You all right, Gibby?" Hildy said.

The door swung open and young man's cherubic face smiled out at them. "We damn well gave it to Jerry! Was that bloody wizard, or what?"

Hildy smiled, but his eyes held a weary expression. "Wizard, all right. Need anything?"

"A pint and a bit of slap and tickle will put me as right as rain. Everybody all right?"

"Farley bought it," Hildy said, his face clouding.

"Oh, Christ." Gibby shifted his gaze to Thorley. "This mission had better be bloody damned important. Farley was a good man."

"It's more important than you can imagine," Thorley replied, knowing that it offered nothing in the way of solace.

"Ease up, Gibby," Hildy said. "Farley knew what it was all about. So do you."

Gibby nodded, his anger dissipating. "Sorry, Major."

"It's okay," he said, feeling awkward.

He wanted to say something else, anything to make it all right. But, of course, there was nothing he could say that would change a blessed thing. Farley would still be dead.

Hildy tugged on his sleeve. "Come on. I've got to get back and plot us a new course."

Hildy pulled out his sextant, aimed it at Polaris, and made a few calculations on his flight computer, a small round plastic device similar to a slide rule. After double-checking his figures and taking into account the depletion of fuel during the dogfight, he gave the Flight Lieutenant their new heading. Amazingly, after all their evasive maneuvers, they were only off their original course by five degrees.

Then came the grim work. Both the nose gunner, a man whose name Thorley never knew, and Farley had been killed. Flight Lieutenant Mullins had them wrap the bodies in tarpaulins and place them next to the bomb bay. It took considerable effort for Thorley not to throw up, especially when he caught a glimpse of the ruin that had been Farley's head.

With the bodies stowed and the spent shell casings swept up, Thorley curled up on his parachute and tried to nap. But sleep refused to come. Adrenaline from the dogfight still pumped through his body, making his heart pound, his hands tremble, and his mind reel. He couldn't rid his thoughts of Gibby's accusations, especially the unspoken ones that blazed from a young flier's eyes grown old before their time.

For the remainder of the flight Thorley sat in silence staring at the wrapped bundles that had once been living men, praying that he would never have to join them.

7

It was nearly dawn when the Vickers-Wellington made its final approach into Lisbon's *Lisboa Aeroporto*. An early morning fog blew in off the ocean, spreading ghostly tendrils through the city and into the surrounding hills. Though low on fuel, the Wellington had to make one circular pass before being allowed to land on the single oil-streaked runway.

When it taxied to a stop in front of the civilian terminal, Thorley watched as a cadre of Portuguese troops frog-marched out of the building and surrounded the plane. Flight Lieutenant Mullins powered down, appraised the bullet-smashed cockpit and the blood splashes on the instruments with a sad shake of his head, then climbed out of his seat and opened the hatch. Warm, sultry air wafted up through the hole, smelling of dead fish and aviation fuel. About to drop through, Flight Lieutenant Mullins hesitated, then turned to Thorley, eyeing him coolly.

"Ordinarily, I'd wish you luck, Major, like I do for all the others I've put down on foreign soil," he said, his voice tight with anger. "Lord knows, it's a tough, bloody war. But something about this mission has smelled to high heaven from the very start. Whatever it is you're supposed to find, I hope you find it...and bloody well choke on it." And then he dropped through the hatchway and was gone.

Thorley stood, smoothed out his uniform, and followed the pilot out of the aircraft in time to see him disappear into the terminal, escorted by two Portuguese soldiers. He couldn't blame the man for his anger; he'd lost two good men, men for whom he cared deeply. Still, Thorley couldn't hold back his own anger. After all, as Hildy had said, they all knew the risks when they signed up. So, what did the Flight mean when he said something about the mission smelled?

He was about to go after him to demand an explanation then decided against it. No doubt the man would refuse to speak to him, and besides, the Portuguese soldiers didn't look as if they would let him pass. Suddenly tired, Thorley leaned against the skin of the Wellington and used the moment to scan his surroundings.

The plane sat fifty yards out from the terminal, a squat two-storey Mediterranean style building with stucco walls and red tile roof. Except for the equipment that would identify it as part of an airport, it looked like someone's ramshackle villa. Beyond the terminal lay a chain-link fence and Lisbon proper. The city consisted of mostly low-profile Spanish-style buildings, radiating outward toward the hills where expensive homes sat perched on the hillsides. It seemed that every square block contained a church, for bells were ringing all over the city, calling the faithful to morning mass.

Thorley glanced at his watch. One hour till sunrise.

A moment later a Mercedes staff car rounded the building and headed for them. The Portuguese soldiers parted to let the Mercedes through, then closed ranks. The car came to a halt in front of Thorley, the rear door opened and out stepped a wiry little man in a charcoal pin-stripe suit carrying an attaché case. His eyes blinked rapidly behind gold-rimmed pince-nez, and his hair was so saturated with pomade that it looked as if it were lacquered. The man smiled and stepped toward Thorley, his hand motions reptile quick.

"Ah, Major Thorley!" he said, his English almost impenetrable. "Did you have a pleasant flight, Senhor?"

Thorley couldn't believe the man. Either he was supremely myopic, or unctuous in the extreme. All the little fool had to do was look at the plane.

"Senhor Velasquez, I presume?"

Velasquez positively beamed, convincing Thorley that the man simply did not wish to acknowledge the gore-spattered Wellington, the mark of a true diplomat.

Velasquez bowed from the waist. "At your service, Senhor Major. Please, come with me."

Thorley hesitated, staring back at the plane and its crew. "What about them?"

"They will be taken care of, Senhor. Everything is arranged."

"No doubt," Thorley said, shooting him a cold look.

"Major, please, we must go."

Thorley moved toward the Mercedes. "Let's get on with it, then."

Once they were ensconced inside the car, it sped off toward the other end of the airport. Thorley took a last look at the Wellington, hoping Velasquez was as good as his word. The little man seemed to have put the matter behind him, as he began speaking volubly about everything from fine wines to expensive cigars. Finally, his monologue returned to more serious matters. "...I do hope you realize that this is all highly irregular. Entertaining members of belligerent nations on neutral soil.... Very, very awkward. I have taken considerable risks to facilitate this...."

"It's a little late to renegotiate your fee, Velasquez."

The little man threw up his hands in a placating gesture. "No, no, Senhor! You misunderstand. I am happy to oblige, but I do not wish our neutrality to be challenged."

"You have nothing to fear from us...."

The rest of Thorley's retort died on his lips as he spotted the plane up ahead parked inconspicuously between two corrugated steel hangars. It was a Heinkel He 111, the pride of Göring's *Luftwaffe*. Powered by two 1350 horsepower Jumo engines, with a wingspan over seventy-four feet, it was capable of bombing London from deep inside France with over 4400 pounds of explosives—a devastating payload whose destructive force Thorley had experienced far too many times.

His throat went dry when he spotted a *Luftwaffe* Major inspecting the aircraft with the plane's pilot. As the staff car halted a few yards from the right wingtip, the Major looked up, appraising them with a cool and calculating eye.

Inside the staff car, Thorley reached for the door handle. "It's been a pleasure, Senhor Velasquez. Just make sure that I never have cause to regret that statement."

Velasquez blanched, but said nothing. Thorley walked quickly toward the *Luftwaffe* Major, who pulled a cigarette out from an expensive-looking silver case, lighted it with a wooden match, and blew the smoke out the side of his mouth, all the while keeping his eyes riveted on Thorley.

Square-shouldered and a little under six feet, he wore the standard issue blue-gray tunic and jodhpur breeches, along with black leather riding boots polished to a mirror gloss. His peaked cap sat at a jaunty angle, and a Knight's Cross—with Oakleaves and Swords—dangled at his throat. A host of other important ribbons and badges decorated the left side of his tunic like a metallic smorgasbord.

The German blew out another cloud of smoke, and as Thorley drew closer, he saw dark circles under world-weary eyes set into a face sporting a day's growth of beard and a jagged scar on one chiseled cheek.

The pilot held out his silver cigarette case. It had a diamond-encrusted *Luftwaffe* eagle affixed to the lid.

"Have one, they're American," he said in German. His tone was affable, though his eyes remained wary.

Thorley studied the man a moment before he spoke. "No, thank you," he replied. "They give me a headache."

The Major smiled, revealing a gold crown covering one of his molars. "That's a shame, Herr Major. They're quite good; and as rare as a trustworthy man these days, *ja*?" The man's accent was clearly Bavarian. Though the major had done well for himself, enough to win Germany's highest award, he was not a Heidelberg man, not one of the vanishing Junkers that still ruled the German Officer class. This major was of a new, more pragmatic breed.

Thorley heard Velasquez drive off and the Major took this as his cue. "Warm up the plane, *Herr Leutnant*."

"*Jawohl, Herr Major!*" He climbed into the plane through the belly hatch, while the Major turned his attention back to Thorley. Behind him the Heinkel's two Jumos fired up, idling with a deep throaty grumble.

"The letter, please."

Thorley reached into his tunic and pulled out a single sheet of vellum, folded once, and handed it to the Major.

The contents were a simple paragraph beginning and ending with a prearranged coded phrase. The rest of it identified the bearer as one Michael Thorley. MacIlvey had penned the letter himself.

The *Luftwaffe* Major scanned the document, and for a fleeting moment Thorley feared he would pronounce it a forgery, ending his mission there and then. But the Major merely nodded and handed it back.

"All is in order," he said, a sardonic grin creasing his face. "Come, time is short."

Thorley followed the Major into the aircraft and was directed toward an empty seat. There lay the field gray uniform of a German Army officer, with the white piping and epaulettes of an Infantry Major. Back at 54 Broadway, when MacIlvey and the others had outlined the mission, Thorley had wondered about the uniform switch. Why not wear the German uniform from the beginning? The answer, when it came, made him feel like the neophyte he was. The British uniform was necessary, they said, because if for some reason the Wellington was brought down in occupied territory, he would end up in a POW camp, rather than in front of a firing squad.

Thorley had barely pulled on the boots and buttoned the tunic when the plane began its takeoff run. The Heinkel was a faster, sleeker plane than the Wellington, reaching flying speed in nearly half the time. By the time he'd seated himself and strapped in, they were at two thousand feet and climbing. Minutes later, they leveled off and the long flight to Finland commenced.

For a time, he amused himself with comparing the similarities and differences between the Wellington and the Heinkel, but that quickly proved boring—the planes were more similar than not. He tried to go over the details of his mission one last time. In minutes, his eyelids drooped and he fell into a deep and dreamless sleep.

❖ ❖ ❖

Thorley awoke three hours later as the Heinkel began making a descent, the pressure in his inner ear building, tugging him toward consciousness like a vicious little terrier. He opened his eyes just as they hit a downdraft. It threw him against the bulkhead, slamming his shoulder into one of the stanchions. Christ, it hurt. Gritting his teeth, he rubbed it, making sure he could still move it.

He glanced out the small observation window and saw the earth moving up to meet them. A few seconds later, the wheels met the runway with a screech. Something wasn't right, he thought, something about the light. Frowning, Thorley glanced at his watch, and realized that the position of the sun differed from the time on his watch. Could they be in Finland already?

The cockpit door opened, and the Major came through it looking fresh, as if somehow he'd managed a shower and a shave. "Did you sleep well, *Herr Major?*" he asked. "Would you like to stretch your legs? We have a few minutes."

Thorley shook the last vestiges of sleep from his mind, then rubbed his own face, feeling the sharp rasp of the stubbles against his palm. "Where are we?"

"Just outside The Hague. A refueling stop. We're halfway there."

The Netherlands, known to some as the Low Countries.

An early casualty to Hitler's armored *Blitzkrieg*, the Dutch homeland had fallen, along with Belgium and France, the year before, and was now a part of the "Greater German Reich. *Lebensraum* for the Master Race." Rubbish.

Thorley swallowed his anger and followed the Major out of the plane onto the runway. The land was flat and featureless, stretching for miles in all directions. He thought he could see a farmhouse in the distance, a lone windmill its one distinguishing feature. From what he remembered from his school days, most of this land was reclaimed from the sea by the complex system of dykes and sea walls used to hold it at bay. If ever the fight came here, Thorley thought, all the Germans would need to do to halt an advancing army would be to blow up the dykes. It was a thought that chilled him as much as the cool breeze that blew in from the sea, where a bank of ugly gray clouds sat hovering over the water like some giant carrion eater.

Because of the threat of bad weather, it appeared that they had the airport to themselves. The only other people, aside from the Major and the flight crew now doing stretching exercises a few yards away, were the two Dutch ground crewmen hooking up the hose from the fuel truck to the nozzle on the wing. Two *Luftwaffe* guards attached to the airfield stood nearby, rifles pointed at the ground, their eyes dull with boredom. Thorley watched the two Dutchmen for a moment, noting their furtive glances, glances that barely masked the hostility they felt. It made his skin crawl.

Out of the corner of his eye, he saw the Major move up beside him, an unlit cigarette dangling from his mouth. The Major stared at the ground crew, watching them with a bemused expression, and then he spoke, his voice thick with irony. "How does it feel, Herr Thorley?"

"What do you mean?"

"I think you know."

They were silent again for a moment.

"I think perhaps I'll have one of those cigarettes, after all," Thorley said.

The Major smiled and motioned for him to move away from the plane. At a safe distance, the Major extended the cigarette case, Thorley took one, placed it between his lips and bent toward the flaming match the Major offered. The German then lit his own, and they spent a moment of silence watching the ground crew work. Thorley coughed. The cigarette tasted dry, acrid, as if it had lain in a box for years. Still, it was a welcome respite from the thoughts and feelings that ran through his mind. "What's your name?" he asked, breaking the silence once again.

"It is better you do not know," the Major said, picking a piece of tobacco from his teeth. "Let us say that my being here is because I choose to aid a cause that needs my help. Honor demands it." He faced Thorley, his ice-blue eyes narrowing. "My country was founded on the concept of honor, *Herr Major*, the concept that a man was as good as his word. Now, certain *factions* are doing their very best to destroy what honor we have left. And I can't stand by anymore.... Do you understand?"

Thorley nodded. "I believe I do. What I can't understand is how your people allowed all this to happen in the first place."

The Major coughed, then spat out another piece of tobacco. "That is something historians will debate for generations," he said, smiling bitterly. "The truth is that we Germans are a race that worships power and those who wield it. This time, I'm afraid, we've gone too far."

Before Thorley could reply, the ground crew signaled the refueling was finished. The Major threw down his cigarette, squashed it out with a twist of his highly polished riding boot, and walked back to the Heinkel without another word. Thorley followed him into the plane. Five minutes later, they were airborne, and Thorley's thoughts and emotions became a jumble. Now, more than ever, he was afraid of what he would find at his destination.

8

They crossed over into Finnish airspace just after 1 p.m. local time. The Heinkel hugged the landscape, giving Thorley a dramatic view of the untamed forests of thick evergreens, of snow-capped mountains and deep valleys dotted with lakes and the remnants of ancient glaciers. It was a land that few had mastered.

Half an hour passed, then the Heinkel banked left and dropped lower. The pilot throttled back the engines and the aircraft shuddered as the landing gear caught the airstream.

Thorley's anticipation rose, fighting for supremacy with another feeling that was all-too-familiar…fear. He was flying directly into the maw of the beast, and protection or not, once he landed, once he placed himself in their hands, all bets were off. The thought of it chilled him.

The plane swooped down into a shallow valley, making a rough landing on an airstrip hewn directly out of the virgin forest: an earth-brown gash in a field of verdant green. Off to the side, he saw mountains of tree stumps waiting for burning, mute evidence of a grueling effort to wrest the airstrip from the grip of nature.

The pilot taxied the Heinkel to the end of the airstrip and turned about, parking the aircraft next to a makeshift fuel dump. While the plane rolled across the craggy ground, Thorley used the time to collect his gear and position himself near the exit hatch. As soon as the aircraft came to a stop, the engines powered down, plunging the cabin into an eerie silence broken only by the soughing wind. The Major emerged from the cockpit, his face drawn with concern.

"We're getting reports of a weather front moving in by six p.m. tomorrow. We will wait until four. If you're not back by then, we take off without you."

"That's not what was agreed."

The Major waved his hand impatiently. "That does not matter. I will not jeopardize this plane and my crew—"

"For a *verdammt Englander?*" Thorley said, voice tight with anger. "Where's your honor now, Major?"

"That's not fair—"

"And war is? You will wait for me, weather permitting or not, or I shall see to it that those responsible for my being here will know of your cowardice."

The Major's lips compressed, and Thorley could see the man was deeply offended; but there was something else behind his eyes: *the knowledge that Thorley spoke the unblemished truth.* Either he was the man of honor he claimed to be, or he was a worthless hypocrite who didn't deserve even the slightest regard.

The Major stared back at Thorley, his left eye quivering with anger and, for one long unbearably tense moment, it seemed to Thorley that he might lose his only means of leaving this godforsaken place.

And then it was gone.

The Major shook his head, his expression one of a man who has had to make too many hard choices. "You are right, of course," he said, rubbing the bridge of his nose between his thumb and index finger. "It's this fucking war; it makes people say and do such appalling things— things they never would have dreamed possible before. But that's just an excuse, like all the others.... I will wait. But if we have not taken off by the time this weather moves in, then we shall all be stuck in this shithole together."

Thorley smiled and twisted open the hatch. It clanged against the hull then swung lazily back and forth several times before coming to a stop. "I wouldn't have it any other way, Major," he said. He dropped through and began walking away from the plane toward the woods.

When he came to the edge of the runway, the desolate nature of the landscape was even more apparent. Aside from the thick forest of tall pines that hemmed-in the strip on three sides, a mountain range lay to the north at a distance he judged to be at least fifty miles. It was from that direction that he caught sight of a dust cloud moving toward him. Several moments later it became recognizable as a *Kübelwagen* staff car.

Painted with camouflaging paint in a random pattern of green, brown and gray to simulate foliage, its odd sloping bonnet, corrugated siding, and jutting wheel wells made it look ungainly, even clumsy, yet the sturdy little vehicle seemed well-suited to the rough, rocky terrain. It bounded onto the dirt runway and raced toward him with alarming speed, sliding to a stop and throwing up a cloud of dirt that stung his eyes and made him want to gag. He forced himself to ignore it, concentrating, instead, on the two men occupying the vehicle.

The driver, a sergeant, had skin like leather and a sinewy face whose every line appeared chiseled from granite. He kept his gaze averted, his attention on the area immediately surrounding them, and appeared nervous, watchful, as if he expected someone might attack them at any moment.

The other occupant was a *Wehrmacht* Captain in his mid-twenties. Tall, blonde, and youthful in a fresh, innocent way, he radiated an undeniable charisma—the exact opposite of the brooding Luftwaffe Major. The young Captain smiled with genuine warmth, bounding from the *Kübelwagen*, his hand extended in greeting.

"*Guten Tag, Herr Major*," he said, his brown eyes twinkling. "I am *Hauptmann* Friedrich Rainer, and I am pleased you could come. You cannot know how much your visit will mean. What should I call you?"

Thorley thought for a second, then remembered something from his briefing at MI6. "Major Weiss will do," he replied, giving Rainer a final appraisal.

The young Captain grinned. "Ah, yes, *Der Weisse Adler*. Quite apropos." He paused then, his mood turning serious. "We had best be on our way. It's a long drive."

He started to climb back into the *Kübelwagen* and Thorley grabbed his arm. "Wait," he said, his tone urgent.

Rainer turned back to face him.

"What can you tell me?"

"I'd rather you saw it all for yourself," Rainer said, his expression troubled. "Words will only trivialize it. Come, we only have a few hours of daylight left."

They drove for an hour before hitting the mountain road that led to their destination. All through the ride, Thorley kept his own counsel, preferring to watch the passing scenery. It was a study in contrasts. The land grew rockier as they rose in altitude, the pine trees thinning out and giving way to low-lying scrub. Wildflowers grew everywhere, splashing the land in striking hues from the brightest yellow to the deepest violet. It was breathtaking, yet there was blight on the land; it took the form of endless columns of German soldiers, Panzers, supply trucks, and horse drawn artillery. Because the road was so narrow, they were forced to fall into the column until they reached the other side, where it widened enough to allow them to race ahead.

They reached the site by mid-afternoon, passing more columns of weary, battle-bloodied troops trudging toward the rear. The *Kübelwagen* pulled into a makeshift parking lot filled with all manner of vehicles, mostly troop transport. Up ahead, through a stand of trees, Thorley could see a mass of men moving about in a large clearing. In the distance he heard the steady rumble of artillery, the front a mere five miles to the east. Too bloody close.

Climbing out of the *Kübelwagen*, Thorley suddenly found himself reluctant to move forward. Rainer took the lead. They moved quickly, and as they neared the clearing, the first thing Thorley noticed was the smell: heavy, pungent, cloying—the smell of death... and rotting flesh. And it took every ounce of his will not to vomit.

They arrived at the clearing's perimeter and Rainer bent down, reached into a bucket and pulled out a wet handkerchief that he proceeded to fold and hold over his mouth. When Thorley hesitated to follow his example, he pulled out another and handed it to him. "It's soaked in a mixture of camphor and water," Rainer explained. "I suggest you use it."

Thorley clamped the cloth over his nose and mouth and moved forward, his stomach churning. The camphor had its own unique odor, but it was more tolerable than the one it masked.

Passing through a cordon of guards armed with MP40 machine pistols, Thorley saw a group of thirty-odd soldiers in coveralls using shovels to carry refuse to a six-foot-deep trench. He estimated it must be at least forty feet long and twenty feet wide. Another smaller group—accompanied by a clique of Swiss civilian observers in red armbands with white crosses—photographed the actions with Leica cameras and a newsreel crew photographed the goings-on with a battery-powered Arriflex camera fitted with a high-capacity magazine. Except for the whine of the Arriflex and the occasional clank of shovel against rock, the area was eerily silent. It all sank in as he realized what he thought to be "refuse" was in actuality the decomposing bodies of soldiers.

Hundreds of them.

The entire clearing lay covered in a jumble of arms and legs jutting out of ragged uniforms caked with grime—many with patches of putrid flesh still clinging to them. The faces were the worst: gaunt and eyeless, they faced skyward, mouths frozen in twisted grins mocking all who gazed upon them.

Mixed in with the bodies were rust-spotted rifles, dented helmets and dirt-encrusted backpacks. Bayonets and boots, along with cartridge belts and magazines lay strewn about with no rhyme or reason.

"You must understand that we did not do this," Rainer said, his emotion-laden voice muffled by the camphor-soaked handkerchief. "We are not butchers."

Thorley's mind reeled. "My God, there must be an entire battalion here."

"More than that. We have counted over a thousand bodies thus far...."

Thorley stumbled away but stopped when something small and metallic clinked against his shoe. Looking down, he spotted a shiny object. He reached down and brought it up to his face. His hand trembled and he had to squint to bring it into focus.

Cast out of a metal that resisted rust, the design consisted of a laurel wreath surmounted by a King's crown. In the center of the wreath stood a rampant Wyvern, a mythical dragon-like creature, its teeth and claws bared. At the bottom of the badge, on a scroll, ran a motto in raised lettering: *Royal South Wessex Inf. Reg.*

It was a cap badge, a *British* officer's cap badge.

Stunned, Thorley placed the badge in the pocket of his tunic and trudged back to the *Kübelwagen*. He threw the handkerchief to the ground and leaned against the car, gulping lungfuls of air, anything to clear his aching head and take away the stench of death.

"Major White?"

Rainer was walking toward him, the wary sergeant by his side. "Are you all right? Perhaps you would like to rest a while?"

Thorley stared back at the man; his eyes felt as if someone had scoured them with steel wool. "Let's get the bloody hell away from here."

The camp was a five-minute drive back the way they'd come. It occupied five acres of cleared land and consisted of two dozen prefabricated buildings of raw pine with tar-paper roofs arranged in a quadrangle. The largest building stood in the center; a sign above the door read: Mess Hall. A plume of white smoke rose from its chimney, and as drab as it was, it was a welcome respite from the horror they'd left behind.

The sergeant pulled the *Kübelwagen* into a space next to a BMW motorcycle with attached sidecar, and Rainer indicated that they should go into the Mess.

The inside of the building was a boxy affair with electrical wiring strung between the exposed rafters, smelled of boiled cabbage and potatoes, and was jammed with both officers and enlisted men, and even a few of the Swiss civilians. The somber mood at the massacre site was reflected here, as well. Men quietly consumed their meals, drank their ersatz coffee, smoked, and some even played cards. Conversations were few and carried out in a low murmur, the only other sounds being the clink and clatter of utensils and the muted strains of classical music emanating from a portable radio at the far end of the room. For a fleeting moment, Thorley considered waiting outside, but the sun had dropped behind the mountains and a chill breeze had blown up. All he wanted was some coffee, with perhaps something a little stronger poured into it.

The sergeant left them to join a group of his compatriots, while Rainer led him through a sea of tables, nodding to some of his men as he went. Thorley saw they were heading for a semi-private area near the back. At an empty table, Rainer pointed to one of the stiff-backed chairs. "Please, sit down."

Thorley eased himself into the chair with a weary sigh and threw his cap onto the table.

"Would you like something to drink?"

"I'd ask for a Schnapps, but I don't think that would go over very well."

Rainer's eyes twinkled. "You might be surprised. Out here, we tend to view things with a little less severity than they do in Berlin."

"Oh? Then make it a double," Thorley said, with the ghost of a smile.

Rainer turned to a passing soldier and spoke to him. The soldier nodded and hurried off, appearing moments later with two tumblers and an unopened bottle of Akvavit. Cracking the seal with a twist of his hand, Rainer poured a generous amount of the colorless liquid into both glasses, then raised his own. "To our families. May they never know the horrors we have seen."

Thorley clinked his tumbler against Rainer's then drank deeply, feeling the fiery caraway-flavored liquor burn its way down to his stomach, where it sat warming him like the dying embers of a once roaring fire. "Christ, that's bloody strong," he said, his eyes watering. "And I probably shouldn't ask where you got it, either."

"One learns to keep one's own counsel if one wishes to remain above ground," Rainer replied, his eyes fixed on the sparkling reflections inside his tumbler.

Emboldened by the brandy, Thorley leaned closer to Rainer. "Who did this? Who killed them?"

"Are you sure you really want to know? And will your people act on it?"

"You asked them to send someone, they did. So why are you playing coy with me?"

Rainer exhaled. "Forgive me. I've become far too paranoid for my own good. May I ask you a question?"

Thorley nodded.

"What did your people tell you?"

"That the man who would contact me was a member of—" he stopped and looked around, afraid to mention the name.

Rainer raised his hand in an assuring gesture.

"Please, you have nothing to fear. I trust my men implicitly. You may speak freely."

"They told me that you belonged to *Der Weisse Adler*, The White Eagle, and that this was an organization of junior officers dedicated to ending the war and bringing democracy back to Germany. Do I have that right?"

"You do."

"They also told me that they had no idea why you wanted someone sent."

"And now you do."

"Yes. Now I do. And I wish to God I didn't." Thorley paused to take another generous swallow of the 180-proof brandy, then asked the question that had nagged him ever since they'd left the site of the massacre. "How long have they lain there?"

Rainer gulped the rest of his Akvavit and poured another two fingers into his tumbler. "Our medical man estimates that they've been dead for about six weeks."

This last revelation surprised Thorley. "My God, if what you're saying is true, that means they were here—"

Rainer nodded. "Since the before the beginning of our campaign against the Russians. Exactly."

"But you chaps have been in Finland all this time, why has it taken you so long to find them?"

"We're not in Finland, Major, we're more than twenty kilometers inside Russia.... I would say your government owes you an explanation."

Though the rebuke was a mild one, Thorley understood its import. Britain's policy regarding the Winter War between Russia and Finland had been one of emphatic refusal to become involved, a fact at odds with what they had just seen. But before Thorley could comment, someone turned up the volume on the radio as a popular song began. The tune was mournful and the voice was at once familiar and strange, a husky feminine contralto that could turn a man's knees to water.

"Vor Der Kaserne, vor dem grossen Tor. Stand eine Laterne und stedt sie noch davor. So wollen wir uns wiedersehen, Bei der Laterne woll'n wir stehen. Wie einst Lili Marlene, wie einst Lili Marlene...."

Marlene Dietrich. A woman without peer.

Some of the soldiers began taking up the tune on the second verse, and very soon most of the men were singing it.

"A sad song for a sadder age," Rainer said, smiling wistfully.

"It's popular in Britain, too."

Rainer's expression became inquisitive. "Is it really?" He pursed his lips, then laughed. "I guess we all have someone waiting for us."

"Family?"

"Just Gerda, my wife. We wanted to have children right away, but the *Führer's* war got in the way."

The sarcasm in his voice was unmistakable.

"Does she know about—"

Rainer shook his head. "No. And the less she knows, the safer she will be."

"That must be an awful burden, keeping secrets like that."

Rainer's glass was empty again, but he made no move to refill it. "And I would bear it for eternity if it would keep her safe."

"What about the Gestapo?"

"Those *Schwein!* If I didn't have to deal with them, I wouldn't make the effort to spit on them." Rainer's eyes bulged as he spoke these last words in a low voice taut with anger and bitterness. "It is they who will bring down Germany. It is they who sully our honor."

A chilling thought ran through Thorley's mind. "Was it them? The SS? Did they do this?"

"No," Rainer said, shaking his head and reaching for the Akvavit. "It wasn't them. It was—"

Rainer stopped speaking and listened. A sound like that of a banshee screaming dopplered overhead. And then the explosion came, rocking the mess hall to its makeshift foundation.

A soldier stood up, his face flushed red from fear and excitement. "IVAN!"

The room erupted and Thorley felt the hard fist of panic punch him in the solar plexus when another banshee screamed overhead. It sounded closer.

They were being shelled.

"Bloody fucking Ruskis!" Rainer bellowed.

The next explosion took out part of a wall and caused a stampede for the door. Thorley snatched up his cap when Rainer grabbed him by the scruff of his tunic, propelling him toward a side door. In moments they were outside.

Soldiers were running every which way in a blind panic to find shelter. More incoming rounds shrieked overhead and one smashed through the roof of a building. It flew apart in a cloud of wood splinters and dirt, and Thorley felt Rainer tug on him again. "Come on!" he screamed.

They ran with other soldiers toward a series of trenches. At best, it was marginal protection, and none at all if it suffered a direct hit. Suddenly, a lorry careened around the side of a building and sped toward them, weaving erratically as the panicked driver fought to maintain control.

A shell hit the lorry dead center, blowing up the cab, shredding the driver, and setting it on fire. But instead of checking its momentum, the explosion only seemed to accelerate the wreck in its headlong rush.

More shells screamed earthward, stitching a line of craters that passed within fifty feet of where Thorley and Rainer lay sprawled in the dirt.

"We've got to get out of here!" Thorley shouted, trying to be heard over the incredible din.

Rainer shook his head vigorously, his brow knitted in a deep frown. "The safest place is where a shell has already struck."

Rainer pointed to a large crater and the two of them crawled on their bellies until they reached the edge of the shell hole, then dove in.

"Welcome to Man's folly, Major White," Rainer said, as another explosion shook the earth, throwing clods of dirt on them.

The shelling went on for another half an hour before it petered out to an occasional lob that ended as dusk fell. Thorley and Rainer crawled out from the crater and surveyed the devastation. Five of the dozen buildings were destroyed, and four others looked as if they would need extensive repairs. Prefabricated to begin with, they wouldn't take long to rebuild. Fortunately, the Mess Hall had mostly been spared, and everyone gathered there to lick their wounds. By eight o'clock that evening, the camp cook, a stocky Bavarian with a perpetual smile had cobbled a meal of potato soup, boiled cabbage, black bread and ersatz coffee from what hadn't been blown up or incinerated. Everyone, including Thorley ate their portion greedily, remarking to themselves and to each other that nothing had ever tasted so grand.

After the meal, Thorley accompanied Rainer back to his quarters, a cramped six-by-ten-foot room with bunk beds, a footlocker, and a shadeless window that looked out onto the quadrangle. Pale moonlight filtered in, casting ghostly shadows that made the austere little room feel like a monk's cell. None of this made much of an impression on Thorley, who felt as if he might collapse from the weight of the day's events. "Which bunk is mine?" he said, his voice drained of emotion.

Rainer pointed to the bottom bunk. The mattress was a moth-eaten affair that looked as lumpy as the Alps, and was covered with a field-gray blanket woven from a rough, homespun fabric. As uncomfortable as it looked, it beckoned. Thorley pulled off his boots, let them clatter to the floor, and crawled onto the bunk, feeling his muscles ache in protest as the mattress, true to its appearance, dug into his lower back. He grimaced at the musty odor of mildew and forced himself to ignore it. In moments his fatigue overcame everything, and he was fast asleep.

❋   ❋   ❋

It was the light that woke him: a gray and featureless day swathed in wreaths of morning mist, overcast and dreary. A light rain pattered against the window. White noise that both soothed and grated. Sitting up in the bunk, Thorley's head throbbed, a leftover gift from the Akvavit.

I've got to stop drinking, he thought. *I can't bloody take it.*

But that was not what was bothering him. He'd dreamed of the bodies, the eyeless faces staring at him, accusing him, saying, *"You're to blame, too...."*

Blame for what, though? For casting his vote for Tory instead of Labour—for supporting a government that had sent these men to their deaths? War was war, he understood it instinctively, yet these poor sods had been here prior to Germany's invasion.

Why?

He wanted to ask Sir Basil and the others that very question. Why then was he suddenly more afraid of going home than being in the lion's den itself? Rainer seemed to be an honest chap, but could he really trust him? After all, they were still enemies. Common cause or not.

Above him, Rainer shifted his weight and the bunk creaked softly while he settled into his new position. It was just after dawn. Reveille, or whatever passed for that here, would be sounding at any moment.

Boots clattered in the hallway and the door burst open. A wild-eyed private barreled into the room.

"Herr Hauptmann, Herr Hauptmann!"

Rainer bolted awake, instantly alert. "Yes, what is it?"

"We've just received word that *Obersturmbannführer* Müller is approaching the camp."

This news galvanized Rainer. "How far away?"

"Two miles, sir."

"Get back to your post." The private saluted and beat a hasty retreat, slamming the flimsy door behind him. Rainer hopped onto the floor and began throwing on his uniform, his movements quick and practiced, as if he'd had to do it this way many times before. "Get up," he said. "We must leave immediately."

Alarmed, Thorley jumped to his feet and began pulling on his boots. Fate had lent him a helping hand: he'd slept in his uniform. "I don't understand, what's wrong?"

Rainer snapped his collar closed and began buttoning his tunic. "Perhaps you didn't hear the man. The SS are coming."

"Christ."

"We have to get you back to the plane. I just hope those *Luftwaffe* boys are on their toes. If Müller finds you here everything is lost."

"Wait a minute. I'm just one among hundreds. For this man to notice me would be a minor miracle. And even if he does, my papers are flawless, and I speak German like a native."

"The man was born suspicious, my friend. He knows when the slightest thing is amiss. He'll smell you. And when he finds you, he *will* make you talk. And I can't risk that. There's too much at stake. Let's go."

Rainer led the way out of the room and the building. Not surprisingly, the *Kübelwagen* awaited them just outside the door, exhaust billowing out of the tailpipe. The leather-faced sergeant sat hunched behind the wheel, his expression grim and wary, the stub of a cheroot clenched in his yellowed teeth.

Thorley was barely inside the vehicle when the sergeant tromped down on the accelerator and the *Kübelwagen* fishtailed, sending up plumes of mud from both tires as it sped toward the airstrip. When they crested the first rise, they saw a Maybach staff car flying SS pennants drive into the camp. It slowed for an instant, then sped up, heading on the road toward them. Rainer whirled back to the sergeant. "Go!" he said, slamming his fist on the dash.

The sergeant grimaced, slapped the gearshift into first, then popped the clutch; the little *Kübelwagen* lurched forward, its Porsche engine racing. The car nosed over the rise and plunged down the road at breakneck speed, its metal frame shrieking and clattering in protest as it jounced and joggled over rocks and deep ruts in the muddy track. Thorley gripped the edges of his seat, every muscle in his body tensed, his jaw aching from the effort.

Rainer swiveled to face Thorley his face contorted as he shouted over the engine noise. "The Maybach is a fast car on city streets. However, it can't hope to match our agility. With any luck it will break an axle or rip out its sump." He smiled then, the thought apparently pleasing him.

The rain had stopped some minutes before, and the clouds boiled overhead, pushed eastward by a brisk wind that made Thorley shiver.

The rest of the drive back to the airstrip was made in silence, except for the occasional curses from the sergeant as he negotiated the rocky ground. Always there was the Maybach behind them, tailing them at a distance that varied from one to two miles, moving steadily and inexorably. Rainer's previous confidence drained away. Müller, it seemed, would not be deterred.

As the airstrip came into view over the last rise, the weather-beaten sergeant, his cheroot long since chewed into oblivion, began leaning on the horn. It sounded like a goose with a head cold: loud and obnoxious. "This'll wake the bastards up!" the sergeant laughed, his voice a guttural growl.

Rainer's expression remained grim, while Thorley let himself smile in spite of their dire situation. He couldn't help admiring a man who laughed adversity in the face. He scanned the road behind them, but the rise in the landscape blocked his view. Ahead, he saw the Heinkel's engines spewing blue-colored smoke, the propellers beginning to turn. They quickly picked up speed, and the mighty roar of the two Jumo engines was reduced to a high-pitched buzz. Still, the sound made his heart race, knowing that his salvation lay a scant quarter mile distant.

The sergeant brought the *Kübelwagen* to a sliding stop yards from the plane and all three hopped out. The sergeant drew a P38 from a holster and thumbed off the safety.

Rainer shook his head. "Put it away, Axel."

The sergeant looked crestfallen, but obeyed the order, his jaw grinding angrily. Thorley felt the same. From what little he knew of the SS, they deserved to be hung, drawn and quartered, much less shot. Rainer motioned for him to move to the plane.

"This is goodbye, my friend," he said, offering his hand. Thorley took it and smiled warmly. "I think you now realize what's at stake here. Churchill and the others *must* be shown that they cannot trust the Russian Bear."

"I'll do what I can, but I can't guarantee my government will believe your people had nothing to do with this."

"This will convince them," he said, reaching into his pocket and pulling out a roll of Leica film. He dropped it into Thorley's out-stretched palm. It felt surprisingly heavy and warm to the touch.

"Perhaps.... But even if they do, they'll never deal with any of you, as long as Hitler is in power. You know that."

Rainer fixed him with a burning gaze. "Those of us within *Der Weisse Adler* do not hold with *'Der Führer's'* policies. To have at-tacked in the east is madness."

"But if he had not done that, he would have invaded England."

Rainer looked guilty. "Yes, it is a nasty business. Take the film, show them. We are willing to negotiate, anything to—"

"They are coming," the sergeant interjected.

Rainer and Thorley turned and spotted the Maybach racing toward them, spurts of mud streaming out behind it. Rainer reached inside his tunic and pulled out a buff-colored envelope and thrust it into Thorley's hands. He leaned forward and began shouting over the engine noise. "These are the names of those within *Der Weisse Adler*. Put it in a safe place. If we are not successful, then the world must know the truth. Good luck, my friend. The fate of millions rests with you."

Thorley nodded and started to speak, but Rainer silenced him. "Go. Now!" he said, pushing Thorley toward the Heinkel.

The Maybach staff car was closer now, and Thorley could now see the SS pennant—two silver lightning bolts laid against a field of black—flying from the antenna. He turned and dashed for the plane.

The instant his feet cleared the rim of the hatch, the Major slammed it shut and the Heinkel's engines throttled up to a full-throated roar. In moments they were airborne, heading back to Lisbon. Settling back into his seat, Thorley felt his pockets for the film and the documents, then remembered the badge. He took it out once more and held it in his hands, the dim light inside the plane casting tiny shadows across it. If nothing else, Thorley mused, this and the names of Rainer's co-conspirators would be his insurance that his government would do the right thing. Not surprisingly, Thorley had a sneaking suspicion that he would need it.

❈　❈　❈

Friedrich Rainer watched the Heinkel disappear into the cloud bank and felt a great weight lifting from his shoulders. They were not alone anymore. *Der Weisse Adler* could now carry out their mission with the sure knowledge that there would be others working toward the same goal. As Major White had said, he couldn't be sure that those in charge of Britain's government would heed the warning, or would aid them directly. There were powerful elements in England who were still sympathetic to Hitler.

But the seeds had been planted and he had to be content with that. And even more so, Rainer felt as if he'd made a fast and true friend. The irony of that made him smile.

The smile died when he faced the approaching staff car. It slid to a halt, its brakes squealing. As soon as it stopped moving a tall whippet-thin man dressed in the new field-grey uniform of the *Waffen*-SS leaped out.

The new *feldgrau* was meant to make the SS look more like soldiers, the old black uniform having become an object of scorn to those who felt the SS was shirking its duty by remaining home instead of fighting at the front. Now, ever since Hitler had decreed that the SS would carry arms into battle, it had taken supreme acts of will to tolerate their presence. This one made the task all the harder. He was the officer in charge of their military district.

You might have changed your spots, Müller, but you're still scum.

Rainer plastered a conciliatory smile on his face and watched while Müller marched up to him, his polished boots gleaming. He strutted rather than walked, carrying himself with the air of the congenitally arrogant, blue eyes staring out of a face that was all sharp angles and jutting planes.

"*Obersturmbannführer* Müller, what a surprise," he said. "I must confess that I did not expect you until this evening."

One of Müller's long-fingered hands stabbed the air in the direction of the departed Heinkel. "Who was that man, Herr Hauptmann?"

Rainer arched his brows in mock innocence. "Why that, *Obersturmbannführer*, was Major Wenner...from the Inspector General's Office."

This spurious revelation only seemed to make Müller even angrier. "You should have reported his arrival to me, at once. I was ordered to contain the situation here!"

"And I was ordered to cooperate. Perhaps Berlin has its wires crossed?"

Müller sneered at Rainer, then looked toward the sky where the Heinkel had disappeared. "We shall see whose wires are crossed, *Herr Hauptmann*, Berlin's...or yours."

Müller turned back and fixed him with a piercing glare. It made Rainer's blood run cold. For in the man's ice-blue eyes he saw only death, destruction, and rivers of his countrymen's blood.

THE SON:
1984

9

Friedrich Rainer awoke from a restless night of vague and disturbing dreams, covered in a sheen of sweat and feeling every minute of his sixty-eight years. Muscles in his lower back spasmed painfully, and his prostate throbbed with a dull and persistent ache that radiated down through his rectum. Perhaps the most annoying of all was that it now took several minutes for his tired eyes to focus every morning, even after putting on his trademark pair of eight-hundred Mark tortoise shell-rimmed bifocals.

Getting old was shit, but that all paled in comparison with what ran through his mind this mild June morning.

Hans Kleisner was dead, killed by some Arab fanatic they said. Hans had become a controversial writer known the world over for his searing fictional portraits of real-life despots and other politicos, a man who had made many enemies and very few friends. But mere words had not motivated the nervous ascetic young man to wrap his arms around him as the semtex strapped to his youthful body had detonated, blasting them both to atoms.

Rainer knew the real truth: what had killed Hans Kleisner was not his books, but his membership in a nearly forgotten cabal of young German officers dedicated to wresting control of their country from a sputtering madman bent on world domination, a group dedicated to restoring true democracy. Hans Kleisner, like Rainer, had been a member of *Der Weisse Adler*: The White Eagle.

Rainer put on his glasses, squinting while he eased himself off the mattress, careful not to awaken his wife. He turned, looked down on her and smiled.

Thirty years his junior, she'd come into his life two years before during a Lufthansa shuttle flight from Bonn to Frankfurt, where he'd been traveling to close a deal on new factory space for his company. The closing had gone exceptionally well, and Ilse, one of the flight attendants on the return leg of the journey, had flashed her expensive capped teeth and her ample cleavage, leaving no room for doubt that she found the distinguished-looking industrialist to her liking.

And the truth be told, Rainer hadn't been looking.

Managing to survive both the war and Hitler's purging of the *Wehrmacht* officer corps in the wake of the assassination attempt on July 20, 1944, Rainer elected to stay and help rebuild his ravaged country after the surrender, rather than flee to the Americas as others had done. His patriotism paid off in an opportunity to join a fledgling pharmaceuticals firm, which soon became the preeminent company in West Germany. And his beloved Gerda had been there every step of the way, indispensable to both his life and his business, until breast cancer stole her beauty and her life at the age of fifty-four.

A widower now for nearly a decade, he'd grown accustomed to his solitude, preferring to satisfy the occasional urge with discreet high-priced escorts who knew how to pleasure a man and asked for nothing but their fee in return. The rest of his energies he devoted to his business. Now the "Direktor" of the firm of Horst und Freideke, he was one of the most respected businessmen in Germany, and one of the richest. Still, he hadn't realized how lonely it all had become... until Ilse.

With her, there had been an immediate attraction, which surprised him as much as it had delighted her. They'd dated for six months, getting together whenever their hectic schedules permitted, spending most of that time in bed. Ilse turned out to be a consummate mistress in the art of lovemaking, approaching the act with a joyous abandon and a practiced hand. She was what his old *Wehrmacht* comrades would have called a *Nerz*, after the libidinous weasel-like mammals farmed for their luxurious pelts. That she also loved to wear mink coats was an irony not lost on Rainer.

They were married after a short engagement, and the wedding made the society pages of all the major papers. The *Frankfurter Allgemeine Zeitung* called it "a zestful and elegant affair." But what surprised nearly every one of those invited to the ceremony was that Ilse was an intelligent, well-bred woman who had a great sense of humor, and knew how to throw a party.

Now, after two years of wedded bliss, Rainer was beginning to wonder if he would be able to keep up with her for much longer. Their lovemaking the night before had been as strenuous and as deeply satisfying as always, but now he felt like a pugilist's punching bag: bruised and pummeled. He sighed, thinking that if she killed him with her appetites it would not be such a bad way to go.

Smiling again, he walked to the window, wincing when the muscle in his back spasmed yet again. He stifled a groan and focused his attention on the black Mercedes idling just inside the gate of his estate. Including the man in the house, and the two roamers on the grounds, the two men in the car brought the number to five. He'd hired them after the first of his old comrades had died mysteriously six months before. That crime remained unsolved, a seemingly random mugging.

Oh, these bastards were clever, he had to give them that. They were meticulous in making sure that every death appeared to be the work of a common criminal or the cruel hand of fate. Kleisner was only the most recent, and the most personal. He'd been a close and dear friend. Rainer had kept in touch with the others in *Der Weisse Adler* only sporadically. They never held reunions. Their secrets were still feared by many in power. Now, it looked as if their existence would no longer be tolerated.

How long could he hope to elude them? How long could he hope to remain alive?

He forced those questions from his mind, turned from the window, and limped into the bathroom, his bare feet slapping against the rose-colored Tuscan marble that covered the four hundred square foot expanse. He examined himself in the full-length mirror, appraising his physique with a critical eye:

Waist a still trim thirty-four inches.

Hair still full, though now a luxuriant white.

No ugly wattle under the chin.

All in all, not bad for nearly seventy.

He turned and stepped into the multi-nozzle Swedish shower and turned on the water, adjusting the temperature to just this side of scalding, and let the spray sluice over his aching flesh. It felt like a tiny bit of heaven.

While he lathered his body with the scented soap his wife insisted he use, he went over his schedule for the day: 9:00 meeting with his board of directors, 10:00 conference call with the *Wehrmacht Veterans Association* to help gain additional funds for disabled soldiers, 11:00 meeting with the engineers planning the new robotic production line, Noon lunch with Ilse. He smiled, remembering her lusty cries from the night before and felt himself growing hard.

Not now, you old fool.

Then again, why not? Men of his age had to count themselves lucky they could perform at all.

Rinsing off the soap lather, he turned the water cold, not surprised to find the old cold shower cliché had the desired effect. He toweled off and dressed in one of his charcoal gray double-breasted suits, accenting the robin's-egg blue shirt with a yellow paisley "power tie." He laughed at the American expression. Power had nothing to do with one's tie, and everything to do with one's actions.

He then snuck past Ilse's still sleeping form and took the wide curving staircase down to the ground floor.

The house man, a thuggish-looking Westphalian named Rudi, sat at the kitchen table thumbing through the newspaper, a steaming cup of black Turkish coffee resting on the table next to his Hechler & Koch MP5K machine pistol with integral silencer. Rudi raised his dark eyes as Rainer entered the room and started to stand up. "Please, sit down," Rainer said, motioning with his hand as he moved to the walk-in larder. "And please put the gun away. If we are attacked by marauding hordes, I think you will have time to draw it."

"Sorry, *Herr* Rainer," he said, slipping the "Hech" back into a shoulder harness.

As he did every morning, Rainer fixed himself a simple breakfast of Muesli cereal and hot black coffee. He joined Rudi at the small circular table and they conversed while he ate, each talking about the other's experiences. Rainer nodded at the tiny demitasse cup filled with the acrid Turkish brew. "How can you drink that, Rudi? It tastes like something a camel spat up."

Rudi shrugged, an easy smile softening his rough features. "Got used to it when I lived in Istanbul. Now, I can't drink anything else."

"You're lucky there's a Turkish contingent in the Fatherland, now. Otherwise, I'd think it would be hard to come by."

Rudi nodded, his face suddenly clouding. "Maybe so, but I wish they'd stay home. Too many of 'em here now."

This last comment disturbed Rainer, not only because the young security man seemed like a pleasant fellow, but because it sounded exactly like the neo-Nazi drivel that so many of the young were spouting these days. Didn't history teach them anything? Then again, perhaps it was human nature to trivialize the advice of one's elders. Either way, it amounted to the same thing. Hate was making a comeback. Rainer decided to change the subject. "Anything in the paper?"

Rudi knew what that meant. He shook his head. "Nothing new, anyway. The latest on your friend is that no terrorist organization is claiming responsibility. They're saying the bomber was some kind of lone wolf."

Rainer nodded, his mind churning. *It's them. It's them. It's them....*

Rudi started to say something, then cocked his head, listening intently to something coming in over his earpiece radio. The microphone, into which he now spoke, was hidden inside his sleeve. "*Ja....* All is quiet.... *Jawohl*, I'll be right out." He turned to Rainer. "That was Baldric. Our shift is ending. I'm to meet him outside. Erich will be right in."

"Very good. I'll see you tonight."

Rainer watched the big man lumber out of the kitchen, then turned on the tiny *Blaupunkt* television resting on the counter. He switched channels until he found the news, hoping to hear more about Hans, but knowing that if he did it would add nothing to what he knew to be the truth. He sat staring into his cereal while listening to the latest statistics of rapes and murders.

"How can you watch that drivel, Freddy?"

Rainer turned and saw his wife standing in the doorway, her satin robe barely containing her womanliness. *Christ, she looked good in the morning,* he thought. *What does she see in this old soldier?*

"I wanted to see if there was any more news about Hans."

Ilse moved across the floor, her hips swinging invitingly, her green eyes flashing. "Can I persuade you to be a little late this morning?" she asked threading her arms around his waist.

Rainer smiled and caressed the back of her neck, something that always made her purr. "You probably could, but Erich will be in any minute. Besides, if I were to succumb to your charms, as I so often do, you would then have to answer to my board."

Ilse's eyes widened. "My God, I forgot. Today is the day."

"Yes, today is the day. And if I don't get going, it will likely be my last as Direktor of Horst and Freideke. Besides, if the vote goes my way, I'll want to celebrate at lunch."

A wicked smile crossed Ilse's face. "Is that a promise or a threat?"

"Both. Now let me go, or I shall not be responsible for my actions." He pinched her bottom, making her squeal, and walked toward the front of the house, collecting his briefcase from his office on the way. She followed, still playing the seductress.

Reaching for the door, he stopped, remembering something. "Is it all right if I take your car again? I think something is wrong with the BMW."

"I hate it when you drive my car," she said, the seductive mood spoiled. "The last time, you let some idiot put a dent in the door."

"My dear, it's not as if I wanted him to do it. It just happened."

"But if something *is* wrong with yours, how will I meet you for lunch?"

Rainer bowed to her inimitable logic. "You're right, I'll take mine."

He opened the door and walked onto the circular drive, his gait slowing as he noticed that the black Mercedes was gone, the gray BMW belonging to the next crew not yet in its place.

Strange. Shift changes were always overlapping. And where was Erich? He glanced at his watch and frowned. If he did not leave right now, he would be mired in traffic and would be late for his board meeting, the consequences of which would be fatal to his career. He looked back and saw her standing there, one bare, well-formed leg showing through the slit of the robe.

I am a lucky man, he thought.

"Stay inside until the next shift arrives, all right?"

She nodded and blew him a kiss. "Good luck, *Liebchen!*"

Waving, he opened the driver's side door of his jet-black BMW 750IL and tossed his briefcase onto the passenger seat, climbed inside, and placed the key into the ignition.

Sighing at the injustice of Hans' death, Rainer twisted the key, completing a circuit that led to a detonator plugged into a half-pound of semtex wired to the BMW's undercarriage. There was a nanosecond's delay before the massive explosion shattered the luxury car into a million fiery fragments, blowing out every window in his fifty-room mansion and leaving his hysterical widow to watch helplessly while his shredded corpse burned to cinders.

10

Fumbling with his keys, Michael Thorley, Jr. locked the door of his South Kensington mews flat and dashed out onto the pavement, a sweat already beading his brow and staining the underarms of his starched Harrod's shirt.

He was going to be late again.

Cursing when he stubbed the toe of his wingtip shoes on a tilted paving stone, he managed to grab a lamppost in time to steady himself. He took a moment to glance at his watch.

8:35 a.m.

He was going to be very late.

A middle-aged woman approached, her beefy arms laden with two bulging bags of groceries displaying the Tesco logo. She smiled, a pleading look in her eyes.

"Need a hand there, Mrs. Herrick?" he said, trying to sound as if he had nothing better to do. He had to stop being so bloody nice. The older woman grinned, the lines around her eyes crinkling like tissue paper.

"Oh, you're such a dear, Michael. Just up the steps, I know you're a busy lad."

"Never too busy for you, Mrs. H."

"Oh, you're just saying that because I'm your landlady," she clucked, her blushing face belying her words.

90

He took the bags and started up the paved walk to her townhouse, a white stone affair that adjoined his mews flat. "Never. You're the light of my life," he said.

"Ooh, now you're just trying to flatter an old girl," she said, following him. "Well, I won't lower the rent. But I will introduce you to my niece. She's asked about you, you know. I think she rather fancies you."

Michael placed the bags on the top step and managed a pleasant smile. Mrs. Herrick's niece favored purple hair and safety pins through the nose. "I'd appreciate that Mrs. H, but I'm really not looking to—"

"Now, now," she said, patting his arm in a motherly way. "You've got to stop squirreling yourself away, get out more often...."

She began to prattle, and Michael became even more nervous. He felt a rivulet of sweat trickle down his spine.

Really late.

He began backing down the walk. "Mrs. H, I really do have to be running."

"I'll tell Tilly that you're dying to meet her!" She said, waving.

Turning, he ran toward the corner, where he saw the Number 11 red double-decker idling by the curb, an advert for Player's cigarettes plastered along its side panel. He might make it. Putting on a burst of speed, Michael reached the rear platform of the bus just as the driver gunned the engine and began steering back into traffic. He leaped on and grabbed the stairway railing, breathing an overheated sigh of relief.

I've got to start exercising, he thought, feeling his heart thudding against his rib cage. Dizzy from the unseasonably warm weather and the undue exertion, he trudged into the lower level and settled in one of the seats that faced the aisle, his back to an open window.

The bus picked up speed, and Michael closed his eyes when he felt a cooling breeze play across his neck, glad for a moment of relief. He pulled out a handkerchief and wiped his brow, just when the Conductor, a rotund black man with a wide smile and swinging dreadlocks, waddled up to him.

"Where to, Mon?" he asked, his lilting voice betraying its Jamaican roots.

Michael reached into his trousers and extracted a handful of change.

"Horse Guards, please."

The Conductor deftly set the dial on his portable dispenser and rolled out the appropriately priced ticket. Handing him a few coins, Michael noted the man's checked shirt open at the neck. The lack of a tie made for an odd look with the standard London Transport uniform. Like so many other aspects of modern life, the lack of regard for traditional dress was becoming the norm.

The ride to London proper lasted ten minutes and Michael got off the bus in Whitehall at Horse Guards Avenue and walked the rest of the way to the Commonwealth War Graves Commission.

Occupying a tiny one-room office behind a frosted-glass door on the second floor at number 45 Whitehall Court—a rambling pile of white stone and gargoyles—it boasted bilious-green walls, a battered partner's desk surrounded by wall-to-wall filing cabinets of a uniform battleship gray. A fifteen-year-old air conditioner wheezed tepid air from the single window, making the air smell faintly of mildew.

Michael entered the room, shed his jacket, and placed it on the coat stand next to the door. The water cooler burbled a greeting as he slid into his chair and began to study his phone messages. His coworker, Ferguson, lounged across from him, scanning *The Daily Mail* with disdain, a lit cigarette dangling from his lips.

"*Another German War Hero Murdered*," the headline screamed in large bold type.

Everything about Ferguson was rumpled, from his patched tweed jacket and his threadbare corduroy trousers, to his wild thatch of dark-brown hair and affable hang-dog face. Even his desk looked as if it had been visited by a tiny tornado, papers and personal knick-knacks scattered about with careless abandon.

"'Ere listen to this!" Ferguson said, dropping his "H's" in his inimitable Cockney fashion and slapping the paper with his free hand. The ash from his cigarette dislodged, plopping unnoticed onto his tea-stained tie. "'The Prime Minister announced today that talks with the USSR will commence next month as scheduled, despite rumors to the contrary.' Bloody contrary this!" he said, making masturbatory motions. "Those bloody Slavs'll have her for breakfast."

Michael looked up from his work, his nose wrinkling at the stench of Ferguson's cigarette. He noticed the overflowing ashtray, a cheap ceramic dish with the Brighton Pavilion painted on it—had crept onto his side of the desk, otherwise as neat as an army recruit's footlocker. "Don't you ever empty that thing?"

"Sorry, mate," Ferguson said, lifting the ceramic dish and overturning it into the waste bin. It raised a noxious cloud of ash, making the room smell even worse. "You call that number I gave you?"

Michael didn't answer, his eyes fixed on the paper he was desperately trying to study.

"You didn't, did ya?"

"I had work to do," he said, still not looking up.

Ferguson threw the paper aside. It landed in a heap on the floor, drawing Michael's attention.

"Work? Blimey! That's all you do, Mike. What about having a little fun?" He shook his head and leaned forward across the desk.

"Maisy was just about a sure thing. She likes the studious type, she says. And you don't call the number?"

Michael shrugged. "I lost it."

"Now that's a bleedin' good one," he laughed. "The neatest man alive and 'e loses the phone number to the easiest bird in Kensington!"

"I don't want the 'easiest bird in Kensington.' I want someone with a bit of breeding, someone I can relate to."

"You want a bloody fossil, you do. They don't make 'em that way anymore. Now, it's all flash and trash."

"Then I'd rather do without," Michael said, getting irritated. "I swear to God, you and my landlady should open up a dating service. In fact, she's got a niece. You want flash and trash? Have I got the girl for you!"

Before Ferguson could offer a retort, the phone rang. Michael snatched it up, shooting Ferguson a nasty look. "Commonwealth War Graves Commission.... No, I'm sorry Mrs. Petrie, we haven't located the grave as of yet. We're waiting for files from our main office in Maidenhead. I believe we'll know for sure in about a week.... Yes, I wish we could send it over the phone, too.... Thank you, I'll call you as soon as I have the information."

Michael hung up just as Ferguson pulled out a buff-colored envelope from under a pile of file folders. "We got another one of those letters in this morning's post. *Dear Sirs. I know this is a trifle late for such inquiries, but I am trying to locate the grave site of my late father, Sergeant Major Arthur Woodley of His Majesty's Regiment, Royal South Wessex....*'"

Michael frowned. "Hmmm.... South Wessex.... Did you make those inquiries about the last ones we had in?"

"I should say so. Took bloody forever and a day for those

wankers to get back to me. If I wasn't such a bureaucrat myself, I might have gotten—"

"What did they say?" Michael cut in, impatient with Ferguson's usual banter.

Ferguson threw up his hands in disgust. "That's just it. They didn't. The bloke said, and I bloody well quote: "er Majesty's government have no record of such a regiment.'"

"What?"

"That's what I said. Then the bloody arse told me to mind my own business and hung up on me."

Michael leaned back in his chair, his eyes focused on a crack in the ceiling, and tried to make sense of what Ferguson had told him. On the one hand, it was conceivable that someone could have remembered the name of his father's regiment incorrectly. But this letter made the fifth one in six months, and everyone had unerringly inquired about that selfsame regiment: *The Royal South Wessex*. Far too many to be mere coincidence.

So that left the man Ferguson had spoken to. Knowing Ferguson as he did, Michael knew that it was quite possible he'd rubbed the fellow the wrong way and been told to piss off for his troubles. That didn't mean there wasn't a Royal South Wessex regiment buried somewhere in the files.

He sighed and rubbed his temples where a dull throbbing had begun some moments before. What was the use, anyway? Without any leads, there was no way they were going to solve the problem now, or at any time hence.

So why did it bother him so much?

Shaking his head, Michael let the chair fall forward, the spring shrieking for lack of oil.

"All right, then," he said, as he began straightening his papers.

"We'll put it aside for now, maybe I'll call the man myself later on. Let's not worry about it."

Ferguson stubbed out the butt of his cigarette and pulled out another, lighting it with a flick of his battered Zippo. "Fine by me, mate. I've bloody well had it with those tossers. I should've listened to me Dad and become a bleedin' accountant like him. Prob'ly own a bloody Jag by now."

Turning back to his work, Michael allowed himself a tiny smile as he imagined Ferguson tending to someone's books, his office a blizzard of paper.

The phone rang again, and Michael snatched it up, grateful for the distraction. He pushed all thoughts of phantom regiments and incompetent accountants from his mind and put on his best phone voice. "Commonwealth War Graves Commission, Michael Thorley, Jr. speaking.... Yes ma'am, the information came in yesterday, and I was about to ring you up...."

11

Sir William Atwater stood in the crowd of eager tourists cradling a wiry Jack Russell terrier in his arms. Dressed, as was his custom, in a dark blue pin-stripe Savile Row suit, starched white shirt and his Hussars tie, he stood straight and tall in resolute defiance of the infirmities of old age. His snow-white handlebar mustache was precisely waxed, and his Dunn's bowler hat placed at the proper jaunty angle. Gray lambskin gloves covered the large liver spots on his hands and a tightly furled black umbrella hung from the crook of his arm.

The dog, all pointed ears and darting eyes, quivered with anticipation that mirrored his master's.

The tourists around him reacted with awe and a whirring and clicking of shutters as the first of Her Majesty's Horse Guards rode into view, the sun glinting off their highly polished breastplates and helmets. As always, they rode to the strains of the "British Grenadiers," a sprightly tune that never failed to make Sir William swell with pride.

"Watch now, Watson, that's a good lad," he said to the little dog. "This is the best part, isn't it?"

Watson yipped in reply and Sir William chuckled. Ever since his Evie had passed away five years before, Watson had been such comfort. Today, as he'd done every day for the past twenty years of his retirement—Good Lord, had it really been that long already—he'd awakened at 0600, dressed and taken his breakfast at the club. At precisely 1100 hours, he could be found standing on this very spot watching the Changing of the Guard—every day—rain or shine. One must stand on tradition, after all.

When the ceremony ended, he would stroll through St. James's Park, let Watson do his duty, and then spend the afternoon sitting in his study writing his memoirs.

Of course, they would never be published, as much as he secretly wished they would be, for as the former Director of MI6, he was the guardian of his nation's secrets, and therefore still bound by the Official Secrets Act. No, they would never see the light of day. His executors had instructions to burn the lot the very hour of his death, and he intended to see it done, even if it meant haunting the bloody fools. Sir William chuckled to himself. He rather enjoyed the thought of being a proper English ghost.

As the last of the Horse Guards passed him, their mounts swishing their coiffed tails in unison, Watson began to whine, squirming in his master's arms like an eager puppy. Sir William eyed the terrier with mock disdain. "You must learn to hold your waters, old boy. England expects every dog to do his duty…discreetly."

Sir William chuckled again, placing the dog on the pavement and attaching his leash. "Come, Watson, let us take our leave."

They began walking toward the Horse Guards barracks through the dispersing crowd. The tiny dog pulled and strained at his leash, anxious to place his mark on familiar territory. "Easy, old boy, easy," Sir William admonished. "We're almost there."

Passing under an archway between two barracks buildings, they entered Horse Guards Parade where the Guards drilled, and on to St. James's Park, a large area of green crisscrossed by footpaths and dotted with trees. Most of its interior was dominated by a large artificial lake, and here and there were families of ducks trolling about, leaving trails of ripples to mar its otherwise glassy surface.

As with the Changing of the Guard, St. James's Park reinforced Sir William's belief that tradition still reigned, even if common sense in government had long since fled. And that was the rub and the main reasons he'd resigned his position at what was then considered an early age. He'd lost his stomach for the fight, especially when Harold Wilson's Labour government began sniping at MI6's heels, questioning every blasted move they made and calling them imperialist throwbacks.

The nerve of the man! The utter gall! It was even thought, in certain circles, that he made his frequent trips to Moscow only to receive new orders. As a result, the sixties had turned into a quagmire, and it had all gone downhill from there.

Suddenly depressed, Sir William released his hold on Watson's leash, collapsed onto one of the ubiquitous benches and watched as the little terrier scurried over to a favorite tree, letting loose a stream of urine that darkened the bark where it hit.

"Not a moment too soon, eh Watson?" he said, absently.

As if noticing them for the first time, Sir William scanned his surroundings. A few yards away a group of young nannies clucked over their diminutive charges, while further on a pack of scruffy youths clad in black leather, their waxed Mohawks dyed the colors of the rainbow, listened to loud Heavy Metal blasting from a giant portable radio. There were other elderly people scattered about. Some appeared oblivious to their surroundings, lost in some private hell, while others actively engaged in conversations with those they'd only just met.

Sir William smiled wistfully, envying them their gregariousness. That was something he'd never been very good at. It was Evie who'd made all their friends.

Hearing Watson's bark, Sir William looked up and saw the little dog staring past him. He turned to find an elderly man standing next to him.

Where the blazes had he come from?

One moment he'd been alone, and the next...there the blighter stood, clutching his frayed umbrella in rough, gnarled hands. Thick and heavyset like a pillar box, the man wore a baggy suit that was at least fifteen years out of date. The hat was a rumpled moth-eaten fedora pulled low over his beetled brow, nearly hiding his intense brown eyes. It was the man's thick ratty beard, however, that finally put him off. He could never abide a man who let his whiskers run rampant like some creeper vine on a trellis.

"Lovely day, isn't it?" the old man said.

Sir William squirmed, letting a wan smile flicker across his lips. "Quite."

The old man pointed toward the seat. "Do you mind if an old soldier rests his weary bones?"

The man's accent was strange. It sounded like South London, yet something else, the way he rolled his "R's" sounded foreign. Oh, well, there were plenty of them running about these days. Why, oh, why did the blighter have to pick *him* to be friendly with?

Sir William forced himself to look at the old man once again. "It's a free country."

The old man eased himself onto the bench with a heavy sigh, leaning forward onto his umbrella.

"Is it? I often wonder."

"What do you mean?"

The old man shrugged. "Just that times have changed. Not like the old days, eh?" He nodded toward the group of punks cavorting several yards away. "In our day those boys would be in uniform, fighting for King and country.... Not bloody tit-suckers on the dole, eh what?"

Watson stood off to the side, eyeing both men with a wary expression. Sir William snapped his fingers. "Come on, Watson, heel to."

But the little dog remained where it was, staring at them. Sir William began to feel strangely anxious. There was something odd about the other man—something about his face.... "You were in the war?" he asked, not really wanting to know.

The old man smiled, his eyes devoid of warmth. "Yes.... You might say I was...."

"Really, where?" he said, growing impatient with the man's queer manner.

"I was with the Royal South Wessex."

Sir William felt the earth tilt on its axis. Blood pounded in his ears, and he suddenly found it very hard to breath. "W—who the bloody hell are you," he whispered, hating himself for the note of fear in his voice.

But he *was* scared—deathly afraid to the very marrow of his bones, which now felt as if they might crumble to dust.

The old man stared back at him, those mirthless brown eyes now burning with a mad glimmer. "Just someone come to put things right...Sir William."

Sir William gasped. "How do you know my name?"

But the time for talking was past. The old man leaped to his feet with surprising agility, raised the umbrella and aimed the tip square in Sir William's face.

Sir William saw it all in the microsecond it took for the old man to push the hidden button on the umbrella's hand-carved handle.

Oh God, not now, not no—

Atomized to a fine mist by the spray mechanism hidden inside the umbrella, the poison rushed up Sir William's nose and entered his system through the mucous membranes. In a fraction of a moment, his brain lost the ability to breath and his vital organs began shutting down. Sir William tried reaching out to the man who'd killed him, but his arms would not respond. They spasmed like someone with palsy, and he could no longer feel his feet. With a sigh that sounded like a pig whose throat had been cut, Sir William Atwater, late of Her Majesty's Secret Service, pitched over dead.

Watson began barking frantically, and the old man looked quickly about him. The punks, more interested in playing games of macho one-upsmanship, hadn't noticed a thing, and neither had the nannies, still cooing over their slobbering brats. And the best thing of all, that decadent music still blasted at ear-shattering volume, neatly covering any undue noise. And that included this insufferable little mutt.

Bending down to the dead body, the old man sat him up and leaned him against the back of the bench, arranging him so it would appear he'd fallen asleep. Then he reached into the pocket of his own suit and brought something out, which he placed into the pocket of Sir William's jacket.

Satisfied, he stood up, making sure his false beard was still in place, and gazed upon his adversary one last time. In perfect accentless German he said, "The Eagle Flies."

Then he turned and walked out of the park, whistling "The British Grenadiers," leaving the corpse alone with its tiny mourner.

12

The Number 11 Routemaster bus heaved to the curb, its brakes hissing. Michael exited, along with three of his fellow passengers, and the bus moved on, its diesel engine chugging with effort. Sunlight dappled the sidewalk, shining through the lime trees lining the pavement, and the air smelled of curried rice and lemon grass from the Indian and Thai restaurants that abutted each other on the corner. Moving to the newsagent's kiosk, Michael nodded to an acquaintance, threw down his pound coin, and accepted his change and a copy of the *Evening News* from the grizzled agent. "Don't read it all in one place," the old agent joked with a toothless grin. Michael returned the grin, tucked the paper under his arm, and began the short walk home. He passed a Wimpy's and debated stopping in for a hamburger, but changed his mind. He'd been having far too much of that, lately, and he knew it would do him no good. He caught himself, as he thought of his mother's chiding him over his solitary eating.

"At least go out with your friends," she'd say. "It does a body good. Helps the digestion."

He hadn't called the old girl in a while, and he missed her gentle, if incongruous, words of admonishment. Then again, aside from being old enough and having a job, those very words were the reason he'd moved out of the house and came to London. Lillian Thorley could be a formidable woman. It came with having raised a son all by herself at a time when women were expected to cleave to a man, an accomplishment not to be lightly dismissed. That he'd turned out all right was further testament to her skills and raw determination, for life had been hard in war-torn London when he was a baby, and improved only marginally when they moved to Sussex after the destruction of their Brixton terraced house by a German bomb. Now, if he could only keep her from badgering him about getting married.

Michael passed Mrs. Herrick's house and held his breath, hoping the old dear wouldn't spot him and insist he come in for tea, as she had on so many previous occasions. Besides, he was afraid she might actually have her niece there one day, the one with the purple hair.

Rounding the corner of the house, he walked the half block to the alley and turned. His mews flat lay twenty paces in front of him. Once the carriage house and stables to Mrs. Herrick's house, it had been converted to living space in the fifties, when housing in London became a premium. With a kitchen and sitting room on the ground floor, a modest bedroom and bath overhead, and its own entrance, it offered a measure of privacy no regular flat could provide. And to top it off, the rent Mrs. Herrick charged was well below market rates.

Pulling out his keys, Michael unlocked the front door, flipped on the lights and the television, and made his way into the kitchen, where he turned on the gas oven to preheat. The kitchen was separated from the main sitting room by a length of countertop covered in a Flower Power motif; it was the only garish element in an otherwise understated decor.

The sitting room had polished wooden floors covered with a faux Persian throw rug. Furnishings were minimal: a leather-covered couch and two easy chairs arranged around a glass-topped coffee table. A gas fireplace stood at one end of the room and his teakwood "entertainment center" at the other.

Pulling open the door of the tiny refrigerator, he reached into the freezer section, pulled out a TV dinner and popped it into the oven. Something on the television caught his eye, and he went out into the sitting room and turned up the volume. The program was BBC 2's evening news. The reader, Gordon Honeycombe, was in the middle of his report.

"...Federal German Police are still investigating the brutal murder of War hero/Industrialist Friedrich Rainer. Current theories held by the *Bundespolizei* presume that he may have been assassinated by members of the Red Brigades in protest for alleged crimes against the people. Rainer, a manufacturer of controversial pharmaceuticals sold in Third World countries, has long been thought to be on a radical 'hit list.' Thus far, no one has claimed responsibility." Honeycombe paused, shuffling his script. "Authorities have also continually refused to comment on the similarities between Rainer's death and last month's murder of writer Hans Kleisner...."

"In local news, the body of Sir William Atwater was found today in St. James's Park, dead of an apparent heart attack. Sir William, wartime head of MI6, was knighted by King George VI in 1946 and was a member of the Order of the Garter. Private services will be held in Westminster Abbey on Friday...."

"In a moment, after a brief word, we shall return with the weather for the coming week, and the garden report...."

"Same old bloody crap," Michael said, switching off the set. He went over to the entertainment center and turned on his hi-fi system's Audio Research pre-amp. The two MacIntosh monoblock power amps he left constantly powered to save wear and tear on the delicate valves. While the pre-amp warmed up, he selected one of his favorite records, Emerson, Lake and Palmer's 1973 tour de force: *Brain Salad Surgery*. A moment later the first strains of William Blake's incomparable *Jerusalem* trumpeted out of the dual sets of Altec-Lansing speakers and Michael felt himself transported.

So enraptured was he by the piece's end, he almost missed the soft, persistent knocking at his front door. He turned down the music and went to the door, his standard abject apology to Mrs. Herrick's delicate sensibilities on the tip of his tongue. The words died on his lips when the door swung open bringing him face to face with a goddess.

She stood with her weight on one hip, a long-fingered hand poised to knock. Dressed in jeans and a snug-fitting t-shirt, she was slender and tall, even without the high-heels she wore. Blunt cut blond hair swept past her shoulders, framing a sharp, angular face. Prominent cheekbones set off an upturned nose, which in turn magnified the effect of ripe, sensual lips, lips that parted to show even white teeth. But the most unsettling thing about this vision standing before him was her eyes. Almond shaped, with a feline slant, they were of such a startling blue he was unable to find words to describe them. Electric, azure, sapphire, and ultramarine, all fell miserably short.

Michael snapped out of his trance-like state when he realized she had spoken to him. He shook his head, an awkward smile forming on his lips. "I'm sorry, the music was a bit loud."

"Emerson, Lake and Palmer," she said, with a warm syrupy voice heavily flavored with a German accent. It sent a chill running up his spine.

"Y—you know them?" he said, feeling butterflies skittering across the inside of his stomach's lining.

"*Ja*, they are my biggest favorite."

There was an awkward silence.

"Uhh, can I help you?"

The young woman nodded, a hopeful look on her perfect face. "*Ja, ja*, is Michael Thorley living here?"

I couldn't be this lucky, he mused. He said, "You've got him."

"That is not possible," she said, frowning. "I am looking for a much older man."

"I assure you, I'm the only Michael Thorley here."

The young woman bit her lower lip, and Michael felt a sweat break out on the back of his neck. Reaching into the pocket of her jeans, she pulled out a slip of thin white paper, obviously ripped from a phone directory. "I am sorry. I have just driven over from Germany and I found your name in the phone book. Perhaps your father?"

A wistful look came into Michael's eyes. "My father died a long time ago."

Tears flooded those cerulean eyes, her pouty lips quivering with desperation. "I—I was so sure.... Now, I have nowhere to go."

Michael felt awful. Here he was entertaining lusty, if hopeless, fantasies and this girl, this incomparably lovely girl was crying her eyes out on his doorstep. He reached out to her, at first reluctant to touch her out of some irrational thought that she might disappear, or that he might wake up from some dream induced by a long, tiring day at the office. He only hesitated a moment, then grasped her arm. Her skin felt silky, warm, and inarguably real.

"Please, come in, won't you?" he said. His throat felt tight and his pulse throbbed in his ear.

She shook her head. "No. I must go. I'm so sorry to have troubled you."

She pulled from his grasp and started away, making him even bolder than he'd ever thought possible. "Please wait."

He almost lost his nerve, then forced himself to continue. "I feel terrible that you've come all this way. Come inside, I insist." When she looked doubtful, he added, "Besides, it's not a good idea to be roaming about when you're upset. You might accidentally walk in front of a lorry, or something."

Or not so accidentally, he thought.

The young woman studied him then, as if for the first time, and Michael knew what they meant by the term: *under a microscope.*

Wiping her tears, she nodded and walked past him into the flat. Michael quickly closed the door and followed her inside. "Would you like some wine, Miss...."

She turned to face him, a guilty look on her face. "Please, forgive me. My name is Erika, Erika Rainer. My father was Friedrich Rainer...."

The name sounded familiar. And then it hit him as he glanced inadvertently at the television. "My God...the news.... I'm so sorry."

Erika nodded, her eyes again brimming with tears. Remembering the wine, Michael hurried into the kitchen, switched off the oven, and uncorked a bottle of Chardonnay he'd been chilling for dinner, pouring a generous amount into a whiskey tumbler. Back in the sitting room, he handed it to her and watched as she took a healthy gulp. She closed her eyes and placed the cool glass against her forehead, a deep sigh escaping her lips. Her eyes opened, fixing Michael with another penetrating gaze. "Thank you," she said. "You're very kind. My father told me that if anything should happen to him, I was to come to London and find Michael Thorley...that he would know what to do...."

"Do what?"

"I don't know, he wouldn't tell me!" she said, almost shouting, frustration bringing frown lines to her face where they ought never to be. "All he said was that your father was a true friend, and the only man he ever trusted enough to tell his secret, and to tell him that 'The Eagle Flies,' or something like that. Do you know what it means?"

That hopeful look once again.

Michael shrugged. "No, I'm sorry, I don't. Sounds like something out of a bad spy novel."

Erika shot him a hurt look, making him want to shrink into a tiny ball and blow away. He started to say something, then changed his mind. He'd put his foot in it enough for one day.

Draining the tumbler of wine, Erika set it down on the glass-topped coffee table and walked over to the fireplace, where she stood staring at one of the framed pictures standing on the mantel. It was the one photograph of his father that remained, a copy of the one his mother kept by her bedside. It showed him standing by the Thames Embankment. He wore his Royal Guards uniform and the expression on his face was one he could never quite interpret. The sun struck him full in the face, which of necessity made him squint. But there was something else in those long dead eyes staring out from silver halide crystals. Was it a call for help?

And though it was the only picture Michael possessed, it always made him ineffably sad to look at it for any length of time. Yet, he could never hide it in a drawer, either.

"Your father?" Erika finally said.

"Yes."

"You look very much like him. Very handsome."

In spite of his embarrassment, Michael felt a thrill shoot though his body at those words.

"I never really saw the resemblance, myself," he said.

"Oh, *ja*, it is there, in the eyes, I think."

Michael joined her at the mantel and let his gaze trace the lines of his father's face.

"He died fighting in Egypt in 1941...about three months before I was born."

Erika turned to him and the air in the room thickened, became harder to breath. "You never knew him, then," she said, "Now, it is I who am sorry."

"Don't be," he said with a shrug. "My mother told me stories about him all the while I was growing up. In a way, I feel as if I really do know him."

Erika covered his hand with hers, an excited look in her eyes. "Your mother. Perhaps she would know something?"

All Michael could think about was that slim hand with its long tapering fingers laying lightly on top of his own, shooting sparks through his skin.

"I—I've no idea...."

"Surely, she might remember something he told her, something that would give me, how you say, a lead?"

Michael wanted very much to help this beautiful, enigmatic young woman, more than he'd ever wanted anything in the world.

"I suppose it couldn't hurt to ask. Perhaps we should pop down and see her?"

"Really? I do not wish to impose...."

Michael smiled, then motioned toward the door with a courtly flourish. "No imposition at all," he said. "Besides, the old girl's always pestering me to bring home a pretty girl for her to dote over. And you most definitely fit the bill."

Erika smiled for the first time then, her face lighting up with an incandescence that made Michael's heart stumble. It was like a solitary shaft of sunlight knifing through the boundless gloom—a supernova of the soul.

And it was the scariest bloody feeling he'd ever known.

13

Simon Welles hurried out of the Communications Room, a long sheet of fax paper trailing from his right hand, and a look of alarm spread across his youthful face. Turning right at the first hallway junction, his pace increased, and he had to force himself not to run. Not only would it be a breach of etiquette, but anyone seeing the Deputy Director running might draw the wrong conclusions, might start rumors that would be hard to quash. And Welles had built his career on keeping rumors quiet.

Approached discreetly by a recruiting agent eight years before, right after finishing his degree at King's College, Welles had been dazzled by thoughts of dashing about in Aston Martins and bedding scores of exotic women. Of course, he knew it was all rubbish; he knew the reality would be a lot drearier, but the one thing he knew beyond a doubt: he loved England more than life itself and would do anything to protect her from her enemies.

Now, as he rushed toward the end of the hall, the fax clutched tightly in his fist, he had a funny feeling, the kind he got when he knew something momentous was just over the horizon. These feelings had guided him unerringly since childhood. Call it a sixth sense, ESP, or whatever, it didn't matter. What did was that it always meant that the ground was about to shift beneath his feet, heralding opportunities for the man who knew how to read the signs. If Simon Welles played his cards right, he would be the youngest Director in the history of MI6.

Reaching the end of the hall, he hesitated only briefly as the SAS guard standing in front of the Director's office, his L85A1 Bullpup rifle held in constant readiness, took the time to open the door for him. Welles slipped inside and the door clicked closed behind him. It was after five and the secretary's desk was empty. He barely registered this as he made for the large set of mahogany double doors, his fist rapping the door twice. There was only a moment's pause before a gruff voice said: "Come in."

Welles pushed open the doors and walked into a spacious room paneled in solid mahogany, a breathtaking view of the Thames and the Houses of Parliament through the floor-to-ceiling window that formed the back wall. He went right to the massive hand-carved desk sitting in front of that impressive view and placed the fax onto its leather-trimmed blotter.

The man behind the desk snatched it up and scanned it, peering over a pair of reading glasses perched on his hawk-like nose. Sir Robert Sandon, Director of MI6 for the past ten years, had the look of a well-fed predator, his movements quick and precise. Grunting wordlessly, Sir Robert dropped the fax back onto the desk, picked up a lit Romeo and Juliet cigar from a large glass ashtray and placed it in his mouth, letting the acrid smoke swirl around his leonine head.

"My doctor tells me I should give these up," he said, with measured contempt. "What do you say, Welles?"

His voice was sonorous and velvety smooth, a voice one could trust. Welles knew that it was all affectation. Sir Robert Sandon used that magic voice and his considerable charm to cultivate loyalty and trust in others. Like a trained politician, he used people without the slightest remorse. It was a weapon that came with the job, and it was something Welles never wanted to forget.

"I would say, sir," Welles replied, "that your doctor should stop buying them for you."

Sir Robert chuckled. "Right you are, Welles, right you are. The bloody bastard has a lot of nerve." The older man sighed, his eyes returning to the fax. "Has this report been confirmed?"

Welles nodded sadly. "Yes, sir, it has."

"Poor, Sir William. A lifetime of faithful service, only to die on some bloody park bench. It only says poison here. What kind?"

"Toxicology says prussic acid. Smells of KGB to me."

Sir Robert's face darkened as he steepled his hands, the cigar still fuming. "Anything else?"

"Just this," Welles said, pulling something from his pocket. "They found it on the body."

Welles placed it on the desk and Sir Robert leaned forward for a better look. When he saw that it was a Royal South Wessex cap badge, his face drained of all color. "My God.... They've come home to roost, at last."

Alarmed, Welles took a step forward. "Are you all right, sir? Would you like some brandy?"

The older man waved the suggestion away, a frown of annoyance turning down the corners of his mouth. "No, I've got to think." Sir Robert's frown deepened when he leaned forward to take a closer look at the cap badge. It was such an innocent-looking object, Welles thought. Why did it elicit such a look of horror from a man he'd always considered fearless? He was about to ask that very question when Sir Robert reached for the phone, rapidly punching a series of numbers on the dial with the eraser end of a pencil. Dropping the pencil, Sir

Robert leaned back in his chair, his eyes focused on some distant imaginary point in space. Welles could hear the ring of the phone through the handset, measuring his superior's rising anxiety with every passing moment. Finally, someone answered on the sixth ring.

"Roger? Yes, I'm sorry to bother you at this late hour.... Yes, I know there is a vote coming up, but a rather delicate matter has arisen. I must see you...." Sir Robert's eyes flicked to Welles. "It has to do with a D-notice.... Right, I'll be there within the hour."

Sir Robert hung up and reached for a decanter of brandy sitting toward the front of the desk on a silver tray. "I believe I will have that brandy after all," he said, his hands shaking as he poured two fingers into a snifter and pushed it toward Welles. He then poured as much for himself into another snifter and downed it in one gulp. "I'm told Churchill used to drink a quart of this a day during the war. I don't know how he kept it all straight."

Welles looked worried and Sir Robert took it as his cue to wave him toward one of the leather-covered chairs arranged in front of the desk. "Sit down, Welles, there's something you need to know...."

❈ ❈ ❈

An hour later, a profoundly disturbed Sir Robert sat slouched in the rear of his chauffeur-driven Rolls-Royce limousine as it shot across Westminster Bridge, speeding toward his meeting in the House of Commons. The tires on the car made a rhythmic clacking sound as they ran over the bridge sections, and it made him want to scream.

Why now? After all these bloody years, why was it surfacing now? Being the natural pessimist that he was, he briefly toyed with the irrational idea that this was somehow aimed at getting to him, that someone was doing this deliberately to discredit him. But, of course, he knew this to be utterly false. The stakes here were far higher than the career of a petty bureaucrat. The fates of nations rested on this.

And although he was used to handling crises, this one had unhinged him. It was the one thing in his entire career that he'd been afraid of, the one thing he'd known deep down that he couldn't handle. Now, here he was, running for help. It didn't matter that it was mandated as part of protocol and procedure that he consult with the Home Secretary; he hated the very idea of running to MacKinnon. The man was a pompous ass who took supreme pleasure in talking down to everyone, except for the Prime Minister, and only because she was a lady—iron or not. Roger MacKinnon was a man who would think nothing of cutting another man off at the knees if it meant the furthering of his career.

As for his own career, it was less-than-stellar because he preferred it that way. Things at MI6 ran smoothly because he'd worked like the devil to keep it that way. Now, it all looked as if it would go to the devil, after all. Sighing, Sir Robert picked up his snifter of brandy from the built-in cocktail cabinet and took another healthy swallow, recalling earlier times when his beloved service had stood on the brink of disaster.

As a young field agent recruited during the early post-war period, Sir Robert saw MI6 mire itself in one scandal after another. There was the Kim Philby affair, and the defections of Burgess and MacLain to Russia, which had done incalculable damage to Great Britain's security. And though there was no direct threat, the Profumo Scandal of 1963 with all its lurid underpinnings rocked the British government to its core and presented wider ramifications when it was discovered that Christine Keeler, one of the two girls involved, was also dallying with a Russian diplomat.

MI6 took the flak full in the face.

Knowing that its prestige was tarnished, and its effectiveness compromised, MI6 began a quiet campaign in the late sixties to revamp itself. Scores of older agents were given early retirement, while new agents—many from Sir Robert's recommendations—were recruited from all walks of life. Where in the past, only the cream from schools like Oxford and Cambridge were considered, the leadership of Her Majesty's Secret Service made a concerted effort to seek out and train those who walked a more common road. Their reasoning was thus: *send in the right agent for the right job.* If the mission required a man of the streets, then that was the man who got the job. On the other hand, if a cultured man was needed to infiltrate an area or organization in which the average man would stand out, then the cultured man was sent in. It was a brilliant concept, brilliant because of its simplicity.

With a move to bigger, more spacious and secure quarters across the river in Century House at 100 Westminster Bridge Road, MI6 was ready for its new role on the world's stage, a role it began to play with vigor under Sir Robert's able guidance.

A car horn blared, ripping Sir Robert out of his daydream. The Rolls pulled around a minor accident at the foot of Westminster Bridge, made the left turn, and eased through the gates to the entrance of the House of Commons. The chauffeur jumped out and opened the door for Sir Robert, who tossed back the last of his brandy, his face flushing from the effect of the alcohol in his blood.

"Should I wait for you, sir?" the chauffeur asked, trying to keep the note of disapproval out of his voice.

Sir Robert glanced at his watch as he climbed unsteadily out of the limo. "I shan't be more than half an hour, Giles," he said. "Amuse yourself as you see fit."

And with that Sir Robert marched toward the entrance to Parliament with a determined gait.

Giles watched him until he disappeared inside and shook his head. "Bloody lush."

Inside, Sir Robert walked past a group of MPs and nodded his greetings to those he knew. One or two tried to buttonhole him to ask his advice on certain foreign policy matters that were up for debate. He put them off politely, but firmly, pleading an important appointment. For once, it was the truth.

He found Roger MacKinnon standing outside the Common's Chamber, an impatient look on his well-fed face. Standing well over six feet, he was nearly bald, with wide bushy eyebrows overhanging hard merciless eyes that gave no quarter. This was a man who never forgave a slight received, nor a favor owed.

"What have you got, Sandon? I've got to be back in for the vote in five minutes."

Sir Robert chose to ignore the man's obvious contempt for his peerage, something he knew grew out of envy. It was no secret that MacKinnon was jockeying for knighthood himself. He'd bloody well earn one, now.

Sir Robert glanced over his shoulder.

"Out with it, man, time's a-wasting."

Bloody peasant!

"It's about Sir William's death," he said, stifling his anger. "They found something on his body."

MacKinnon gave Sir Robert a withering glare that clearly said: *stop wasting my time.*

Sir Robert pulled out the cap badge and pressed it into the cool flesh of MacKinnon's palm. To his credit, the man barely reacted, but Sir Robert saw the pupils of MacKinnon's flinty eyes dilate and his pasty skin turn a shade whiter. A moment later the iron-willed self-control was back.

"I'll inform the Prime Minister of this, though I'm sure she will wish the D-notice to stand. Relations with the Russians are quite tense these days, as you well know."

"But do you think that's wise?"

"It will be my recommendation."

"But surely with Sir William's death—"

"His passing is a great loss to us all, a bloody shame." He glanced at his watch. "But Sir William knew the risks of his profession...as do you."

"Then I am to do nothing?" Sir Robert asked, incredulous.

MacKinnon took a step toward Sir Robert, who resisted the urge to retreat. "You are to monitor the situation and keep me and the PM informed." He paused as a thought occurred to him. "Anyone else know of this?"

"Aside from the Germans?"

"Yes."

"Just some bureaucrats who have been making inquiries about war graves. I'm having my Deputy handle it."

MacKinnon nodded. "Good. We can't afford to have it splashed in the bloody tabloids just yet. This mess can still embarrass us. I want it nice and tidy. Is that understood?"

All too well, you bloody popinjay.

"Perfectly, sir," he said.

But MacKinnon was already hurrying back into the Common's chamber. Watching him, Sir Robert knew with a certainty that came with his years of service that no matter what happened, Roger MacKinnon would somehow see to it that none of the shit splashed onto his natty Savile Row suit.

14

Dark gray clouds hung low and heavy over East Berlin, especially over Stasi Headquarters on *Nonnenstrasse*. Taking up nearly the entire block, the nerve center for the *Deutsche Demokratisch Republik's* Secret State Police never slept. Even now, at just after six a.m., the offices hummed with activity, lights shining out from nearly every window.

On the top floor, at the northeast corner overlooking the twice-life-size statue of Karl Marx, a man stood gazing out of his office window, his expression bemused.

Time had not been kind to Gerhard Müller. His once jet-black hair was now nearly white, the sharp planes of his handsome face had softened and bloated from years of overindulgence of black-market food and drink. But the eyes remained the same: greedy, all-consuming, merciless. They were still the eyes of a predator, a survivor.

And survived he had. As the war neared its end, Müller—now a *Gruppenführer*—saw the ways the winds were blowing. On the one hand, fleeing to the West would offer salvation of a sort, though he knew he'd spend his life running from both the Jews and those in the Allied governments determined to make the SS pay for its alleged crimes. Unfortunately, he had no funds saved with which to make that flight, and Müller had no intentions of living like a beggar.

D-NOTICE

And despite rumors of an organization forming to help SS members evade justice, he knew this was not an option open to him, for he'd never been popular with those in power.

On the other hand, fleeing to the East seemed just short of suicide. The Russians hated the SS. He knew the part of Germany captured by the Russians would never be given back, and any government set up in their zone of occupation would be as ruthless as the one for which he now worked. And they would need skilled practitioners in forming the new state.

The decision was obvious: he would flee to the Russians. With the armies of the Allies moving ever closer to Berlin, Müller had set about remaking an identity for himself. Identity papers were prepared showing him to be a former member of the *Kriminalpolizei* who'd been drafted into the army to fight in the east in the last desperate offensive. He then had his blood group tattoo removed from under his left arm—a mark that would positively identify him as a member of the SS—disguising it as an old bullet wound, which was duly noted in his false papers, along with an award of the Black Wound badge.

When the end came in April 1945, the late *Gruppenführer* Müller donned his ragged Wehrmacht uniform and disappeared into the Eastern Zone of Occupation, spending a few days in hiding.

So, it was *Hauptwachtmeister* of Police Werner Mueller who "surrendered" to a Russian patrol, and after a few months of interrogation and imprisonment, he was brought before an ad hoc committee comprising a Political Commissar and two high-level Russian officers. Mueller smiled inwardly as the committee pointed out his previous "experience" as a policeman in the Reich, their eyes taking on a greedy gleam.

They then gave him a choice: spend the rest of his life in a gulag, or serve the budding *Staatspolizei*, an organization that would soon be feared under its diminutive name: *Stasi*.

For Mueller, it was no choice at all, but he made it look as if the struggle with his conscience was genuine. He asked to have twenty-four hours to think it over, and then after a presumed night of hard contemplation, told the committee that he accepted their offer.

Within weeks he found himself in Moscow undergoing "reeducation" and training not unlike he'd received in the SS. A year later he was back in East Berlin as a *Leutnant* in Stasi. Now, after nearly forty years of political toadying—something he abhorred—he ran the organization. Men who would bridle with rage if they knew the truth about his Nazi past, now took his orders without question. He was respected.

Feared.

Somehow, it was fitting.

Werner Mueller's mind came back to the present when his eye caught sight of a lone peddler pushing a cart laden with fruit and day-old baked goods up the street, his back bent with age, his clothes little better than rags. He watched the old man struggle with the weight of his wares and briefly toyed with the idea of ordering him brought before him. He could picture the scene: the old man trembling, his soiled tweed cap twisted in his callused hands, a look of silent pleading on his wizened face. He would approach the man and ask him a single question, the first question he always asked during the course of an interrogation: "Do you love the state?"

Invariably, the subjects reacted in one of three ways. Some would trip over their tongues trying to spit out their love for the DDR and of President Honecker, thinking the more they said, the better off they would be. What they didn't know is that the more they said, the more the noose tightened around their cowardly necks, because

Mueller knew they were lying, as surely as a hound could smell the prey he tracked. These people he would either imprison or shoot, depending on his mood.

The second group, when asked this innocent question, would stare at him open-mouthed, as if the very question itself were some abstraction that could not be apprehended by anyone of less than genius IQ. These he would bore into, knowing, as he did from his years in the SS and Stasi, that these people had something to hide. A little judicious pressure and they spilled their guts, denouncing their grandmothers as traitors. They would later become the perfect informers, eager to prove that they now loved the state in all its proletarian glory.

The third group would sneer at the very idea of loving the state, spitting at the ground in wordless contempt. From these, he would extract the information he needed, then shoot them. These people were the true dangers to the state, possessed of a free and stubborn will.

"And which one would you be, Grandfather?" he said to the old peddler down in the street. The old man could not hear him, of course, continuing on his way with grim determination.

Mueller smiled and turned from the window, returning to his desk and the just delivered copy of *Frankfurter Allgemeine Zeitung* waiting on his desk. It lay unfolded to the front page, with its large black and white portrait of Friedrich Rainer bordered in black with the dates: 1916-1984. Underneath the picture the small headline read: RAINER FUNERAL SNARLS TRAFFIC.

Mueller stared down at the picture, his expression dour. "So, my old foe, they finally got you.... *Verdammt* Bolsheviks!"

Grabbing up the paper, he tore it in two, tossing both halves into the metal waste bin at the side of his desk. He sat down and gazed at the latest teletyped reports from the major stations around the world and ignored all but the West Berlin report. It simply said: GREEN.

Mueller reached for his intercom and pressed the button to summon his assistant. A moment later the door opened and a slim young man with washed-out blonde hair and a corpselike complexion walked through carrying a steno pad. Mueller waved away the pad.

"Never mind that, Aldo. Tell me what's happening."

"The London office reports that the Atwater situation has proceeded as planned."

"*Sehr gut.* Tell Karl he is now assigned to Thorley, and to await further instructions. Is that clear?"

"*Ja sicher*, Comrade General."

"Have we heard from Mallory?"

Aldo shook his head. "No, Comrade General. However, we have another South Wessex letter prepared. Shall I send it to England in the pouch?"

"No, destroy it...." Mueller brooded, his eyes staring out at his assistant. A moment later he came to a decision. "Make arrangements for me to travel to the Western Zone, at once. Use the Abelard identity."

Aldo looked surprised. "How long?"

"Indefinite."

"The Politburo will ask questions."

Mueller's lip curled into a sneer. "Then you shall give them the appropriate answers, or I shall be forced to tell them all about your little boyfriend in Leipzig."

Aldo paled, his eyes blinking even more rapidly than before. "Comrade General, I—"

"You thought I didn't know?" he asked with a scolding look. "Shame on you, Aldo, for underestimating me."

Aldo hung his head, embarrassment coloring his cheeks a bright red.

"Now, now, we must never hang our head, Aldo. You have nothing to fear, unless you cross me. Is that clear?"

Aldo's head snapped up, his eyes shining with relief and renewed purpose. "Perfectly clear, Comrade General."

"Good, now get to those arrangements. I will be leaving within the hour."

"*Ja sicher*, Comrade General!" he said, snapping a salute.

Mueller returned the salute with a relaxed wave and waited until the young man had left the room. Then he returned to the window and looked eastward, his eyes narrowing with hatred.

"Now, you Slavic bastards will pay...for everything...."

15

The red Mercedes 500-SL sped along the narrow two-lane road, its high beams cutting through the mist that had sprung up after nightfall. The German two-seater effortlessly hugged the turns on the twisting road with nary a squeak from its wide Pirelli tires.

Inside, Erika slapped the shift into cruise gear, eyed the rearview mirror, then turned to Michael. He stared out through the windscreen, his eyes focused on the road, his mouth a tight thin line.

"Are you all right?" she asked.

"I'm fine. It's just a bit unnerving sitting here on the right with no wheel in front of me."

Her full lips curled with amusement. "I'm an excellent driver."

Michael turned to her, a blush rising on his cheeks. "No doubt you get a lot of practice dashing about on the Autobahn."

Erika ignored the subtle dig, offering one of her own. "My father taught me well."

Michael sighed. "Christ, I'm sorry. That was callous of me."

"That's all right. I sometimes want to forget it, myself," she said, falling silent again.

When would he ever stop putting his foot in it? Of course, she was an excellent driver, most of the Germans were.

And the Mercedes was not exactly a piece of crap, either.

Why was he so bloody uptight?

It wasn't Erika, though Lord knew she was the kind of girl that could make a man sweat a bit. No, it was something else, something he really didn't want to admit to himself; it came forth unbidden, nevertheless.

He was afraid to take her to his mother's home. He was afraid she would draw the wrong conclusions, and afraid she wouldn't. It was all so bollixed up in his mind he didn't know which way was bloody up. As silly as it was, he was fearful that his mother would find Erika wanting somehow. And the most absurd thing of all was that he'd only just met her two hours before. Surely, if she knew what was going on in his mind right this moment, she would laugh in his face.

"Is it much further?" Erika asked, breaking into the stream of his thoughts.

"It's about a mile further up the road," he said. "You'll take a right at the crossroads."

Ten minutes later they pulled into the long drive leading to his mother's cottage nestled into a stand of fir trees. The Mercedes' tires crunched over the gravel and Michael winced as he heard several stones glancing off the doors. Why his mother had never had it paved was like asking why they celebrated Boxing Day after Christmas when they didn't have servants to give gifts. "It's tradition," his mother would say with an arched eyebrow. "We've always done it."

The car rounded the circular drive with its concrete birdbath set into the tiny island garden, coming to a halt directly across from the front door.

"Welcome to Woodhaven," Michael said, opening the car door and climbing out.

Erika followed suit; her eyes filled with wonder as she examined the cottage. It was typical English two-storey red-brick construction, built in the late 1800s, boasting a genuine thatched roof that needed replacing every five years, as well as leaded-glass windows that sparkled like rainbows when the afternoon sun arced through them every day.

"It's lovely, Michael. But what did you call it?"

"Woodhaven. My grandfather built it in 1891 with his own hands and thought it should have a proper name. People did that back then."

"I think it's charming," she said, flashing that hundred-watt smile again.

The front door opened, and Lillian Thorley emerged, a tentative smile on her face. Though, it had been nearly six months since he'd last visited, he noticed she'd changed her hairstyle. It was a shade darker and was now off her shoulders in a soft perm, making her look at least ten years younger. Her dress, too, was more contemporary, more stylish than he recalled her wearing.

Had she finally found someone to replace Michael's father?

He felt a strange mixture of emotions. Happiness, envy, and perhaps more than a little shock. After all, one did not like to see one's mother having a fling.

Lillian came forward and enfolded him in her arms. "Michael, darling," she said, patting his back. "So good to see you."

At least one thing hadn't changed. She still wore the same fragrance she'd always worn—Chanel No. 5. It was her one extravagance, and he could never smell it without thinking of her. It was the main reason he'd never been able to date a woman that wore it.

Breaking the embrace, Lillian turned to Erika, appraising her with a cool eye. The moment stretched for so long that he found himself growing uncomfortable, though he could see no such discomfort in Erika, who returned his mother's gaze with a level stare of her own. Just as he was about to intervene, Lillian broke the mood with a warm smile. "It appears my son has good taste, after all."

Erika laughed, and Lillian and Michael joined in.

Lillian put her arm around Erika and led her inside. Michael followed, shaking his head.

The cottage remained unchanged; the same cozy room, fire in the hearth, stuffed chairs with lace antimacassars, the grandfather clock ticking away the hours, and dozens of photos of a growing Michael atop the baby grand piano in the corner.

Lillian motioned for Michael and Erika to sit on the love seat, while she took one of the hard-backed chairs. Between them lay the remains of her evening meal on the coffee table.

"You must forgive me," she said. "I would have fixed you something, I'm quite embarrassed."

Erika smiled and shook her head. "That is not necessary, Mrs. Thorley."

"You have such a lovely accent, my dear. Where are you from?"

"Germany."

"Beautiful country, I'm told, but such a troubled place. I've never traveled there, you see, but I've heard that the Oktoberfest is such fun."

"Mother," Michael interrupted. "Erika and I need your help."

"You do?" she asked, with a puzzled frown.

"Mrs. Thorley, it's not what you think. Michael brought me here because he thought you might be able to help me find out who killed my father."

"What? Oh, my poor dear child." She turned to Michael. "How long have you two known each other?"

"Michael and I met this afternoon."

And then Michael listened as Erika retold her story to his mother. To Erika's credit she kept her story emotionless, though he knew the retelling of it must be tearing her up inside. As for his mother, she listened patiently, her expression becoming more and more grave.

"...So, you see, Mrs. Thorley," Erika said, "I've nowhere else to turn. I'm sure my father would not have told me to come to England, unless he knew that your late husband could help."

Lillian glanced at Michael. "But surely he must have known that my husband died during the war...."

"I don't know what to say." She paused, her eyes clouding with tears. "My father was a meticulous man. He had to have known...and yet his instructions were explicit."

"Perhaps Dad left something," Michael offered, trying to defuse a situation that was becoming more and more awkward. He was beginning to think the whole idea of bringing Erika here was a fool's errand. And yet, he couldn't—didn't—want to give up so soon.

Lillian shook her head, as if trying to remember. "It was all so long ago. I put all of your father's things in the attic. I couldn't bear to look at them after the army sent them home.... We had so many plans." Her expression saddened, aging her badly, and making Michael's heart ache.

How could she stand the loneliness all these years? he wondered.

"May we go up and look?" he asked gently.

He saw the briefest look of panic sweep across his mother's face.

"But it's so dangerous up there. I've been trying for months to get the local carpenters to have a go...." She turned to Erika. "The beams are weakened with dry rot, you see."

Erika leaned forward in her chair, her eyes taking on a desperate look. "It would mean the world to me, if you would let us."

Michael watched as his mother stared into Erika's eyes. A moment passed, and then an understanding.

"Very well. But do watch your step around the north corner. The beams are most precarious there."

Michael grabbed an electric torch from a drawer in the kitchen and the two of them left Lillian to the remnants of her supper and clambered up the narrow stairs to the second floor.

✽　✽　✽

Lillian tried to remain calm, but the knot twisting her stomach would not let her relax. She had hoped Michael wouldn't go up into the attic, had even lied about dry rot in the beams, but to no avail.

And now he was going up with that young woman, and God only knew what he would find. She should have thrown it all out years before. But she could never bring herself to do it. Just as she could never give up Paul.

What would she tell him about this? Nothing, that's what. What he didn't know wouldn't hurt him—or her and Michael.

Her mind returned to the young woman. She could tell Michael was infatuated with her. She could see it in his eyes. After all, what kind of mother would she be if she couldn't? And though Erika seemed to be a nice young girl this mystery of her father's death was all so unsettling.

Taking a bite of her dessert, she realized that she felt calmer. There was nothing to worry about. Michael had gone through all his father's things years ago, despite her admonitions to the contrary. Boys will be boys, after all.

✽　✽　✽

At the top of the stairs, Michael reached for the light switch. A click, and the single bare bulb hanging from a wire nailed to the roof's peak snapped on, casting a harsh unforgiving light. It was more cluttered now than he remembered it, and the dust seemed thicker, as well. Still, it brought back a pang of old memories when he saw the old tailor's dummy, recalling his imaginary drills and hand-to-hand combat with it.

"My God, it will take us hours," Erika said.

Her voice echoed, giving it a plaintive quality.

"Not when you know what you're looking for."

Erika frowned, puzzled.

Michael stepped around her, a mischievous smile on his face, headed for a pile of steamer trunks. "I spent many a rainy day up here when my mother thought I was otherwise occupied with my homework."

Erika joined him as he began pulling off first one trunk and then another. Near the bottom they found a sand-colored footlocker with the legends, "MAJ. MICHAEL THORLEY" and "WD," stenciled on the lid in black paint. As a child, Michael had always wondered what the "WD" meant, thinking it was some mysterious designation for those killed in action. He now knew it stood for *War Department*. There was a hasp for a padlock, but if there had been one it was now long gone.

Michael unsnapped the other clasps on the lid and then reached for the handle, hesitating at the last moment, unsure if he really wanted to go on.

"I used to come up here quite a lot when my Mum was out. Got quite a tanning the one time I was caught. You'd think a boy would have a right to look in his dead father's footlocker...."

He sighed, as Erika laid her hand on his shoulder and squeezed. Suddenly aware of nothing else, he turned and looked into her eyes. She smiled her reassurance and Michael returned it. "What the hell," he said, throwing back the lid with a loud clatter. "Might as well have a go."

A feeling of nostalgia returned as he went through the locker's contents. When his hands closed around the German Pilot/Observer Badge and the box marked, "Military Cross," he resolved to take them with him this time. In fact, there was no reason not to take the entire footlocker with him. After all, he was the man's son, wasn't he?

And then his fingers closed around another familiar object. Pulling it out into the light, he blanched. It was the Walther PPK. And except for a few spots of rust, it appeared to be in excellent working order.

"Exactly the sort of thing a boy would want to play with," he said, recalling the times he'd held it in his hands. It felt so much lighter now. "It's no wonder my mother didn't want me to play up here," he continued. "I wonder why she never got rid of it?"

"May I see it?" Erika asked, extending her hand.

Michael dropped it into her palm and watched, amazed, as she removed the magazine and checked it. It appeared to be full. She then pulled back the slide, locking it into place, causing the round in the chamber to be extracted.

"My God, it was loaded."

"There's only six rounds here," she said. "It holds seven, plus one in the chamber."

"Probably been there since my father's death. I wonder who he captured it from? Poor sod. Where'd you learn your way around guns, anyway? Your father?"

Erika nodded. "He always believed a woman should know how to defend herself. And a *pistole* is the ideal equalizer for a woman to possess, *nicht wahr?*"

"Well, you'd definitely get my vote for Miss Self-Defense 1984."

Smiling wryly at his joke, Erika snapped the slide back into place and then pushed the loose 7.65mm round back into the magazine and slid it back into the butt. She pointedly put the pistol on safety and laid it carefully onto the pile of clothing and accoutrements piled next to the footlocker. A few minutes later, the footlocker was empty.

"That's it, then," Erika said, resigned.

"I'm sorry.

Erika grabbed his hand. "Don't be. You did your best. And I am forever grateful."

Michael's heart thudded against his rib cage and his ears filled with a buzzing sound, as if his head had become a hive of bees. He wanted to kiss those lips, drown in the oceans of her eyes, taste the essence of her.

Without thinking, he leaned forward, excited to see her moving to meet him. Good Christ, it was really happening! He could feel her breath lightly dusting his mouth. And then—

"Michael?" Lillian called from the bottom of the attic steps. "Are you two all right up there? I was beginning to worry."

"I feel like I'm back in school," Michael whispered.

Erika leaned back, stifling a giggle.

Cocking his head toward the steps, Michael said: "We're just fine, Mother!"

"Anything turn up?"

"No, nothing.

He felt Erika grab his wrist, her grip surprisingly strong. "Michael!"

The urgency in her voice made him snap his head around, prepared to see some rodent the size of a cat sitting on its haunches regarding them with hostile black eyes. Instead, he followed her gaze to the footlocker, noticing that a corner of the patterned paper lining the trunk had come loose on the inside of the lid. Leaning forward, he spotted the corner of a yellowed envelope poking out from underneath.

Ripping the paper aside, Michael yanked out the envelope, his eyes eagerly devouring the four words written on the front in a faded cursive script: TO MY UNBORN CHILD.

"Open it, Michael!" she said, when after a long moment he'd failed to do anything.

He looked up at her, his eyes flaring. "No. There's someone else who should have that honor."

He stood then and clattered down the attic steps. Erika followed him down into the parlor and watched while he threw the envelope into his mother's lap. Lillian looked up at him, a startled look on her kindly face.

"Something turned up, after all, Mother," he said, his voice smooth and controlled. "Open it."

"But it says—"

"I know what it bloody says. Open it!"

"Michael!"

He whirled to face Erika who looked at him with a look of outrage.

"Please...don't," she said.

Michael sighed, nodding once, then fell into a nearby chair, a look of exhaustion spreading across his face. "I want you to read it, Mother. I don't know if I can."

He watched as she gently tore the aged envelope and pulled out a sheaf of equally yellowed pages covered on both sides with the same flowing script. Then, with a pleading look that spoke volumes, Lillian Thorley looked down at the pages in her trembling hands and began to read.

THE FATHER:
1941

16

The Heinkel hit rough weather over the Baltic and Thorley spent most of the harrowing flight strapped into his seat, trying to hold back the contents of his stomach. As the plane pitched and yawed, buffeted by the high winds and lashed by icy rain, he tried his best not to think of the events in Russia.

But this was impossible.

The images and sounds came unbidden: the explosions of the artillery shells as they ripped up the camp, the decomposing bodies and the god-awful stench that clung to everything, permeating to the soul where it festered like a disease. The thoughts piled on top of one another, wave after wave, until his stomach let loose with a torrent that felt as if his entire insides were coming up through his throat. Gasping, for breath, he unsnapped his restraints and tried his best to vomit where it would be the least offensive, but this did little good. The entire cabin now reeked of bile.

Wiping his mouth on the sleeve of the *Wehrmacht* uniform he leaned back in the seat and closed his eyes, feeling his head throbbing with a dull ache that somehow made the feeling in his guts less noticeable. A trade-off. One pain for another. Too bad it didn't expiate the deeper one.

What am I going to tell them?

D-NOTICE

What indeed? That a British regiment was massacred in a country where they should not have even been in the first place? These were the facts, but they still didn't add up. Why had they been there? Were they there to help the Finns or the Russians? And did the Germans really kill them and plan this whole charade as a ruse?

Why were they there?

The more he asked himself that question, the more the question itself sounded like a string of nonsense syllables, like a Hindu mantra spoken over and over again to focus the mind inward toward enlightenment, the words themselves meaningless.

The door to the Heinkel's cockpit banged opened and the Major stepped out. His face twisted into a grimace as he caught a whiff of vomit. He disappeared back inside and a minute later reemerged with a hip flask. Caught by a vicious downdraft, the plane dropped like a stone. The Major snarled and grabbed for one of the struts, as the pilot fought to pull up the Heinkel's nose. The Jumo engines howled, and something heavy broke loose behind where Thorley sat and began banging against the bulkhead. Lightning flashed outside the plane, casting ominous shadows throughout the cabin, and the resultant thunder answered almost instantaneously. They were now in the heart of the storm and Thorley felt a knot of fear in his already beleaguered gut. The plane finally righted itself and began to climb, a moment of calm ensued, allowing the Major to reach him. Balancing himself against the bulkhead, the Major offered the flask.

Thorley shook his head, grimacing when the plane vibrated from a peal of thunder that sounded as if Thor's hammer had torn open the heavens. "No...thanks," he said, feeling his guts roiling.

"Take it," the Major shouted over the noise, and thrust the flask into Thorley's hands. "It's tea and sugar. It will prevent dry heaves."

Thorley felt a wave of nausea swimming up from his battered

stomach and grabbed for the tin flask as a drowning man for a life-line. He brought it to his mouth and began to swallow the syrupy brew.

"Easy," the Major said, grabbing for the flask. "Take it slower."

Nodding, Thorley took one more sip and returned the flask to the Major. "How much longer?"

"About two hours. The storm has the whole of the continent socked in, so we shouldn't have any trouble from your people," the Major said, alluding to the ubiquitous RAF.

"That's assuming we make it through all this."

The Major allowed himself a smile. "Johann and I have flown through far worse than this, and Johann is the best. I'd rather fly through a fucking gale than what we went through over Dover in 1940." He paused, his jaw working as he mulled something over. It became obvious to Thorley that something was bothering the man other than a concern for his well-being. A moment later it became all-too-clear.

"What did you see down there?" the Major asked, his face a somber mask, the words almost inaudible.

Anger flared through Thorley until he remembered what these men had risked flying him in, and why. "I'm still trying to piece it all together myself."

"They were *your* people, weren't they?"

Thorley nodded, the words sticking in his throat.

The Major sighed. "I was afraid of that. It's all fucking madness." Rising to his feet he returned to the cockpit and Thorley spent the rest of the flight trying to keep down the tea and sugar.

Fate, or whatever it was that smiled down on them this day, decided to clear the weather ten minutes out from Lisbon and the landing went without a hitch. Grateful to get back into his own uniform, Thorley folded the German one carefully, placing it back onto the seat as he'd found it. The plane taxied to a stop and the pilot emerged from the cockpit and exited through the hatch, while the Major hung back.

"We were told on the radio that your plane is ready and waiting for you. It seems that a certain Senhor Velasquez has asked that you be informed that your original crew requested to be allowed to take you back. They are waiting with the plane."

Thorley smiled, feeling better knowing that the oily little diplomat had kept his word. "I guess this is goodbye, then," Thorley said, feeling awkward.

"We Germans prefer, *auf wiedersehen*."

Thorley smiled and stuck out his hand. "Until we meet again...."

The Major took his hand and gripped it firmly. "It's Hartmann, Klaus Hartmann. And it's been an honor to fly with you, *Herr* Thorley."

"*Danke schön,* Klaus. I feel the same."

Thorley started for the hatch.

"Wait."

Turning, he watched as Klaus unpinned a badge from his tunic and pressed it into his hands. It was a badge consisting of a silver-toned flying eagle clutching a swastika in its talons, overlaying a gilt wreath of oak and laurel leaves.

"It is our combined pilot and observer badge," he explained. "I think you've earned it."

Here was a man who'd put himself on the line for an abstraction, and would now be going back to what might mean certain death if his mission failed.

"I wish I had something to give *you*," Thorley said pocketing the badge.

Klaus gave him a sober look. "You already have—hope."

Outside the plane, he found Velasquez's Mercedes staff car waiting for him a few yards away from the Heinkel. Michael wasn't the least bit surprised to find that Senhor Velasquez had delegated the chore of escorting him to a lower functionary. This one, a stocky man of indeterminate age and a propensity for wrinkled linen suits and garlic-flavored breath, was as taciturn as Velasquez was loquacious, for which Thorley was sincerely grateful.

A few minutes later, he was aboard the Vickers-Wellington, where he greeted Hildy and the others like long lost brothers.

"Good to see you, sir!" Hildy said, clasping his shoulders in a comradely embrace. "We'll get you back right as rain. Göring's given the goons the night off. The storm front has settled over the Continent, so it'll be smooth flying all the way back to Blighty."

They were airborne ten minutes later and headed north across the Bay of Biscay.

As tired as he was, and as disturbed as he was by what he'd seen, Thorley felt a sense of exhilaration knowing that he was going home.

He wanted nothing more than to be debriefed and to return to his wife and his safe, boring job as a translator. Let Sir Basil and the others debate the complexities of what he'd found. He was not involved; he was just the messenger.

It was dusk when they touched down in Chipping Ongar. After saying his farewells to Flight Lieutenant Mullins and the rest of the crew, he entered the blockhouse and changed back into his civilian clothes. He carefully placed his major's uniform into a suitcase, which had been provided, and after one last look around, he left the building. Outside, as it had been in Lisbon, a car waited, the exhaust fumes like white clouds in the cool night air. Unlike Lisbon, however, Thorley found the rear of the car empty, save for a basket filled with a supper of cold chicken and a bottle of brown ale. In a way, he was relieved, for he was not relishing his appointment with MacIlvey and the others, did not want to relive those hellish moments yet again. Yet, he knew this meeting would be the last of it; that afterwards, he would be free to return to his old life.

That was the odd thing. He'd begun to think of his life prior to this mission as his "old life." And what that meant exactly, he couldn't say. Perhaps it meant nothing more than one more bit of growing up he'd needed to do. Then again, it might mean that going back to business as usual would be impossible. And that was what underlay his feelings of unease.

The whole of his existence had become...uncertain.

Pushing these thoughts to the back of his mind, Thorley opened the bottle of ale and took a long cool draught.

Alcohol was very likely the worst thing for him after what he'd gone through, but it felt good, and the light feeling of euphoria made him less nervous and more fatalistic about the immediate future. He pulled a leg off the chicken and gnawed on it slowly, savoring the mild flavors of sage and thyme. He didn't realize how exhausted he was until he woke up outside 54 Broadway.

He sat up too fast, feeling the blood rushing out of his skull. "How long have we been here?" he asked the driver.

The man turned, eyeing him with profound disinterest. "Only just got here, Gov."

"What time is it?"

"A little after eight."

They would be up there now, waiting for him.

Stepping out of the Humber, he waited for the driver to pull away. He wondered if he should call Lillian first. He wanted to call her, *needed* to call her, yet duty dictated otherwise. His instructions were to return to Broadway immediately for debriefing. And he knew it would last most of the night. They would ask him to tell and retell every detail of the mission he could recall, over and over again, until they had every bloody moment of it noted down on reams of transcript.

One more night, and this will all be over.

He identified himself to the young lieutenant and was once again escorted up the stairs to the fourth floor. He found the door to the Director's office open, the flickering light from the hearth warm and inviting.

Sir Basil was the first to see him. "Ah, Thorley, prompt as always. Do come in."

Thorley managed a wan smile and stepped into the room. When he scanned the faces of the three men seated in front of him, he noted their outward calm. But their hard, glittering eyes betrayed their true intent. He knew then that the pleasantries were about to end.

17

Unable to sleep, Lillian lay in bed studying the track of the moon across the bedclothes. And she wanted to sleep—oh, so badly. Not because she was tired, which she was, but because she wanted to blot out the all-consuming terror sweeping through her, if for only a brief respite. But that was not to be. She replayed the scene with Sir Basil over and over until she could pick out the minutest details.

My God, she thought, *was it only two nights ago?*

She'd just returned from the tryst with Paul when the knock on the door came. Paul had been in a foul mood when she revealed her news about the baby. He'd screamed at her, rebuking her for her carelessness, his words like slaps.

Shaking with anger, she'd started to leave, and he'd grabbed her, enveloping her body with his muscular arms, his hot kisses numbing her. Anger gave way to passion and then...to guilt.

Oh, God, where would it end?

Why didn't she have the courage to tell Paul the truth? Instead, she'd lied to him, let him make love to her, then fled. She'd even refused a ride from Paul's bewildered chauffeur, preferring to take the Tube directly to Stockwell Station. Ordinarily, she couldn't abide the crowds and the smell of sweat and bad breath in the narrow, tightly packed trains. But while sitting amongst her fellow Londoners, she'd found a measure of solidity and calm. Etched into the tired lines of their faces, were problems other than her own, problems no doubt far worse than an errant husband and petulant lover. And it humbled her.

Enduring the short walk from the station, she arrived home just after nine, removed her coat and froze when she heard the sharp, insistent rapping at the door. Could Paul have followed her home, already contrite and wanting her? He wouldn't dare, she thought. It would be far too risky for him to be seen in this neighborhood, though she had to admit the thought of it titillated her, but he would send his chauffeur, never himself.

With mounting unease, she tore off her scarf and coat, threw them onto one of the overstuffed chairs and went to the window, where she pulled aside one of the blackout shades and peered outside. What she saw looked like nothing more than a tall black shape outlined against the gray of the outside wall. She saw the flare of dull red light as the man sucked on his pipe, revealing his handlebar mustache and white hair.

Sir Basil.

For a brief moment she was paralyzed by panic. Had he followed her from Paul's hotel? Did he know about them, and if so, was he here to admonish her not to risk her husband's career by her selfish transgressions? Hot anger shot through her, and then melted away as fast as it had come.

He wasn't here because of her.

Something was wrong with Michael.

Stifling a cry of alarm, she went to the door, shot the bolt and flung it open. His eyes held a warm twinkle.

"Hello, my dear. You're looking lovely. May I come in?"

She'd stepped aside and let him enter. He was solicitous, as always, and that only increased her silent terror. Closing the door, she followed him into the sitting room where she found him tapping out his pipe into the fireplace.

"Where is Michael?" she asked.

When he didn't answer right away, Lillian felt a sharp knot of fear twisting inside her stomach that steadily worsened while she watched him refill his pipe and relight it with excruciating deliberateness, taking extra care to tamp the full-bodied tobacco down just so.

"Something's happened to him, hasn't it?" she said, at last giving voice to her deepest fear.

The old man looked shocked. "My Lord. Is that what you think?"

"Why else would you be here?"

"Please forgive me," he said, shaking his head. "I get so wrapped up in my own little world that I scarcely think of what others must think. Michael's fine, my dear. But there is something we need to discuss."

He'd gone on to tell her that her husband had been sent to Lisbon on a special mission to translate documents captured from a German courier, documents, he said, that were far too valuable to risk being sent by the usual channels. And that he would be gone for two days.

It sounded reasonable, and totally within the purview of Michael's job with the Foreign Office; but something in the older man's manner gave her pause, made her realize that he wasn't telling her the whole truth. She'd pressed him, then, asking pointed questions; and that had only made Sir Basil vague and evasive. At every point, he begged off, citing the Official Secrets Act. It was infuriating; and it took every ounce of her will not to lose her temper and throw him out of the house.

Now, two nights later, with her fear and worry at fever pitch, she thought of one other question she'd neglected to ask, and now seemed horribly obvious in the light of 20-20 hindsight: *What if something happens to him?*

Even now, the question brought hot salty tears to her eyes. Of course, Sir Basil would not have been able to answer it. And even if he had, she knew the answer would have been as dissatisfying as all the others.

A sound outside the window interrupted her thoughts. For a moment she couldn't identify it. And then she knew: It was the sound of a car door closing.

Throwing off the bedclothes, she ran to the window, pulled aside the blackout curtain and looked out in time to see Michael walking up the front walk, his little red Morgan parked at the curb. His gait was slow and measured, the pace of a man weighed down by exhaustion and the pressures of his job. Her heart went out to him.

Racing down the stairs, she waited until he'd opened the door, then flung herself into his arms. She buried her face into his neck and sobbed, her tears as much from joy as they were from fear. Startled, at first, Thorley embraced her.

"Oh, God, Michael, I was so worried, I—"

Her sobbing renewed itself, the tears coursing down her cheeks, as she collapsed against him.

"It's all right, now," he said, rocking her back and forth in his arms. "I'm all right, I'm fine."

She kissed him then, ignoring his sour breath, tasting him hungrily, greedily. He started to speak, to protest, and she shut him up with another passionate kiss that left no doubt as to what was on her mind.

He pushed her back gently, and her hurt and puzzlement must have shown on her face, for he immediately took her back in his arms, caressing her as he said, "Don't you even think that I don't want you," he said. "Not for a bloody moment. But we have to talk. Something's come up."

She felt the panic all over again and pulled away from him.

"Sir Basil came to see me two nights ago."

Michael nodded. "He told me he would."

"Why did he lie to me, Michael?"

He looked at her strangely. "What did he tell you?"

"That you were going to Lisbon to translate some documents."

She saw his lips tighten with anger. "I might have expected as much."

"What *really* happened?"

"I can't tell you," he said, sounding exhausted.

"Don't start with the damned Official Secrets—"

Michael stalked into the sitting room, throwing his hat and coat onto a chair. "I have no choice, Lillian. I can't tell you anything!"

"I'm your wife."

"It doesn't matter. I gave my word."

His hard, determined look brought her up short, and she forced herself to calm down. "You're right, I'm sorry. It doesn't matter anymore, anyway. You're home, and you're safe. That's all that matters."

Michael walked to the hearth and studied the dying embers. His little boy lost look tore her heart. She went to him, enfolding him in her arms. "I can tell something else is bothering you. What is it?" she asked, after a moment of tender silence.

He looked away, as if to marshal his thoughts, then he turned back to her. "I don't know how to tell you this, so I'll just say it. They're sending me to Egypt...to the front."

His words rocked her.

"What?" she asked, standing back from him, her eyes like saucers.

"I leave for camp in three days."

This was all too much. If she didn't know Michael as well as she did, she would've sworn that this was some hideous practical joke. But the look in her husband's eyes told her it was all-too-real.

"But how—how can they do that? You're not a soldier."

A heavy sigh. "Actually, I am. The only way they would let me go on the mission to Portugal was to accept a commission. I'm now a Major in the Royal Guards."

"You could have refused. Why didn't you? How could you do such a thing?"

He stared at the floor—his eyes focused on some imaginary point. "Because I was tired of sitting in dusty rooms listening to life going on around me. Because I couldn't sit by anymore while thousands of my countrymen were dying. That's why. And now the bastards are using it as leverage to put me where I can't do them any harm."

She grabbed him by his shoulders, forcing him to look her in the eye. "You know something don't you? Wherever it was they sent you, you saw something they want to keep quiet."

Michael nodded wearily and moved over to the brocaded love seat. He fell into it and the springs under the cushions groaned in protest. Lillian joined him, taking his hand in hers.

"They grilled me for eight hours, Lily. Eight bloody hours, asking me the same questions over and over again. And all through it I kept asking myself: Why is this so important? Why are they so bloody concerned about this one incident?"

"Was it that bad?"

He looked at her with haunted eyes. "I hope I never see anything like it again."

"So, you asked them."

"That was my mistake," he said, shaking his head in disgust. "As long as I played the game their way, I was fine. But as soon as I showed them that I was more than their little wind-up toy, it was all over. They stared at me like I was some sort of bug, Lily. Even Sir Basil."

"What did they say?"

"That I had no *need* to know. After all I went through for them. I had no *need*." He shook his head. "And that's when they told me that I was being transferred to Egypt, that a certain general officer required the services of a translator. Bloody crap. And they knew I knew it, too."

"We'll talk to Sir Basil," she said, her voice taking on an edge. "We'll make them rescind the order; we'll threaten to tell their bloody little secrets...."

"You know I'll never do that."

"So, you're just going to let them pack you off to the war, like a good little soldier. Let them have their way. Is that it?"

"Yes."

Her lips trembled as the tears threatened to flow anew. "But, why, goddamnit?"

"Because I made a commitment, Lily. Because I *want* to make a difference. And they know it. Are Sir Basil and the others a bunch of treacherous bastards? Too right, they are. But I'm not going to stoop to their level. I can beat them at their own bloody game."

"And what if you don't?" she said, hating the quaver in her voice.

"My chances are better than good," he said, caressing her face. "After all, I'm just a translator. I'll be well back from the fighting most of the time. I'll be fine. The truth is, it doesn't really matter what *they* want. I *need* to do this, Lily, or I'll go stark raving mad."

And there it was, that blasted insufferable male ego that always raised its ugly head whenever reason tried to prevail. Like some prehistoric leviathan lumbering through a forgotten rain forest knocking down everything in its path, it would stumble blindly into whatever trouble it could, taking her husband along with it.

She cupped his face with her hands. "No. You don't need to. You only *think* you do. I'm not blind, Michael. I see all those nasty looks, too. The ones from all those smug, self-important prigs who think they know what's best for everybody else. The ones who think that you must be shirking your duty just because you fight from behind a desk. Somebody has to do that job, or the men in the field would be lost."

Michael smiled at her, took her hands from his face and kissed them. "You're right, dearest. But I don't have a say anymore. I'm in for the duration and these are my orders. Would you rather see me in the glasshouse?"

"You can resign the bloody commission."

"Yes, I suppose I could. And assuming I didn't end up in prison anyway, I would very likely never have a proper job again. Or would you prefer being married to a penniless academic?"

She looked into his eyes and saw that his heart was set, and there was no other way to reach him, save for one.

"I would rather your son have a living father in jail or destitute, than a dead one he'll mourn the rest of his life," she said."

He stared at her, his mouth gaping. It would have been funny under any other circumstances. Now, it only made her want to cry.

"My *what?*" he asked.

"I'm pregnant, Michael. We're going to have a baby. I had it all planned to tell you over dinner the other night. Then this...."

She watched as a panoply of emotions flitted across his face, ending with a sad, ironic smile and a weary shake of his head. "Funny how things happen," he said.

"What do you mean?"

"Just that if I'd known this two nights ago, I would have refused the mission, and they would have given it to someone else. Now, I can't turn back." He reached for her again. "I don't want you to think I'm abandoning you, sweetheart, because I'm not. But I've got to do this. For me *and* our baby. I want him to grow up in a world where he'll be free. And I'll want him to be proud of me. Is that so wrong?"

She shook her head, tears stinging her eyes. "No, it isn't."

"Good. Then, I'll ask Sir Basil to look after you, make sure you and the baby have all you need. It's the least he can do."

It was at that precise moment that Lillian realized she'd lost her own private war, that Michael would be leaving her to follow a destiny that might ultimately rob her of him forever.

Suddenly, she felt the irrational urge to tell him everything she'd hidden from him, the whole truth about her past...and about Paul. But she knew it would destroy him. And that she could never do, for employing that most secret of weapons would destroy her as well.

Swallowing her fears, she vowed to make the next three days the happiest they had ever known in their married life. And yet, even as she made this promise, she'd already begun to think of herself as a widow.

18

Rain fell in torrents out of a gunmetal sky while the squad stood braced at attention, the fifty-pound packs on their backs growing heavier by the second. The Sergeant Major, a stocky bantam rooster with an acne-scarred face and a penchant for smoking stinking cigars, paced back and forth in front of them, screaming out expletives in a gravelly tenor, the cords on his neck standing out like white stalks against the dark brown of his leathery skin. His beady black eyes glittered with a kind of mad glee that made Thorley wonder if the man wasn't shy a marble or two. Certainly, the prospect of a five-mile double-time march through the woods—the second that day—was not the product of a balanced mind.

"...And I bloody swear to God in his bloody infinite wisdom, that I have never seen such a bunch of lazy tarts in all me life. For two fucking weeks we've made this goddamned march, and you're still fagging out like a bunch of fucking infants before we've even gone halfway. Good bloody Christ, my own mother could make this march faster than you girlies! Well, let me tell you this, you worthless strings of piss, you will do this march twice a day until you make it, or so help me, I will rip off your bleeding heads and crap down your necks! Is that clear?"

"YES, SERGEANT MAJOR," they all screamed in unison, their voices already showing the strains of having shouted this many times.

Thorley felt a wave of dizziness wash over him, and he fought to maintain his rigid stance as the rain beat a steady tattoo on his helmet.

He was so bloody tired.

It seemed that, aside from the routine workouts, part of the conditioning involved sleep deprivation. Up at the crack of dawn, they were kept running from one activity to another until they fell into their bunks at 9:00 p.m., exhausted.

There was the two hours of calisthenics every morning, followed by two hours of rifle practice. Thorley didn't mind the weapons training so much; in fact, he rather liked the idea of trying to better his score every day. And after four weeks of intensive daily training, his skills had become considerable: he was one of the few in the squad who'd made Marksman.

But what he couldn't stand was the constant verbal assault. He couldn't see how this made a man tougher. All it did was wear him down, day after day after day. Then again, it made perfect sense. The army didn't want someone with spirit and initiative, they wanted an automaton that followed orders.

Thorley pushed those thoughts from his mind when he realized the Sergeant Major had asked a question. Then he realized those tiny obsidian eyes were burning holes through *him*.

"So glad you could join us, you bloody git, sir!"

There it was, the "sir" spliced in before or after every choice piece of invective. Because Thorley was an officer, the Sergeant Major could not just spew his venom without paying obeisance to his rank. Somehow, the addition of that simple appellation made the rest all right in the eyes of the military. It was just one more bit of craziness in a maelstrom of insanity.

"See, Ladies," the Sergeant Major continued, "we've got ourselves a dreamer, here. Fancies himself quite the soldier, he does." The Sergeant Major stalked over to Thorley, placing his battered nose mere inches from his own, the pores of his skin looking like lunar craters.

"Sir, you are a lazy, good for nothing turd, who spends far too much of his time using his tiny brain to dream about pulling his pud instead of learning how to save his worthless life and the lives of his fellow turds! Am I getting through to you, sir?"

"Yes, Sergeant Major Bell!" Thorley shouted.

"Good! Then get down and give me thirty pushups, you scum-sucking shit—sir!"

Without a second thought, Thorley threw himself down into the mud and began doing pushups, counting them off one by one. The pack on his back, now soaked with the rain, felt twice as heavy, making each pushup excruciating.

It was hard to believe he'd been at Sandhurst for almost a month. Somehow it seemed longer, as if he'd spent half his life there. He let his mind drift back to his goodbyes with Lillian at Victoria Station. He'd told her that he loved her, and when she began to sob even harder, that of course he would return. And that was why he didn't protest when Sir Basil had told him that he'd be going to Sandhurst for a foreshortened course in basic training. He wanted to prove to himself that he could do it. He also wanted to learn as much as he possibly could about being a soldier. The Sergeant Major was wrong about him in that one respect. He didn't dream, he watched...and learned.

In another week, he would leave for Egypt for a stint at Abbassia Barracks in Cairo, where he would learn desert survival techniques at the Officer Cadet Training Unit. From there, it was on to his assignment as Chief Translator attached to the Long Range Desert

Group, commanded by Lieutenant-Colonel Guy Prendergast. The prospect both excited and frightened him, for no matter how much he professed to want it, he still wasn't at all sure that he would pass muster.

Completing his last pushup, he sprang to his feet and resumed his position in line. The Sergeant Major gave him a curt nod. "Very good, Major Thorley, now perhaps you'll lead this march. ALL RIGHT, you gits! Squad...right turn...by the left...Quick march!"

The march lasted for two hours, and Thorley was gasping and wheezing by the time he reached the finish line among the first group to finish. Too winded to care that he'd finally come in first instead of last, he flopped onto the ground and tried to keep from passing out. All he wanted was to lie there and let the rain wash the last vestiges of mud and sweat off his face. But the Sergeant Major had other ideas.

"Get off your bloody arses, you tarts! Do you want to puke your guts out, too? On your feet, NOW!"

Everyone groaned and rose to their feet.

Brady, a rangy Irishman with a shock of carroty hair and a crooked grin, turned to Thorley and whispered, "To know him is to love him, eh what?"

Thorley smiled. In school, Corwin Brady would have been known as the class clown, always offering the witty remark or the pithy observation that had escaped everyone's notice.

But Thorley had to admit he admired Brady, because the man had no fear. He'd done something Thorley would never have done: come right up to Thorley on the train to Sandhurst and introduced himself.

At first, Thorley felt put off. All he'd wanted was to keep to himself. But later, after he'd listened to a few of Brady's raunchy pub stories, he realized that the only reason he'd wanted to be alone was because he was scared of what lay ahead. Brady made him laugh that fear right out of his head. Later, once they'd settled into the routine at Sandhurst, Brady proved to be a good friend and a staunch ally against Sergeant Major Bell's never-ending tirade.

"And I think you should be the one to tell him, Brady, maybe with a bouquet of petunias."

"Now there's a pretty thought," he replied with a characteristic chuckle.

After the last stragglers stumbled to the finish line, Sergeant Major Bell ordered them all to the showers and then to mess. For the third night in a row it was bangers and mash, along with limp cabbage and tea with milk. Sugar, regrettably, had been an early casualty of the war. Thorley longed for Lillian's deft hand in the kitchen, though Brady seemed in his element.

"Cabbage is in our blood," he said. "It's the Irish national flower."

"I thought it was the Shamrock."

Brady scowled. "That's just for the tourists. It's the bloody cabbage."

"You're round the bend, Brady," Thorley laughed. "You've had too much of the national drink."

"There is that." Brady winked and took another mouthful of cabbage. "I've been meanin' to ask you something, if I may. And you can tell me to go to hell if you like, but why's a man like you, a major no less, sweatin' along with us subs and lieutenants? I would've thought you'd have done this a long while ago. Did you tell the wrong general to piss off, now?"

Thorley felt a glimmer of panic. It was one of the reasons he'd wanted to remain aloof from the others in his squad. He decided to tell as much of the truth as he could, knowing that this would be easier to recall than an outright fabrication.

"I got tired of working behind a desk, so I volunteered."

"Spoken like a true patriot. But you can't fool me, Thorley, you volunteered because of *them*, didn't you?"

His expression must have said it all, because Brady leaned forward, his manner becoming conspiratorial. "You know what I mean. Them.... The ones who give you the looks as if to say, 'How dare you stay here where it's safe. Why aren't you in uniform?' Sound familiar?"

This was hitting far too close to home for comfort. Thorley stared into the remains of his food.

"I thought as much," Brady said. "Well, it was familiar to me, too, boyo. Believe me, you, I know exactly what it feels like."

Thorley looked up, intrigued. "What were you doing before this?"

"Me? I own a pub in Dublin, called the Golden Shamrock. Where do you think I got all those stories? Surely you don't think I spent all my time there just for pleasure, do you? Business was boomin'. But more and more as the times got rougher, fewer and fewer of me regulars were comin' in, and soon those that were began to ask me: 'Corwin, me boy, when are you going to fight for the Green?' They never would have said Britain, you see. That would have been too hard on an Irishman's pride. But with so many of us spyin' for the Jerries, the rest of us got our dander up. It's all right for *us* to piss on you Brits, but that's 'cause your ours. It ain't right to have the Jerries hang you out to dry, 'cause as sure as there's blarney in Ireland, we'd be next. So, I decided to come over and join up. And the only reason I'm here is because I went to the University of Dublin. They must have figured if I'm that smart I must be lieutenant material. What rubbish!"

Thorley grinned through a mouthful of sausage. "I never asked you what unit you're being assigned to."

"The Long Range Desert Group, sir!" he said snapping off a mock salute. "Holy Mother of God, it'll be nothing but snotty Oxonians and Scotsmen!"

"And me."

Brady's face split into a grin. "Well, now, that's the first sensible thing I've seen the army do."

The final week of Thorley's training was spent in the classroom and on the field, square bashing for their final parade. At week's end, after a small ceremony where the others in the squad received their commissions, Thorley and Brady packed up their gear and reported to the train station in town. There they waited for over two hours for the train to arrive.

"Some of the lines are up after last night's raid," the stationmaster had stated when asked.

Unconcerned, they spent the time playing cards and talking about their life outside the army. Once again, Thorley avoided saying much about his job at the Foreign Office, making it sound as tedious as possible, prompting Brady to comment. "It's no wonder you volunteered, me boy. Sounds like you were about to go crackers."

When the train chugged into the station, they found the only seats left were in the last car. Filled with smoke and the laughter of other servicemen, Thorley suddenly felt out of place. He remembered Lillian's words of admonishment: *You could have refused.*

His eyes scanned the crowd of uniforms and the flush of excitement on their young faces, and he realized there were tears in his eyes. Some of these boys, a lot of them, would never see Christmas this year.

"You okay, Mikey?"

Thorley turned and saw Brady had somehow managed to come up with a bottle of scotch whisky and two reasonably clean glasses.

Thorley nodded, blinking back the tears. "Too much smoke in here," he said.

"After a couple of these, you'll be as right as rain. It's not from the old sod, but it'll still put hair on your chest." He laughed and handed Thorley one of the glasses, pouring in a generous amount of the amber liquor.

The train ride was spent in a delightful fog with Brady regaling the carload of soldiers with more of his inexhaustible anecdotes. They arrived at Victoria by nightfall. Their orders told them to report to their ship for transport by 0700 the next morning. That left almost twelve hours of liberty. Thorley wanted to go home to Lillian, but Brady cautioned him against it. "She's already said her goodbyes, Mikey. You'd only be throwin' fat onto the fire by showin' up for one night out of the blue like that."

While his words held a certain logic, Thorley's heart rebelled. He wanted to hold her in his arms one last time, he told Brady. For what if it were exactly that—the last time?

"Then you'll never know," Brady replied. "And your wife will always have her memories. Now, come on, you old sod. We're young and alive, and it's time we showed the world what's what!"

Still feeling guilty, Thorley allowed himself to be taken on a tour of Soho dives straight out of a bad B-movie. He drank more than he wanted to and as the night wore on, he regretted his decision not to see Lillian. He left Brady occupied with a couple of painted-up tarts and took a taxi straight to Brixton. It deposited him on his doorstep at precisely 2:15 a.m. The Morgan was parked out front, and house was dark, which of course came as no surprise. But he did notice that none of the blackout shades had been pulled. *That* was strange.

Using his key, he let himself in, closing the door behind him with a soft click of the latch. He knew something was wrong immediately. It was *too* bloody quiet.

Resisting the urge to call out, he crept up the stairs, grateful that they'd never thought to have a gun in the house. But when he reached the top of the stairs, his unease increased. The bedroom door was ajar. One of Lillian's little quirks was to always close the door upon their retiring. The first couple of times she'd done it he'd laughed, claiming, rightfully so, that they were all alone in the house and that no one was about to walk in on their intimate moments. And while she had never been a prude, she put it down to childhood fears that had never released their hold on her. She simply slept better with it closed.

Seeing it yawning open now brought a chill to Thorley's heart, and abandoning caution, he ran into their bedroom, expecting to see the worst: her body on the floor twisted into some horrific pose of death. Somehow, what he found was worse: an undisturbed bed, everything in its place, like some sterile tableau in the home of a famous person long dead, preserved to convey the impression that they'd only just left the room.

Feeling woozy from the scotch he'd consumed with Brady, Thorley sat on the bed and tried to sort out the clutter of thoughts flooding his mind. Lillian was an orphan with no living relatives, so she could not be visiting any family. The only friends they had were university friends, faculty members they'd socialized with as a matter of decorum. On more than one occasion Lillian had remarked as to how stuffy and venal they all were, especially the wives.

I must be really drunk, he thought. *She's in the bloody air raid shelter.*

Thorley retraced his steps downstairs, went through the kitchen, and out into the backyard. The "Anderson Shelter," a structure of corrugated steel, nine feet long by five wide, lay half-buried in one corner of the yard. He opened the door and peered inside. Typical of Lillian, the emergency beds were neatly made, showing no signs of having been slept in.

That left only one other possibility: that she'd somehow been in an accident in London. Perhaps one of the recent air raids had collapsed a tube tunnel while she'd been on her way home. He cursed himself for listening to Brady and not coming home at the first opportunity. But he knew no amount of self-recriminations would bring her back if she were—he forced himself to form the word in his mind—dead. Still, she might only be hurt, might be lying in one of the hospitals.

He picked up the phone and dialed the operator.

"Yes, hello. Would you connect me with St. Thomas Hospital, please?"

The operator took a long, agonizing moment to make the connection, which was filled with static.

"Hello? I can't hear you? Is anyone there?" a woman asked.

The voice had a light brogue, reminding Thorley of Brady. "Um, yes," he said, dreading the question he was about to ask. "Has a Lillian Thorley been admitted?"

"Oh, dear," she said, making Thorley's heart seize for a split second. "Let me see...no, there's no one by that name on the list. Of course, we've had a lot of people come in from last night's raid, you see. We haven't had too much time to identify the dead. Did your wife carry any identification?"

"Yes, she always carries something with her name and address on it, especially now."

"Well, you can't be too careful, nowadays, dearie. If you call back after seven this morning, the admissions list will have been updated. If she's here, she'll be on it by then."

Frustrated, Thorley broke the connection. This time he called King's College, Dulwich, Westminster, and University College Hospitals. None had a record of admission for a Lillian Thorley. With the greatest of difficulty, he'd then asked about the casualties, the ones lying in cold storage. Again, he was told they had no record of Lillian being among the dead. As relieved as he was to hear this, it made his mood even more frantic. Where the bloody hell was she?

He reached up and rubbed the spot above his right brow where a tiny throbbing had begun. A glance at his watch with its glowing radium dial told him that it was now approaching half past three. He'd been home slightly more than an hour and he still knew nothing more than when he'd arrived. He would wait. The ship sailed at 7:00, and if he left no later than six, he would make it. Just barely.

Yawning, he went into the kitchen and put the kettle on for a pot of tea, then made himself a slice of bread with marmalade. When it was ready, he took it into the sitting room and sipped it, his eye on the front door.

He must have dozed, for the sound of a car door slamming awakened him. He saw that the light in the room was gray, rather than black. What time was it? His watch read 5:15. He sprang to his feet, went to the window and saw a large black Daimler just pulling away, a diplomatic "C.D." plate on its rear. It pulled out of sight too fast to see more. But it was the sight of his wife dressed to the hilt in an evening dress that made his heart pound and his body break out in a cold sweat.

When she approached the front door, he faded back into the sitting room, suddenly feeling an irrational urge to hide. He fought it, standing his ground and listening for the scrape of her key in the lock. He watched the doorknob turn and the door swing inward, her silhouetted form a dark gray against the haze of dawn flooding through the open doorway. His hands trembled, and his mouth tasted of ashes.

"Hello, Lillian."

The look of terror and guilt on her face spoke more eloquently than the contents of a thousand volumes.

"M—Michael, my God, you startled me!"

She ran to him, then embracing him. "Why didn't you tell me you were coming home? I—I thought you were in Egypt." He stood there, stiff, as if at attention, watching her silently.

"Where have you been, Lillian? I thought something had happened to you, I called the hospitals, I was bloody frantic."

She disengaged and stood back from him, the look of guilt coming back on her face. She started to speak, and Thorley held up a hand. "No, don't even try. I saw the car. Whose is it?"

Her lips began to tremble, and she rushed past him and up the stairs. The room had brightened even more since she'd arrived, telling him that his time was short. But he wasn't about to leave without having it out. *Let them court-martial me, he thought.*

He took the stairs two at a time and entered the bedroom to find her seated on the bed facing the windows. The sky was reddening, making the room resemble some hellish scene from out of a Bosch painting. She spoke without turning around.

"I never meant to hurt you, Michael.... I suppose you'll want a divorce."

He rounded the bed and knelt down in front of her. Tears had smudged her makeup, making her look like a little girl who'd raided her mother's vanity case. "How long has it been going on?"

She met his eyes for a brief moment, then looked back down at her hands, unable to bear the look she saw in them.

"Five years."

This rocked him. "You've been sleeping with this man since before we met?"

She nodded quickly, a sob escaping her throat.

"Then why on God's earth did you marry me?" he asked, a part of him not really wanting to know.

"Because I loved you, Michael. I still do."

"Then why, for Christ's sake?"

She forced herself to look at him, her eyes like that of a frightened doe. "Because I—" she halted, closing her eyes to gather her strength. "Because I love him, too."

Michael stood, throwing up his hands. "That's just too bloody rich. You love *two* men. Is that what you're asking me to believe?"

"It's true!" she said, her voice filling the room.

"Oh, I'm sure it is," he said, rubbing the place above his right eye. "After all I've been through, why should this surprise me."

Lillian bit her lip. "I'll give you a divorce."

"NO!" Michael shouted, making Lillian flinch. "No divorce. I just want to know one thing. The baby. Is it mine?"

She stared at him, her expression becoming resolute for the first time. "Yes."

"I want to believe you, but how do you know?"

"Because Paul—"

"Please," he said, cutting her off with another wave of his hand. "I don't want to know anything about him, do you hear me? His name, where he comes from—nothing."

"I—I'm sorry. You asked me how I know. I can't tell you in concrete terms. It's just something a woman knows. If that doesn't satisfy you, then you're free to go. I won't stand in your way." She began to cry once more. "I've always thought you were too good for me."

She began to sob in earnest then, burying her face in her hands. Thorley could stand it no longer, for the stunning truth of it all was that he still adored her, even after the knowledge of her infidelity stood revealed in the ugly light of dawn. He reached for her and took her in his arms. She melted against him, her arms wrapping around him with viselike intensity, the tears coming all the harder.

After five minutes she calmed down, and without releasing her hold on him asked, "What do you want to do, Michael?"

He could tell from the tentative sound of her voice, the quaver in it, that she was afraid of what he would say, or perhaps of what he wouldn't. He pushed her back, holding her by the shoulders, her face only inches from his own. He could smell her perfume and the faint scent of something else. *Was it his cologne?*

"What I *wanted* is for our lives to return to the moment before I saw you get out of that car," he said, his voice a gentle whisper. "But I know now that it was all a sham."

"Michael, I—"

He silenced her with a finger to her lips. "Please, hear me out. What I want, now, is for us to remain together, and for us to raise our child in a home that is filled with love...and trust. You said you still loved me. Do you really mean that?"

"More than ever...."

Michael nodded. "All right, then, whoever he is, you will give him up, tell him you'll never see him again. If we are going to make this work, I have to know that you're willing to do this, otherwise when I walk out that door, it's forever. Do you understand?"

"Yes, I'll tell him," she said, nodding. "Today."

For the first time since he'd come home that morning, Michael smiled. He kissed her then. And rather than feeling mounting passion as he normally would, he felt something different and even more profound: a sense that a corner had been turned in their lives, that their love would survive and be stronger for it. It was more feeling than thought and it suffused his body with a warmth that was unmistakable.

The room brightened considerably when the sun peaked over the horizon. Breaking the kiss, he glanced at the clock on the wall. "Christ, it's after six! I'm going to miss the bloody boat!"

"What time does it sail?"

"Seven. From the Prince Albert Docks."

She grabbed for her wrap and headed for the stairs. "We'll take the Morgan. At this hour I'll have you there with time to spare."

Luckily, Lillian had recently filled the tank with their month's ration of petrol. The traffic was sparse all the way to the docks with only a few heavily-laden lorries getting in the way. And while she rarely drove, Lillian handled the little three-wheeled touring car with aplomb, taking turns at speeds most drivers would have avoided. And true to her word, by taking the Blackwall Tunnel, they arrived at the dock gate at 6:45. The gangway to the ship was still in place and Thorley could see a line of soldiers still waiting to be checked in.

"Where're your things?" Lillian asked, noticing for the first time that he had no luggage with him.

"Already on board, though it won't matter very much. None of it's tropical issue."

"I hate these goodbyes."

"So do I," he replied, a lump forming in his throat. "Part of me doesn't want to go."

She reached for his arm and gave it a firm, assuring squeeze. "You don't have to worry, Michael, it's over. I swear it."

"I know."

"And why only a part of you?" A tiny smile had formed on her lovely mouth.

It took him a moment to realize what she meant. "Oh.... I guess there's a part of me that's excited. Silly, isn't it."

"Not at all," she said, kissing him on the nose. "Did I tell you how handsome you are in that uniform?"

Thorley smiled. "No, you didn't."

"Well, you are, just the same. And I'm going to miss you so very much." She clasped him to her, tears coursing down her face once again. "Bloody hell, I promised myself I wasn't going to do this."

"I'll get word to you where to write me. I want to know how you and the baby are doing every day, and I'd like you to move out of London and go down to the cottage."

Lillian nodded, wiping her eyes on the back of her hand, as Thorley climbed out of the Morgan.

"I'll be back before you know it," he said.

Turning so she wouldn't see his own tears, he walked through the gate toward the gangway. It was only when he heard the Morgan's engine revving up that he allowed himself a look in time to see the tiny car disappear around the corner.

"I love you, Lillian," he said, not caring if anyone heard him or not. Then he turned and made his way onto the ship.

19

Sailing was delayed twelve hours due to a mechanical fault in one of the diesels, and during that first night on board, the bombers came over, dropping their high-explosive and incendiaries on the docks again. The ship, an old troop carrier commissioned in the last war, slipped out without a scratch, passing down the Thames silhouetted against a background of a London in flames.

There was one near miss, hitting the leading tugboat, which went down in less than two minutes. Most of the ship's compliment missed the excitement, however, as they were far too busy retching their guts out, due to a bad batch of fish served up by the less than sanitary ship's galley. Some, like Brady, who seemed to have cast-iron intestines, had an uncomfortable night of mild cramps, while the rest lay in unrelenting agony.

The trip out of the Thames Estuary and into the North Sea went without incident. The only aircraft spotted were the occasional Catalina on submarine patrol. It was when they reached the Channel, hugging the English coast, that the drone of approaching bombers could be heard overhead. And the sight was awesome.

About a hundred Heinkel 111's and Dornier 17's blackened the sky like a plague of locusts, their fighter escort weaving vapor trails that crisscrossed the sky as they dodged the flight of Hurricanes the RAF had scrambled from Manston. The coastal Ack-Ack opened up with an ear-splitting "whack-whack" and the troop ship joined in with its aft gun. One Heinkel went down, orange flame and black oily smoke spewing out from one wing. It passed overhead disappearing over land to crash somewhere in a Kent field.

As suddenly as it started, it was over, the bombers moving on to London as a part of the second wave. The remainder of the voyage was uneventful.

On the fifth morning, his legs feeling like rubber bands, Thorley staggered onto the deck, his hands grasping for the rails as the ship gently rolled. The sun, a blazing red ball, hung above the North African desert, casting reddish glints off the water. It was already beastly hot, and his clothes stuck to his skin. The air smelt of dead fish and diesel fuel. In spite of the odor, his stomach growled, and he realized he was ravenous. The ship's doctor had told him to drink water or tea, and nothing else. It had kept him from being dehydrated, but he'd lost ten pounds in the bargain and now his body was crying out for compensation.

He went below and headed for the galley, a part of him growing wary as he neared it. But the smells coming from there—brewing tea, frying bacon and eggs—made him forget his unease. He entered the galley, picked up a sectioned tray and filled it to the brim with everything in sight. Brady found him ten minutes later gorging on his fifth kipper.

"Back to the land of the living, I see," Brady said, his grin widening.

Thorley washed down his mouthful of food with tea and responded. "For a while I wished I *were* dead. What about you? You look entirely too cheerful this morning."

Brady sat across from him, his manner becoming conspiratorial. "I've been on a winning streak, old sod, like you've never seen. I've just about cleaned out all the high-rollers on this tub." He laughed and swatted the table with his hand. "I'm tellin' you, Mikey, you've never seen a sorrier bunch of poker players in all your days."

"No doubt, but some of them might be wanting to make you sorrier still. I'd watch your back."

"Not to worry, lad. This old sod's been kicked around a time or two enough to know who might be a sore loser. The trick is not to be too smug about it. Otherwise they begin to get ideas, you see."

"So, what are you going to do with all of these ill-gotten gains, my friend?" Thorley asked, not really wanting to know, but having nothing else to say. He felt worlds better after having eaten, but his head still throbbed and the close humid air inside the ship made his skin itch.

"I've been talking to some of the crew, and they said the best places to see the sights, as it were, were the Gezira Club and the Dug Out. One lad mentioned the Kit Kat, sayin' it was off-limits. Now, that's the place for me."

Thorley shook his head, a tiny smile forming on his lips. "Somehow, I'm not surprised. What about a place to sleep? We don't report to Abbassia until the twenty-first. That's two days *after* we disembark."

"From what I've been told it's Shepheard's Hotel, hands down. Of course, it costs a few quid, so I hear."

"We don't need to waste our money on luxuries."

"And why not? Do you think you'll be needin' it out in the middle of nowhere? Besides, it be my money that's to be wasted. And I say we stay at Shepheard's."

Thorley was in no mood to argue and let it go. He spent the rest of the voyage resting, conserving his strength for what he knew would be a strenuous course in desert survival. He also wrote a letter to Lillian. Or tried to. He'd wasted three sheets of his precious writing paper by the time he realized that who he wanted to write to was not his wife, but his son or daughter. The thought of his child had kept him from going out of his mind all during his time at Sandhurst and while he was suffering from the food poisoning. And it was only now, faced with disembarkation the next day, that he wanted to put all his thoughts on paper, thoughts he never confided to anyone, even Lillian. It was three in the morning Egyptian time when he began, and he stopped writing only when the announcement came for everyone to head up on deck. Packing the precious, unfinished missive away in his footlocker, he joined the throng on deck and watched while the ship made its way into the harbor in Alexandria.

Once off the ship, Thorley joined Brady and the two of them took one of the river barges for the trip to Cairo, eschewing the regular transport. Aside from being cooler than the back of a truck, it allowed them to soak up some of the "local color," as Brady put it. They arrived in the city just after noon.

The streets of Cairo presented an interesting mix of both the ancient and the modern. Military transports, sleek Daimlers and Rolls-Royces competed with oxcarts and bicycles of every description; peddlers shouted from makeshift stalls hung with everything from dead chickens to pre-war Paris fashions. And the smell. The air was redolent with all manner of spices, cooking odors, and fresh dung. Flies abounded everywhere, and Thorley found it both amazing and repellent that the average Egyptian ignored them as they crawled over their flesh.

Grabbing an ancient Austin taxi with a wheezing engine, they told the driver to take them to Shepheard's Hotel, not knowing that it lay less than a quarter mile from where they stood. The journey took over an hour, however, caused by the snarl of midday traffic, and the driver's good-natured attempt at showing them "the sights."

Thorley was more than grateful when they finally reached Shepheard's. Hot and gritty from the ubiquitous dust, he wanted nothing more than to climb into a tub of tepid water, the last he would probably see once he reported to Abbassia. Alighting from the taxi, Thorley and Brady headed into the hotel.

The lobby, cool, dark, and quiet, was a delightful mixture of high Victorian elegance and Middle Eastern pragmatism. Overstuffed chairs and chaise lounges lay scattered about amongst priceless antique paintings and statues, while belt-driven ceiling fans turned lazily overhead stirring air that reeked of Turkish tobacco and oiled leather. Taking all this in, Thorley realized that the war never felt farther away, and that made him feel guilty.

Brady had already gone over to the registration desk and was talking to the dark mustachioed manager. It didn't strike Thorley as strange until he was closer and noticed the familiar way they were conversing—as if they were old friends. When he reached the desk, Brady turned and clapped Thorley on the shoulders. "...Now, Abdul, I want the best you've got for me and my comrade in arms, here."

Abdul bowed lightly from the waist. "Very good, Mr. Brady. So glad to see you again." The little man darted off behind the key slots.

"I thought you told me you'd never been out of Dublin until you joined up."

Brady laughed. "You must have been listening with half an ear, old sod. My father was an inveterate traveler, used to take all of us along. Cairo was a favorite port of call."

"Yes, but Abdul, there, knew you."

Before, Brady could answer, Abdul returned with two keys. "As I suspected, Mr. Brady, the keys to the suite had not been placed back in the slot. Enjoy your stay."

"That's a good lad," he said, heading for the lifts.

Thorley followed, deciding to let the matter drop. After all, Brady had told him a lot of things about his life, most of it after they had consumed more than the usual amount of alcohol. It would be surprising if he *hadn't* gotten something mixed up.

After that much-looked-forward-to bath, Thorley dressed in the lightest weight uniform he possessed and joined Brady downstairs in the bar for one of its famous gin martinis. He found his friend sitting with another officer at a dimly lit corner table, two empty drinks apiece already before them.

"Come on, boyo," Brady said, waving him over, "you've got some catching up to do."

Thorley managed a smile, then sat in the one empty seat left at the tiny circular table, thinking that if he managed to survive the war, he'd end up a raging alcoholic.

"Mikey, may I present Lieutenant Reginald Herter of the 22nd Guards."

"Call me, Reggie," he said, extending his hand.

Thorley took it, trying not to wince under the other man's nutcracker grip. "Michael Thorley," he said.

"Reggie, me boy, tell Mikey what you just told me."

Reggie leaned forward and it was then that Thorley caught the heavy scent of gin and noticed the other man's eyes drooping at half-mast. "Auchinleck's got us all hopping, old boy. New offensive, probably in mid-November or thereabouts. Very hush-hush." The man burped, his hand rising to his mouth too late to cover it. Thorley felt a wave of embarrassment for the man and annoyance at his carelessness.

"If that's true, why are you telling us?"

Reggie waved it off as he snatched up his tumbler of gin. "Not to worry, old boy, Jerry's too bloody busy trying to take Tobruk to worry about what's coming up his bum." Reggie laughed, causing his drink to spill on his tunic. "Bloody hell," he cursed, trying to sop up the liquor with a wad of cocktail napkins. Thorley used the moment to signal Brady that it was time to go. He nodded his acknowledgment, then turned to Reggie, who appeared to have forgotten what they'd been talking about. "Sorry, Reggie, but Mikey and I must be on our way."

"Oh, do stay for one more round, old boy," he said, belching between words. From Thorley's perspective, the man looked as if he might keel over at any moment. Without answering, he and Brady left the man to his own devices and headed out into the night.

In prewar days, it was said that Cairo at night was a sight that would dazzle the eye of the uninitiated. Now, with blackout regulations in force, it was all one could do to navigate in near pitch-blackness. He caught Brady as he was about to jump into a cab. "What the hell was all that about?"

Brady grinned. "Just having a little fun."

"You call encouraging a man to betray his comrades a little fun?"

"Oh, come now, Mikey, it wasn't all that bad. The man was the talkative type. If it wasn't me, it would have been someone else, perhaps someone less than trustworthy."

"That's still no excuse—"

"Mikey," Brady said, his voice mildly scolding, "relax for God's sake. We've got one last night of freedom. Let's make the best of it."

Right then, Thorley decided that he'd had more than enough of Brady for one evening. "You go, I'm completely knackered. I'm going to get some rest."

A look passed over the Irishman's features that in the deepening gloom Thorley could have sworn was the hot flash of anger. And then it was gone, replaced by the devilish gleam that was pure Brady. "Have it your way, Mikey," he said, patting Thorley on the shoulder. "I'll see you when I see you."

And then he was gone, the cab roaring off in a blue cloud of oily exhaust. Thorley returned to their suite and stripped off his uniform, glad that he'd decided to stay behind. If he knew Brady at all, before the night was through, he would have made every attempt to pair Thorley off with some woman of less than sterling repute, encouraging him to dip his wick.

He preferred not to think of that. It reminded him of his last hours with Lillian. Even though they had reconciled, there were still those nagging tendrils of doubt in his mind. Had she given the man up, as she'd promised? There was no way to know, of course, now that he was thousands of miles from home. He would have to trust her; and he could never do so if he himself were unfaithful.

Driving all of these thoughts from his mind, he pulled out the letter he'd started on the ship and reread what he'd written. It was good, it said most of the things he wanted to say, including the instructions to follow in case of his death, but something was missing. He spent the next two hours attempting to form these vague feelings into words, but the words, as obstinate as Sergeant Bell, refused to come. Frustrated, he put the letter away, doused the lights, and went to the windows. When he raised the blackout shades, cool night air blew in off the Western desert.

A sliver of moon shone high in the sky and the blanket of stars overhead shone like a bright pinpoint tapestry. Cairo stretched out before him, a dark gray mass creeping over the landscape, every window dark as his own. It made him feel as if he were in a mausoleum.

Looking off to the west once more, he tried to imagine what

it would be like living out there day after day on patrol with the L.R.D.G., sleeping out under that vast canvas of light, the air crisp and clean, and silent as the grave. A part of him realized that he was scared, and yet he was also more excited than he could ever remember. Shivering, he turned from the window, padded to the bed and climbed in, careful to replace the mosquito netting so that none of the pesky little blighters could dive-bomb him as he slept. Sleep, however, came hard. His mind raced with all manner of thoughts, and in spite of the cool breeze, his body felt tense, causing him to toss and turn for what must have been hours. The last thing he remembered before falling asleep was the sound of Brady stumbling in sometime before dawn, accompanied by the soft titter of feminine laughter.

20

Thorley awoke, his mind in a fog of vague nightmares. The light in the room told him it was well after dawn, and a squinty-eyed glance at his watch confirmed it.

6:13.

Their orders were to report to a Lieutenant David Lloyd Owen at Abbassia Barracks at precisely seven. That left precious little time to dawdle. Shaking the last vestiges of sleep from his brain, Thorley staggered to his feet and made his way over to the door that separated his room from Brady's. It lay ajar, and he could see that the blackout shades were still drawn. From the light coming through the door of his own room, he saw Brady sprawled across the bed, his arm around a dusky Egyptian woman with coal-black hair and the ample proportions of a belly dancer.

Good old Brady, true to form. He would have been disappointed to have discovered his wild and wayward friend any other way. Remembering the time, he suppressed a grin and walked into the room, throwing open the blackout shades as he went. Light flooded the room and Brady groaned, trying to bury his face in a pillow. His companion reacted differently, springing awake in an instant, her dark sloe-eyed face filled with fear. She spotted Thorley and her expression turned wanton, mocking. She didn't bother to cover herself, either, letting her heavy breasts with their large, nearly black aureolas and taut nipples advertise their availability.

"We've got to be at the barracks in forty minutes, Corwin. Let's get cracking."

Brady groaned again, motioning Thorley away with a limp-wristed wave.

"Not on your life, let's go."

"Bloody Christ, why don't you just shoot me and get it over with," Brady said, rolling over onto his back. He spotted his companion, and rolled his eyes. She smiled, revealing a broken front tooth. "Go on, me darlin', time to be shovin' off."

The woman threw off the bedclothes and reached for her dress, a shabby print that had seen better days. Thorley spotted a tattoo on her capacious rump, the design both inscrutable and unfamiliar. After she dressed and left, Brady crawled from the bed and stumbled into the bathroom, where he doused his head under a stream of tepid, faintly brown water.

Soon, they were outside the hotel, where they hailed a cab and instructed the driver to take them to Abbassia Barracks.

Located in the center of Cairo, the barracks had been built in the late nineteenth century; and its imposing edifice of stone and iron occupied an entire city block. Home to various regiments over the years, it was now the main headquarters of the Long Range Desert Group, as well as the Officer Cadet Training Unit.

After a mad dash through downtown Cairo, narrowly avoiding catastrophe no less than five times, the cab pulled up in a cloud of dust and deposited Thorley and Brady at the main gate. Thorley paid the driver, who thanked him profusely in a rapid stutter, and roared off.

After identifying themselves at the gate, they reported to Lieutenant Owen in the main office overlooking the dun-colored quadrangle. Owen, a slight man of medium height with a warm, easy manner, gave them the cook's tour of the barracks, ending up in what was to be their room, a narrow warren at the southwest corner they would share with two other men who had not yet arrived.

To Thorley's surprise, the ensuing week went rapidly. Unlike the tyrannical Sergeant Bell, the officer in charge of training them in desert survival techniques, was calm and patient. He tutored them, making sure that every one of the fifteen men undergoing training understood what was at stake.

"Remember," he said, over and over again, "the desert will never forgive the mistakes I will. If you want to survive out there, pay attention here."

There were other, less vital, aspects that others had learned from bitter experience: The serge battle dress uniforms issued to the British army, for instance, were wholly inadequate for wear in the desert. Soldiers had found that while it would keep them warmer at night, sand coupled with sweat would become ingrained in the fabric, causing severe chafing. And once they were out in the field for weeks at a time, any discomfort would become magnified tenfold. In addition to the uniforms, the regulation leather shoes had given way to soft suede ankle boots with rubber soles, drill trousers at night, shorts during the day. For headgear, it varied. Some liked to wear berets—different colors to signify a particular unit—and others their issue peaked caps, the last vestiges of their official uniform. For the L.R.D.G., comfort was all-important.

At the end of the week of training, Lloyd Owen called Thorley into his office. With him in the tiny cramped space was another officer. Older by at least fifteen years, with salt and pepper hair and a stiff military bearing, it was obvious to Thorley that the man had seen the horrors of war firsthand: one sleeve of his immaculate uniform lay slack and empty.

Owen waved him to a chair, the only one unoccupied. "Good of you to come, Thorley," he said. "This is Lieutenant-Colonel Callum Renton, my superior."

Thorley made to stand, and the older man signaled for him to remain seated. "At ease, Major, you've earned a rest. From what Lloyd Owen tells me, you've done a first-rate job of acclimating yourself."

"Thank you, Colonel," he said, beginning to wonder what this impromptu meeting was all about. It was as if Renton had read his mind at that moment.

"Right, I'm sure you're wondering why we've asked you up here, then," he said.

He didn't have a chance to speak before Renton continued in his clipped Oxonian accent. "Sir Basil has instructed us to fill you in on your mission...."

Thorley sat up straighter, his attention now riveted on the one-arm man.

"I thought I was being assigned to Colonel Prendergast."

"Oh, quite right on that. However, Guy is in the midst of moving his entire base of operations to Siwa—getting a bit nasty, there, you see—and thought it best that we fill you in, as well." He paused, and Thorley thought he would go out of his mind as he listened to the lazy squeaking of the ceiling fan overhead, the only sound to break the agony of silence. Finally, Renton cleared his throat and continued. "As you may have heard, we're going on the offensive in just over a month. General Auchinleck is very concerned about security, and wants very much to be sure that Jerry hasn't caught wind of our plans, or if he has, that it's the disinformation we've been spreading.

"To that end, we've been sending out the patrols to key locations to do road watches. It's their job to spot any and all enemy movement and to report it back via wireless."

"So you want me to—"

Renton raised his one arm. "Hear me out. You're much too valuable to send on a road watch, Major. We're assigning you to one of the Guards patrols. It's their mission to get you as close to Rommel's Panzers as possible.

"It seems that something called 'skip' is being picked up from their tank radio traffic. It's something I don't understand, but it seems that on certain normally short-range radio frequencies, the signal bounces off the Heavyside Layer, resulting in it being picked up thousands of miles away.

"Some radio ham in America tuned in by accident and heard German. He reported it, of course, thinking it could be a spy in his hometown. But the Americans found out it was Rommel's Panzers. They, in turn, informed London, who also tuned in. Unfortunately, because of sunspots, or some such rot, it's so bloody filled with static that they can't make head or tail of it enough to have one of their translators make a go of it." Renton leaned forward then, his dark eyes blazing. "We want you right on top of the bastard. We want you to listen in on exactly what they're saying, then we'll know for sure if Rommel is planning any nasty surprises come November."

"When do I leave, Colonel?"

"Tomorrow morning. First light," Lloyd Owen said.

"You and Lieutenant Brady will be riding to Siwa with supplies on one of several new Chevrolet 30-cwts. It's a three-hundred-and-fifty-mile journey, and you should be there two days hence. You'll report to Guy immediately."

Thorley stood, sensing the meeting had come to an end. Renton offered one last piece of advice. "I envy you, Thorley," he said with genuine emotion. "The Long Range Desert Group is the best of the best, and you'll be in the thick of it. Stay on your toes."

Thorley thanked them both and then returned to his barrack room. Brady was already packing, his characteristic grin plastered on his face. "Looks like we'll be together through thick and thin, Mikey," he said, stuffing a pair of socks into his duffel. "Like two peas in a pod. Must be fate, eh?"

Thorley dropped onto his bunk, feeling drained all of a sudden. "Yeah, fate."

It was funny. A few moments ago, he was itching to go, and now that the opportunity presented itself, the doubts began to flood his mind. Could he do the job? Would he survive? What he'd heard from a couple of veterans was that the biggest danger to the patrols came from the air. Otherwise, the distances were so vast out there in the trackless desert that skirmishes between patrols and the enemy were rare. This time, however, he and his patrol would be going directly to the enemy and putting his ear to their keyhole. The prospect was daunting.

Brady seemed to sense his mood. "You all right?"

"I'm fine, just feeling a bit dicey."

Brady continued to pack his footlocker. "I've got a feeling, Mikey. You and me are going to come out on top of this one. You'll see."

After a night of restless attempts at sleep, Thorley sat up in his bunk shortly before five, his mind racing. It was all clear to him now. The sudden switch to a field assignment and the mention of Sir Basil's name at his impromptu briefing with Lloyd Owen and Renton had clinched it. Though the mission on which they were sending him was vital, they fully expected him to become a casualty of war, and he would no longer be a threat to their precious security.

His anger growing, he climbed out of his bunk, padded across the cold stone floor, and pulled the unfinished letter out of his footlocker. Unfolding it, he quickly scanned what he'd written, then tore it to shreds. What he'd written before was no longer adequate. He reached into the desk, pulled out a fresh sheet of foolscap and began again, the soft scratching of his pen the only sound within those dark stone walls.

He wrote quickly, the words flowing directly from his heart to the page. Half an hour later, as he was struggling with the best way to end the letter, he heard Brady stirring, a soft moan escaping from the Irishman's lips. A quick glance at the window revealed the sky had turned from a deep blue-black to dark charcoal gray. Dawn was perhaps ten minutes away. That meant the patrol would be leaving shortly thereafter. No turning back now.

Thorley grabbed for an envelope, placed the folded letter inside and sealed it. He then wrote on the front: *To my Unborn Child*, and sat staring at it feeling uncharacteristically weepy. Brady moaned again.

"What time is it, Mikey?"

"Almost dawn," he replied, hiding the note under some other papers.

"I'll never get used to this shit."

A few minutes later, Brady stumbled from his bunk and trudged out into the hall, headed for the bathroom. Thorley used the time to open his footlocker and place the note in the space he'd prepared earlier in the day. The backing paper had come loose inside the lid and Thorley had worked more of it loose, careful not to tear it. Now, he shoved the letter as far in as he could and then used some chewing gum to fasten the paper back in place. When he was finished, he examined his work carefully from several angles until he was satisfied that nothing showed. Except for a minor bulge, nothing did. He only hoped that his child, his son, God willing, would be able to find it. More doubts assailed him then, making him wonder if perhaps he'd hidden it too well. But he could already hear Brady returning to the room, whistling some bawdy drinking song. By the time Brady had reentered the room, the footlocker looked as if no one had disturbed it and Thorley was busily packing his last remaining articles.

They left the room for the last time at half past six and hurried to the quad, where six 30-cwt. Chevrolet trucks stood end-to-end, engines belching exhaust into the hot, dry air. The rear beds of every vehicle were piled high with gear: explosives, ammunition, food, petrol, water, spare tires, everything they would possibly need for the journey to Siwa, and then beyond into the Libyan desert and Rommel's tanks. Thorley had learned that a typical patrol could cover over fifteen hundred miles and last for as long as three weeks. Thorley's patrol would be much more surgical: find Rommel's tanks, find out their plans, and get out.

Brady tossed his duffel bag onto the back of the lead truck, gave Thorley a hand with his footlocker, and then climbed up onto the bed, finding seats on a pile of tires wedged in next to the petrol cans. A few minutes later, all six trucks drove out the front gate and headed west. They stopped for lunch at the Fayoum Oasis, a collection of date palms surrounding a brackish watering hole. A group of Bedouin watched them cook their lamb stew with an amused curiosity.

True to his nature, Brady invited them over with a wave and soon the Bedouin were laughing as Brady told them obscene jokes using an impromptu sign language. An hour later they were back in their trucks. Shortly before nightfall they camped out within sight of the Qattara Depression, a huge canyon that stretched northward toward El Alamein. Here the desert became rockier, looking far less like the gently rolling dunes so familiar to audiences of Hollywood films. Dinner consisted of more stew.

The next morning, everyone awoke at first light and ate a quick breakfast of dried dates and tea. They waited for the patrol's navigator, a stocky Welshman named Craddock to use the Theodolite and get their position relative to the sun. He carefully calculated their exact latitude with a slide rule and a dog-eared notebook. They were just mounting up when an Italian Macchi fighter came into view over the horizon. It made several passes, and everyone made as if everything were normal, even to the extent of waving to the plane. Thorley breathed a sigh of relief when he saw the fighter turn back toward his base in Libya without strafing them. Either the pilot believed they were friendly forces, or had not wanted to waste his ammunition.

After the Macchi disappeared, the patrol commander, Lieutenant Fitzhugh, ordered everyone to mount up and they were soon underway. Delays were few, only two of the trucks required tires changed. They managed to avoid any sinkholes, traps that could mire a vehicle for hours, or if it was severe enough, break an axle.

By nightfall they pulled into Siwa, a community of adobe buildings so tightly packed together, and so haphazardly constructed, that from a distance the town appeared to be a natural rock formation. It was only when they were within a mile of it that the hand of man became apparent.

Prendergast's headquarters occupied a small stone building next to the airstrip, collectively known as "Rest House," for its cool interiors and hospitable cuisine. Patrols coming in after a three-week outing could expect to find all the comfort lacking in the desert, except for women.

The six trucks pulled up to Rest House and everyone dismounted. Thorley watched Fitzhugh march into the building and a moment later another soldier came out. Short and slight, he was tanned a deep mahogany color and his face looked as if it had been run through a tannery. He wore the uniform of a sergeant, and unlike Thorley's, it was clean and crisply pressed. He scanned the trucks and the other men milling about smoking and chatting, then began walking toward them.

"Which one of you is Major Thorley?" he said in a pronounced Manchester accent.

They didn't waste any time, did they? Thorley mused.

"I am," he said, raising his hand.

The sergeant saluted, a snapping movement. "Right, Colonel Prendergast wants to see you straightaway, sir!"

Thorley returned the salute and motioned for him to lead the way. The sergeant turned on his heels and walked back toward the building. Once inside, it took a moment for Thorley's eyes to adjust to the light. The interior was Spartan to the point of austere. The room he now stood in looked to be a common room of a sort, the furniture consisting of a few rough-hewn wooden chairs and tables that looked as if they'd been designed by someone who'd never seen a proper chair. Ornamentation was minimal. A map of Egypt and Libya occupied one wall and a picture of the King hung next to it. And that was it. He'd seen some prison cells that looked cozier, but it was meticulously swept, and Thorley could smell fresh tea brewing.

"You must be Thorley," said a deep gravelly voice.

Thorley turned and found himself face to face with Colonel Guy Prendergast.

In his early fifties, Prendergast was of medium height, with square shoulders and a straight spine. Like everyone else, his face was deeply tanned and crisscrossed by scores of lines and wrinkles, and the pencil mustache he wore was precisely trimmed. He studied

Thorley with a pair of hazel eyes curiously devoid of warmth, as if he were a specimen. He'd been told that Prendergast could be a cold fish. Some said he was humorless, while others said it was because he was shy. And while no one could agree on why the man stayed aloof, all agreed he was a first-rate commander.

"Major Michael Thorley, Royal Guards, reporting, sir," he said, saluting.

"Very good, Major," Prendergast said, returning the salute with a casual wave of his hand. "But we don't stand on too much ceremony out here.... Gets in the way. Won't you sit down?"

Thorley pulled up a chair and sat down. A moment later the sergeant rolled in a tea cart, its dainty lines looking very out of place. "Tea?"

Thorley realized that his mouth was dry, parched from the last fifty miles of their journey. "I'd love some, Colonel."

"Please, call me Guy."

"One lump, no milk, please."

Prendergast nodded to the sergeant, who poured the tea. It tasted surprisingly good, a piquant Darjeeling, if his memory served. The older man began to speak.

"I assume Callum briefed you on the situation?"

Michael nodded. "He told me you wanted me to listen in on Rommel's radio traffic, try to assess their knowledge of our offensive."

"Right." He leaned forward, his face flushing. "We have to know if they've caught on to us. Crusader depends partially on surprise. If we lose that we could lose everything. I've got a topnotch radioman who will travel with you on patrol. He'll be operating a special wireless. The problem is you have to be within line of sight of the tanks or you won't pick up a thing. You see what I'm driving at?"

Thorley said nothing, taking a sip of tea as Prendergast stood and went to the large map. He pointed to an area in Libya with a thick finger. "Our last intelligence put Rommel in the area of Hatiet el Etla, just south of Tobruk. Auchinleck feels that his position gives him a good chance of retaking the city." He returned to his chair across from Thorley, his expression grave. "Sir Basil told me how good you are. He and I go way back. You get me anything you can from that German bastard, and you may be saving thousands of lives. Rest up for tonight, you and the patrol will be leaving at first light."

Outside Rest House, Thorley sought out Brady, finding him at a small café that was little more than a hovel with a covered terrace and some battered tables and chairs. He was sipping on something that looked cloudy, almost like watered-down milk.

"It's something the Bedouins brew up for the infidels. I believe its fermented camel spit, or some such. Whatever it is, it packs a punch. Come, sit down, Mikey, you look parched."

Thorley took the unoccupied chair across from him, and a moment later a young Arab boy came up to the table, his nut-brown face creased with a cheerful smile. Brady said something to him in Arabic and the boy bowed and ran off.

"Arabic? I'm impressed," Thorley said.

Brady shrugged it off. "Always had a penchant for languages, enough to get by, anyway." He took a sip of his drink and grimaced as he swallowed. "I'm going to have to get the recipe for this. I know a few boys back in the pub who would take to this like fish to water."

He laughed, and Thorley smiled, imagining a bunch of swackered Irishmen swimming in a vat of Brady's Camel Spit elixir. The Arab boy reappeared and slammed down a tall earthen mug of the same drink and stood smiling from ear to ear.

"He's waiting for you to try it, Mikey. Better tip it back, or you might offend the local sensibilities, if you be catchin' my drift."

Thorley stared at the milky brew, feeling his stomach roiling. The look of it was bad enough, but its odor was far worse, reminding him of the pungent smell of a men's locker room after a hard game of Rugger. Gritting his teeth, he raised the mug to his lips, careful to hold his breath. Then he knocked it back, feeling the lukewarm liquor burning its way down his throat like liquid phosphorus. He gagged and began coughing. The Arab boy clapped his hands and said something and ran off.

Brady chuckled and took another gulp. "The boy says that Allah blesses your name."

"Oh, that's bloody wonderful," he said, still coughing. After wiping his eyes, he took another experimental sip and found that it tasted far better than it smelled, and it was somehow familiar.

"Dates?"

"Very good, Mikey," Brady said, raising his glass. "You might just make Honorary Irishman, yet." He winked then turned serious. "I heard we're moving out tomorrow."

Michael nodded. "Prendergast gave me the poop."

"What are we going to be doing, then, besides catching flies and burning ourselves black?"

Michael detected a note of bitterness in the man's voice that made him uncomfortable. The question bothered him too, as did his friend's semi-drunken glare.

"I don't think—"

"Come on, Mikey, what's the big secret, here? Tomorrow we're both going into the mouth of the beast. I've a right to know what we're going to be doing."

"There's a briefing tonight. I'm sure all your questions will be answered."

"Fuck the bloody briefing, I want to hear it from you."

He was right, of course, he had every right to know. They were on the same team, weren't they? And unlike when they first met, this was not something under the cloud of secrecy. Nobody had specifically ordered him not to talk.

Thorley took another gulp of the date beer. This time he barely noticed it going down. "All right, it's like this...." He went on and explained why he'd been sent to Egypt, leaving out his mission to Finland, and how they would be getting closer to Rommel's Afrika Korps than any patrol had ever done thus far, and why. When he was done, Brady leaned back in the chair and whistled.

"Christ, Mikey, you mean to tell me that it's just going to be you and this radioman creepin' up on old Erwin?"

"We can't risk the rest of the patrol," Michael said slugging back the rest of his drink. He slammed the empty earthen mug onto the table. "You and everyone else will be about two miles behind us."

Brady leaned forward, all evidence of intoxication suddenly gone. "It's madness. You've got to have at least one other man to keep an eye out—watch your back, for cryin' out loud. You'll both be occupied, him with the radio, you listenin'. What if you're spotted?"

"Then it's better that only two are captured."

"Killed, you mean."

Michael didn't respond to that, preferring not to think of the worst case. "It's not up to me, Corwin."

Brady slouched back into his seat, disappointment and frustration plainly evident on his face. "It never is, Mikey. We signed on for the duration and they'll do whatever they want with us, even if it's the stupidest thing possible."

Brady finished his drink and they both stood up, Brady leaving a few Egyptian coins on the table. After dinner that evening, all those patrols not already out in the field met in Rest House, and each was briefed on its assignment. When it came to their patrol, Thorley kept his eye on Brady, afraid the headstrong Irishman would voice his protest about his mission. Fortunately, he kept his own counsel, but Thorley could tell it was eating his friend up inside. Strangely, a part of him wanted Brady along, figuring the man's presence would bring him luck. His practical side knew it was a foolish thought. Two men would travel faster than three.

Everyone turned in early. After making sure the letter to his child remained secure in its hiding place, Thorley went to bed. It took him a while to find a comfortable position on the hard floor. His head throbbed from the date beer and his mouth tasted musty. After a while he drifted off, the sound of the desert wind in his ears.

21

The patrol left Siwa at six a.m. heading northwest toward Giarabub, which they reached late in the day. The town lay in a small depression on the edge of the Great Sand Sea, and where Siwa was pleasant, Giarabub was dismal. Aside from the domed mosque where the founder of the Muslim Senussi sect lay buried, there was little else, a collection of squat buildings that appeared ready to collapse at any moment. Flies and mosquitoes were everywhere, buzzing their faces relentlessly.

The patrol found sanctuary in an airplane hangar abandoned by the retreating Italians some months before. Fitzhugh hopped off the lead truck. "We'll stay the night here. I want everyone to stay close at hand and for God's sake don't even think of drinking the bloody water."

While others went to the oasis, Thorley used the time to get to know Byron Wilson, the radioman who would be trekking across those last two miles to Rommel's base near Hatiet el Etla.

A warm and humorous man, Thorley took an immediate liking to him. After small talk, Wilson showed him the radio. It was remarkably compact, arranged in a backpack format for ease of carriage, yet it weighed almost fifty pounds. "It's the batteries, you see. They're more than half the weight of the blighter." He then went on to show how both he and Thorley would have a pair of headphones to listen in. Wilson would home in on the frequency of the signal and Thorley would verify that it was the correct one. "The last we've been told is that the tanks are using 27 megacycles. It's a low frequency on the 11-meter band and it has to be 'line of sight,' or we'll never hear it. That's why we've got to be up their bums on this one."

"How long do the batteries last?"

Wilson shrugged. "Oh, if you left it on continuously...about half an hour. The valves suck up a lot of juice."

That meant they would have to be judicious about the radio's use, survey the situation, and wait until the traffic became heavy. That might take hours, and they would be vulnerable to detection the longer they remained in position. "What about spare batteries?" Thorley asked.

Wilson shook his head. "We've got a total of four. Two will go with us; the other two stay with the patrol. We can't risk taking them all because these same batteries run the main wireless. Without them we've lost our ability to report back to Siwa. If that happens, we might as well turn tail and head back."

The rest of the day crawled by and the men grew anxious. Fortunately, someone had a deck of cards and they all occupied themselves playing Whist and Old Maid until nightfall. Dinner was another stew and quite forgettable.

The next morning, the trucks pulled out of the hangar and continued the journey north. An hour out of Giarabub, one of the trucks broke an axle in a sink hole, and the stores and men had to be redistributed to the other five trucks, necessitating a delay of several hours in the broiling sun.

It was noon when they began moving again. They were now in Libya proper in the area known as Cyrenaica. Vast and trackless, it seemed to Thorley that this is what the moon would look like if it had an atmosphere. Hot, dry, lonely, and silent. The trucks found a flat area, picked up a bit of speed and Thorley eased himself down into the stores, prepared to sleep away some of the monotony.

The Macchi C.202 fighters came out of nowhere, streaking overhead at what would have been treetop level. One moment the desert had been as quiet as a grave, the next the two planes roared overhead, banking to get a better glimpse of the patrol. Several of the men waved, but something about the way the pilots flew their aircraft gave Thorley a bad feeling. He turned to Wilson, who lounged next to him. "Get the Vickers out."

Wilson scrambled to his feet and tore off a tarpaulin. The Vickers Gun was a relatively light tripod-mounted machine gun that fired .303 caliber bullets at the rate of 450 rounds per minute. Primarily produced for use with tanks, the LRDG found it extremely useful on their patrols, especially for road watches.

Thorley kept his eyes on the Macchis as they each did a split-S and came around facing the patrols head on.

They were making a strafing run!

"Get that bloody gun cocked!" Thorley screamed.

He heard Wilson curse and then the sound of the bolt pulling back and slamming home. Ahead and behind him, Thorley heard others pulling out their guns, but his was the only one battle-ready.

The Macchis began firing from half a mile out, their 12.7mm Breda SAFAT machine guns blazing. He saw the muzzle flashes before he heard them, and the bullets striking the desert floor, kicking up plumes of sand in straight parallel lines that raced toward them.

"Fire!" Thorley shouted.

Wilson wasted no time. The Vickers chattered, and he pivoted the gun as the Macchis blurred by.

"Jesus C—Christ!" Wilson stammered, eyes wide with terror.

The Macchis rolled and came on again, Bredas roaring. The guns from the other three trucks joined Wilson's and Thorley saw a smattering of hits in the engine cowling of one of the planes, bits of debris flying off. Black smoke streamed out, and the plane nosed to the ground, exploding into the sand in a large orange-black fireball. The pilot never had a chance.

Sobered, Thorley watched the other plane make a pass without firing. Someone from one of the other trucks yelled out: "Go on, you yellow Eyetie bastard, turn tail like you all do!"

It was almost as if the pilot had heard. Instead of going off the way he'd come, he turned for one last pass. He came in lower this time, as if daring them to hit him with their Vickers.

Suddenly, Thorley realized Wilson wasn't firing, he turned, ready to scold the man and froze. Wilson sat back, his hands still on the trigger, a neat half-inch hole drilled through his forehead. Behind him the canvas tarpaulin was spattered with gore. The worst of it wasn't the blood and the brains, it was the tiny smile of surprise frozen on his face. Screaming, Thorley tore Wilson's hands from the gun and began firing, following the Macchi as it flew by. It was a lot like the skeet and trap shooting he'd done as a young boy with his father in the Midlands. One just had to lead the bird and let him fly to meet the projectile. Instead of waiting for it to make another strafing run, he waited for the plane to pass by. Aiming just ahead of the nose, he squeezed off the last of the magazine. He watched, amazed, as the .303 slugs tore into the side of the Macchi, raking down the fuselage in an almost perfect line. For a moment it seemed that it would have no effect, and then in a bright flash the plane disintegrated. Hundreds of pieces plummeted to the ground.

The men cheered.

Wilson had been a good man, and now he'd spend eternity in

a lonely grave far from his family and friends. It was all too bloody much. Thorley reloaded the Vickers and stowed it away. He then set about wrapping Wilson's body in the tarp stained with his blood.

"You all right there, Thorley?"

He looked up and saw it was Fitzhugh, a look of solemn concern on his face.

"I'll be okay."

"Right. I'll send someone to help you with Wilson. We'll stay here tonight. I don't think we need worry about the Eyeties any longer."

He walked away, his head bowed.

At sunset, the men gathered and buried Wilson, his beret lying atop the shallow mound. They stood around it in a semicircle and Fitzhugh pulled out a tiny dog-eared Bible and read one of the Psalms in a voice heavy with emotion.

Next came dinner, though no one felt much like eating. It was Fitzhugh who brought up what no one wanted to voice.

"Right. With Wilson done in, there doesn't seem to be much point in going to Hatiet el Etla." The flames from the fire reflected in his brown eyes, making him look demonic. "We've no one to operate the radio. We'll get a good night's rest, and in the morning, we'll head back to Siwa."

"Excuse me, sir, but how about letting me take a crack at it?"

It was Brady who'd spoken. Thorley thought he looked uncommonly grave. Then again, what was there to be jocular about?

Fitzhugh frowned and stared back at Brady with an intensity that would have made most men look away. Brady met his gaze head on. "You have radio experience?" Fitzhugh asked. The tone of his voice belied his suspicions.

"I've enough to get Mikey and me there and back with what we came for, and not make this whole patrol and Wilson's life a bloody waste, if that's what you be gettin' at."

Fitzhugh's jaw clenched and Thorley could tell the older man was angered by Brady's brash remarks. But he couldn't help admiring his friend's audacity. He also noticed the others were nodding in agreement.

"Has anybody checked the radio for damage?" Fitzhugh asked.

That prompted two of the men to run off and retrieve the radio and bring it back to the fire. He motioned for the two men to hand it to Brady.

"Let's see what you can do with it." Fitzhugh said, his gaze level.

To his credit, Brady studied the panel for a moment and then reached for the "on" switch. A jeweled red light went on as did a light behind the frequency dial. A moment later the hiss of white noise could be heard through the built-in speaker. He then twisted the dial until a stream of Italian issued forth. He listened for a moment, then said. "That's radio traffic from Italian Headquarters in Benghazi," Brady said. "Heard enough?"

He switched off the radio and zipped it back into its carry pack. Fitzhugh still looked unconvinced. "Obviously you found that quite by accident. We can't afford lucky accidents out here."

"Excuse me, Lieutenant," Thorley cut in, "but there won't be any lucky accidents, as you put it. I know the frequency we'll be monitoring. We've come this far, let us have a crack at it. And as Corwin said, it's better than turning tail."

Fitzhugh caved in, throwing up his hands. "All right," he said. "Let's just hope we don't get caught with our pants down again."

The next morning, they all voted to forego breakfast so they could make Hatiet el Etla by midmorning. Their last intelligence put the bulk of the Afrika Korps about five miles north of the town.

They decided to skirt the tiny settlement on the off chance that any Germans might be in the town. By noon, they were as close as they dared to get. Now, it was up to Thorley and Brady to hike the rest of the way on foot.

They waited until after lunch when the sun began to wane, then they set off. Brady carried the radio, and Thorley carried the compass and the spare battery, as well as the food and water for the both of them. By Fitzhugh's estimation, Rommel's tanks lay in a shallow depression due north from where the patrol had set up camp. The hike, though only two miles, felt like two hundred. The weight of the stores they'd taken, enough for two days if needed, began to take its toll on Thorley's body within the first half mile. Part of the problem was the terrain. Extremely rocky, it took longer to go a given distance because one had to step carefully over and around the countless obstacles strewn in their path. And then there was the relentless heat. They could only take so much water, because of weight and rationing. Already, Thorley could feel his throat crying out for it, knowing that if he gave in too soon, they would run out.

For his part, Brady appeared to be in his element. He moved over the rocks like a mountain goat, his pace never flagging, a continual grin on his face. They reached their destination at three o'clock and found the tanks just where intelligence said they would be. Putting down their supplies, both men crept to the top of the rise and looked over. Down in the depression they counted over three hundred tanks parked in even rows across from an equally large area filled with tents. They could see hundreds of German troops going about their business.

"Go get the radio," Thorley said.

"There won't be anything now, Mikey, they're all parked."

"Let's try it, anyway."

Brady shrugged and slid down the rise. He returned a moment later with the radio in hand. Unzipping the front of the carry pack, he erected the special antenna with its neatly coiled length of copper wire, turned the radio on and the two of them huddled around the speaker as Brady tuned the radio to 27 megacycles. There was nothing but static.

"I told you, Mikey," he said, flipping off the radio. "Sure as God's in his Heaven, they'll be firing up those tanks come morning. That's when we'll hear something, if there's anything to hear."

They spent the night huddled next to each other for warmth, proximity to the enemy making a fire impossible.

The sun was creeping over the horizon, casting its crimson light across the steamy desert, when both men awakened to the sound of hundreds of tank engines revving. Grabbing the radio, Thorley and Brady scrambled up the small rise. The German camp was breaking up, tents folded and thrown into the backs of trucks, men running every which way shouting orders. From their position high overhead, it resembled a busy anthill. The tanks began pulling out of their neat rows and into formation for traveling.

"Blast this infernal thing!"

Thorley turned at the sound of Brady's curse and saw him tinkering with the radio. A stab of fear pierced his heart.

"What's wrong?"

Brady looked up from the radio, a sneer curling his lip. "This bloody contraption has decided not to work, that's what's wrong!"

Thorley decided to leave well enough alone and turned his attention back to the tanks. From his vantage point, it looked as if Rommel was sending the tanks north, toward Tobruk, but that was a guess, and not a very educated one. Still, unless they got the radio working, they would have very little else to report.

"Got you, you little bastard!" Brady said triumphantly. "Radio's up, Mikey."

Brady tossed him the headphones, which he plugged into the jack and then placed onto his head. He nodded and waited as Brady tuned the dial to 27 megacycles. From what little he knew of radio, there could be a thousand working frequencies between 27 and 28 megacycles, all with separate conversations going on. It would take a steady hand on the dial to tune into them all. What worried Thorley were the odds involved in actually hearing what he came to hear, odds that someone would actually talk about it over the air, unlikely at best. If they did, Thorley might miss it simply because he wouldn't be listening on the correct frequency at the precise moment it was spoken. It was obvious the Panzer units were moving out of the area. That meant they would have perhaps half an hour, forty-five minutes at most before the last tanks were out of range. And that would be that, for there was no way for them to shadow the tanks on foot. And the patrol would be vulnerable if they tried to follow as a unit. It was clear they would just have to muddle through.

Thorley held up his hand as he heard a flash of conversation. "Go back, slowly."

Brady barely tweaked the dial and the headphones squawked to life. *"Anton Übermut Nordpol, Dies ist Zachari Fünf. Verstanden? Aus."*

The reply came back tinged with static. *"Ja, Dies ist Anton Übermut Nordpol. Ich habe Verstanden. Nächster Punkt Viktor. Aus."*

"Jawohl. Aus."

The radio fell silent and he pulled one of the headphone cans off one ear, leaving the other covered.

"What was that frequency?" Thorley asked.

"27.135 megacycles."

"Make a note of that one and keep scanning."

"You heard something. What did they say?"

Thorley shook his head. "Routine. One of the Panzers identified themselves and the base commander ordered them to proceed to a point they're calling Viktor."

"So, what does it mean?"

"I don't bloody know. I was afraid of this."

Brady looked puzzled, prompting Thorley to explain.

"The Germans use radio codes, phonetic words that stand for actual German words. Just as we use, 'Abel, Baker, Charley,' they use the German equivalent. They also use them as vectors on a map, point Viktor, or 'V,' being one of them. And every branch of the *Wehrmacht* uses a different code. Unless I have access to a German map, I can't tell you where Point Viktor is."

Thorley watched the tanks forming ranks for traveling.

Brady shook his head, exasperated. "Bloody Christ. All this work and they're speaking gibberish. What about what you just heard?"

"Like I said, routine. There was no reason for the code, except for their destination. That could mean any place."

"Like Tobruk."

"Yes, like Tobruk," Thorley echoed, his mood turning dark. He readjusted the headphones. "Let's keep going."

They caught another snippet of conversations between two tanks and like he feared, it was almost entirely in code, something about *"Sago"* and *"Kurfürst"* and *"Indianer."* The words themselves, though formal German vocabulary, he knew were being used to mean something entirely different here and now.

The first column of tanks began moving out of the depression. There was more coded chatter intermixed with some joking between the Panzer crews. Thorley turned to Brady. "What's your frequency?

"27.225."

"Go back to 27.135."

Brady nodded and turned the dial. At first there was nothing. And then Brady must have nudged the dial one way or the other because his headphones suddenly filled with laughter and then a question.

"Dort sollen die Frauen gutaussehen. Aus?"

The reply came in a guttural Bavarian accent. *"Ja, sehr gut. Du wirst Jamila kennen lernen. Sie besizt das beste wirtshaus in Alamein. Ich war dort bevor dem Krieg. Sie wird sich freuen, uns zusehen. Aus."*

"Oh, ja. Das ist ausgezeichnet."

Thorley was riveted. Someone in one of those tanks had mentioned El Alamein, as if they planned on being there sometime soon. Either this meant Rommel was planning his own offensive and these lovesick tankers had just given away the objective, or it was all idle chatter, wishful thinking on the part of two war weary men. One thing was for sure, he needed to hear more, something of a more military nature. No one had mentioned anything about General Auchinleck's offensive. Thorley returned to the conversation between the two tankers, eager to hear more. By this time, however, the talk had degenerated into bathroom humor that was soon ended when an officer cut in on them and demanded they stop jabbering.

Thorley ripped off the phones and began writing on a tiny notepad. Brady watched, his tense expression giving away his eagerness to learn what Thorley had heard. Thorley resisted the urge to smile, enjoying his newfound power over the impetuous Irishman.

"You're about ready to burst, aren't you?" Thorley asked, allowing himself to smile.

Brady looked annoyed. "Bloody right. Now spill it. What did you hear?"

"Basically this. Two men were discussing the merits of Egyptian women and one of them promised to introduce him to the tart that runs his favorite bar in El Alamein."

"It's not much to go on, Mikey."

"No, it isn't."

"Did they say anything about Crusader?"

Thorley shook his head wearily. "Not yet, so I suggest we keep listening. The tanks will all be gone in a little while, maybe someone else will let slip with something."

"Fine by me," Brady said, staring after the departing tanks.

Thorley replaced the headphones and listened as Brady ran through the spectrum between 26 and 28 megacycles. They caught a few more conversations, mostly in that blasted code. He transcribed what he could, hoping that something would jog his mind later, but without knowing what the clear German words were, it would be a guessing game at best.

The tanks took longer to evacuate the area than they had anticipated, and Brady had to change the battery. They scanned the frequencies one last time and Thorley caught the tail end of another conversation. The word Alamein was mentioned again. That clinched it for him. Rommel was up to something, and had no idea that Auchinleck was about to mount a major offensive. The information they had would be invaluable, and from what he knew of El Alamein, it was the perfect ground for a confrontation, the advantage going to those who would be ready and waiting.

After the last tank had disappeared over the next rise and all possibility of surveillance had ceased, they packed up the radio and moved out. The sun fell toward the horizon and a cooling breeze had sprung up when they made their way back toward the spot where the rest of the patrol had encamped. Thorley shivered and made an effort to pick up the pace. He had no desire to be caught out in this godforsaken place after nightfall.

Winded and feeling the cold, they reached the camp under the light of the full moon. Fitzhugh and the others greeted them like long lost brothers and feted them with hot lamb stew and a fresh bottle of Scotch someone had brought along contrary to regulations.

After he and Brady had eaten, Fitzhugh asked them what had happened. Thorley told him what he'd heard, and Fitzhugh listened intently.

"I think you're onto something, Major," he said when Thorley had finished recounting their mission. "General Auchinleck will be pleased. Good work."

The whisky hit them all hard and everyone turned in soon after. The next morning the trucks retraced their route to Siwa. They arrived back at Rest House a little after dawn the next day. Michael was called upon to debrief for Prendergast, who seemed a little less than enthusiastic at his findings. By now, Thorley knew that Prendergast's lack of emotion was not a reflection either on him or his information, simply a part of the man. But Thorley knew he'd scored a coup by the twinkle in the man's eyes when he shook his hand.

"I spoke with General Auchinleck this morning," Prendergast said. "He wants you in Cairo day after tomorrow to brief him personally on your mission. You and Brady will leave on the outgoing supply truck. You also have three day's leave, by the way. Good show, Thorley."

After his debriefing with Prendergast, Thorley took a much-needed bath and changed into a fresh uniform, taking time to shave off the four days growth that stubbled his chin. He'd noticed some gray hairs in his beard and for some reason it bothered him. It was as if the war and his recent experiences were taking an inevitable toll— the theft of his youth, his innocence long since gone.

Outside Rest House, Thorley found Brady waiting for him next to the idling supply truck, which ran back and forth from Cairo every other day to bring petrol and travel rations for the patrols. Usually, the drivers would then take outgoing mail or passengers bound for Cairo.

Brady clapped him on the shoulders. "When you and me hit the big "C," boyo, we're going to have us a grand old time. You just leave it to Corwin." He winked and climbed up on the back of the truck and Thorley joined him. The driver, a nervous sort, glanced at his watch and shook his head. "One more minute and you blokes would have been left behind, General or no General." He then climbed into the cab, started the engine, threw it into gear and they were off.

Unlike their journey to Siwa, the return to Cairo seemed far shorter. Thorley reasoned that the supply truck drivers knew the best and fastest routes, and knew where to avoid the sinkholes and other pitfalls so common in the desert. They reached Cairo and the hospitality of Shepheard's by nightfall. Brady made several phone calls. When he got off, he clapped his hands and laughed.

"I just got the poop. There's a little spot on the other side of town where the girls are easy, and the liquor is cheap. What do you say, we paint this town a new color?"

"Thanks, but I think I'll pass on that one. I've got to see Auchinleck at 0700, and I'd rather not be nursing a hangover. "

"Come on, Mikey. We're in Cairo, for Christ's sake. You've just been given three days to put the war and the dirt behind you. Besides, I'll not have me friend mopin' about on his night of glory."

"What glory, we just listened to the radio."

"It was a lot more than that, and you know it. I'm standin' you drinks, boyo, and the least you can do is come along, drink up and enjoy yourself. If you're not wantin' female companionship, that's okay by me."

Thorley sighed. There was no getting out of this one. "All right, *boyo*," he said, putting on a fake Irish accent that made Brady wince. "Let's be going then."

The "little spot" Brady mentioned was the Kit Kat Club, a splashy nightspot on the opposite side of Cairo from the hotel. Decorated in a cross between Art Deco and Egyptian motifs, it boasted a seventeen-piece band up on its own stage, and two full bars with enough exotic concoctions to melt the brains of several armies. It was packed when they walked in, smoke hanging thickly about the dimly lit room. Pools of light dotted the floor in between tables covered in crisp white linen. To Thorley it all looked like something out of a Hollywood B-movie.

Wading through the smartly dressed crowd, Brady found them an empty table near one of the bars just vacated by an amorous couple heading for the door. A young Egyptian busboy came by, scooped up all the empty glasses, replaced the linen and the table lamp, and scurried away. Thorley took his seat and let his eyes run over the crowd, already regretting his decision to come. The club was too dark, the band too loud, and the smoke made his eyes water. Moments after they'd taken their seats, a white-coated waiter came up to them and took their drink order: two scotches, neat.

When the drinks came, Thorley took a generous sip and let the fiery liquor flow down his throat, feeling it warm his stomach. It felt good. And he was beginning to think that it was just what he needed. He realized Brady was talking to him and leaned forward to hear over the band's rendition of "Little Brown Jug."

Brady was grinning like the Cheshire Cat and pointing toward the bar. Thorley followed his gaze and noticed two women seated at the end drinking tall glasses of what looked like champagne. Brady grinned at them and they returned the smile with toothy ones of their own.

"There's a couple of ripe ones, eh, Mikey." Brady's voice was thick with desire, and Thorley felt his stomach twist as his anxiety level rose a notch.

The girls were voluptuous in the classic sense: narrow waists book-ended by large breasts and derrieres. The word "Junoesque" came to mind. Both were darkly complected with raven hair and chocolate-brown eyes that smoldered with frank invitation.

"A feast for the eyes, as well as the soul," Brady said, raising his glass to the girls. They took it as their cue and began threading their way through the crowd toward their table. Each wore a slinky cocktail dress that clung to them, undulating with their every move.

Thorley fumed.

"I told you I didn't want this, Corwin. I'm married, for God's sake!"

"Just relax," he said, a sly grin on his face that made Thorley even angrier. "No one's twisting your arm, here. Let's enjoy their company. Nothing has to happen. Okay?"

Thorley felt as he'd been neatly boxed into a corner: Leave and be the party poop, the bloody stick-in-the-mud, or stay and risk—what, temptation?

He sighed, shaking his head at the absurdity of the situation. "All right, you win. I'll be a good boy."

Brady clapped him on the back and smiled. "That's the way to play it!"

When the women drew closer, Thorley saw they were both very young, probably under twenty-five. Their smiles widened when they reached the table. Both men stood.

"Ladies, may I present Major Michael Thorley, and I'm Lieutenant Corwin Brady, both of His Majesty's Long Range Desert Group. And we are honored to meet you."

He made a mock bow and both girls looked at each other and laughed. The taller of the two girls spoke first. "Hello, British, my name is Aziza and this is my friend, Femi." Aziza's accent was thick, but understandable. Femi, however just smiled and giggled. Apparently, Aziza would have to do the talking for the both of them.

They sat down and Aziza moved her chair closer to Thorley, her spicy perfume hitting him like one of the L.R.D.G's trucks. Subtlety was obviously not this girl's strong suit.

"What are you girls drinking?" Brady asked, his smile widening as Femi stroked his arm.

"Champagne," Aziza purred, her eyes drilling through Thorley.

Brady waived to the waiter and rattled off the order in rapid Arabic. The waiter nodded and scurried off, returning moments later with two more flutes and an iced magnum. Brady raised his glass. "A toast. To my good friend, Michael Thorley, who has very probably saved his country single-handed!"

Thorley was embarrassed; not only because of what Brady had just said, which was patently foolish, but because the man was already drunk and drawing unwarranted attention to the both of them.

And then there were the girls.

Femi continued to become overly familiar with Brady, who lapped it all up like a thirsty dog, while Aziza's mere existence and close proximity was enough to upset Thorley's equilibrium.

"Corwin, likes to joke," he said, shooting his friend a disapproving glare.

Brady drained his glass of champagne and laughed, and Femi joined in, perhaps thinking that she should. "Ahh, Mikey's a modest one, that's for sure. Now take me, for instance." He paused for dramatic effect, his eyes moving from one girl to the next. "I'll tell you I'm the best and to hell with you if you disagree. Hah!"

The girls laughed and Thorley shook his head, taking a long gulp of the champagne. It was surprisingly good, and he quickly drained the glass, then refilled it. He let Brady dominate the conversation, as he usually did, and watched him regale the girls with a series of his infamous pub stories, alternating between both English and Arabic. He soon had the women hysterically laughing. Bored and not a little sad that his big moment in the desert was already behind him, Thorley kept refilling the glass with the bubbly wine. A quick glance at the label nearly brought him up short: Dom Perignon—1932.

Not a cheap wine, to say the least. It was then he decided to throw caution to the wind along with his money. After all, hadn't he come close to death once this week already, and hadn't he completed the mission his superiors set out for him, and successfully at that? He bloody well deserved to at least enjoy an evening out.

Twenty minutes later, he realized he was drunk, and when the band came back from its break and began playing a fast-paced Swing tune, he impulsively asked Aziza to dance. She practically dragged him out onto the floor and began a frantic jitterbug that would have been the envy of any teenager at the Hammersmith Palais. Reticent at first, Thorley let loose and began to mimic her moves, surprised that he was able to pick them up so quickly. And then the music changed, the tempo slowing. Aziza came to him, vital and brimming with her youth, and cleaved her curvaceous body to his. Unlike Lillian's, her body meshed effortlessly with his, like a jigsaw puzzle made of flesh.

Lillian.

All at once, like a bad omen, she intruded, her face welling up in his mind, along with a flood of guilt. But instead of backing off, instead of coming to his senses and leaving the nightclub for the safety of Shepheard's, he began to respond to Aziza's none-too-subtle overtures. A part of his fogged mind knew it was wrong, knew it even as he succumbed to it. But the one image that kept him traveling down that inexorable road was that of the faceless man sitting in the back seat of that black Daimler with the C.D. plate. The man who'd held Lillian exactly as he now held this dusky jewel, the man who'd nearly stolen his wife from him.

As the mood of the music became more romantic, Aziza pressed even harder against him, her long crimson nails digging into his back; he felt himself growing hard against her. He looked down and saw that she was gazing up at him, a lost, pleading look in her dark eyes. A sweat broke out on the back of his neck and the room began to tilt. The band seemed unbearably loud; the smoke impossibly thick.

He needed to breathe.

Leaving Aziza on the dance floor, Thorley pushed through the crowd, oblivious to the angry snarls of those he elbowed past, his eyes focused on the exit. He burst through it, welcoming the cool breeze that caressed his face like a soft hand. His heart hammered against his ribs and he found that he needed to lean against the stucco wall of the nightclub or risk fainting.

It was the champagne.

He wasn't used to drinking that much that fast. It still bubbled through his brain, making him feel surreal, otherworldly. But he had to admit, part of it was the girl. That she was attractive was obvious, but there was something else about her, something primal. And it had affected him in a way that scared him to the core.

"Are you okay, British?"

She was there, right next to him, her breath against his face—

unavoidably sexual. She caressed his cheek, and a shock passed through his body, as if her fingers were electrified.

He wanted to hold her.

He wanted to kiss her.

He wanted to run.

Oh, God, Lillian, a man can only resist so much!

"I'm fine," he said, his voice barely above a whisper. "Just a little winded." He avoided looking at her, afraid of what he might do.

"It is hard to be so far from home, yes?"

She sounded different, less predatory, and it was the note of empathy in her voice that made him turn and face her. She smiled and it made her glow with a genuine warmth he would have thought beyond her.

"Yes, it is."

"You are married?"

Thorley nodded, and he found that he parted with that information reluctantly, as if some portion of his being did not want to alienate the girl.

"My husband was killed by the Germans, because he tried to help the British."

Thorley studied her now, seeing the gleam of tears in her eyes. "I'm so sorry," he said, hating the phoniness of those three words. A moment went by before he spoke again. "You must hate us, awfully."

She shook her head, slowly. "No, I do not. You fight to save us, as Reshef did. He was a good man, and I think that you are a good man, too. I cannot hate you for that."

She drew closer and planted a soft moist kiss on his lips, her hand cupping his chin. The dam broke in Thorley's heart and he took her in his arms, kissing her with all the unspent passion within him. She groaned and melted against him, her agile tongue filling his mouth with hot expectant wetness. The kiss seemed endless, a total world unto itself. Moments, or hours later he couldn't tell, they broke, staring into each other's eyes, knowing that it wouldn't end there.

"We can't go back to where I'm staying," he said, breathless. "I'm sharing a room."

She put a finger to his lips. "I live nearby. Let me tell Femi that we are going, yes?"

He looked off toward the Pyramids, the outlines of those ancient tombs barely visible in the darkness, then turned back to her. "Yes, tell her."

She retreated into the nightclub, leaving Thorley to the fury of his thoughts. When she returned clutching her purse, they began walking down the street, her arm through his. For the briefest of moments, he felt like a schoolboy on his first date.

Aziza lived in a tiny three-room apartment over a café, consisting of one bedroom, a modest bath, and the main kitchen/living area. Furnishings were scant: an ancient overstuffed sofa, a couple of straight-backed chairs, and a lot of gaudy throw pillows scattered about on what appeared to be a high-quality Persian rug. And while the apartment was by no means a palace, it was clean and cozy.

Aziza's bedroom overlooked the street and had a small balcony, reached by a set of French doors trimmed with lace curtains. Aside from a bureau heaped with cosmetics, the room was barely big enough to fit the bed, a large full-sized affair also covered with pillows, and which sat directly on the floor without benefit of box springs.

Leading him by the hand, Aziza pulled him inside and began undressing him, her nimble fingers working patiently at the buttons of his shirt and trousers, kissing each new area of his exposed skin with her warm full lips. When he was naked, she gently pushed him back onto the bed. The moon poured through the window, its pale light throwing the pattern of the lace curtains onto his body.

Without taking her eyes off of him, Aziza moved to the bureau. She picked up a box of matches, struck one, and lit a fat candle. It sputtered at first, then settled into a steady flame that cast a romantic glow throughout the tiny space. She turned to him, eyes shining with lust. And then she began to disrobe.

Starting with her evening dress, she teased each strap off her shoulder, slowly, sensually, then let the dress slide off her body to the ground. Thorley inhaled sharply as he saw her body now fully exposed, save for her panties and brassiere. Unlike so many Western women who insisted on starving themselves into sticks, Aziza was full-figured, curvesome—womanly. And she seemed to delight in his rapt attention. Smiling, she reached for her bra, unsnapped it from behind and tossed it aside, her generous breasts heaving. Thorley noticed the nipples and aureolas were a dark chocolate color against the unblemished café au lait of her skin. She caressed them, kneading them together, her eyes closed, her mouth pouting with pleasure. Aroused, she stepped up the pace of her striptease, her own eagerness overcoming her desire to titillate. She tore off her panties, then kicked off her high heels, revealing long, gracefully curved toenails polished a bright red to match her fingernails.

She climbed onto the bed and slid into his arms, encompassing him with her ripe body. He kissed her and again felt that swirling vertiginous feeling, as if the entire universe began and ended there. Pulling away from her mouth, he began to trail his lips down her body, feeling her back arch as he reached her pubic mound. Her hair was thick and dark, like wool and he filled his nostrils with her musk as he began to make love to her in earnest.

Sensing that her desire now matched his own, he rolled her onto her back and mounted her. Her groan as he entered her was deep and throaty. He began to thrust, slowly at first, marveling at her tightness, then increasing his speed as she began to respond. She moaned and writhed beneath him, beads of sweat breaking out on her dark skin. Her musk permeated the air and she began to buck against him. He could feel the tightness beginning in his scrotum and knew that would not last long. Scant moments later he ejaculated with a groan and fell onto her, his breath coming in ragged gasps.

After he'd caught his breath, he rolled onto his back, feeling the first onrush of guilt, his wife's face once again before him. He wanted to shrivel up and blow away, melt through the mattress, anything to get the bloody hell out of there. His mind worked furiously, wondering how he would extricate himself from the situation gracefully. Then he realized that there was no need. All he had to do was get dressed and walk out, without another word or glance.

But as rotten as he felt for betraying Lillian—and himself—he couldn't bring himself to be quite so callous.

Aziza spoke suddenly, as if reading his mind, her voice a husky whisper. "I am not quite so beautiful to you now, am I, British?"

Christ, what was it about women that they could sense when a man was thinking about another?

He turned to face her and was about to answer when the light snapped on in the room. Aziza scrambled to cover herself as Thorley whirled to face their intruder. It was Brady.

"Jesus bloody Christ, Corwin, what the hell are you doing here?"

The normally loquacious Irishman stared at him, a hard expression on his narrow face, then he raised his right arm. Clutched in his hand was a Walther PPK pistol with a silencer attached. He fired once, catching Aziza just over the right eye. She issued a strangled cry and flopped onto the mattress, blood spouting from the wound like a tiny geyser. Thorley was too stunned to move.

"My God, what are you doing? W—why did you shoot her?"

Brady kept the gun trained on him as he padded into the room. He went to the lace curtains, pulled them aside and looked out. Apparently satisfied, he returned his attention to Thorley, who watched him with saucer eyes.

Brady smiled without a trace of humor. "What are you talking about, Mikey? *You* shot her."

"W—what?"

"You had a row after making love and you shot her, then, in a fit of remorse you took your own life.... I'm sorry, Mikey, you were a real friend."

Brady raised the gun just as Thorley opened his mouth to scream, providing the perfect target. The gun coughed once more and the 7.65mm bullet caught Thorley squarely in the mouth, blowing out the back of his head. Without a sound, he fell across Aziza's corpse, his body spasming in a grotesque parody of their lovemaking.

Working quickly, Brady unscrewed the silencer and wiped the gun down, then placed it firmly in Thorley's right hand.

It was perfect.

The fact that he'd shot him in the mouth would make it hard to disprove suicide, except for the lack of powder burns. And he knew from experience that the incompetent Egyptian medical examiners would not bother looking for them, that is, if they even bothered to examine the bodies to begin with.

Standing back from the bed, Brady stared at Thorley a moment, a sadness creeping into his eyes, then he turned and left the apartment, taking the back stairs, careful not to let any of the early risers in the building see him leave.

Three hours later, he stood on the aft deck of a tramp steamer bound for Dublin, watching the shoreline as it pulled out of Alexandria harbor.

Another job well done.

Another job made neat and tidy for King and country.

This one, however, had left a bad taste in his mouth. He couldn't wait to get back to the old sod and hide away in his farmhouse in Kerry for a month, or until those right old bastards in MI6 called him again. In any event, he'd had enough of sand, sun, and friendships to last a lifetime.

THE SON: 1984

22

"*Dearest One... If you are reading this letter, it means that I have not survived the war, something I now fear is intended by those who wish to insure my silence. I want you to know that your father loves you with all of his heart. If you are a girl, I have asked your mother to name you after her. If you are the son I have prayed for, then...after me. However you turn out, please know that you are wanted and loved.*

"*A great deal has happened in the last two months, so much that I can scarcely comprehend the consequences. All I know is that after returning from a successful and highly secret mission to Finland—that I was ordered to undertake—I have been hastily reassigned from a comfortable job as a translator in the Foreign Office to a post within Hell itself....*

"*I write you now from my barracks in Cairo. I leave tomorrow for Siwa, where the temperature reaches an ungodly one hundred twenty-five in the day and plunges to near freezing at night. God only knows why the war has been brought to this godforsaken land....*

"*My coming journey will take me right to the heart of the enemy, and I fear this will be my undoing. If that be so, I can accept an honorable death in battle. What I cannot accept is the treachery of my own government.*

"*Now comes the difficult part. Though we will probably never meet, I must ask you to do your father a favor. My solicitors, Cadwallader and Soames, are holding certain items for me in safekeeping. If I fall, they are instructed to release them only to my heir. That is you, my child. Aside from providing the solicitors with a copy of your certificate of birth, you must utter these three words, 'The Eagle Flies.' These items hold the key to the peace and security of the world, my child. When you see them, you will know what to do. Use them wisely, and well. Love, your father...."*

❄ ❄ ❄

The yellowed pages fluttered to the floor, resembling leaves scattered by the wind on a raw Autumn day. Michael watched his mother reach for them, her delicate, liver-spotted hands grabbing for them with sharp, desperate movements. She held them to her breast, her breath coming in great sobs, her eyes brimming.

"I had no idea this was up there, Michael," she said. "No idea at all. I'm so dreadfully sorry."

Michael nodded. His father, who had been little more than a dusty photograph and a collection of stories his mother had told him over and over again, had suddenly taken on flesh and blood, had called out to him from the grave and asked his help. Part of him yearned to reach out and tell his father that he'd loved him all his life, but the thought of it also left him feeling a trifle silly, as if he were contemplating confessing to a statue. And then there was the fog of mystery surrounding his death. What had he meant by the "... key to the peace and security of the world?" Certainly, whatever the problem was, the urgency was long past; it couldn't be more than an historical curiosity, by now—a mere footnote. And yet the passion behind his father's words continued to resonate within Michael. He hungered to know more, any scrap that would reveal more of this man who still remained partially hidden by the shadows of time.

I want you to know that your father loves you with all of his heart....

"Where are Cadwallader and Soames located, mother?" Michael asked, breaking the silence.

Lillian looked up, a look of panic flitting across her face. "I—I'm not sure. I believe they used to be in Piccadilly, but I stopped using them after your father...."

"Then they could still be there?"

"I don't know, I suppose so, but would they even remember something from so long ago?"

Michael stood, and began moving toward the door, his lips compressed into a thin line. "Let's go, Erika."

"Surely, you're not going back tonight? Let me fix up your old room. Miss Rainer could stay in my room on the chaise lounge—"

"No."

Erika reluctantly followed Michael, her expression mirroring her extreme discomfort with the mounting tension in the room. Lillian joined them, her hand reaching out to her son. "Please, Michael, don't go."

He whirled on her. "How could you not know of this? You were his wife, for God's sake! And that letter.... Waiting in that dusty attic all these bloody years! Something happened to him out there, something they've covered up! And you've just let them bloody do it."

A panoply of emotions swept across Lillian's face: shock, anger, outrage, then...sadness. "No, I didn't! I loved your father."

"Bloody crap! They send all his worldly possessions home in a tidy little box, and you just tucked him away in the attic and never looked back. How could you do that to him? How could you do that to *me!*"

Before she could answer, Michael turned and stormed out, letting the weathered oak door slam against the wall. There was a moment of silence before Lillian spoke, a moment where the two women listened to Michael's feet crunching across the gravel drive.

"I should have expected this," Lillian said, with a sigh. She turned to the younger woman and fixed her with a level gaze. "With just he and I all these years, it's been so very, very hard. All we had was the memory of his father.... We tried to forget the disgrace...." Lillian paused and watched her son, who sat leaning against the red Mercedes, brooding. "I should have remarried. I had plenty of suitors. Good men they were. But after Michael, I—I just couldn't. Lord knows little Michael needed a man around to teach him how to become one."

"I think your son is a fine man," Erika said.

"You're kind to say that."

"I mean it."

Lillian stared at the younger woman again, her aged eyes searching Erika's face for some indefinable something. "I believe you do," she said finally. "I just wish Michael could see it.... And what I had to do...."

Erika nodded, looking toward the door. "I'll talk to him."

Lillian wiped a stray tear from her eye and smiled. "You're a dear. I do hope we shall get to know one another better."

Erika reached out and gave the older woman's arm a gentle squeeze. "I hope so, too. Good night, Mrs. Thorley.

Erika turned to go, and Lillian stopped her, her grip surprisingly strong. "Be careful, my dear, history is such a restless beast."

Puzzled, Erika nodded, then walked out and joined Michael. A moment later the bright red car tore out of the driveway and headed back toward London.

✵　✵　✵

It had been a long time since Pavel Kolenkovich Hedeon had felt his career teetering on the precipice. And it was a feeling he hated. After all he'd been through in the last forty-five years: Stalin's purges, Beria's aborted coup attempt, Khrushchev's bullying, Brezhnev's pig-headedness, he was now about to be undone by a phantom.

Under any other circumstances, he would have welcomed Sir William Atwater's death, would have itched to do the deed himself, yet someone else—someone outside his network—had killed the old goat and made it so the finger pointed straight at him.

Why?

And why now?

Atwater was no longer a threat to anyone, save his own country, though he wouldn't put something like this past those bastards at MI6.

The phone rang, and Hedeon moved his stocky frame toward it with surprising grace. Still well-muscled for a man in his late sixties, he also boasted a mane of shocking white hair, a vanity of which he proudly proclaimed. His face, though lined with a thousand wrinkles like a fine old painting, showed strength and determination in the firm set of his mouth and the feral gleam in his ice-blue eyes.

The phone sat atop an exquisite and very original Louis XV table at the far end of the suite. It never ceased to amaze him that the Dorchester Hotel, one of the best in London, refused to put more than one phone in a suite, and in the wrong room, no less. Still, Hedeon counted himself lucky. As the senior KGB man in Britain, he had the choice of living either in the embassy compound, or in any residence of his choice. He liked the Dorchester for its sense of history and because the Penthouse floor he rented could be secured without becoming obtrusive to the rest of the hotel's guests. He also liked it because it tweaked Moscow's proletarian nose. And if they ever complained, he could always point out the fact it helped to bolster his image as the Chief Russian Cultural Attaché.

He snatched up the receiver on the fifth ring, already annoyed at the lateness of the call.

"Yes...?" He listened, his eyes softening. "Speak English, you know better.... Yes, I know all about the girl. My operatives picked her up when she boarded the ferry at Ostend.... I won't make any promises. If she can be separated from young Michael, then any unpleasantness can be avoided.... Yes, I will keep you apprised. Do not worry. Good night."

Hedeon hung up the phone and walked to the large picture window overlooking Hyde Park, his gait less graceful, almost lumbering, as if a large weight had deposited itself on his wide shoulders. The fierce expression on his face moments before had changed to one of deep sadness, the blazing light in his eyes dull and flickering low. This business was a dirty one when it concerned ones you cared about. It was a weakness for which Moscow would be ruthless and unforgiving, and one against which he'd fought his whole life. Sentiment had no place in the craft.

Reaching a decision, he returned to the phone and picked it up, dialing a special series of numbers from memory. He waited until the person on the other end picked up, and then said, "It's Hedeon.... *Da*, I know.... I want everyone on his toes. This Atwater business was directed at us. I want answers...."

He hung up a moment later and returned to the picture window, easing himself into a comfortable overstuffed chair, a tiny bitter smile creasing his lips. He would find whoever was responsible for this mess, and when he did, Pavel Kolenkovich Hedeon would take great pleasure in wringing his fucking neck.

23

The young girl moaned and bucked beneath him, her normally plac-id face now twisted into a grimace of ecstasy, sweat gleaming off the stud in her nose.

"Oh, God, Fergie!" she screamed, digging her rather generous claws into his back. "Fuck me harder!"

Biting back the pain, Ferguson thrust into her harder in retali-ation, his wolfish grin widening. This one was a real tart. He'd seen her round the pub often enough, squawking and giggling with her girlfriends, always giving him the "sly eye." And she was a real treat for the jaundiced eye: sort of Punker meets Sloan Ranger with a touch of leather. She had style, all right, but she couldn't resist the odd touch, like the stud in her nose and garish makeup that made her look like something out of Madame Tussaud's. It was like a mustache on the Mona Lisa, or mooning the Queen, a rebelliousness that appealed to Ferguson's contrary nature. Unfortunately, he'd always managed to be with someone else, either another woman, or his drinking buddies.

He'd hit the pub right after work and gotten lucky.

Absorbed in his pint of MacEwan's, he'd been thinking of Mike and how much of a screw-up the poor sod was with women, when he chanced to glance up and found her staring at him from the other end of the bar.

226

Neither her friends, nor his buddies, were anywhere in sight. Bloody perfect.

He smiled back and lifted his glass in a toast. She took it as her signal and sidled over, a little unsteady for the drink. She must've started early. Then again, it could have been the six-inch spike heels.

After another half a pint and a bit of meaningless conversation, they'd headed over to his flat, three streets away.

That had been two hours ago, and the bird was insatiable—wanting to do it in every imaginable way (even up her bum), bending herself into shapes that would make a Chinese acrobat jealous.

She screamed again, and Ferguson gamely thrust harder, feeling as if he were in a long-distance race. Well, he was game if she was. After all, as his Mum once said, *"Be careful what you wish for, son, you just might get it."*

"Too right."

"What?" the girl said in between grunts.

"Nothin', love," he said, thrusting harder still, "just daydreaming."

She was too swept up in her pleasure to notice the sarcasm behind his remark, which made Ferguson all the giddier. But his pleasure was cut short when a pounding began on his front door two rooms away. It sounded as if someone were storming the bloody Bastille. He tried to ignore it, hoping it was just one of the local hopheads mistaking Ferguson's flat for that of a dealer's, but the pounding only increased in tempo and volume.

"Who's that, Fergie?" the girl said, breathless.

Ferguson climbed off of her and slipped into his pair of leopard-print briefs and an old ratty robe. "Never mind. Stay here."

The girl sat up in the bed, her kohl-rimmed eyes blazing. "You got another woman coming here, don't ya? Well, I don't do that stuff. I've got breeding, ya know!"

Ferguson snorted in annoyance and stalked into the sitting room. Here the pounding was louder, shaking the flimsy door on its loose rusty hinges.

"Bloody gits," he mumbled. "All right! Why don't ya just bust the bleedin' thing in? Hold your horses!"

When he reached the door, he refrained from opening it, suddenly nervous. What if it *was* some crazed addict angry for some imagined slight, or a rival dealer thinking his nemesis lay behind the door he was pounding on. Christ! He might have a bloody machine gun, or some such nasty, waiting to mow him down. Realizing that he made a rather large target in front of the door, he quickly stepped to the side, like he'd seen done in all the cop shows.

"Who is it?" he said, hating the nervous quaver in his voice.

"Open up in the name of Her Majesty's government," came the firmly stated reply.

Ferguson frowned. What had he done that would merit this?

"Open up, this is our last request."

Ferguson fumbled with the two locks and swung the door open. Three men stood before him. One of them, obviously the senior man, stood about an inch taller than Ferguson, had blond hair combed boyishly over to one side, a thin ascetic face and a nose as sharp as a spear. He looked like some pompous public school proctor, the kind that would as soon kick you in the arse as smile at you. And then he did smile, only confirming Ferguson's assessment.

"So sorry to intrude, Mr. Ferguson. But I wonder if we might have a word?"

The accent was all oil and polish, and so smooth it would have the average idiot eating out of the man's hand. It made Ferguson want to throttle him.

"Who the bloody hell are you? And what do you want?"

The man smiled again, and Ferguson frowned. Was that contempt he saw in the man's blue eyes?

"Forgive me," he said. "I'm Simon Welles, MI6."

Ferguson looked dubious. "MI6 is military. I was a bloody washout. How about some ID?"

"Very well."

Welles reached inside the jacket of his olive-tan suit and pulled out a wallet made of expensive Morocco leather and flipped it open, revealing a picture ID. Ferguson made a big show of taking it and looking it over. A moment later he handed it back.

"So, what do you want?"

"Just the answers to some questions."

Ferguson leaned toward Welles conspiratorially. "If it's all the same to you," he said, nearly whispering, "I'd rather wait until morning. I've got some company...if you catch my drift."

Welles smiled again then shook his head. "I'm afraid it can't wait. Please come with me."

Welles nodded to the two large men, who moved toward Ferguson with alarming swiftness. Each one grasped an arm and began dragging him out.

"Hey! Now, wait a bleedin' moment! I've got rights ya know! You can't be pullin' a man out of his bed like the fucking Gestapo. Let me go, you bloody gits!"

The door slammed shut and Ferguson's protests faded away, leaving the flat eerily silent. A moment later the girl's voice rang out from the bedroom. "Fergie? Where are you? You coming back to bed? I've got an itch needs scratching.... Fergie?"

* * *

The Mercedes responded like a trained tiger under Michael's hands, hugging the winding Sussex roads with practiced aplomb, its engine growling contentedly. It felt good to drive it, felt good to let the car's power infuse his mind and body. And he needed to feel good at the moment. Staring through the windscreen, he watched the darkened landscape streak toward him, taking him farther away from the cottage.

He glanced in the rearview, then, seeing the white lines receding into the distance, like some giant pair of apron strings that would never run out, never exhaust their hold on him. But was that why he'd gotten angry? Was it as silly as feeling that his mother had ruled his life—that even knowledge of his own father had come through her? And here they'd uncovered something new, something both terrible and wonderful and he felt as if his heart might explode.

He shifted gears then looked over at Erika. He could feel her anger coming at him in waves. Obviously, he was a total fuck-up when it came to women, including his own mother. The mere thought of Lillian and his anger renewed itself. Could she really have not known of the letter's existence all these years? And if she had, then why hadn't she'd told him about it sooner? It didn't make any sense. After all, hadn't she always said she loved him, said it that very night?

Michael stole another glance at Erika. She sat stiffly in the soft leather bucket seat, her luminous face staring out through the windscreen, a tiny frown furrowing the skin just above the bridge of her nose. Even with as dour an expression as this, she was breathtaking.

He turned his attention back to the road and noted a pair of headlights in the rearview mirror. The car joined them not long after they'd left the cottage and had stayed about a quarter mile behind them the whole way. The lights were low to the ground, suggesting some kind of sporty model.

"That was a shitty thing you did," Erika said, breaking into his thoughts.

He turned, fixing her with a puzzled frown. "Was it?"

"Yes, it was. She's your mother, not your enemy."

"Sometimes I wonder," he said, downshifting as they rounded a curve. "She made Dad into some kind of hero all those years. He was like a god to me...perfect. And now this."

"You can't blame her for not wanting to deepen her wounds, Michael. My God, she'd just lost a husband, and was pregnant. She needed to survive."

Erika was right.

And knowing it only made Michael feel worse. Even in his righteous rage, he'd known he'd treated his mother unfairly, lashed out at her with forty years of a young boy's anger at losing his father—blamed her for it, in fact.

Leaning back in the seat, he exhaled a long breath, as if expelling four decades of accumulated poisons from his body. He shook his head.

"You're right. I've been a right bastard. She's done her best, Lord knows. There's a pub a few miles up the road. We'll call her from there."

Erika's expression softened. "What about Cadwallader and Soames?"

"You're as curious as I am, aren't you?" he asked, a sly smile turning up the corners of his mouth.

She nodded, returning the smile.

"We'll try them in the morning. Nothing we can do till then."

A flicker in the rearview mirror made Michael glance up into it. He frowned. "What the bloody hell is this?"

As if on cue, the car behind them snapped on its main beam and roared forward, closing the quarter mile gap between the two cars in seconds. It pulled up to within a foot of the Mercedes' bumper.

From what Michael could see, the car looked to be a late model Lotus Esprit, either black or midnight blue. And because of the glare on the Mercedes' back window, it was impossible to tell who was driving. Erika turned in her seat and squinted into the glare.

"Maybe they want to pass," she said, her voice sounding unconvinced.

Michael shot her a look. "If they'd wanted to do that they would have done so. The road's deserted."

The Lotus made its move. With a growl from its powerful 300 horsepower engine, the car nudged the Mercedes, forcing Michael to grip the wheel harder to remain in control. Erika screamed and Michael took this as his cue to step on the gas. The Mercedes leapt forward, its eight-cylinder engine winding out until he remembered to shift gears. Now in fourth, the 500 SL streaked forward into the night, the white line now taking on a greater significance. As long as he stayed with it, Michael knew he would be all right. The problem was, the Lotus looked as if it had every intention of running them off the road.

"Pull over, Michael!" Erika yelled.

The Lotus smashed into the back of the Mercedes, making Erika scream again.

Michael stomped on the accelerator, pushing it to the floor. The 500 SL responded like a bullet shot from a gun, the tires screeching as the car rounded a tight curve.

"Slow down, you'll kill us!"

"And I suppose the men in the Lotus won't?"

Her answer was her hand on his arm, her grip like a vise.

The two cars reached a straightaway and Michael caught sight of the Lotus in the driver's side mirror as it swung out and shot forward, coming alongside the Mercedes. They rode side by side, each car jockeying for position. To the uninitiated, it would appear that the two cars were having a "drag race," but Michael knew without having to be told that the stakes were a lot higher than macho bragging rights.

Keeping his eye on the road, he saw a bend about a mile ahead. He turned his head and tried to see into the Lotus's windows. Unfortunately, they were tinted a smoky black, making an identification of the driver and any passengers impossible.

Returning his attention to the road, Michael tried pulling ahead. The Lotus stayed with him. He then tried to drop behind, hoping to give the exotic car some of its own medicine, but the Lotus merely matched his speed. The problem was the straightaway was rapidly diminishing, and any moment someone could come around the bend. A trickle of sweat ran down the side of Michael's face, and his hands felt slippery on the wheel. He looked for a turn off, but there was nothing, just a narrow strip of road lined with stone walls.

"Michael!"

He looked into the distance and spotted a pair of headlights as it rounded the bend in the road up ahead. A bad situation had just gotten worse.

And then the Lotus began smashing into them, trying to force them into the stone wall. Michael shot a smoldering glance at the Lotus then wrenched the wheel toward it, sending the right wing of the Mercedes into the Lotus. The screech of metal as the two cars collided was music to Michael's ears. He imagined that the men inside, professionals though they must be, were nonetheless a little flustered as he bashed into them. Perhaps they were even a little worried.

He smashed the Lotus again; the other car approaching them was now flashing its lights.

Michael turned to the Lotus. "How do you like that, you bastards?"

Now, the Lotus tried to back off and Michael matched their speed, keeping the other car on a collision course with the oncoming car.

"Michael, NO!"

Her words ripped into his brain, and hearing them, he realized what it was he'd been about to do. Pushing on the accelerator, he sped forward allowing the Lotus to squeeze in behind him, just as a white Mini Cooper streaked by, its reedy little horn howling. A second later, the Lotus was back beside him. Michael didn't wait for it to try to force him off the road. He began smashing into the Lotus again.

It was then that the passenger side window of the Lotus rolled down and an automatic pistol fitted with a silencer poked out gripped in a ham-sized fist. The barrel turned down, aiming for the Mercedes' tires. The pistol coughed twice, and the right front tire blew out, then shredded and fell away from the steel rim. Erika screamed while Michael fought to control the hurtling car. When the car left the road, the steering wheel tore from his grasp and the car veered toward a massive tree.

At the last second before impact, something gave, and he managed to wrench the wheel to the right. The car shot past the tree, so close the side mirror sheared off, clanging against the door before flying off into the night.

Michael tromped down on the brakes, bringing the car to a lurching halt against a low outcropping of rocks, accompanied by a loud ripping sound. The last thing he saw before the curtain of darkness descended was the hub of the steering wheel hurtling toward his face.

�֍ ✖ ✖

The car listed slightly to the port side and Erika struggled with the seatbelt, finally forcing the buckle to open. Turning to Michael, she saw that he was unconscious, his head resting against the steering wheel. A trickle of blood seeped from somewhere on his scalp, tracing the line of his jaw. She eased him back, letting him collapse against the seat.

Suddenly a familiar odor assaulted her nostrils.

Benzine.

There was a leak!

Working quickly, she unbelted Michael and then climbed over him. She tried his door and found it jammed shut. Bracing herself, she reached under his arms and heaved him over the passenger seat and out of the car. His feet hit the ground and she heard him groan.

Good. The fact that he was only lightly unconscious meant that a concussion was unlikely. Straining, she pulled him to what she judged a safe distance from the Mercedes, laying him out of sight from the road behind some brambles. She felt his pulse.

Slow and steady.

She returned her attention to the road, freezing when she spotted the Lotus pulling over to the side. Two men got out and stared at the Mercedes. In a moment, they would be coming to investigate.

She remembered her purse and reaching inside, she pulled out a pack of matches and crawled toward the Mercedes, careful to keep as low to the ground as possible. She was grateful there was no moon out that night, or the two men from the Lotus would certainly see her.

Raising her head, she looked at the two men. They still stood watching the car. They wouldn't wait much longer. Despite this being a lonely country road, someone else might happen by. And that could not be left to chance.

She saw one turn to the other and say something.

Hurry, you fool. Do something!

Scrabbling the last few feet to the Mercedes, Erika, pulled one of the matches free from the pack, lighted it, then touched it to the remaining ones. The matches flared and Erika tossed it beneath the car near the ruptured fuel tank. In the same motion, she tumbled backwards and pushed her face into the earth. Even with her eyes closed the flash of flame was bright, making stars dance behind her lids. Opening her eyes, she saw the Mercedes totally engulfed, the tongues of red-orange flames dancing skyward. She could hear the sizzle of the leather seats and smelled the burning rubber of the tires. The heat made the flesh of her face feel parched and crackling, as if she'd spent the whole day lying in the sun.

Another sound caught her attention. The two men had returned to the Lotus. The engine roared again, and the midnight blue car streaked away.

She'd done it.

She stood then, feeling the blood rush from her head, making her momentarily dizzy when she made her way back to where Michael lay. She knelt beside him and ran her hand across his cheek. His eyes snapped open and he bolted upright, his attention riveted by the burning car.

"Erika!"

"Here, I'm here," she said, touching his arm.

He visibly relaxed. "My God, I thought you were— What happened?"

"Take it easy, we're all right. I set fire to the car. They think we're still inside."

"Who were they?"

"I don't know," she said, shaking her head. "But they followed me from Dover, and I think they were on the boat over, too."

Michael's eyes widened and she immediately regretted telling him this.

"Why didn't you say something?"

"I didn't want to alarm you. I didn't think they would follow me here."

"Erika, who *are* they?"

The night had turned colder, and a mist had begun forming on the ground. Michael helped her to her feet and then put his jacket around her shoulders. She leaned against him, shock and exhaustion finally taking their toll.

"My father had enemies," she said finally, her eyes focused on a point far in the distance, "competitors who will stop at nothing to gain control of what is now my company."

"Including murder?"

Erika said nothing, not sure if she could trust him, even after all they had been through. What would he say if he knew the whole truth? Would he still be willing to help her, or would he walk away?

"The pub I mentioned isn't far from here," Michael offered. "About a mile and a half. We'll hike there and hire a cab to take us into town. I suggest we take a room at a hotel for the night. They might be watching my flat."

"But surely they think we're dead...."

Michael shook his head. "I don't think they're that easily satisfied. At best, your little deception has bought us some time. Eventually, possibly tomorrow if they check the car again, they'll know they've been had. In the meantime, we need to find out what my father left for me. Perhaps then we'll be able to make some sense of all this."

Leaning on each other, they hobbled back to the road and headed off toward the pub.

24

It was after one in the morning by the time they checked into the modest-looking hotel in East London.

"No one will look for us in a place like this," Erika said.

She was right. The hotel lobby looked tired and threadbare around the edges, like a child's once-favorite toy now relegated to the back of a closet. Cheap red carpeting dotted with dark oily stains, clashed with vomit-green walls and furniture covered in orange and black leatherette upholstery. The whole effect was of a room in some hideous corner of America's heartland—the furthest thing from London's East End. The only giveaway was a framed portrait of the queen staring sternly down from her perch on the wall above the soot-stained mantel.

After paying in cash, Michael and Erika trudged up to their room, the manager dogging their heels. A gnomish man of indeterminate age, he babbled in his thick Birmingham accent, pointing out various aspects of the hotel. A moment later, he was gone, his admonishment not to play the television after nine fading down the hall.

"Bloody depressing," Michael said, wiping his finger along the top of the dresser. It came away smudged with grime.

"You've obviously never been to Berlin. There are places even a rat wouldn't live in." Erika stripped off her blouse, revealing a frilly lace bra, her generous breasts threatening to spill out of the cups. "I'm going to take a bath."

She walked past Michael, her heady fragrance filling his nostrils. A flush of heat rose up from his collar.

Bloody Christ!

"Uhh, fine…. I'll check the message machine at my flat."

Erika nodded wearily and disappeared into the bathroom. A moment later the sound of the water splashing into the tub filled the room. Shaking his head, Michael went over to the bed and sat down, reaching for the phone that sat on the battered nightstand. He grimaced when he noticed the rubbed-in filth on the ear- and mouthpieces. Wiping them off on the bedspread he dialed his number.

"Hello, you've reached Michael's answering machine. Though I'm not at home, you may leave a message after you hear the tone. Cheerio!"

It sounded insipid now that he heard it as others did. He made a mental note to change it when he got home—if he ever did. And the bit about not being home, a bloody invitation to any thief who cased by phone.

The machine beeped and Michael punched in his three-digit code. He heard the machine click and the message tape rewinding. Three seconds later the first message played back: *"Michael, it's mother, I'm sorry again about what happened. Please call me when you get back. I think we need to talk."*

The machine beeped and then the second message played: *"Michael! Where the bloody hell are you? Everything's all mucked up. Call me as soon as you get home."*

He listened for a few minutes more then hung up when he realized there were no more messages. He would call his mother back and apologize. It was the right thing to do, after all. But she could wait. Ferguson was another matter. Picking up the phone, he dialed again.

❈ ❈ ❈

Ferguson leapt for the phone when it rang, knocking it off the table. Cursing, he snatched it up and put it to his ear, suddenly nervous.

"H—hello?"

"Hi, John, it's Michael."

Ferguson rocketed to his feet and began pacing, the ratty robe flapping open as he walked. "Dear God, man, where have you been? I've been going out of my mind."

"I'd rather not go into it. What's the problem, someone misplace a grave?"

Ferguson rolled his eyes. "You know, Michael, sometimes you're a real shit. I've just spent the last five hours sitting under a bleedin' hot light answering the same damn questions over and over again. Christ! It was like something out of a bad Yank movie. We opened a real can of worms, mate."

There was a long moment of stunned silence. "What are you talking about?"

Ferguson's motions became more frantic. "What the fuck do you think? The bloody South Wessex crap. There's a *D-notice* on that! These wankers aren't fucking around."

"Who? Special Branch?"

"MI-bloody-Six! They kept asking me where you were. They want you to come in and talk to them, Michael." Ferguson stopped pacing and listened. "Michael, are you there?"

"I'm sorry you had to take the brunt of this, John. But there's something strange going on with all of this, something I'm convinced is tied in with what happened to my dad. They're hiding something— the D-notice confirms it."

"Never mind all that," Ferguson said, pacing again. "If you want to keep your bloody job, you'll tell them everything you know with a pretty-please-and-a-cherry-on-top. As for me, I want nothing more to do with this. As far as I'm concerned, the Royal South Wessex can bloody well rot." Ferguson slammed the phone down and screamed, "Bloody gits!"

Suddenly exhausted, Ferguson trudged back toward the bedroom. It was then that someone began pounding on the door. Sharp, insistent, and as relentless as before. Livid, he stormed toward the door and flung it open. He noticed that the lights in the hall were out, obscuring whoever it was standing outside his door.

"Bloody Christ! I've had it with you bastards. I told you all I know." Ferguson squinted into the gloom. "Where's Welles, anyway? The shit too lazy to come himself this time?"

Before he could say anything else, a silenced automatic pistol was thrust into his face. It fired once, sounding like a loud cough. A spot of red flowered on Ferguson's forehead and he toppled to the floor. A moment later, the pistol coughed once more, and a heavily accented voice intoned, "The Eagle flies...."

※　　※　　※

Michael hung up the phone and sighed, running his hand through his now unruly hair. He felt as if the four puke green walls of the room were closing in on him. Nothing made sense, not a bloody thing. And yet, there was a glimmer of hope that somehow it would all fit. The key was Cadwallader and Soames. Would they still have the things his father left in their care? After all, it had been forty-three years. Coming out of his thoughts, he heard Erika singing in the bathroom, her husky voice barely able to hold the tune. He recognized it as something by Duran Duran. A moment later the singing stopped.

"Michael?"

He looked up and caught sight of her standing in the bathroom doorway, wrapped in a damp towel. A wave of hot soapy air filled the room, raising the humidity to the saturation point. He didn't notice. Every drop of water stood out on her skin like tiny liquid diamonds, and her hair, now wet and scraggly, hung over her smoldering eyes, making her look like some world-weary waif.

"The bath's free," she said, running a hand up her arm.

Without realizing that he was doing it, Michael stood up and walked toward her. It felt as if some outside force were operating his body and he was along for the ride, watching as if through a pair of reversed binoculars. A heart-stopping moment later he stood in front of her, inhaling her scent and losing himself in her eyes. He could hear his heart beating in his ears and his head felt as if it were filled with wet cotton. He saw something in her face, a longing that matched his own, and yet a part of him wanted to run, wanted to hide from her. He raised a hand to touch her and stopped himself. What was he doing? Was he daft? They'd only just met. It was then that he realized that the room had returned to normal perspectives and the look he saw in her face had fled. Had it really been there to begin with, or was it just post-adolescent longing? Feeling awkward, he fumbled with the bathroom door.

"Why don't you order up some food. I'll just be a minute."

❋　❋　❋

Erika watched Michael disappear into the bathroom, her mind a tangle of conflicting thoughts and emotions. Michael was clearly attracted to her. That much was obvious. The problem was she was beginning to reciprocate those feelings, and that was not something she'd bargained for.

Mein Gott, what am I to do? There's no room in my life for this.

She sighed and waited until she heard the sound of the shower, then went to the phone, picked it up and dialed.

"*Ja,* it's me," she said.

And then she began to speak in rapid German.

※　　※　　※

The remnants of their carry-out fish and chips lay on paper plates strewn on one of the twin beds. Michael sat back against the headboard, his arm thrown over his eyes, his breathing deep and regular. Erika watched him; her expression neutral.

"Are you awake?" she asked.

"Mmmmm.... Just trying to sort everything out."

"What's a D-notice, Michael?"

He dropped his arm and looked at her with tired eyes. "You heard me?"

"I didn't mean to.... Your friend, he is angry with you?"

"Scared was more like it."

He spent the next few minutes telling her about his conversation with Ferguson.

"So, what does 'D-notice' mean?"

Michael sat up and crossed his legs. "It's a restriction the British government places on information it deems 'injurious to the public good.' Sort of like 'Top Secret' or 'Eyes only.'"

"And you think our fathers were involved in some way?"

"I'd almost bet my life on it," he said, his eyes burning with a fierce light.

A flicker of worry crossed Erika's face. Michael touched her hand, a brush of flesh against flesh. "I said...almost.... I've got to find out what happened to my father...and why. And to hell with the bloody government!"

"It was wrong of me to come here and ask you to become involved in my problems," she said.

Michael shot her a look of disbelief. "What?"

"Let's forget the whole thing. Go back to your life, Michael... while you still can...."

"Go back? Are you mad? After all that's happened, you want to quit?"

She touched him then, and it jolted him like an electric cattle prod. "Yes, please...."

He looked into her eyes, and again he saw something there, a longing. "There's something you're not telling me."

She withdrew, shaking her head. "No, it's nothing. We'll keep going. I've no right to prevent you from finding the truth about your father. It's what *my* father would have wanted."

Confused, Michael was unprepared when Erika leaned over and caressed his face, placing a delicate kiss on his nose. She then moved over to the other twin bed and lay down, her face turned away from him.

Michael stared at her, his mind aswirl. A moment later his puzzled frown changed to a boyish grin. Sleep eluded him for the rest of the night.

25

The offices of Cadwallader & Soames, Solicitors, occupied one of the white stone buildings on a quiet corner of Regent Street several blocks from the bustle of Piccadilly Circus.

As Michael and Erika's cab pulled over to the curb, his anxiety rose. What if they'd lost what had been entrusted to them? And what if they had it, and refused to relinquish it? These thoughts and others raced through his mind while he stared at the building's forbidding facade.

"Are you all right?" Erika asked.

He nodded. "I'm fine, let's go."

Michael handed the cabby a five-pound note and didn't bother to wait for the change. Erika clambered out after him. They passed through the stout wooden doors and disappeared inside.

The entry way led up a short flight of stairs covered in a thick forest green carpet that gave underfoot. The walls were paneled in a dark wood and lit by filigreed light fittings that gave off a pale amber glow. It was obvious the firm was no longer the one his mother remembered. It resembled a mausoleum. It was only later he learned that it employed over 200 attorneys.

On reaching the first floor, Michael spotted the receptionist's desk, a semicircular modern piece wholly out of place with the rest of the decor, yet it added an ominous tone of authority to the woman seated behind it. Middle-aged and dressed severely in a dark suit, the receptionist was everyone's nightmare schoolmarm: sharp face, graying hair pulled into a tight bun and secured with a carved ivory comb. She wore a headset with a built-in microphone that allowed her hands to remain free to perform other tasks; and she was typing now as she spoke, her thin bloodless fingers a tangled blur.

"Cadwallader and Soames. Yes, Mr. Halleday is expecting your call. Please hold." She stopped typing only long enough to hit a series of buttons on the compact switchboard. "Mr. Halleday? Mr. Richardson on line five.... Cadwallader and Soames. No, I'm sorry, Mr. Bridges is on holiday until next week. Do you wish to leave word?"

Michael watched while she scribbled something on one of the preprinted pink message slips, tore it off its pad, then slipped it into one of the slots behind her already bulging with messages.

"Excuse me," Michael said, leaning over the desk, "I'm looking for Mart—"

"Cadwallader and Soames. Yes, Mr. Prentiss. I gave Mr. Gaylord your message over an hour ago. No, I don't know why he hasn't returned your call."

"Excuse me, Ma'am, but—"

"Cadwallader and Soames. Yes, sir. The writs were delivered well before the filing deadline...."

Michael shot Erika an annoyed look, his patience nearing its end. One thing he could never stand was rudeness in any form, especially from those who were supposed to be greeting the public. Erika shook her head and shrugged, apparently at a loss as to what to do. That was fine, for he knew *exactly* what to do.

Reaching across the desk, Michael grabbed the cable leading from the receptionist's headset and yanked it out of the switchboard. The receptionist jumped, as if someone had jabbed her with a needle. She lunged for the cable's end, her eyes blazing. Michael deftly moved it farther away.

"You give me that back, or I shall call security at once."

Erika smiled at Michael's audacity.

"That might be a little difficult," he said, holding up the cable.

The woman fumed. "What is it you want?"

Michael put on his best smile. "So sorry to trouble you, but we're looking for Martin Cadwallader, a matter of utmost importance."

The receptionist smiled then, and its cold, merciless expression sent a chill through Michael. She grabbed the cable back and plugged it in. Nearly every light on the switchboard was blinking.

"I'm sorry. Mr. Cadwallader retired some years ago."

"But surely, someone would be familiar with our business...." Michael couldn't keep the disappointment from out of his voice. It turned to anger when he saw the gleam of pleasure in the receptionist's eyes. He wanted to slap her.

The receptionist tapped a series of buttons on the switchboard. "Mr. Ripley to reception."

Michael started to say something else, but Erika's tap on his shoulder silenced him. There was no point in trying to win a game of one-upmanship with this woman. They went over and sat down on a leather-covered sofa. It felt cool against the skin of his arm and the smell of leather conditioner was a soothing balm to his spirit, something homely and familiar. A few moments later, a slight young man appeared. He looked as if he'd slept in his too-tight herringbone polyester suit, which clashed with his checked shirt and regimental tie. The young man stopped at the reception desk and spoke with the receptionist, who pointed a long finger at Michael and Erika. He smiled and nodded his thanks and walked over to them, his hand extended.

"I'm Halbert Ripley, so glad to meet you," he said, in a reedy voice. It sounded as if he'd been breathing helium. Michael just managed to keep a straight face as he took the man's hand.

"Michael Thorley, and this is my friend, Erika Rainer."

Ripley's flaccid hand felt like a dead fish. He cracked a wan smile and pushed the thick black frames of his glasses back up the bridge of his pudgy nose. "Well, then, how may I help you?"

"Perhaps we should go round to your office," Michael said.

Ripley nodded sharply. "Of course. Follow me."

They walked past the reception desk and Michael couldn't resist giving the old girl a wink.

Ripley led them through a maze of offices to a stairwell that took them down into the basement past rows and rows of files. At the end of the stacks, they came upon a door that Ripley held open for them. Inside was an eight-foot-square room lined with filing cabinets and a prim desk more at home in a schoolroom. Ripley, motioned for Michael and Erika to take the two straight-backed chairs facing the desk, then took his own seat behind it. Michael noticed the top of the man's desk was perfectly neat, with pens and papers at perfect right angles to each other.

Ripley made a show of shuffling papers and then smiled, folding his hands on the desktop. "So, what can I do for you, Mr. Thorley."

"I'm here to pick up something my late father left in your firm's care."

"Ahh, I see," Ripley said, his glasses slipping down his nose again. "Of course, I'm happy to oblige, but you see, Mr. Thorley, I've only just started my employment here, and I'm really not quite up to speed, so to speak."

He shrugged and attempted another smile. Michael noticed that the man's hands twitched nervously, as if he wasn't comfortable with them unless they were occupied. A moment later they began shuffling more papers, and Michael began a slow burn. The receptionist had deliberately handed them off to the most incompetent fool she could muster. Surely there was a circle in hell just for the likes of her.

Michael sat forward in his chair. "I can appreciate that, Mr. Ripley. But what we're looking for would have been kept under Mr. Cadwallader's personal care. Surely those records are handy."

Ripley brightened, his hands ceasing their busy work for the moment. "Oh, yes, quite handy, indeed. Those records are even now being gone through and collated by my assistant for microfilming, you see."

"Good, then what we seek is more than likely stored in whatever boxes are marked 1941."

Ripley's practiced smile faltered. "Oh, dear me. Did you say, 1941?"

"Yes," Michael said, not liking the man's tone one iota.

"Those records were destroyed in 1944. A stray buzz bomb, I'm told. Nasty business. Everything from the firm's founding up until that time. All gone. Nearly unraveled the firm altogether, I might add."

Michael collapsed back into the chair, feeling as if someone had kicked him in the gut. The room seemed to tilt on some unseen axis, nauseating him.

Erika, seeing his distress, broke in. "The woman upstairs said that Mr. Cadwallader had retired some years ago. Is he still alive?"

"Last I heard," Ripley replied.

"Then perhaps you can tell us where we can find him. It's very important."

Erika smiled at him and Ripley blushed a deep shade of crimson. Reaching into his desk, he pulled out a notepad and scribbled on it with one of his ubiquitous pens, tore it off, and handed it to Erika.

"You'll find him at that address. Although, I'm not at all sure he'll be of much help to you."

❈　❈　❈

"You see anything?" Michael asked.

Their car was parked outside the East Grinstead Convalescent and Retirement Home, a sprawling two-story brick building occupying two manicured acres at the end of a quiet cul-de-sac. Its nearest neighbors were blocks of dreary low-income housing that resembled concrete bunkers.

Erika scanned the road leading to the mouth of the cul-de-sac and shook her head. "No, nothing."

Michael watched a group of elderly residents arrayed on the home's front lawn. They slouched in lawn chairs, each consumed with their own thoughts, or lack thereof.

He faced her and nodded. "Let's go."

Exiting the car, they hurried across the street. Ever since they'd left London, Michael had eyed the rearview mirror, looking for the Lotus, or any other car that stayed with them too long. Of course, whoever was interested in them might have managed to remain undetected despite his vigilance, a thought that renewed his sense of unease.

When they reached the glassed-in entrance, Michael gave the street one last look, then motioned for Erika to go inside.

❈　❈　❈

The Nikon's motor drive wheezed as the camera snapped off several excellent shots of Michael and Erika through the car window when they entered the Home. The photographer, a burly man with a bullet-shaped head and mean piggish eyes, lowered the camera and stared at the building, his jaw working methodically on a piece of gum. His companion, the driver, tapped the steering wheel impatiently, his ferretlike eyes darting between the building and the entrance to the cul-de-sac. He didn't like being in a place without at least two ways to get out of it. Here, if something happened, they were trapped. He didn't like it one bit; it wasn't professional. Still, what choice did they have? They did what they were told. And they'd been told to wait until young Thorley and the girl showed up. If they did, then they were to act accordingly. Unfortunately, they'd had to wait nearly four hours.

"You get them, Karl?" he said, in German.

The photographer nodded, and put the camera away, lovingly wiping the large telephoto lens with lens tissue. "Ja. Good shots. Now, let's get out of here."

The driver shifted in his seat, then checked his watch. "Shouldn't we wait for them?"

Karl shook his head. "No. I have enough, and there is nothing I can do until this evening. Besides, I'm hungry. Killing always makes me hungry."

The driver laughed and started the car's engine. "I know exactly what you mean," he said.

A moment later the silver-gray Jaguar XJ-12 pulled out from the curb, made a U-turn and sped away.

※　※　※

Although it shouldn't have surprised him, the inside of the home was even more depressing. Extremely utilitarian, it looked for all the world like a cross between a college dormitory and a hospital, with hard linoleum floors and painted brick walls. Their feet echoed as they walked.

Stopping first at the front desk, they asked the duty nurse where Martin Cadwallader's room was located. The woman had sneered, shaking her head. "It's on the second floor," she said. "Just follow the bloody music and you'll find him."

Michael thanked her and got a grunt in return. Dodging carts piled high with dirty dishes left over from lunch, they ignored the lift and took the stairs. On the second-floor landing, Michael heard the music, and recognized the tune as Glen Miller's "Moonlight Serenade." It made him smile in spite of his dark mood.

They found Cadwallader's room at the end of the hall, the door standing ajar. The music was so loud, Miller's trombone made the walls throb. Peering in, Michael spied a frail-looking old man sitting in a sagging easy chair, eyes closed and a blissful smile on his face, his half-eaten lunch on a tray in front of him. A quick scan of the room revealed a lifetime of knickknacks crammed into every available space. There were also several ancient wooden filing cabinets lining one wall. Michael was wondering what they might contain when the music ended. Taking advantage of the silence, he knocked on the doorjamb. The old man remained oblivious and he knocked harder. This time Cadwallader cracked open his eyes and turned toward the door, an expectant look on his face. When his eyes connected with Michael's, they widened in astonishment, his lips trembling.

"M—Michael? Michael Thorley?"

Now it was Michael's turn to be astonished. *How could he know me? Had Ripley called ahead? It would seem unlikely, but—*

The old man spoke again. "Dear God, Man, you look bloody wonderful. But I thought the Jerries got you last year."

A wave of disappointment rushed through him. Cadwallader was confusing him with his father.

Michael and Erika approach him, not quite sure what to expect.

"Mr. Cadwallader? I'm Michael Thorley, Junior. Michael's son."

The old man looked nonplused. "Junior? Michael's son?"

Cadwallader suddenly began to cry, big fat tears coursing down his pale wrinkled face.

Panicked, Michael looked to Erika, who knelt by the old man and comforted him. His manner abruptly changed. He eyed her with suspicion and began to sniff the air around her.

"You're German, aren't you?" he said, continuing to sniff. Michael could see Cadwallader's question and his odd manner had taken her off-guard. She backed off from him, a puzzled frown on her face.

"How did you know?" she asked.

Cadwallader's eyes were wild.

"Can smell 'em. I know a Jerry from their stink!" He turned to Michael and screamed, "Why have you brought one of them? You've gone over, haven't you? A traitor to King and country!"

Suddenly fearful the old man would draw attention—the last thing they needed—Michael moved to the door. "Mr. Cadwallader," he said, returning to his place in front of the old man, "I've come for what you've been keeping for my father."

Confusion flashed across Cadwallader's face, and then he appeared to relax, a friendly grin creasing his face.

"Michael? Michael Thorley is that you? Where's that beautiful wife of yours?" He turned to Erika, the smile widening. "Lillian! You look absolutely ravishing! I'm always telling Michael he should bring you round when he comes to visit. I'm so glad you're here."

Erika shot a glance at Michael, who nodded for her to play along.

"It's good to see you, Martin. It's been much too long."

Michael winced inwardly at Erika's atrocious English accent. Fortunately, Cadwallader was submerged too far into his fantasy to notice.

"Michael and I have come for the items you have been keeping for him," she continued. "Do you remember what they are?"

"Items?"

Erika leaned close to the old man's ear. "The Eagle Flies," she whispered.

Cadwallader stiffened and the glaze left his eyes, replaced by a measure of lucidity and a sly smile.

"Damn doodle-bug hit the firm in '44. Blew it all to hell. For some reason I can't explain, something made me remove certain items from the firm's safe beforehand. Yours were among them. I put them in a safe place." The old man grinned like a schoolboy and tapped the side of his head.

For one horrifying moment, Michael believed the old man meant that he'd memorized whatever had been in the safe. And then Cadwallader struggled to his feet and hobbled over to one of the file cabinets. He kept up a steady patter of muttering while he pulled open drawers and rifled through them, sometimes extracting a file, brown and crumbling with age. Each time the old man yanked open a drawer, wood shrieked against wood, making Michael wince. It was like the proverbial chalk on a blackboard. He looked to Erika and saw that she wore an eager, expectant expression. His own face must look much the same, he thought.

"I know the bloody thing's around here somewhere...." Cadwallader said. "Blast! They've been mucking about in here again." He turned to Michael and Erika. "So sorry for the inconvenience, Michael, but I can't keep a decent secretary anymore. Practically a different one every day. And these white uniforms they insist on wearing! No style at all."

Cadwallader turned back to his cabinets and opened another drawer. It howled in protest. Michael began to wonder if they'd wasted their time. For all he knew those filing cabinets contained nothing more ominous than old time sheets. Suddenly the old man straightened up. "Aha! Knew I had the blasted thing!" He raised his arm in triumph, revealing a yellowed file clutched in his gnarled fingers.

Bringing it over to a small table, he opened the folder, extracted a sealed envelope, and handed it to Michael, who wasted no time in tearing it open, and dumping out its contents into the palm of his hand.

It was a key to a safe deposit box.

And on it was the box's number and nothing else.

Cadwallader squeezed Michael's hand, his aged eyes burning with fervor. "Barclay's Bank," he whispered. "Trafalgar Square."

A surge of adrenaline raced through Michael's body. He cradled the key in his hand like a holy relic, feeling it warm to his touch. The gentle pressure of Erika's hand on his arm told him she felt the same way. A troubling thought occurred to him and he looked up at the old man.

"How will I get into the box if it's under your name?"

"It isn't. It's under *yours*."

Michael's eyes widened. "But how could you know that I'd come?"

Cadwallader clapped him on the back affectionately. "Kept tabs on you, my boy. From very early on I knew you were your father's son."

Michael felt a wave of emotion wash over him. "Thank you, sir. I am in your debt."

"Of course, you are," the old man snapped, "you haven't paid your bill in months."

The dark veil had descended over the old man's eyes again, and Michael signaled to Erika that they should leave. She nodded and walked out the door, leaving the two men with a moment of privacy.

"I wish you well, sir," Michael said.

The old man remained silent, staring out into space, his mouth hanging open as if in the middle of forming a word. It made Michael's skin crawl. Feeling awkward standing there, he turned to go. He'd barely taken a step when Cadwallader called out.

"M—Michael?"

He turned to face the old man and found that the light had returned to Cadwallader's eyes, along with an expression of wistful sadness.

"Your father was a good man," he said, moving to the ancient record player, "a man I was proud to call my friend.... He just trusted the wrong people."

The smile that had come to Michael's face faded as he walked out of the room. Once again, the music of Glen Miller blasted out into the hall. This time its lively rhythms and happy-go-lucky sound grated on his nerves.

Trusted the wrong people.

The old man's words sent a chill up his spine. He hadn't wanted to admit, even to himself, that there might be a grain of truth to it. And if that were true, what did that bode for him now that he was dogging his father's footsteps?

Erika fell into step next to him, and remained silent, sensing his darker mood. Back on the ground floor, she stopped him when they reached the front door, her face etched with concern. "What is it?"

He sighed, shaking his head. "Nothing, just something the old man said about my father."

Erika squeezed his arm. "It's hard to hear unexpected things about someone you love."

Michael frowned. "What do you mean?"

"I'm sorry, I am not trying to be, how you say, enigmatic. My father had secrets that I am just now finding out. It's hard—" She stopped as tears welled up in her eyes. "I'm sorry...."

"Me too," he said, laying his hand over hers. "It's all a lot of bloody crap." He looked out on the street until he was satisfied that nothing was amiss, then held open the door. "Come on, we need to hurry if we're going to make the bank before it closes."

In a few moments they were back on the A22 headed for London. For the entire drive, Michael was very much aware of Erika's presence in the car. It was palpable, as if the air pressure had increased somehow. Part of him wanted to pour out his feelings to her, feelings that were growing by the hour. The other part of him resisted the urge, fought it tooth and nail, as if his life depended on it.

When are you going to grow up and be a bloody man? he thought bitterly. When, indeed? Perhaps his father had asked himself the same questions, and the answers had placed him inevitably in harm's way. And that was when another thought came to him in the form of an old quote from George Santayana, one his old philosophy professor at Cambridge had drummed into his head: *Those who cannot remember the past are doomed to repeat it.*

He only hoped the old goat was right, and that he would have the time to learn enough about what had happened to avoid the same fate.

26

The coarse wool of Werner Mueller's pea coat made the back of his neck itch, as did the rough denim of his shirt. Thank god the shoes fit, at least. They were stout, hobnailed boots, the kind a laborer wore on a construction site, which was precisely the image he was out to project. Ignoring the tickling on his neck, Mueller adjusted his hard-hat and squinted toward the guard shack up ahead. He'd been standing in the line at Checkpoint Charlie for slightly over an hour. And it had barely moved. He cursed the *Grenzpolizei* and their damned painstaking efficiency. The bastards were cracking down, checking every *umlaut* in every passbook. No doubt this was due to his own efforts as Stasi Chief to reign in the rampant escapes to the West. He'd never understood the Communist mentality, even after all these years working for them. On the one hand, they extolled the worker's paradise and how great it was to live in it. And yet, they were so bloody paranoid about some grandmother going to West Berlin and not coming back. So what? If anything, they should encourage the malcontents to leave, give them all amnesty and say you have a choice: stay or go. Mueller was willing to admit that more of them than not would elect to stay. Human nature always dictated that people would not want something as much if they were given it freely. They would think it tainted.

Unfortunately, the party never thought in such flexible terms.

Dogma ruled and that was why the *Grenzpolizei* were so vigilant. It was a vicious cycle of repression and escape. If it went on long enough there would be no one left. But Mueller saw the handwriting on the wall. He could see that the days were numbered. And like the last time, in the days when he'd been SS-*Gruppenführer* Gerhard Müller, he intended to land on his feet.

The line began to move, and Mueller saw that the *Grenzpolizei* were waving several people through. The next person was hauled off, his protestations of innocence sounding like the bleating of sheep. Mueller smiled. He always found this sort of scene entertaining.

After another fifteen minutes, it was his turn. One of the guards, a pasty-faced man with the breath of a bear, thrust out his meaty paw and glared at him with witless intensity. "Papers," he said, his voice edged with fatigue and boredom.

Mueller handed over his identification and watched the guard with a steady gaze. The man glanced down at the passbook, comparing the grainy picture with Mueller's face. The photo had been taken some years ago, and Mueller realized it was time to update it. Too much Bratwurst had changed the lines of his face. That and time, the grand thief of all that was good.

The guard then checked "Heinrich Abelard" against a list of names on a nearby clipboard. Suddenly the man straightened up, his eyes filled with newfound respect.

Mueller leaned toward the guard. "Act normal, you fool," he whispered.

The guard stiffened, glanced around him quickly to be sure that no one else had heard, and then began shouting. "Why can't you get a job in your own country, you shirker! Go on and go before I turn you over to Stasi!"

Barely suppressing a smile, Mueller walked through the gate

and marched across the no-man's-land to the American side of the checkpoint. He showed the MP his papers and was waved through. He walked straight down the street until he was out of sight of the checkpoint, then turned into a small side street. The black BMW was waiting, its engine idling. He climbed into the back and the driver turned to face him. "Any trouble?" he asked.

Mueller shrugged. "Nothing I couldn't handle."

The driver laughed, put the car in gear and swung away from the curb. A moment later it was lost in the crush of the late afternoon traffic.

❈ ❈ ❈

They were being followed.

He was sure of it. Ever since leaving the convalescent home in East Grinstead, Michael had not been able to shake the feeling that someone was watching them. It made his skin tingle, as if touched by a small charge of electricity. The maddening thing was that he couldn't be sure what car it was. He'd caught site of a silver-gray Jaguar several times, but unlike other cars it didn't maintain a consistent distance. It would loom in the background, sometimes easing forward, other times it would be lost in the maelstrom of traffic.

Forced to concede the possibility that he might be imagining it, he nevertheless kept swiveling his eyes to the rearview mirror every other moment. Even Erika noticed it. He gave her a lame sounding excuse about being a nervous driver, but he didn't think she believed him. The real question was why he didn't give voice to his suspicions. Could it be that he didn't really trust her? That was absurd, of course, because he not only had no choice, he *wanted* to trust her. Perhaps that was silly, but there it was.

They reached London at 2:45 and the traffic became thickly snarled the closer their goal became. Up ahead, he saw Nelson's Column and Trafalgar Square and knew he was only moments away. Somehow, that made the last few minutes crawl by even slower. Gritting his teeth, they drove the last quarter mile and were fortunate to find a parking space, sliding into it just as a Rolls vacated it. Switching off the motor, Michael turned to Erika. "I don't mean to alarm you, but I believe we've been followed."

"I know. Silver-Gray Jag. Five cars back."

"You knew?"

She smiled in spite of his surprised expression and the import of what he'd said. "*Ja.* They were clumsy."

"Clumsy?"

"They kept trying to appear, how you say, nonchalant. But I spotted them right away."

"Why didn't you tell me?"

"I didn't want to upset you. You seemed...nervous."

Michael laughed. "I suppose I was. Are they gone?"

Erika leaned forward to get a better perspective in the side view mirror. She studied the reflected landscape for a few minutes, her lovely brow knitted in concentration.

"Yes, I think they are."

Michael let out a sigh. "Good. Come on, we'd better be going.

The interior of the Trafalgar Square branch of Barclay's Bank, like so many old banks in England, was a study in stuffy elegance. Marble floors stretched across a wide entranceway that led into the main lobby carpeted in a deep blue pile. Teller's cages in carved mahogany and brass bars stood arrayed against the back wall and the floor was dotted with islands where customers could fill out their transaction paperwork. The room gave off the illusion of stability and strength. Here, one's money was safe from the vicissitudes of daily life.

Michael and Erika crossed the room and headed directly to a section off to the side of the regular teller's cages. A sign hung above it that read: Deposit Boxes, and behind the window, Michael saw the open door of the vault. His pulse quickened.

In a moment, he would know the truth.

The Safe Deposit Teller looked up and spotted them approaching, his bulbous nose wrinkling in distaste. It was clear the man was counting the minutes to closing and now he would have to work.

Reaching the window, Michael pulled out the key and shoved it through the window.

"Good afternoon, I've come about my box."

The Teller got up from behind his desk. "Your name?"

"Oh, sorry. Thorley. Michael Thorley, Jr."

The teller picked up the key and frowned. "That's an old one. Hold on a minute."

With growing anxiety, Michael watched the teller waddle over to a file cabinet, pull open a drawer, and slowly flip through the hundreds of signature cards. It was agony.

"Is this going to take long?" Michael asked, not really wanting to hear the worst.

The teller shook his head, jowls wobbling. "Can't say. These old files have never been properly indexed. Could take a while. You sure you don't want to come in the morning?" The hint was painfully obvious, but Michael wasn't giving any quarter.

"No, I can't, I'm sorry."

The teller grunted and returned to his task. Frustrated at this last-minute delay, Michael turned to Erika. She stood beside him; her eyes riveted on the door. He followed her gaze, a feeling of dread stealing over him. Two men stood at one of the islands. From their studied nonchalance and furtive glances at him and Erika, it was obvious they were not there to make a deposit, or anything else related to bank business.

"Do you know them?" he asked from the side of his mouth.

Erika shook her head. "No. But I know their type. Ever since my father died, men like them have been shadowing me."

Michael saw she was trembling and turned to the teller. "You know, maybe we'll come back—"

"Got it!" the teller cried, holding up a yellowing card and hurrying back to the window. "Since there is no signature provision, it says here that the bearer of the key must give the password."

"You must be joking." He turned to Erika, suddenly angry. "That's not what that old man said." He turned back to the teller. "Doesn't it say the box is owned by a Michael Thorley, Jr."

"I'm not at liberty to say, sir. Not until the password's given."

Michael saw a gleam in the man's eye. Probably thought this was all some silly game. Probably made his bloody day. But what was the password?

He felt Erika's breath on his ear as she whispered to him. Shrugging, he leaned toward the teller. "The Eagle Flies."

The teller's eyebrows shot up. "Quite right. Mr. Thorley, I presume."

"Yes."

"Right. Walk this way, sir."

The teller unlatched a door leading into the vault area and both he and Erika went through. A quick look over his shoulder revealed that the two men still stood at the island pretending to fill out forms. He was wondering what they would do when they came out, when the teller handed him back his key and led the way into the vault carrying his ring of master keys.

The box proved to be lighter and smaller than he'd imagined.

Grasping it in his arms, he carried it to one of the viewing rooms and waited until Erika closed the door behind them before opening the box. He hesitated a moment, or rather his hands did. They hovered over the latch, finger flexing, reaching, yet refusing to do their owner's bidding.

"What?" Erika asked.

"Just had a silly thought," Michael said, his throat tight with anxiety. "That after all we've been through, there'll be nothing in there. That I'll lose my Dad all over again. Stupid, huh?"

Erika hugged him, the scent of her silky hair filling his nostrils. "It's all right to be afraid, Michael," she said, whispering into his ear. "As long as you never let it paralyze you. The men behind all this have every reason to be afraid, because whatever is in that box...will set us free...."

He pulled away from her, a look of newfound purpose in his eyes, as if some invisible line had been crossed. Letting out a breath, Michael lifted the latch and threw open the lid. Inside, were two envelopes. One was a large manila type with a tie-string. The other was business sized. And there was something unusual about them. It took a moment for his brain to interpret what it was seeing, but it came together like the snap of a rubber band. Both envelopes were engraved with the national symbol of Nazi Germany: an eagle clutching a wreathed swastika in its talons, its wings spread wide. Underneath was the legend: *Oberkommando des Heeres*. The Army High Command.

Intrigued, Michael picked up the smaller of the two envelopes and carefully unsealed it, mindful of its age. He pulled out a sheaf of papers, made of the same heavy cream vellum matching that of the envelope. The first sheet had a list of six names:

1) Friedrich Rainer

2) Werner Reinholt

3) Wilhelm-Franz von Schliefen

4) Baldar von Arnwolf

5) Ludwig Jarmann

6) Manfred Valdemarr

The rest of the sheets held a lengthy typed message:

"My Dear Comrade: Now that you have seen the Russo-Finnish tragedy for yourself, I now entrust you with our lives.... The list you hold in your hands contains the names of those of us who have, for years, opposed Der Führer's expansionist policies, knowing as you do, that they could only result in catastrophe.

"We have met secretly for these many years in order to establish ties with the West, and work within this tyrannical system in order to bring about its demise. Alas, the Gestapo is far too vigilant. It is wholly ironic that because of this madness our Führer calls "The Great Struggle," the opportunity for us to act has arisen.

"The attack on Russia in these past weeks has produced massive victories that have lulled the populace into a temporary state of euphoria that we know cannot last. For Herr Hitler has forgotten the hard lessons Napoleon learned over one hundred years ago, lessons that are even now being learned at a terrible price in human currency. I pray that your government will listen, and realize that with Hitler out of the way, Stalin is our real enemy. For if we fail, the world will suffer under the yoke of Communism as it has never suffered before.

"I pray that fate will be kind to both our countries and that after this conflict has ended that you and I can reunite in friendship. If anything should happen, tell the world. They must know that we tried to save it from two madmen. With the evidence I have given you, I trust action will be taken. Godspeed, my friend. Hauptmann Friedrich Rainer, OKH."

Stunned, Michael handed Rainer's letter to Erika. He watched her face while she read it, registering every nuance of her reaction. He waited until she'd finished, then reached for the larger envelope, untying the ties with hands that trembled with suppressed fear and excitement.

He then upended the envelope and watched as a sheaf of photographs spilled out onto the table. Under the glare of the fluorescent lighting, the stark black and white images seemed to pulse with a sort of hyper-reality. There were only a dozen prints, each carefully mounted on a board and captioned in German on the piece of paper glued to the back. There were shots of the overall scene: bodies piled on top of each other—the cliché of cordwood came to his mind, closeups of eyeless faces and arms and legs twisted in horrific postures impossible during life. One picture brought him up short, a photo of his father wearing a German Army uniform standing next to another German officer, their faces grim and haunted. It had to be Rainer, Michael thought. Aside from the oddity of seeing his father in a German uniform, it was doubly strange to see him in any other context than the one picture he'd known his entire life. The smile was missing, and that changed the whole complexion of the man, made him seem vulnerable, less godlike.

Suddenly weary of it all, Michael picked up the envelope to replace the photos. It was then the last item fell out, sliding onto the table with a metallic clatter. It was a cap badge, its silver luster now tarnished nearly black. He brought it up for a closer look and felt the world drop out from under him. The letters fairly screamed at him: *Royal South Wessex Inf. Reg.*

"Oh, my God," he said in a strangled whisper.

"What is it, Michael?"

He handed her the badge and began scooping up the photos.

"I don't understand. What does it mean?"

"It means this is bigger than we thought. Come on, we've got to get out of here."

Michael rose and opened the door to the cubicle. Erika grabbed his arm. "Wait. Let's see if there's a back way."

They returned to the front of the vault and caught the eye of the teller.

"Is there another way out of here," Michael asked him.

The teller barely registered any surprise. "I'll take you through the lunchroom. Follow me."

After walking through a minor labyrinth of corridors and storerooms, they found themselves back out on the street around the corner from their Toyota. Moments later, they were safely away. For the next few minutes, Michael drove around in circles, taking left and right turns at the last possible moment, all in an effort to ascertain whether they were being followed. He saw at least two silver-gray Jaguars, but neither one was the same model as the one that had tailed them from East Grinstead.

Erika, who had remained silent since they left the bank, finally spoke, her voice tight with fear.

"Tell me what we have, Michael. What was that badge?"

"It's from a regiment my government says never existed. Except it did...once. Those photos were all that was left of them. Your father and the people he worked for, invited my father to come and see for himself, and to report back to his government."

Erika shook her head in confusion. "But it doesn't make sense. You're telling me that my countrymen invited their enemy into captured territory during wartime in order to view this massacre? Why?"

"Because they wanted the world to know *they* didn't kill those men."

"Then who did?"

Michael ignored the question, his eyes scanning the rearview for any suspicious vehicles. Everything looked normal.

"You ever hear of *Der Weisse Adler?*" he asked.

Erika shrugged. "The White Eagle? No."

"I remember reading about them in school. They were a cabal of *Wehrmacht* officers dedicated to Hitler's overthrow; officers determined to have a democratic Germany join with Britain to defeat the Russians. It was a pipe dream, of course, but you had to admire them for what they risked. Except for a few sacrificial lambs, the group's core somehow survived all the purges, even the one after the failed attempt on Hitler's life in July 1944.... Your father was a member."

Erika's eyes widened.

"The people behind the massacre don't want any loose ends," Michael continued. "That's why your father died.... Mine, as well."

"But who killed them?"

He turned to her, fixing her with a level gaze. "The Russians."

"My God, if that's true—"

"Then they will go to any lengths to keep us quiet, including killing us. What I don't understand is why that regiment was there in the first place. The British weren't involved in the Russo-Finnish War. There was no bloody reason for it!" He slammed his hands against the steering wheel repeatedly, his anger boiling over. "Damn them! Damn them all to hell!"

"Michael, please!" Erika shouted, grabbing the wheel when the car began to swerve.

He pushed her back and pulled the Toyota over to the side of the road, then turned to face her, eyes blazing. "Never do that again! You want to kill us?"

"Maybe you should ask yourself that question," she said, opening the door and stalking away from the car.

Michael sighed and shook his head. "Bloody idiot you are, Thorley." He threw open the door and went after her, catching up to her outside an Italian restaurant. He reached out for her arm and she wrenched away from him. "Erika, wait.... Please."

She stopped and turned, her eyes tearing and her mouth a delicious pout. "I'm sorry," he said. "I shouldn't have yelled at you. But you can't imagine what this all means to me."

"Yes, I can.... I lost a father, too."

Michael nodded, feeling even more foolish. "Of course, you did, and you know I'm sorry for that. But at least you knew him." He paused, searching for the right words. "I didn't tell you this.... There was evidence that my father's death was self-inflicted. Neither my mother nor I believed he could do that, but nothing existed to prove otherwise...until Dad's letter."

"Then that is what your mother meant by 'disgrace.'"

Michael stared at the ground and nodded.

"Christ," Erika said.

"My God, Erika, did that letter sound like the letter of a man about to blow his brains out?"

"No, it didn't."

"Then you can see why I have to pursue this, why I have to find the truth, no matter what it means?"

Erika reached across the gulf between them and squeezed his arm affectionately. "We'll find it together."

They started walking back to the car, and Michael's determined mood intensified, his gestures becoming more and more animated as he spoke. "I think our salvation lies with one of the remaining four men on that list. There's nothing in what your father gave to mine to indicate it, but I'm certain there has to be one more piece to the puzzle, otherwise I think we'd be dead by now.

"We have to go to Germany, Erika, as soon as possible—tonight." They reached the Toyota and he locked eyes with her. "I know you want to help, and I'm so very glad you're here. I hope you know that. But we have to get to those men on the list before the Russians do...or we're doomed."

27

The sight that greeted Michael and Erika when they entered his mews flat, stopped them cold. Everything that could be moved had been turned upside-down and scattered to the four winds. All his books had been ripped to pieces, his records pulled from their sleeves and cast about, one so hard it stuck partway into the wallboard. Furniture had been reduced to kindling and the leather sofa he'd owned and loved since his university days had been slashed, the horsehair stuffing yanked out in ragged tufts that spilled onto the floor.

The kitchen had not been spared either. Mason jars full of sugar and flour had been dumped out on the linoleum, the jars then smashed to slivers. Even the stove and refrigerator had been wrested out of place and now sat in the middle of the tiny space. It was all too much.

"Bloody fucking hell!" Michael said.

Erika remained silent while she moved about the room, her eyes scanning everything. She picked up an Emerson, Lake, and Palmer record that had been broken in half, then let the pieces fall back to the floor.

"This is all my fault," she said. "I'm so sorry, Michael."

He shot her an angry glance when he caught sight of his university diploma ripped into five ragged pieces. He sighed, shaking his head wearily. "Sorry, doesn't cut it, love, but it's okay."

She nodded, her lips trembling. The phone rang then, and it took a moment for Michael to locate it under an overturned bookcase. Throwing it aside, he snatched up the receiver and brought it to his ear.

"Hello?" His voice was harsh, unapologetic.

"Michael? My God, are you all right?"

Lillian sounded frantic, and Michael frowned, puzzled.

"Why wouldn't I be, mother?"

"Turn on the telly. Now!"

Michael nodded to Erika. "The telly, turn it on."

"What?"

"The television. Turn it on."

Ironically, the television was one of the few items that appeared no worse for wear. Erika moved over to it and snapped on the power switch. In a moment, the staid image of Gordon Honeycombe filled the screen.

"...Once again, police are searching for anyone with information on the murder of John Ferguson—late of the War Graves Commission—who was found shot late last night in his home in Streatham. The Police refuse to comment on the motive, saying only that robbery is not indicated."

"Oh, God," Michael said.

He couldn't believe his ears. Ferguson murdered? It was insane—incomprehensible. But then again, the last two days had been exactly that.

His mother shouted through the earpiece. "Michael? What's happened, what's going on?"

He put the phone to his ear. "I'll call you back, mother," he replied.

Michael hung up the phone over Lillian's filtered protests and it began to ring almost immediately. Ignoring it, he headed for the bedroom.

The condition of the bedroom was no better than the sitting room had been. His bed had been tossed, and his dresser drawers pulled out and overturned. Clothes and other personal items lay scattered all over the floor.

Cursing silently, he moved to the nightstand. The drawer hung halfway out, the contents a jumble of nose sprays, tissues, and old manicure sets. He pawed through the mess; his mouth set in grim determination. He smiled when his hands closed around a familiar shape. He pulled it out and glanced briefly at the British coat of arms embossed on the leather passport case. And then he frowned. Something wasn't right. It was too light.

He tore it open and snarled, tossing it aside. "Blast!" he said, standing up and kicking his overturned mattress. "Fucking bastards!"

"What's wrong?" Erika called out.

He stalked back into the other room and headed for the bar. "They stole my bloody passport."

Throwing open one of the cabinets, he grabbed the Courvoisier, twisted off the cap and drank right from the bottle. Erika joined him, resting a hand on his shoulder.

"It's bad enough that I'm having my life turned upside-down. But what really gets me is the feeling that I'm being manipulated like some bloody puppet."

He took another slug of brandy and began coughing.

"I—I'm sorry."

"Please, stop saying that," Michael said, annoyed. "It's no more your fault than mine. And if I had it to do all over again, I'd do the same damn thing. The one *good* thing about this whole mess is you."

Erika smiled, her eyes tinged with a curious sadness.

"What about your passport?" she asked.

Michael scowled. "Take it from a bureaucrat who knows. It'll take weeks to get a new one. We haven't anywhere near that long. We're finished."

He took another drink, recapped the bottle and replaced it in the cabinet, slamming the door.

Erika squeezed his hand, her eyes shining with purpose. "Maybe we're not," she said. "I know some people who can help."

"Who?"

She shook her head and kissed him on the mouth. "Do you trust me?"

Michael nodded, a puzzled look on his face.

"Good. Then don't ask," she said, moving toward the phone.

※　※　※

An hour later, Erika nosed the Toyota to the curb in front of a crumbling terraced house in Whitechapel. When they climbed out, Michael scanned the area, his eyes darting to the alleys, as if he half-expected an army of muggers to descend on them. It was silly, he knew, but a lifetime of hearing about the horrors of Whitechapel could not be overcome by mere logic.

Situated near the docks in East London, Whitechapel was still the home of the poorer classes, as it had been for two hundred years. And even though Jack the Ripper was almost a hundred years in his grave, his specter still haunted this borough of winding streets and decaying, tightly packed edifices. Street lighting was poor, and shadows dominated. As for the immediate neighborhood where Michael and Erika stood, it was populated primarily by Indians and Pakistanis, as evidenced by the plethora of Hindi signage and the smell of curry in the air.

"I don't know why I let you talk me into this," he said, locking the passenger door. "And just how does the spoiled rich daughter of a German industrialist know where to find a passport forger in Whitechapel?"

Erika came around the car and joined him, slipping her arm through his. "We spoiled rich girls have to be resourceful at times, especially in fending off the fortune hunters and gigolos." She grinned at her little joke. "Besides, Jalil is an old art school chum who fell on hard times. He was a mediocre painter but turned out to be a master forger. Now, come on, we don't want to be late."

Shaking his head in both admiration and exasperation, he let Erika lead him into the building, neither of them aware of the silver-gray Jaguar that had parked across the street.

Inside the hallway of the terraced house, the smell of curry and dried urine increased to nauseating proportions. Michael wrinkled his nose when he stepped over a battered plastic tricycle that had one of its wheels missing, marveling that people could stand to live this way. Erika led the way up the stairs and Michael heard a cacophony of sounds when they passed each door: loud Indian music, a couple arguing, a baby squalling, a television tuned to a war movie.

Erika stopped at a door at the end of the hall. A small sticker was adjacent to the knocker: *Artists do it with style!* it said in bright splashy colors.

"Typical Jalil," she laughed.

Erika extended her arm and rapped sharply on the door. Somewhere inside the apartment, they heard footsteps pounding down a hallway, and then a high-pitched voice. "Who is it?"

"Your favorite Kraut."

A second later the door flew open and there stood a gnomish man with dark chocolate skin and pop-eyes wearing a white turban, a tie-dyed t-shirt featuring a picture of Jimi Hendrix burning his guitar, and a pair of stonewashed jeans covered with brightly colored patches. When he caught sight of Erika, he cracked a smile that split his face from ear to ear.

"Rika! My goodness gracious! You are too good looking for humble words!"

Erika giggled, then remembered why they came. "I need a favor, Jalil," she said, turning serious. "My friend has lost his passport. We need a replacement—fast."

Jalil became all business, turning his sober black-eyed gaze on Michael, appraising him at once. He turned back to Erika and nodded. "To you, I owe everything. Come, come," he said, waving them inside."

Jalil's flat was best described as student eclectic. There were the obligatory gallery posters on the walls advertising art shows from ten years in the past, some of Jalil's art—a pastiche of early Andy Warhol—sat on an easel near the large bay window that dominated the room. As for furniture, the room was alive with pillows of every description, some as big as sofas. But nothing resembling conventional tables and chairs could be found. The only concession to modern living was an obscenely expensive stereo powered by valves and a door leading to a darkroom that held the best and most expensive equipment for the manipulation of photographic images.

The next few hours went by in a whirlwind of motion. Minutes after they'd arrived, Jalil had Michael filling out a forged passport application, which included a space for a signature. He told Michael to leave everything but the signature space blank.

Unlike passports from other countries, where the bearer signed his passport after receiving it, British passports had the signature re-photographed and made a part of the photo, presumably as means of preventing forgery. It was then pasted into the passport in the proper place, and laminated.

As Michael handed the form to Erika, Jalil brought out his photographic gear and set it up facing a light blue backdrop. Michael vaguely remembered when he had his original picture taken that it was the same robin's egg color. Jalil, looked up from the viewfinder of his Hasselblad camera with a critical gaze. "Oh, my, this will never do," he said, clucking like a mother hen.

Michael frowned and turned to Erika, who seemed to be staring at him with the same appraising eye. "He thinks you look too good."

"What?"

"Please not to be misunderstanding. You must remember when you have a picture taken for a passport you are never at your best. Please do not smile and do look as if you have been standing in line for three hours."

These people are bloody crazy, Michael thought, but he stared back at the camera with what he hoped was an expression of mild hostility.

"Perfect!" Jalil shouted and snapped the picture.

Blinking from the spots before his eyes, Michael watched while Jalil stepped into his darkroom and closed the door. A second later the red light over the door popped on, signaling to those outside that it was unsafe to enter. Half an hour later, Jalil emerged with a print about the size of a wallet photo. He was smiling broadly.

"The Passport office has a special prismatic camera that will photograph both the subject and his signature simultaneously," he said. "Of course, I cannot get one of these marvels and must be content with my humble equipment. They forget the art of collage. I must be telling you that the gods have smiled on their humble servant this day."

He proffered the photo to Erika, who nodded approvingly, and then passed it to Michael. The signature was seamlessly married with his photograph, laminated, then cleverly embossed with a forgery of the official Passport office embossing stamp. It would no doubt stand up to even microscopic examination. As for his image, he cringed when he saw his wide-eyed grimace. He looked like a bloody criminal. "Maybe we should do it again," he said.

A look of annoyance flashed across the Pakistani's face "No, no," he said. "It is exactly perfect, my friend, exactly perfect."

Next came the blank passport form that Jalil withdrew from a strong box he kept in a hidden compartment in the back of one of his closets. It was one of the old blue ones, with the gold coat of arms, before the changeover to the brown Common Market type.

"I have a friend at the firm who printed these magnificent items. He slipped me several after every run." Jalil said, smiling proudly. "This one is among the last."

"What about other countries? Does your friend have those, as well?" Michael asked.

Jalil wagged his fingers. "That, my inquisitive friend, is better left unsaid. Now, where would you like to have been?"

"Excuse me?"

"We must have a travel history, unless, of course, you want a new passport, in which case we will have to start over."

"Oh, now I understand. I don't care."

"Have it show trips to the United States and the Orient," Erika said.

Jalil nodded. "Very good."

"What about East Germany," Michael asked. "What if we need to go there?"

"That is quite the impossible, my adventurous friend. The DDR changes its stamps every month. It is too hard to keep up with. I would need the right stamp for the right month that you supposedly traveled. If it were wrong...."

The implication hung in the air and Michael shook his head. "Fine, we'll deal with that if and when we need to. Carry on."

Jalil then set about putting in the requisite stamps.

"What time of year do you take your vacation?" he asked, about to apply the first one.

Michael thought a moment. "Usually in early June."

Jalil put down the stamp he was holding and picked up another. He pressed it onto a red ink pad and then into the passport. For some reason this made Michael nervous, as if he were taking some irrevocable step into uncharted realms. It was another silly feeling, but it persisted. He moved over to the window and looked out onto a tiny courtyard and the back of the building on the next street.

"You have any way of looking out onto the street in front?" Michael asked.

Jalil paused in his stamping, his expression grave. "Have you been followed here?"

"Not that we know of."

"Then not to worry. We will be done here very soon." He then picked up another stamp and pressed it onto a black ink pad.

After another twenty minutes, Jalil closed up his ink pads and put away the stamps, then drew out what looked like a fountain pen and used it to sign the name of some obscure Foreign Office functionary. He blew on the ink and then handed it over to Michael. He whistled. It was a bloody work of art. Erika had been right; her friend had produced a flawless document that would pass muster anywhere.

"There is only one problem, my friend," he said tapping the passport with a long-fingered hand. "If they are checking numbers, you will be caught. That is the one part I cannot forge perfectly, for it would mean having access to their computers. I am sorry."

Erika took Jalil in her arms and hugged him. "Thank you so much, old friend. You may have saved our lives."

Jalil's eyebrows arched. "Where are you going?"

"It is best you do not know," she replied, shaking her head.

The little Pakistani shrugged and smiled, taking her hands in his own. "Take care, my child. The gods smile on you."

Erika kissed him on the cheek, eliciting a deep blush. He then turned and fixed Michael with a level stare. "You would be wise to treat her well."

"I intend to," Michael said, extending his hand. "Thank you for all your help."

When Jalil reached to grasp his hand, the front door exploded inward, knocked off its hinges by four black-clad men holding a battering ram. More figures dressed in black ran in around them brandishing Enfield automatic rifles. Michael instinctively grabbed for Erika and moved away from the door as the men barreled into the room screaming.

"ON THE FUCKING FLOOR, NOW!" they shouted. "HANDS BEHIND YOUR HEADS!"

Michael, Erika, and Jalil hit the floor simultaneously, their hearts racing, while the black-clad men encircled them, weapons aimed for their heads. It was obvious these men were Special Air Service. Their timing and efficiency spoke of military training, where split-second decisions were the rule rather than the exception. Special Branch would have knocked first. The question that remained was why the SAS were operating in a civilian environment? All this went through the back of Michael's mind, though he barely had time to think before those questions were answered.

Directly on the heels of the SAS came a tall blond-haired man, who strode into the room with a pleasant smile and a confident air. He stopped and stared down at the three people on the floor and his smile widened. "Mr. Thorley, I'm Simon Welles, MI6. So sorry to intrude, but I thought it high time we had a talk." He nodded to the SAS men. "Take the wog to Scotland Yard and have him booked on forgery charges; the others will come with me."

Jalil was dragged to his feet, twisting and squirming, his dark eyes flashing with anger. "The gods will curse your children, you petty bureaucrat!" he said, spitting at Welles's feet. "You have no honor."

"Now, there's the pot calling the kettle black," Welles replied, chuckling.

Jalil misinterpreted the statement as a slur against his color and began hurling invectives in his native tongue at the top of his voice. The two burly SAS men hauled him out the door, his feet kicking at the air.

When Jalil's curses faded away, Welles turned to Michael and Erika. "On your feet." He saw them eyeing the automatic rifles and nodded to the SAS men, who stepped back and pointed their weapons at the ceiling. Michael then helped Erika to her feet.

"You two can make this easy, or not, it's up to you."

"What do you want with us?" Michael asked.

"I'm under no obligation to tell you anything; however, I think it would be in your best interest to cooperate."

Michael shot Erika a glance. She appeared inordinately cool, and he found that both inspiring and worrisome.

"My car's waiting downstairs," Welles said, motioning toward the door. "We can talk freely there."

Out on the street, they found a large Daimler Limousine waiting, its engine idling. The driver sat behind the wheel looking bored, while beefy MI6 agents stood by the open passenger door. One had his hand on the door's handle and one on a holstered pistol. The other had his pistol drawn and held at the ready.

Welles let Michael and Erika enter first, then followed them inside. The two MI6 agents brought up the rear and took their places on either side of Michael and Erika. A moment later the driver stepped on the accelerator and the car glided away from the curb, headed back toward central London.

Michael and Erika sat facing Welles, who examined Michael's new passport, flipping through it with the same infuriating expression of smug amusement on his face. Michael wanted to punch the man. Welles reminded him of all those arrogant bureaucrats who used the system to heap abuse on those less powerful. He'd run into them his entire working life and he hated them with unspoken passion. Here was one, however, that had real power. And it scared him.

Welles closed the passport and tossed it onto the seat beside him. "A nice job, really. Too bad your friend won't have the opportunity to enjoy the fruits of his labors. Forging a British passport is a serious offense. Of course, so is using one...."

"You can't prove I was going to," Michael said.

That smile again. "Perhaps not.... But I believe Scotland Yard would very much like to see you right about now."

"I don't know anything about what happened to Ferguson."

"Didn't presume you did, old boy. But the murder of the old man at the East Grinstead Home is another matter entirely."

The tone in Welles's voice made his blood turn cold. "What are you talking about?"

Welles drew out the moment like a consummate actor.

"Martin Cadwallader was found dead this afternoon. Someone injected the poor old sod with air. Left the bloody syringe right next to his head." He paused again, letting the silence do his work. "The nurse also found your business card on the floor."

"We visited the man earlier today, I didn't—"

"And these were delivered to Scotland Yard not two hours ago.... Anonymously."

Welles reached into a pocket built into the car's door and pulled out a collection of black and white 8x10s showing Michael and Erika exiting their car and entering the East Grinstead Home. Seeing these, Michael lost his self-control.

"I'm being set up!" he shouted.

Welles stared back, his gaze cool and penetrating.

"I know."

"You *know*?" Michael stared back, incredulous. He felt the reassuring pressure of Erika's hand on his arm.

Welles reached over to a console of buttons and pressed one. The whine of a motor behind him told Michael the privacy window was being raised between the driver's and passenger's compartments. Welles leaned forward, his eyes taking on a predatory glint.

"We've been monitoring you ever since your office began inquiring about the Royal South Wessex business."

Erika's grip tightened on Michael's arm. "Then you admit it did exist," he said.

"Oh, quite. But that's all I can tell you."

"Then what are we doing here?" Erika asked, speaking for the first time since entering the limousine.

Welles glowered at her, but his voice remained icy calm. "You've no doubt heard about what happened to Sir William Atwater?

Michael nodded, sensing the MI6 man was about to reveal something important. Welles continued.

"We believe he was killed by Russian agents bent on not only keeping a lid on this business, which could prove to be very embarrassing for them, but also to keep a sleeper agent from being discovered. Someone who has been in place for a very long time. It's imperative we discover who the sleeper is."

"Then why don't you bastards go public?" Michael demanded. "Tell the world. Make them squirm."

Welles sighed and looked out through the tinted windows at the passing landscape. They were coming to the market section of Whitechapel, now as quiet and deserted as a churchyard.

"I wish I could. But it could be embarrassing for us, as well...."

Michael sat forward on his seat, his anger returning. "Why? What was that regiment doing in Finland?"

He asked the question reflexively, not really expecting the man to answer, and yet, Welles appeared to consider it. A moment later, he nodded.

"All right, you deserve to know at least that much," Welles said.

Michael's pulse raced. Now, at least he would know why people were chasing him, why people were being murdered, why his father had died.

Welles smiled. This time it was warm and relaxed. "I know it's hard to believe, but we're on your side."

"Really. You people all look the same to me. And you all play the same dirty tricks with no regard for anyone. Like Jalil."

Welles's expression hardened. "Your friend is a criminal. And he'll get what he deserves."

It was Michael's turn to smile. "Us, too, I imagine."

"You've got nothing to fear," Welles said, opening up the bar.

He extracted a crystal decanter and poured himself a whisky into a glass tumbler. He nodded to Michael. "Would you like one?"

"No, thank you," Michael replied, shaking his head. "Just get on with it. Why was the Royal South Wessex in Finland?"

Welles was about to speak when a small hole appeared in the window next to his head, sending a spider web of cracks running to all four corners and the patter of broken glass on the leather upholstery. Welles's eyes widened, suddenly devoid of all expression. Then his mouth dropped open like a trap door releasing a torrent of blood. The car jounced and Welles slumped against the door, dead.

Erika screamed when the silver-gray Jaguar roared out of nowhere and slammed into the side of the limousine, sending it into a fishtail. The driver twisted the wheel in the direction of the spin and tromped on the accelerator. Tires screeched and the car rocketed forward, the Jaguar keeping pace.

They raced side by side for two city blocks, each trying to gain the advantage. Because of the late hour, the streets were nearly deserted.

Reaching a portion of the road that narrowed, the Jaguar fell behind and Welles's driver used the opportunity to make an evasive maneuver. He slid the Daimler into a sharp left turn, tires screaming. The Jaguar made the turn easily and closed the distance between them, staying half a car length behind.

Inside, Welles's body had been thrown against the opposite side of the car and threatened to topple off the seat.

The chatter of machine gun fire rent the air and bullets slapped into the limousine, another piercing the window next to Welles's lolling head. It continued through the car, shattering the privacy shield behind Michael and Erika. Without a moment's thought, Michael grabbed her and hurled her to the floor.

"Stay down!" he screamed, throwing himself on top of her. She squirmed, fighting him.

The two MI6 agents, having gotten over the shock of their superior's untimely death, tried to lower the windows and found them inoperable.

"Kick them out!" the driver yelled, putting the Daimler into another sharp turn.

Not wasting any time, the two men kicked out the windows and fired at the Jaguar from both sides. The Jaguar fell back behind the limousine, making itself a more difficult target. The agents leaned farther out. Suddenly one of them screamed and fell back into the car, his hands clutching at his throat where a bullet had pierced the carotid artery.

Erika, covered with the man's blood and screaming hysterically, threw Michael off of her, and clambered up the seat, wrapping her arms around the driver's neck.

"Stop the car!" she shouted. Stop it, now!"

The driver struggled, trying to keep control of the car. "Get her off me! Goddamnit!"

The car began to swerve and the men in the Jaguar took this as their cue to start ramming the Daimler from behind. This made Erika even more frantic. "Stop the car, I have to get out! I have to get out!"

"Get this bloody bitch off me, or we're *all* going to die!" the driver said, his voice almost choked off.

Bullets slammed into the car again and the driver took the next right turn, throwing Erika over and nearly succeeding in choking him. Michael reached up, wrapped both arms around her waist and pulled her back. The driver rubbed his throat and checked the rearview.

Erika, still in a panic, began hitting Michael with her fists. "Let me out! Let me out! Let me out!"

He had no choice. Rearing back, he slapped her across the face, hating himself when he saw the raw look of betrayal in her eyes.

"What's the matter with you, are you trying to get us killed?"

More bullets hit the limousine, sounding like hailstones.

"You don't understand!" Erika shouted. "I can't be here!"

"What the bloody hell are you talking about?"

An odd look flashed across her face and she began to cry. "I'm sorry...I didn't mean for this to happen. I—"

Michael grasped her shoulders. "Of course, you didn't," he said.

The two cars were now traveling through the market district, each side of the road lined with empty stalls that, during business hours, offered fresh produce and other sundries.

Michael frowned, remembering something. "We've got to take the next left to Tower Bridge," he shouted, "or we'll end up in a dead end."

"I know, mate," the driver said, eyes flicking to the rearview. "We'll take the next left." He paused as he saw a truck backing into their path. He smiled. "We got the bloody bastards now!"

He stepped on the gas and Michael saw what he was trying to do. If he could get past the truck, the Jaguar would be trapped, forced to go a whole block out of its way in order to find them. By then, they would be long gone. But the driver didn't see what Michael saw: a long piece of metal hanging off the back of the truck.

"STOP!" Michael yelled.

The driver, seeing the problem, stomped on the brakes. But it was too late. The limousine went into a spin, and the driver tried frantically to compensate when it careened into the truck with a frightening sound of tearing metal. Michael was thrown against the seat just as a piece of steel plunged through the windscreen neatly decapitating the driver.

Dazed and bruised, Michael saw his passport jutting out from beneath Welles's body. He grabbed it, shoved it into his pocket, and got up to look out the window. Outside, the silver-gray Jaguar screeched to a halt fifty feet away, the doors popping open. Two men leaped out and moved forward, Skorpion machine pistols clutched in their hands. Through the shattered window he heard one of them speak German to the other, a joke, something about English scrap metal. The one who'd spoken, the taller of the two, had a head shaped like a bullet and walked with a swagger in his gait.

The surviving MI6 agent struggled to reach his weapon, which had flown out of his hands on impact and now rested on the road three feet from him. The bullet-headed German reacted, instantly riddling the agent with .32 caliber slugs.

Erika whimpered, her eyes shut against the horror, and Michael placed himself in front of her. It was a noble if futile gesture, he knew it, but if he was going to die, he wanted to face it head on. He realized his knees were shaking. The bullet-headed man stopped ten feet from him, and Michael could see the blackheads in the man's nose.

The man raised the Skorpion machine pistol and grinned, revealing short stubby teeth.

The driver of the Jaguar leaned out of car and called out in German, "Karl, we must leave, there is no time."

"I'm going to end this crap, now," he replied, his voice sounding harsh and guttural.

Michael felt Erika grab onto him as she rose to her feet and stood beside him. Suddenly, the one called Karl straightened up, his eyes widening.

"Karl! Let's move!" the driver of the Jaguar shouted.

Karl took one last look at them, eyes round with fear, and then he ran to the Jaguar. Tires spun when the driver stomped on the accelerator, and a moment later it was gone. Erika stared after the departing Jaguar, her expression oddly calm.

"Are you all right?" Michael asked.

She gave him a wan smile. "Yes."

Sirens wailed in the distance.

"Come on, there's a tube station nearby."

Grabbing her hand, they started for the station, which lay a block away. A large club crowd had gathered, heading home on the last train, making it easy to lose themselves within it. Michael bought tickets with his remaining pocket change, and when they reached the stairs leading to the Underground, he saw Police and Emergency vehicles streak by, their sirens dopplering as they passed.

The Whitechapel Underground station was several degrees hotter than aboveground and packed with travelers staring into space or into the eyes of soon-to-be loved ones. A train had just arrived and was disgorging passengers. Michael checked the sign displaying its destination and saw it was headed for New Cross, completely the wrong direction. Then he remembered the station was a hub for the District Line and would take them back in the general direction of Kensington. He checked the clock, feeling a wave of relief wash over him. The last train to Wimbledon was due any moment, and one of its stops was South Kensington. Erika joined him at the map, her face etched with worry.

"Where are we going, Michael?"

"We've got to get some new clothes," he said, indicating the blood on her dress. "How are you fixed for cash?"

"All the English money I had was back in the limousine."

She pulled out a wad of German Marks and Michael saw that

most of the bills were large denominations. He sighed and leaned against the wall, shaking his head.

"That means we'll have to risk the bank first thing in the morning."

"But surely they won't react that quickly," she said.

"Never underestimate the British government. But you may be right. The bank will most likely be clear. It's the ports we have to worry about. They'll probably have people stationed at all the exit points. It's the chance we'll have to take. The problem is we have no place to go until then. Even if a hotel would take your money, they'd take one look at us and turn us out."

A gay couple clutching each other's derrieres, passed between them, giving Michael an appraising glance. Their eyebrows arched when they noticed the condition of his attire. Erika gave them a withering glare, then turned back to Michael, who drew her over to a spot near the wall.

"I have other friends...in Sloan Square," she said.

"No, I don't want to involve anyone else. It's too dangerous. We'll keep moving until daylight. When the bank opens, we'll exchange some of your money. I only bloody hope they don't arrest us."

Another train pulled into the station, and Michael saw it was the Wimbledon train. "Come on, this is it."

They ran for the train, slipping inside just as the doors clattered shut. Michael let Erika have the one seat available and stood in front of her, holding the bar overhead. He tried not to notice the stares of the other passengers, for he knew they were both a frightful mess. And even though their position was a precarious one, this was not what was continually nagging at his mind. It was the look of naked fear in the eyes of the German gunman, the one called Karl. It was a look of a man who was staring death in the face.

28

"Reprehensible! This is absolutely reprehensible!" Roger MacKinnon shouted. He stalked back and forth across the carpet in front of his desk, his cheeks mottled with rage.

Sir Robert Sandon, the object of his ire, sat facing him in one of the straight-backed chairs, looking grim.

"*You* told me you were handling this situation, Sandon. And I expected you to be bloody well discreet! Now, we have four dead bodies in Whitechapel, the press crawling all over us asking their blasted questions, and nothing to show for it!" He stepped closer to Sir Robert, bending down like a parent scolding a child. "You were told to keep me informed, and you let Welles go off half-cocked on some bloody safari!"

Sir Robert's pushed himself up from the chair and met MacKinnon's fiery gaze, his blood pressure rising.

"I won't be talked to like this! My men were brutally murdered, God only knows by whom, and I will have to be the one to break it to their families..."

"They were East German," MacKinnon snapped.

"...and I resent the implication— What did you say?"

"They were bloody East German! MI5 and Special Branch have been tracking them since they entered the country."

Sir Robert's eyes widened. "And you let them kill my men?"

A little of the hot air seemed to leak out of MacKinnon. He moved behind his desk and dropped into the leather-covered swivel chair. "Up until now, all they were doing was shadowing Thorley and the German woman," he said, his hands toying with a letter opener resembling a miniature Excalibur. "There was no reason to expect that they would try to take them out."

"Then it looks as if MI5 and Special Branch are to blame, doesn't it? Besides, what have the East Germans to do with the South Wessex affair?"

MacKinnon slammed his hand down upon his desk. "That's what MI5 was trying to find out! Welles should never have picked up Thorley and the girl! Not without my approval! It wasn't his province to do so."

"But we have it on good authority that the two of them are about to flee the country."

"Precisely, old man, precisely," MacKinnon said, steepling his fingers and offering a hawkish grin. "I have every reason to believe they're heading for West Germany. And when they arrive, the Russians will resolve the situation. With Thorley and the girl dead, we'll expose the bastards for the bloody savages they are."

Suddenly, Sir Robert understood everything. It was as crystal clear as a bright summer sky. "My God, man.... You don't give a damn about Thorley, the girl, or the bloody D-notice. You want to hang the Russians...."

MacKinnon leaned forward, trembling with excitement. "By their bloody balls. When all this comes out, the PM will make a statement to the press that will absolve Britain of any complicity then...and now. Can't you see it, Sandon? It will mean the end of the Iron Curtain!"

"Yes, but at what price?"

"Bugger the price. We've been crushed between the Soviets and the Americans for forty bloody years. Become a second-rate power begging scraps at their table. No more. It's time we reasserted ourselves and took our rightful place among the superpowers as equals."

"And the PM *agrees* with this?"

MacKinnon remained silent, his eyes blazing.

"You're all out of your minds, it'll never work."

"Oh, it will, Sandon, I assure you. And I've purchased a little insurance to make *sure* it happens."

Reaching across his desk, MacKinnon pressed a button on his intercom. Sir Robert heard the muffled buzz through the wall.

"Yes?" came the reply through the speaker.

"Have him come in, now." MacKinnon ordered.

The door leading to MacKinnon's antechamber opened and in stepped a man in his late sixties. His hair was salt and pepper gray, with streaks of what had once been a fiery carrot-red still evident. And though he was of less than average height, there was something powerful about the man, like that of a coiled spring. It showed in the graceful, catlike way he moved when he walked out of the shadows toward the desk. The man wore a Harris tweed jacket over a chambray shirt and tight denim pants held up with a silver conch belt. His feet were shod with expensive lizard-skin boots in the style of the American West.

The man halted midway between MacKinnon and Sir Robert, his mouth twisting into a crooked grin as he placed his hands on his hips. Sir Robert caught a glimpse of a shoulder holster and the dull gleam of blued metal.

"Well, well, Roger, me boyo, we meet again. And it's been far too long, I might add."

Sir Robert saw the rage in MacKinnon's face transform into his characteristic mask of aloofness. He also saw something else: loathing, and maybe a touch of fear. Somehow, this made Sir Robert feel better for the first time since walking into MacKinnon's office. Any man who could elicit this response from the Home Secretary deserved his respect.

"Sir Robert," MacKinnon said, beginning the introductions. "This is—"

The older man stepped forward and offered his hand. Sir Robert took it and found the Irishman's grip surprisingly strong.

"Corwin Brady, at your service, me lord," he said, his lopsided grin widening.

Sir Robert allowed himself an ironic smile of his own. "Are you always this irreverent, Mr. Brady?"

"Only to those that deserve it, sir." Brady chuckled, releasing his grip on Sir Robert's hand.

MacKinnon interrupted. "Mr. Brady is what you might call our Odd Job Man. From now on, he'll be in the thick of it. Wherever Thorley and the girl go, he'll be waiting in the wings...watching."

"And then what?" Sir Robert asked, already regretting the question.

"If the Russians fail to resolve the situation as we anticipate, Mr. Brady will step in. His orders are to have all evidence point to Moscow. You are to cooperate in every way. Is that clear?"

Sir Robert turned and faced Brady, who now eyed him with the cold gaze of a sociopath. It was at that moment Sir Robert knew that his career hung by a thread. Early retirement was now out of the question, perhaps any retirement at all. He was caught up in sea change far beyond his control, and he was in it up to his bloody neck.

"Very clear, sir," he said finally.

MacKinnon nodded. "Right. Be so kind as to close the door behind you, that's a good man."

His face turning red from MacKinnon's casual rebuke, Sir Robert stalked out of the Home Secretary's office wanting very much to have another drink.

⁂

Brady watched Sir Robert leave, and wondered what it was about the man that made him take the crap that MacKinnon dished out. Fear? Weakness? It didn't really matter. The point that kept raising its ugly head was that he, Corwin Brady, was no better, coming at MacKinnon's beck and call like a prized poodle. It was at the precise moment the Home Secretary had dismissed his underling that Brady decided he'd had enough. He'd spent the better part of the last twenty years on his farm and that's where he wanted to be. Not in this godforsaken country. Oh, he was a hypocrite, that was for sure, taking the odd job over the years—as MacKinnon had so eloquently put it—so that he could maintain himself in the style to which he'd become accustomed. But now, with his diversified investments he didn't *need* the work any longer.

"So," MacKinnon said, easing himself back into his chair, "is there anything you require?"

Brady stared at the man, wanting to wrap his hands around his smug Limey neck. "That is as loaded a question as I've ever heard."

MacKinnon smiled. "Perhaps, but a legitimate one, nevertheless."

"Just a first-class ticket home."

The smile slid off MacKinnon's face. "This is no time for your peculiar brand of humor, Brady. You're needed here."

"Only because you boyos keep getting your Shillelaghs caught in the proverbial crack. I'm retired, MacKinnon. I want to stay that way. So, if you'll pardon an old sod—"

"SIT DOWN!"

MacKinnon's outburst came close to the edge of hysteria, and Brady reasoned it fell short only because the man was holding himself in check. MacKinnon was scared. And that made Brady uneasy. Seating himself into one of the chairs facing the desk, he kept his expression neutral.

MacKinnon leaned forward, his lips a tight angry line. "Understand something, Brady," he said. "You have no choice, here. If it weren't for my predecessors and their largesse, you'd be rotting away the rest of your life in Wormwood Scrubs, a convicted terrorist."

Now it was Brady's turn to anger. His voice remained steady, but the heat could be seen blazing in his eyes. "No one could prove I had anything to do with that bombing."

"We don't need proof, you bloody bastard." MacKinnon said, picking up the phone. "All I need is to make one call and you'll be in prison. How much effort do you think it would take to make it stick for good?"

Brady remained silent, knowing the old sonofabitch was right.

"All right, you win. But I want your assurance that this is it. Once this job is over and all the loose ends tidied up, I'll want a letter exonerating me of that IRA nonsense. You and I both know I was never with that bunch. Is *that* clear?"

"You'll have it."

And though he watched the man's every facial nuance, Brady was sure, as God was in His heaven, that Roger MacKinnon was lying, and that he'd have to go on killing for Queen and country until they decided his services were "no longer required." And it didn't take a bloody genius to figure out the lay of the land on that one.

If it weren't so bloody tragic, Brady would have laughed—right in the pompous old bastard's face.

✖   ✖   ✖

Inside his embassy office, Pavel Hedeon hung up the phone and sighed. The Premier was getting nervous, and that meant trouble for everyone. The man had all but ordered him to end the Thorley business. "What they start, Pavel Kolenkovich, we will finish," he'd said, "This can still embarrass us." And this from the man who'd invented *Perestroika*.

Openness, hah! What a fat lie that was.

The man was just like everyone else with their dirty little secrets... and their fear. And yet, Hedeon was sworn to obey them, to defend the Motherland—the Rodina—no matter what.

If the order came, he would have to kill the girl...and the boy....

Scowling, he reached across his desk, pulled out a Cuban cigar, snipped off the end with his solid silver cutter and lighted it, puffing it until the end glowed like a tiny red sun. The heavy aroma filled his nostrils and he leaned back in the chair, watching the smoke drift upward toward the ceiling.

He thought of his counterparts across Hyde Park in Grosvenor Square, nestled in their block-long building and smiled. No doubt those decadent American bastards would love to know what was going on. And maybe they did. After all, they were always trying to listen in, just as his people tried to listen in on them.

Chuckling at the absurdity of it all, he checked his watch, and saw it was after seven. He would have the car brought around in fifteen minutes to take him back to the Dorchester for an early dinner. He was getting too old for these twelve-hour days. For now, there was time enough to enjoy a fine cigar and try to figure a way out of this mess, one that would satisfy both the Kremlin and the yearnings of his own heart.

A knock sounded on the door. "*Da*, come in."

The door swung open and a young KGB man entered. Hedeon smiled. "Ah, Feliks, sit down, have a cigar."

The young man looked nervous. "I beg to report, Comrade Colonel...."

Hedeon frowned. The formality could only mean bad news. "What is it, Lieutenant Danya?"

Danya cleared his throat. "I have just received a report from Fifth Directorate. Another of the Hitlerite conspirators has been eliminated."

So, perhaps the news was not all bad. "Which one?" Hedeon asked, not really caring.

"Manfred Valdemarr."

"Then the only ones left are Jarmann, and von Arnwolf."

Danya's nervousness increased, irritating the older man. "Out with it, Lieutenant, I cannot abide waiting for bad news."

"Comrade Colonel, von Arnwolf has disappeared. His detail lost him during a visit to the cinema."

Hedeon nodded, remaining calm. "They must be aware they are being hunted by now. Tell Malkovich to notify all informants that the usual reward shall be doubled for any information regarding von Arnwolf's whereabouts."

"Yes, Comrade Colonel."

"What about Michael Thorley?"

Danya hesitated again. Now, Hedeon grew alarmed.

"What, what is it?"

"I—I beg to report that someone tried to kill him early this morning."

Hedeon bolted to his feet, cigar ash tumbling to the carpet. "What!"

"He had been arrested by the British Secret Service. Two men in a silver-gray Jaguar chased them down and killed everyone in the vehicle except for Thorley and his female companion."

"Fools! Idiots! Who authorized this?"

Danya shifted from one foot to the other. "Thorley's tail did not recognize the men but heard them speaking in German."

Hedeon slumped into his chair, the news rocking him. "Mueller...."

The phone rang, shattering the momentary silence.

"I want Thorley watched around the clock," Hedeon ordered. "Do you understand? I want him alive!"

Danya turned on his heels and marched from the room. When the door closed, Hedeon snatched up the phone and brought it to his ear. "Yes." He listened a moment, his expression softening. "Svetlana. I am so glad you called. Yes, I just heard.... I know it was not supposed to happen. It was not our doing. Someone else has interfered, someone I know very well.... I have not forgotten my promise, my love. I will let no harm come to them. This I swear."

❋   ❋   ❋

Dover Harbor stretched out before them, overshadowed by the famous white cliffs, a maze of piers, warehouses, and freighters all crammed together on a spit of land that appeared far too small to accommodate the massive structures. Loading cranes on tracks stood quayside like silent sentinels, their spiderlike arms reaching silently skyward, red lights blinking a warning to passing aircraft. They reminded Michael of the giant insects from the monster movies he'd loved as a child, and that thought offered a moment of amusement in an otherwise strained atmosphere. He watched Erika staring out across the inky-black water toward their destination: Ostend, Belgium. She appeared outwardly cool, yet there was something underneath that studied calm, something he could not put his finger on. It unsettled him. Except for that wild horrific ride through Whitechapel, she'd been the epitome of cool under fire.

"I can't be here," she'd said.

Why had she said that? Not "I *don't* want to be here," but *"can't."* It was an odd thing to say, and at the time, he'd let it go. Now, it boiled up into his conscious thoughts, and he fought the urge to ask her about it. After all, she was panicked, and people often said and did things that made no sense when caught in its grip. And who wouldn't want to get out of a situation like that?

That was it, wasn't it?

Still, he wondered if it would happen again. He needed her cool, steady nerves if they were going to make it through this ordeal. The taxi driver, a reed-thin Cockney with one eye permanently crossed, interrupted his thoughts.

"Where'ya want to be dropped, Guv?" the man said, tobacco-stained teeth flashing.

"The Ferry terminal."

"Right-o, Guv."

The taxi pulled up to the main terminal a moment later, and Michael shoved two five-pound notes into the driver's hairy fist. The man smiled and bowed.

Outside, the damp fetid air embraced them, smelling of equal parts diesel fuel, salt, and rotted fish. Mist rolled in off the Channel, and somewhere off in the distance a ship's horn blew.

For the hundredth time, Michael felt the pocket of his jacket for the passport, taking a measure of comfort from its heft. It also fed his fear of discovery, gnawing at him like a rat desperate enough to chew off its own leg to escape a trap. Erika grabbed his hand and squeezed.

"Maybe we should try the airport," she said. "It might be safer."

Michael shook his head. "First place they'll be looking. The second is here. We'll buy our tickets and walk to the ferry. If anything looks out of the ordinary, there are a hundred places we can get out."

He led her to the terminal, a large ultra-modern building, brightly lit and kept far cleaner than he would have assumed. Even at this late hour it was choked with people.

Michael turned his attention to the ticket counters. Hugging the walls, they fronted a section of glassed-in offices, with each passenger line represented. He scanned the dizzying array of signs until he spotted one halfway down that read: *Dover-Ostend Ferry* in bright red type.

The ticket agent smiled when they approached.

"May I help you?" she asked.

"Two for Ostend, please," Michael said.

The young woman nodded. "That will be twenty-two pounds."

Michael reached for the money in his trousers and felt icy fingers crawling up his back.

Someone was watching them!

He *knew* it. The feeling was strong, nearly corporeal, and it sat on his shoulders whispering into his ear with a tiny insistent voice: Get Out!

While the agent punched up the tickets, he turned first one way, and then the other, trying to discern who among the throng might be surveilling them.

Calm yourself, Thorley, you're getting paranoid. Take it easy.

He took a breath and thought it through. None of the people he saw looked the type, none looked like a trained killer, though perhaps that was what made them professionals.

Stop it.

If any of these people were after them, would they really sit by and wait to act? Not bloody likely. They were safe for the moment. They were—

"Here you are, sir," the ticket agent said, reaching over the counter. "Two for Ostend."

Tickets in hand, Michael and Erika walked quickly through the terminal toward the entrance to the ferry. A line of people waited to check in, delayed by two Immigration officials who were examining each and every passenger, checking their faces against a pair of photos in their hands. Michael pulled Erika up short and they melted into the passing crowd, taking a strategic position next to a newsagent's kiosk.

"What now?" Erika asked, her blue eyes flashing.

Michael pretended to study the newspaper headlines while he pondered their next move. The ferry was out of the question. They'd never get past Immigration without being apprehended. And even if they somehow managed to get by those two goons, it was more than possible that someone waited on board, someone who wouldn't be satisfied with an arrest. And who would miss two fugitives gone overboard in a dark, choppy sea? Suddenly, he smiled as an idea kindled in his mind.

"Come on," he said, taking her hand.

Retracing their steps through the terminal, Michael led Erika out of the gate and down the narrow road leading back into town. The mist had thickened, rolling in off the harbor and wrapping them in its damp arms. Staying to the seaward side, they passed through Dover proper and on to the Prince of Wales docks. It was quieter here, the sounds of the Ferry terminal lost in the lapping of the waves and the groan of the fishing boats against their moorings.

Every craft lay dark and silent, their owners long since gone home. There was nothing to do but go back to London, or try the ferry and risk imprisonment, or worse.

"You wanted to steal a boat, didn't you?" Erika said, giving voice to his idea. It sounded reckless and stupid coming from her.

"I didn't know what else to do. I just realized that I know next to nothing about them." He turned to her. "I don't suppose you know how to hot-wire a boat and navigate through this." He pointed to the fog, now nearly impenetrable.

Erika shook her head. "I'm sorry."

And then he heard someone whistling. Aware that sound carried further on nights such as these, it nevertheless sounded close by. He recognized the tune. Glenn Miller's "Moonlight Serenade."

Motioning her to follow him, Michael led the way further down the quay, taking each step with caution. Up ahead, he spotted the faint amber glow from an oil lamp. The closer he drew to the whistling's source, the more he could discern the outlines of an old mahogany fishing boat, its wood and metalwork gleaming. Painted on the stern in a flowing script, was the name: *Molly's Revenge.*

The whistling grew louder, and Michael spotted a man exiting the hatch leading down to the cabin below. Thin to the point of emaciation, his face resembled toughened leather tooled into deep chasms from years in the wind and rain. A soiled yachting cap sat perched on a balding pate above two kindly eyes separated by a razor-thin nose.

The old man bent down, grabbed a wrench from an open toolbox, and started back down the steps, still whistling. Michael took up the tune, harmonizing with the old man, who

stopped and turned, eyes squinting into the fog.

Michael and Erika stepped forward until the glow of the oil lamp fell on them.

The old man's bushy brow lifted. "Cor blimey. I didn't think anyone knew that one anymore," he said in a thick Cockney dialect.

"It was my father's favorite song...so I'm told." He paused, giving the boat another glance. "I'm looking to hire a boat."

The old man grinned. "Bit early for fishing. The smelt don't run 'til five o'clock."

"We need to get across the Channel...to Ostend," Erika said.

The old sailor studied Erika, his expression sphinx-like. "They have a nice ferry for that, in case you hadn't noticed."

Michael shot a glance at Erika, whose own expression remained as inscrutable as the old man's. Michael decided to trust him.

"We can't exactly avail ourselves of it, at the moment, Mister..."

The old man doffed his cap and bowed. The effect was comical. "Captain Terrence Nye, at your service, Guv'nor." He squinted again, giving his face the appearance of a wizened bird. "You wouldn't be runnin' from the law, would you?"

"In a matter of speaking...."

Nye shook his head, the grin returning to his face. "Never was much for the law.... Bastards always mucking about in me business. I'll take ya across for two hundred quid cash. In advance."

"All right. But it's half now, half when we get there.... Plus, a bonus if we beat the ferry."

Nye's grin widened; he was missing all his back teeth.

"Wouldn't have it any other way, mate. 'Cept this old tub'll never beat that boat, unless we go to Calais."

"Will that delay us?" she asked, turning to Michael.

He shook his head. "It's actually closer."

"Calais it is."

"Come aboard then," Nye said, waving them forward. "We'd best be going."

Relieved, Michael and Erika clambered onto the boat, while Nye threw off the mooring lines and started the engine. It sputtered and coughed, stalled once, then caught, the pistons smoothing out to a deep throaty roar. Water boiled above the propeller, and oily clouds of noxious exhaust belched out of the rusted pipes jutting from the transom. The deck vibrated under their feet, and Michael wondered if the old tub would even make it out of the harbor, much less to Calais. But his fears eased when the old captain goosed the throttle and the boat glided away from the pier. Out beyond the harbor wall, the sounds of the busy harbor faded, leaving only the sound of the engine and the water slapping against the hull. Moments later the tiny craft faded into the swirling fog.

※　※　※

From his perch on the seawall above the quay, Feliks Danya stood smoking a black Sobrani cigarette and watched while Thorley and the woman negotiated with the old sailor, then climbed aboard and motored away.

It would have been so tempting to take him and the girl then and there. But orders were orders. And orders were not to be countermanded, especially those of Comrade Hedeon. Feliks took a long drag and blew out the smoke, shaking his head.

When the dilapidated old boat had gone, Danya turned to the man standing next to him.

"Take the ferry to Ostend and stay with them," he said. "Report to me as soon as you determine their ultimate destination. Is that understood?"

"Yes, Comrade Lieutenant." He turned and lumbered back toward the ferry terminal. Danya sighed.

Above him, he had a superior running an operation, making decisions from his emotions; below him, he had men like "Yuri the Cave Man," whom he had to watch constantly to make sure they did not blunder. It was all too much.

"God help us," he whispered. And then he laughed. Here he was a good communist asking for help from heaven. Hell would have been a more apt choice, for that was where all good communists were going if their mission failed.

Disgusted, he threw down his cigarette and walked away, his tongue already craving the taste of the vodka waiting in his car.

※　※　※

Werner Mueller stepped from the shadows, his foot crushing out the stub of the Sobrani. The two men with him kept watchful eyes on the area around them, poised for violence. Each looked as if he welcomed the opportunity. A moment later another man glided out of the fog, his step as jaunty as the tune he whistled. Karl's whistle died when he saw the look in Mueller's eyes.

"They took the fishing boat?" he asked.

Mueller nodded, staring off into the fog where *Molly's Revenge* had disappeared. "Those Slavic bastards have someone on the ferry." he turned to Karl. "You know what to do...."

Karl smiled, catching the eyes of the other two men.

"Ja, I know," he said, turning back toward the way he'd come.

Mueller waited until he'd gone. "Now, we take a little drive into the country," he said, a smile peeling back his lips. In the sickly glow of the streetlamp, he looked exactly like a grinning skull.

29

Once they cleared the harbor wall, the fog stole away, revealing a clear night of preternatural calm. The water, a sheet of flat obsidian, reflected the stars overhead, along with the dim light of a jaundiced moon.

Leaving Erika in Nye's care, Michael ventured to the Harpoonist's Perch, a narrow plank jutting out from the prow, with a waist-high metal rail encircling its perimeter. Standing at the point, he looked down, watching the prow slice into the water, the incessant hiss of the foam a balm to his soul. The salt air tickled his nose with its complex bouquet, and he reveled in the sting of the spray and the caress of the wind against his face. Visibility was nearly unlimited and, if he squinted, he could see the lights of the French and Belgian coasts hugging the horizon. Tension leaked from him, and for the first time in uncounted hours, he felt relaxed—at peace.

"We're almost there, Dad," he whispered.

He cocked an ear, as if expecting an answer his conscious mind knew would never come; and yet he felt closer to his father than he'd ever felt in his life. It was a feeling that both comforted and left him bereft.

What happened out in that desert, Dad? And how the bloody hell did the Royal South Wessex regiment factor into all of it?

He knew the answer lay across the cold black waters. They had to reach Valdemarr, Jarmann, or Von Arnwolf before the killers did. If fate were on their side, one of these men would hold the key. Only then would the killing stop. Only then would they be safe.

He sensed Erika's presence before he saw her.

She waited for him at the entrance to the perch, trembling from the chill in the air, her delicate brow furrowed with concern. He retraced his steps, went to her and took her into his arms, feeling her body fitting to his like two halves of a mold. Her heart hammered against her ribs, keeping cadence with his own. And then he kissed her. Soft at first, it quickly turned more urgent, her tongue warm and insistent. For Michael, it felt as if nothing else in the universe mattered.

She broke the kiss a moment later, leaning against him, sighing. "You looked so sad just now," she said. "I was worried."

"Just thinking about my father. As much as I want to know what happened, Erika, there's a part of me that doesn't."

She shook her head. "You're afraid he won't live up to your image of him."

"Am I that transparent?"

"Only in a way that is good."

"What about you, Erika?"

"What do you mean?"

"Did your father live up to your image of him?"

Michael didn't get the reaction he expected. Instead of confiding in him, she pulled away and walked to the railing, her head bowed while she stared into the water. He stayed where he was, sensing she didn't want him near just then. After a long agonizing moment, she turned to face him.

"There's something we need to talk about, Michael. It can't wait any longer. I—" she halted, the tears welling anew. "*Scheisse!* It wasn't supposed to be this way."

An icy chill swept through Michael. "What is it?"

"You'll hate me."

"No, I won't. I'm too bloody much in love with you."

An emotional tug of war played across her face. She bit her lip.

"You're married, aren't you?" Michael said, giving voice to his worst fear.

She shook her head. "If only it were as simple as that."

He went to her and grabbed her shoulders, forcing her to look at him.

"I don't care what it is. Do you understand? I don't care. I don't care if you've had ten husbands, or had a fling with the bloody girl next door!"

"You *will* care," she said, her voice a tiny whisper almost lost to the wind.

"Oi, you two!" Captain Nye called out. "It's bloody cold as a witch's bum. Get on back here, I've got some tea brewing!"

Michael saw the relief in Erika's eyes and decided that whatever was bothering her could wait. He took her hand, feeling her frozen fingers dig into his, and led the way back to the wheelhouse.

True to the old sailor's word, a battered enameled teapot sat boiling atop an ancient hotplate, the odor of Typhoo permeating the air. Nye pointed a long bony finger toward two steaming cups, while taking a sip from his own. Michael nodded, picked them up, and handed one to Erika who retreated to the stern, taking a seat on the transom. Michael sat on one of the two swivel chairs and sipped from his; it tasted sweeter than he liked, but the warmth coursing through him was more than welcome. He took another sip and looked up to find Nye regarding him with an expression of cautious amusement.

"I never could understand 'em myself," he said, placing his mug on the instrument panel and grabbing the wheel with both hands.

Michael's puzzled look elicited a soft chuckle from the elderly sailor. "Women. Loved 'em as much as any man. Had one in every port, you see. But they'd drive me bloody crackers with all their demands and their contrary ways. Couldn't abide being with one for longer than a week. By then I'd feel the call o' the sea and back I went." He gave the wheel an affectionate pat. "Molly's the only woman for me. Right old girl?"

Michael smiled in spite of his dark mood. It didn't take a genius to see that the old salt was trying to make him feel better. Funny thing, it was working.

"No regrets?" Michael asked.

Nye shook his head. "Nary a one. Molly and I have an understandin', you see. I don't go foolin' with human females, and she don't never let me down. So far, it's been a perfect match."

Michael nodded, finding the old man's anthropomorphic thoughts about his boat both sweet and sad. To have spent a lifetime—alone.

"In fact," Nye continued, "the last time I made this crossin' was in this very boat back in '40. Oh, Molly was a real looker then, let me tell you. Not that you aren't a fine specimen now, my dear," he said, as if to mollify the boat's wounded feelings. "Molly's been good to me, and she was good to the boys who needed a lift back from Dunkirk, she was." He gave Michael an appraising glance. "I just want you to know I'm not doin' this just for the money."

"Why then?"

Nye's faced turned pensive, his mouth pursing as he mulled the question over.

"Why, indeed.... The truth of the matter is I'm bored, mate—bored to bloomin' tears. I've spent a lifetime on the sea.... Loved her as only and old salt can. And in return, she's given me and Molly a right good livin'. But I have to admit—she's been a trifle tedious, as of late. You and the lady looked as if you might be good for a bit of fun."

"For your sake, Captain, I only hope it isn't more than you bargained for."

※   ※   ※

Karl stared out at the ferry's wake. Twin tails churned up by the two screws pushed the boat at a moderate twelve knots. Out of the corner of his eye, he saw the KGB man move to the railing, his expression one of distress. The *dummkopf* was actually seasick. The Channel was as flat as a schoolgirl's chest and, with the exception of the thrumming of the ferry's two engines, there was almost no sensation of movement. Unless one looked at the wake.

The KGB man leaned over the railing and expelled a stream of vomit.

Idiot. Even a state certified moron would know they sold Dramamine in the snack bar for two pounds, fifty. Still, it provided him with the perfect *entré*. Except for an old man asleep in a deck chair, they were alone.

The KGB man wiped his face, gasping for breath. To his credit he watched Karl's approach, his muscles tensed.

"Chilly night for a boat ride, isn't it old chap?"

Karl's flawless accent has the desired effect on the KGB man, who relaxed. "Yes, very chilly."

Gott in Himmel! Karl thought. *This Slavic boob would never fool anyone.*

Smiling again, Karl pulled a flask from out of his coat.

"Then why not have a nip with me to stave off the cold, eh what? A drink to the Queen."

He took a swig and held it out to the KGB man, who eyed it with ill-concealed suspicion. Then, thinking better of it, he shrugged and took the flask.

"That's a good lad," Karl said, watching the Russian take several large swallows.

The man exhaled, grinned and said, "Cheers!"

Karl returned the smile and then spit something into his hand. He showed the plastic cap to the Russian and laughed. "You know, they finally had to drown Rasputin because the poison he drank wouldn't kill him. I should imagine you won't have that problem."

The KGB man stared at him his eyes clouded by alcohol and incomprehension. Then, with a cry, he hurled the flask into the water and flung himself at Karl. But the poison had already begun its deadly work, robbing the KGB man's muscles of the vital oxygen necessary for a fight. Instead, he began to gag and convulse, bloody foam appearing on his lips. He strained his hands upward, trying to claw Karl's face, but the big German just laughed and batted the man's hands away. Then he reached down and lifted the KGB man by his legs and tossed his limp body over the railing. One last look around, and Karl was satisfied the man on the deck chair was still asleep. He straightened his coat and began a stroll around the deck, the air filling with the sound of his jaunty whistle.

※　※　※

From his deck chair, Corwin Brady cracked open his eyes and watched the burly German disappear around the corner of the deckhouse, his weathered face creasing in a smile. With the way things were going, it looked as if both the Russians *and* the East Germans were racing to do his job for him. Either way, his assignment would soon be over. And then it would be back to his farm in Kerry and away from all this malarkey masquerading as politics. Smiling again, he tipped his rain hat back over his eyes and let sleep overtake him for the rest of the long ride across the Channel.

30

Werner Mueller's Daimler limousine streaked along the A23, exceeding the speed limit by a wide margin. He stared through the windscreen, keeping his eyes fixed on a point far ahead of the vehicle. Next to him sat a Stasi man poring over a map.

"We have just passed through Handcross, Comrade General," the Stasi man said. His accent was thick and guttural, matching his jutting brow and low hairline. He reminded Mueller of a chimpanzee.

Mueller nodded absently, his thoughts resting with Karl. By now he would have eliminated the KGB presence on the ferry and would be in place when Mueller was ready for him. The one piece of the puzzle left lay several kilometers ahead of them in Peas Pottage. *Scheisse*, these foolish *Englanders* had such idiotic names for their towns. It was no small wonder that no one took them seriously anymore. They were still cozy bed partners to the Americans, however. And that relationship should never be underestimated.

"How much further is it, Comrade General?"

It was the driver who'd spoken, snapping Mueller out of his thoughts. "In another five kilometers, you will come to a crossroads with a little stone church on the east side," Mueller said. "Turn left there. The cottage is half a kilometer further on."

The driver glanced into the rearview and gave his superior a curt nod, then returned his attention to the road. Mueller turned to the Stasi man, who folded the map and slipped it into the pouch on the seat in front of him.

"I don't want her harmed in any way, Franz. She is our lure to bring Thorley back to us. Do you understand?"

"*Jawohl,* Comrade General."

Mueller grunted and swung his eyes back to that imaginary point in front of the car.

Soon.... Very soon....

Half an hour later, the Daimler coasted to a stop a hundred yards from Woodhaven Cottage, its lights extinguished. The cottage was dark, save for one dim light that burned in one of the windows. All three men watched for signs of life, then Franz unbuckled his seatbelt and reached for the door. Mueller grabbed his arm, stopping him.

"Wait," he said sharply.

Franz shot him a puzzled frown and Mueller nodded toward the cottage. The Stasi man followed his gaze, his expression turning from bewilderment to eagerness.

Lillian Thorley stepped from the cottage and strode quickly to her motorcar, a white Ford Escort with a scrape in the right front fender. She climbed in and the tiny four-cylinder whined to life. A second later the lights snapped on and the car reversed down the narrow gravel drive.

"Back up!" Mueller shouted. *"Schnell!"*

The driver slapped the shift lever into reverse and twisted in his seat, his eyes squinting to see the road behind them. Then he punched the accelerator and the Daimler shot backwards, weaving back and forth. The driver spotted another driveway and turned into it just when Lillian Thorley's car reached the road. The little Ford bulleted past them, exuding a cloud of blue-white exhaust.

Mueller clapped the driver on the shoulder. "Follow her. And leave the lights off until we reach the main road. I have a feeling I know where she's going."

✳ ✳ ✳

With her running lights extinguished, Molly's Revenge bobbed in the swell a mile outside Calais harbor like a child's tub toy. Captain Nye stood braced against the wheel, staring through a battered pair of Zeiss binoculars, his tobacco-stained lips moving his pipe from one side of his mouth to the other. He lowered them and turned to Erika his expression grim.

"I'm assumin' you wish to avoid any contact with Customs and the like?"

She nodded. "You know this harbor well?"

"Like the back of me hand."

"Then where would you suggest."

Nye cracked a lopsided grin, the pipe still clenched in his teeth. "Well, now, Missy.... If I was not wanting any unexpected greetings, as it were, I would pull in over beyond that quay." He pointed to an area of warehouses swathed in shadow. "Not likely to be seen there. And if you were, it'll be by the sort who know to keep their bleedin' holes shut."

The old man was right. There was no way they could approach the ferry pier without being seen and apprehended. And even with passports, they couldn't risk being detained or spotted by someone with a darker agenda. The choice was clear.

"All right, then," Michael said. "Let's do it."

The old captain's eyes gleamed as he put the engine in gear and goosed the throttle forward. Molly's Revenge nosed into the swell and chugged toward the darkened warehouses.

✳ ✳ ✳

The Daimler kept its distance from the little Ford Escort with ease, but Mueller had to admire the old girl's nerve behind the wheel. She not only didn't drive like an old lady, but took risks, swerving around slower drivers in a fashion that would have given younger drivers pause. He smiled, noticing the beads of sweat on the back of his driver's neck. For once the fat slob was earning his meager pay. He was about to make a comment when his portable phone chirped.

Made from microelectronics years ahead of the consumer markets in the West, it operated on a new "cellular" principle, and also included a scrambler chip that could be coded to match an identically coded mate. Mueller pulled it out from his coat and flipped it open, turning it on.

"Ja," he said, his eyes narrowing as Karl's voice buzzed in his ear. His mouth curled into a cold smile. "I know, they took some fishing boat to Ostend."

"That's the problem," Karl said, sounding tired and frustrated. "I just received a call from one of our French people. Thorley and the girl were seen getting off at Calais."

"Calais?"

"*Ja.* I believe they will be headed for Bonn—to the university."

Mueller drew in a sharp breath. "Jarmann."

"*Ja.* He's the most logical one to reach."

"*Ausgezeichnet!* For once I am glad the old fool insisted on staying put in that decadent institution. What's the situation with the others on the list?"

Momentary static blocked out part of what Karl was saying. "...and the *verdammt* Russians found von Arnwolf."

Icy fingers gripped Mueller's heart. "What happened?"

"The safe house was raided. He tried to run—"

Mueller dropped the phone into his lap and rubbed the bridge of his nose, his entire body trembling with rage. Karl's voice continued to buzz through the earpiece, but he didn't need to hear any more. He could visualize the entire scene in his mind. The old man tottering down the cobbled street, his arms outstretched in panic, the staccato rattle of machine gunfire, the blood pooling in the gutter, eyes glazed by death. Another opportunity gone forever.

Mueller snatched up the phone, his lips curling in contempt. "Karl, I want you to listen to me very carefully. You are to make sure that Thorley makes it to Jarmann. Use whatever means necessary to get there ahead of them. Charter a plane if you have to. I will take care of what is to occur on this end and then make my way to Ostend. *Verstehen Sie?*"

Karl's reply came through entirely free of static: "*Ja,* Comrade General, I understand."

※　※　※

It was nearly dawn when they reached the car rental agency, occupying one of a dozen identical cubicles set into the middle of a giant parking lot clogged with vehicles. After arranging for their car in halting French, Michael used the men's room while Erika went to fetch the car, a late model Peugeot 505. He washed up, trying to avoid the haggard image that stared out at him from the spotted mirror.

Outside, he found the Peugeot idling at the curb. Erika sat in the passenger seat hunched forward, her ear cocked toward the radio blasting a news report. She flipped it off and leaned back.

"The bastards have killed three more on the list since I left Germany. That leaves only one."

"Who?" Michael asked, buckling the seat belt and adjusting the seat back to relieve his cramped legs.

"Ludwig Jarmann," she replied, shaking her head.

"Where do we find him?"

"University of Bonn, College of Geopolitics. From here it should take us about four to five hours."

Michael nodded and threw the car into gear.

"Geopolitics," he said, laughing humorlessly. "I wonder if the Russians appreciate the irony."

They pulled away from the curb and shot out onto the main road. A moment later, back in the parking lot, a midnight-blue Citroen slithered out onto the road and followed in their wake.

❊ ❊ ❊

Mueller smiled when Lillian's car pulled up to the front entrance of the Dorchester Hotel. The valet opened her door and she strode through the glass doors, disappearing into the lobby.

"It would appear that our widow is merrier than we thought," Mueller said, chuckling.

Franz joined his laughter. "What next, Comrade General?"

"Let's give them a moment. It may well be their last."

❊ ❊ ❊

Lillian fought the impulse to flee the hotel back to the safety of her car and, ultimately, the seclusion of Woodhaven. It was a temptation as seductive as any that beguiled the ancient Christian saints. The difference was that her sin would not be the return to the safety of her home, but the retreat from a confrontation she dreaded.

Steeling herself, she crossed the elegant lobby with its overstuffed furniture and priceless objects d'art, her knees feeling like rubber. She felt every eye on her, even though logic and her own empirical observations belied it.

Reaching the bank of elevators, she entered one that stood open and pushed the button for the penthouse, her throat going dry when the doors hissed shut and the elevator shot upwards with stomach wrenching swiftness. The floor numbers swept by, each one announced by a cheery "ding" that grated on her.

The penthouse floor, unlike the others, was decorated as if it were an extension of the ornate lobby: Brass sconces spaced every few yards, cast a muted amber glow on the beige-colored walls. Expensive paintings took up the spots in between, making it appear much like a conservative art gallery or museum. The carpet, a luxurious Wilton pile, squished under her feet when she moved toward the door at the end of the hall. A hulking figure stood guard in front of it, half-shrouded in shadow, his hands clasped in front of him.

The guard stared at her, looking puzzled that a prim-looking elderly woman would be standing there in front of him. She met his gaze, refusing to let his grim, determined glare intimidate her.

"Tell him I am here," she said.

If the man was puzzled before, he was now astounded to see this old lady speaking idiomatic Russian with no accent. He hesitated only a moment before raising his arm and speaking into a radio. Seconds later the door flew open and another giant KGB man beckoned for Lillian to enter. She followed him into an enormous sitting room that looked out onto a breathtaking view of the London skyline. She found Pavel Hedeon standing in front of the window puffing on a Cuban cigar.

"Why have you come, Svetlana? You know it is not safe for you to be seen with me." He had not turned from the window to look at her, and that hurt and angered her. She moved toward him, measuring her words.

"You promised me, Pavel. You promised me that no harm would come to him."

Hedeon whirled to face her. "And I have kept my promise! No harm *has* come to him."

"He's been shot at and nearly killed, twice!" She trembled, hating herself for showing what Pavel would consider a weakness.

"That is the fault of the East Germans!" he said, extinguishing the cigar in a marble bucket of sand. "Those jackals yearn for reunification with the decadent West. They betray the revolution."

"Blast the bloody revolution! I don't care anymore!" She advanced toward him, coming to within arm's length of him. "You are responsible for him. Or had you forgotten?"

Hedeon's anger seemed to leak from him, like sand from a broken hourglass. "No," he muttered. "I have not forgotten."

"Then what are you going to do?"

Hedeon grabbed her by the shoulders, his sausage-thick fingers caressing her. "What I must. There is too much at stake, my dear." He looked past her toward the KGB man who'd let her into the suite and motioned for him to leave. Lillian heard the door shut behind him. Hedeon turned to face her, his fierce eyes boring into hers. "Please, you must let me handle this my way. It is almost over. There is only one of the Hitlerite conspirators left."

The feeling rose up in her again, the nearly uncontrollable urge to flee. Instead, she fell into his arms, her lips burning against his as fiercely now as they had the first time over forty years before. A wave of passion overwhelmed her, and she moaned when he caressed her jaw line in that special way of his. Hedeon broke the kiss after uncountable moments, leaving her dazed, her lips tingling. "Oh, Pavel, it's been so long. I didn't know if I could bear it. When will it all end?"

He tilted her head up with his hand. "Soon, my love, soon. After the loose ends are cleaned up, we are sending you home."

Lillian stumbled back, her world rocking. "W—what?"

"You have been of great service to the Motherland, Ninotchka.

It is time you came home to the honors that are rightfully yours."

"B—but my life is here.... Everything I know, everything I love—is here...."

"Everything? How do you think it has been for me, my love? I sacrificed a fiancée." He moved to embrace her once more and Lillian stopped him with an outstretched arm and burning gaze.

"And I sacrificed a husband!"

"Surely you did not love that royalist swine!"

"He was good to me.... And the son he thought was his.... All these years, Pavel. Alone. It's been so hard. And now this. Don't ask me to sacrifice our son, as well. I won't do it. The Motherland isn't worth it."

Hedeon nodded, saying nothing. He walked back to the window, clasping his hands behind his back. "Never fear, Ninotchka.... The time for sacrifices is almost over...."

A commotion in the next room made them both turn toward the door. Sounds of a door being kicked in followed by the muffled coughs of silenced pistols galvanized Hedeon, who headed for a credenza and removed a Makarov pistol from the drawer. Quickly, but without a trace of panic, he removed the magazine, checked to see it was loaded, slapped it back in, then pulled back the slide, letting it snap back with a resounding clack. He turned to Lillian, motioning her to follow. "There is a back way! Come!"

The door exploded inward before she could move and Mueller and Franz entered, their pistols held at the ready. They were dressed in dark civilian clothes but, to Lillian's eye, there was something decidedly "military" in the way they carried themselves and handled their weapons. Mueller smiled, revealing white even teeth. His eyes, however, held no warmth. "*Guten Abend,* Comrade," he said, his voice edged with sarcasm. "It seems we meet at a propitious moment."

Hedeon wasted no time. He lifted the Makarov and fired, the shot going wild. The slug buried itself in the thick wood molding near the ceiling. Before he could get off another, Franz fired, hitting Hedeon in the hand and sending the pistol flying. Lillian screamed and made a move toward Hedeon. She stopped herself when the Stasi man's pistol moved her way.

Mueller's expression turned to contempt. "I thought you would be smarter than that, old friend."

Hedeon glared at him, his one good hand holding the ruined one. Blood patted the expensive carpet.

"They should have purged swine like you long ago, *Gruppenführer* Müller!"

"So, you know...." A smile spread across Mueller's face.

"We have known since the beginning. You don't think that phony police identity of yours fooled us for one minute, did you? We had records of everyone in the SS. But you were useful in the beginning, but now—"

"But now, I know where all the bodies are buried, *Comrade*." Mueller turned to Franz, indicating Lillian and Hedeon with his pistol. "Take them to the safe house. Wait for my call."

Franz nodded, then pushed Lillian and Hedeon toward the door. When they were gone, Mueller let his eyes roam over the opulent apartment, a scowl on his face. "And he has the audacity to call them decadent."

Turning on his heels, he strode from the apartment, shutting the door with a resounding slam.

* * *

Opposite the Dorchester, two men sat in a black Astin-Martin, their weary eyes trained on the door and the Daimler limousine idling at the curb. They sat up straighter when Lillian, Hedeon, Mueller, and

Franz exited the hotel and clambered into the waiting car. Scant seconds later, the car pulled into traffic and streaked away.

The passenger, a middle-aged man with a hangdog face and premature gray hair, picked up a walkie-talkie, while his companion, a tall man with jug ears, started the car and eased out into the stream of traffic.

"Hutchins, here," the passenger said into the walkie-talkie. "They've just left. They've got Hedeon and Thorley's mother."

"Jolly good," came the answer swathed in static. "Stay with them, no matter what you have to do. Is that clear?"

Hutchins started to nod, then stopped himself. "Right. We'll stay with them. Over."

❋ ❋ ❋

Back at MI6 headquarters, Roger MacKinnon stood over the radio, frowning. "What on earth is Thorley's mother doing there?" he asked, his voice rising in annoyance.

Standing next to him, Sir Robert Sandon suppressed a smile, his heart dancing a jig. For once it seemed things might be going his way. He turned to MacKinnon and fixed him with a sober gaze. "Welles was looking for a sleeper," he said, drawing out the moment. "It seems we've found her."

The look of shock on MacKinnon's face was more than he could have hoped.

31

"We're here," Erika said, shaking him awake. Michael groaned and stretched, feeling a jab in his neck from a kink that had settled in over the past hour while he'd slept. He remembered going through the border at Aachen and not much more after that. Rubbing the fog from his eyes, he squinted out through the windscreen at the Bonn skyline cowering under an umbrella of static gray clouds pregnant with moisture.

A small city at the end of World War Two, it had greatness thrust upon it when it became the seat of the newly created democratic West German government. Chosen because of its academic and bureaucratic tradition, as well as for its distance from the divided city of Berlin, now tainted by its recent past and its encirclement by the *Deutsche Demokratisch Republik*, Bonn had the look of a city suffering from rapid unplanned growth.

Ugly glass and steel monstrosities built over the past four decades sprouted like mushrooms between venerable nineteenth century buildings. And sitting amongst this architectural miasma was the University of Bonn, itself a victim of explosive growth.

"How much further?" Michael asked, massaging the back of his neck.

Erika consulted a map and gestured through the windscreen.

"The College of Geopolitical Science is half a kilometer west of here."

She took the next right turn and brought the Peugeot to an ultra-modern ten-story structure that resembled a child's aborted attempt at using an Erector set. An example of the new "Deconstructionist" school of design, it looked as if the construction crew had gone on strike and never come back. Erika shut off the engine and Michael became aware of the street noise around them. Just after noon, traffic was heavy, everyone impatient to get to their luncheon appointments. As if Erika had read his mind, she said, "Classes don't start again until one. I suggest you go back to sleep."

He shook his head. "Too keyed-up, now. Besides, I still think you're daft. Jarmann would have to be insane to remain here in the open."

"Perhaps that is precisely why he is still alive."

"Maybe," Michael shrugged. "But now that he is the only one left who can harm them, he might not be so secure."

"I don't want to argue, I'm too tired." She shut her eyes and Michael fought off the urge to kiss her.

"I saw a café around the corner where we turned. You want some tea?" he asked.

She grunted her assent without opening her eyes, and Michael stepped from the car. The dampness in the air clung to him, in spite of the chill breeze blowing in from the west. Turning up the collar of his tweed sport coat, he walked back to the corner and into the tiny café two doors down. His nose was immediately assaulted by the seductive aromas of espresso and pastry browning in the oven. His mouth watered. A young woman stood behind the counter reading a newspaper and had all the earmarks of a student: Leather clothes and cadaverous makeup. She looked up at his approach and smiled.

"Two teas, *bitte*," he said, feeling self-conscious at his British accent.

If the girl noticed, she pretended not to care; she went about putting two tea bags into Styrofoam cups, then adding the hot water.

"Could I also have two rolls?" he asked, pointing to the trays of pastries. The girl nodded and grabbed for a paper bag and a sheet of waxed paper. He was about to add milk and sugar to the two teas when his eyes flicked across the newspaper. The German headlines and the text meant nothing to him, but his face staring out from the bottom half of the front page nearly made him spill the hot beverage all over the counter.

Controlling himself as best he could, he reached for his wallet and realized that he'd forgotten to ask Erika for some German money. Panic seized him then. He had to leave. But how was he going to do it without arousing suspicion, and without paying?

The girl brought the two rolls, giving Michael an idea. "How much for three dozen?"

"Seventy-two marks," came the heavily accented reply.

"I'll take it."

The girl frowned, noticing as he had, that the tray was just shy of that amount of rolls. "I will have to check the back," she said.

Michael smiled, "Please do."

When she disappeared, Michael snatched up the paper and left the café, rounding the corner already sprinting. He forced himself to slow down.

Reaching the car, he flung open the door, startling Erika awake. "Where is the tea?"

"Never mind that," he said, thrusting the newspaper into her lap. "Look at this."

She appeared confused, at first, but her eyes widened in alarm when she caught sight of the photograph. "Oh, no, Michael."

"What does it say?"

She scanned the article quickly. "It says that you are sought in the murder of your friend, that you are armed and dangerous, and at large on the European continent, perhaps in Germany."

He pounded his fist on the dash. "Damn those bloody bastards!" He turned to Erika his face flushed a bright crimson. "It's those fuckers in Whitehall. How often do you think a routine murder in England would make the papers here in Germany? Zero. Armed and dangerous, for Christ's sake. They want me dead."

Erika grabbed his hand. "We're almost home, Michael. In a little while they won't be able to touch us."

"You sure about that? Can you guarantee it?"

"Of course not. I—"

Michael held up his hand, silencing her.

"It's okay. It's not as if it really changes anything. It just rattled me."

They decided to drive around the city for a while, rather than stay where they were. This way, they would be far less vulnerable. At least it sounded good in theory. The time crept by, each minute ratcheting up Michael's anxiety level. He kept spotting a blue Citroen in the side mirror pacing them at least half a kilometer back. Coincidence? He didn't think so, not anymore. Whoever they were he hoped they kept their distance. He was getting sick and tired of being followed and chased.

They arrived back at the College of Geopolitics at five minutes till one. Michael checked the street finding no blue Citroens in sight. It did little to relieve his anxiety.

Inside the building, the hallways were choked with students headed for classes.

Erika stopped a militant-looking girl and asked for directions.

She rattled them off in rapid German and took off running, no doubt late for a lecture.

They found Jarmann's office on the fourth floor, a small plastic nameplate affixed to the door the only indication. Michael looked at Erika, his pulse beating a tattoo in his ears. She smiled and nodded. He raised his arm and knocked.

"Ja, herein," came the reply. The voice was low and guttural.

Michael pushed open the door and entered a twenty-foot square room that could best be described as organized chaos. Papers and books stacked on top of each other covered every available surface. Michael cleared his throat.

"Professor? Professor Jarmann?"

Jarmann's eyebrows arched at the unfamiliar sound of English, but his attention remained fixed on the term paper in front of him.

"Yes, young man. You wish a copy of the syllabus for next semester?"

Michael shot an unsure glance at Erika, who encouraged him with a curt nod toward the older man.

"No, Professor, just a message.... The Eagle Flies...."

The effect on Jarmann was immediate. His head snapped up from the paper, eyes ablaze with suspicion, and perhaps a touch of fear.

"Who are you?"

"I'm sorry to upset you, sir, but we've come about an important matter."

"You have not answered my question. Who *are* you?"

"Forgive me," Michael said, moving toward the desk where the old man sat. "My name is Michael Thorley, Jr. My father was an acquaintance of Friedrich Rainer. This is his daughter, Erika."

Jarmann eyed Erika, the hint of a smile on his lips. "What took you so long?"

"Pardon?"

Jarmann stood and crossed the cluttered office to a credenza, pushing a stack of papers aside to reveal a battered coffeemaker. He opened the top, put in a filter and began filling it from an open can of ground Turkish coffee.

"Just what I said, young man," Jarmann said, picking right up where he left off. "What kept you? It seems my erstwhile associates have been dropping like flies, as of late. Do you like cream and sugar?"

Michael couldn't believe the old man's blasé manner.

"What the hell's the matter with you?" he asked, his anger overcoming his decorum. "Aren't you afraid? By our reckoning, you're the last living member of *Der Weisse Adler* left. If they kill you, it will all have been for nothing."

Jarmann paused in his task and stared off into space, his expression saddening. "My God.... I haven't heard that name spoken for over forty years. I'd almost forgotten it."

"The Russians haven't," Erika said, speaking for the first time.

The old man shot her a troubled glance, then resumed making the coffee.

"In answer to your question, young man.... No, I am not afraid. I am too old to worry about such things."

"But surely what you know is important?" Michael said.

"Is it? Would you like to know why they have not killed me, why they *won't* kill me?"

"Yes, I would."

The coffeemaker gurgled, the office filling with the odor of brewing coffee. Jarmann stared at Michael, seeming to take his measure. A moment later he spoke.

"They have not killed me because I am regarded as a crackpot within the academic community, and in the world at large—a drunken lunatic with tenure. Nothing I say is ever taken seriously. Were I to come forward and speak the truth, the world would laugh.... I will doubtless remain in these 'hallowed halls' until I ossify.... Then again, perhaps my colleagues are planning my demise. They've the most to gain, at this point."

The old man roared with laughter, pleased with his gallows humor. He began pouring the steaming coffee into three cracked and dusty mugs. Michael glanced at Erika, who nodded sadly.

"He's right," she said. "No one would believe him."

"Then why the bloody hell did we come here?"

"Because, young man, your pretty Fräulein knows something you do not."

"What?" Michael asked, his patience near its end.

"That my reputation for eccentricity is by design. Friedrich entrusted me with the final proof should this day ever arise. Proof that will forever silence the Russian Bear...."

※　　※　　※

Karl sat behind the wheel of the midnight-blue Citroen, watching the fourth-floor window of Jarmann's office through a compact pair of Zeiss binoculars from his vantage point across the now busy street. He snatched up the compact cellular phone, punched in a long series of numbers, pressed it to his ear and waited.

It was answered on the first ring. "*Ja.* What is your report?"

"They are inside at this very moment, Comrade General."

"Excellent," Mueller replied. "Make sure no one interferes. The Russian swine may still try to take the old man out, just to play it safe. After Thorley leaves the building, you know what to do?"

Karl's bulldog face creased into a smile. "*Ja,* Comrade General, I know...exactly."

✻ ✻ ✻

Michael stared at the old man's wizened face, trying to discern the slightest hint of guile, but the ancient bloodshot eyes were determined—resolute.

Proof!

The eccentric old bastard had proof!

A look to Erika confirmed the measure of his own excitement. Her eyes glittered with a fierce, almost greedy light. Michael watched, breathless, while Jarmann opened a section of his bookshelves, revealing an expensive state-of-the-art fireproof safe. He then raised a gnarled finger toward the digital keypad and entered a series of numbers, so fast that Michael could only discern the first three. The safe beeped, and a second later the door swung open as if propelled by invisible hands. Jarmann wasted no time reaching in and pulling out a yellowed envelope. He handed it to Michael, who cradled it in his hands as if it were a ticking bomb.

Shaking, he tore open the still-sealed envelope and extracted an equally yellowed sheet of foolscap paper. His heart sank.

"It's in Russian," he said.

Erika held out her hand. "Let me see it."

He handed her the paper, and watched as she read through it, her lips moving slightly as they formed the Russian words. She halted, her head snapping up from the page. "*Mein Gott,* if this is authentic—"

"I assure you, it is, *Fräulein,*" Jarmann said, indignant.

"What does it say?" Michael asked, anxious.

Jarmann took the paper from Erika and gave it a quick glance, then handed it back to Michael. "It is an order to Marshall Ivan Tinenko, commander of Russian forces in Finland in 1941. It was found on his body after a particularly vicious firefight with Friedrich's battalion. It is the express order to liquidate the Royal South Wessex Regiment—with prejudice.... For some reason, the Marshall disobeyed orders by not destroying the letter immediately. Perhaps it was the novelty of having his name on an order signed by Stalin himself."

Michael's disappointment grew. "So what? Everyone knows that Stalin was as much a monster as Hitler. Russia's repudiated the man, and everything he stood for. Why should any of this matter, now?"

Jarmann smiled as a teacher would to a dull child. "Indeed, young man, why should any of this matter, now? It wouldn't, except for one not-so-insignificant detail.... England and Russia had just become allies. *Before* Stalin gave the order."

The room seemed to tilt as Michael reached for the desk to steady himself. "Dear God...." he said.

"You see," Jarmann continued, "alliances were very fluid at that time. The English were secretly helping the Finns fight the Russians, who until June 22, 1941, were allied with Germany. Stalin wiped out the regiment as a warning, as a way to ensure that England would never join with Germany to defeat Russia, as British Fascists and Hitler desired." Jarmann slammed his empty coffee mug onto the credenza. "That Georgian lout even had the nerve to inform Churchill of the massacre via a secret communiqué."

"And we did nothing?" Michael asked, already suspecting the answer.

"Churchill's hands were tied. To expose Stalin for what he was risked splitting the alliance and perhaps ultimately losing the war for the Allies. It was far too great a risk to take for men who were already dead."

"If they already knew, then why send my father at all?"

The old man's expression softened. "The proof, my boy, they wanted the proof the Rainer uncovered...so they could bury it."

Michael stumbled over to the window and stared out into the tiny park the building overlooked. Benches surrounded a tiny fountain, and one lone statue of some forgotten academic stood facing it, covered with pigeon droppings.

They'd sacrificed his father, tossed him to the bloody wolves—for nothing! They'd sent him on a mission when they already knew what had happened, and why. All they'd wanted was an errand boy—an expendable one....

He squeezed his eyes shut, trying to stem the flood of hatred that washed over him. All the venom he'd felt over the years, blind anger against faceless unknown men, now finding its true home with those who now professed to have their country's best interests at heart. They weren't as bad as the monsters who'd pulled the triggers in that distant forest. They were *worse*.

I won't let them get away with it, Father. I promise!

"Will you let us take it?" Erika asked.

Jarmann stared at her with a look that was a curious mixture of suspicion and amusement, then handed Erika the paper.

"I would be very careful with that, my dear. Far too many have died for it already."

Erika nodded and turned to Michael. "Michael? What is it?"

He turned from the window. "Our friends have found us."

Erika and Jarmann rushed to the window and followed Michael's gaze. Down in the park, seated on one of the benches, was a large bullet-headed man staring brazenly up at them, a smile on his face.

Erika grabbed Michael's shoulder. "We must go."

She headed for the door, the two men following.

"There is a fire exit down the hall," Jarmann said. "It will take you to the other side of the building."

Erika started down the hall and Michael hung back a moment,

his eyes meeting Jarmann's. "There's something else, isn't there?"

Jarmann nodded, saddened. "Yes. As far as I know...Friedrich Rainer never had a daughter."

Michael didn't say anything, couldn't even *think* of how to respond to that. Was the old man crazy, after all?

"Michael!" she called. "Come on!"

He turned to go and Jarmann grabbed his arm, his grip like a vise. "Good luck, young man."

He nodded, and the old man released him. Out in the hall, he spotted Erika at the end of the corridor holding open a door marked: *Notfall-Ausgang*—Emergency Exit. He ran to meet her, blood pounding in his ears and a brackish coppery taste in the back of his throat.

They took the stairs two at a time, clattering down the concrete steps without concern for noise or decorum. He prayed the door leading out to the campus wasn't alarmed. If it was, they stood the chance of alerting the hulking presence waiting for them on the park bench.

There was no alarm, just a push-bar and a sign in German about fire drills. They blew through it right into the muzzle of a silenced Makarov pistol.

"Good afternoon, *Fräulein*." Karl said, his acne-pitted face splitting into a knowing leer. "Nice day for a jog, *Ja?*"

Erika glared at him, contempt oozing from every pore. Michael's eyes darted from the gun to Erika and then to their immediate surroundings. Surely someone had to see them. And then he saw the cold calculation in the big German's eyes, and knew that it wouldn't matter if someone had seen them. He would simply kill them and walk away, no doubt to the comfort of some safe house.

"What do you want?" Michael asked.

The big German reached into his pocket and pulled out something that resembled a walkie-talkie, except that it had a keypad, like a phone.

"I have someone who wishes to speak with you, Herr Thorley."

Michael frowned, watching as the German tapped out a number.

"It is Karl. Yes, I have them."

He handed the phone to Michael, who put it to his ear.

"H—hello?"

A momentary burst of static startled him, and then he heard a voice. The accent was also German, but sounded far more cultured.

"Ahh, Michael. At last we meet through the wonders of micro-electronics."

The voice was like warm molasses, caressing his ear with its seductive timbres. He wanted to choke it off with his bare hands.

"Who are you and what the hell do you want?"

"Who I am is unimportant, for the moment. As to what I want, why, the same thing as you...the truth."

"Somehow, after all we've been through, I find that rather hard to swallow."

The voice chuckled. "I can well understand, my young friend. Nevertheless, I must ask your indulgence one last time. You and the young lady will meet me on the last outgoing Ostend-Dover ferry at midnight. You will then hand over the letter Jarmann gave you. Is that understood?"

"What letter?"

"Please do not insult my intelligence," the voice said. "Someone's life depends upon your cooperation, someone very close to you."

Michael heard the phone clunk a couple of times as it was handed over to someone else.

"Hello, Michael."

Her voice was calm, almost normal, as if she'd called to ask about the weather or what he'd planned for dinner. And somehow that made it all the worse.

"Mother! What's going on, what's happening?"

Her tone changed abruptly. "Be quiet, son, and listen.... These men are quite serious. They are very capable of killing me with absolutely no reservations, so you are to do exactly what they ask. Do you have what they want?"

Michael closed his eyes and cursed silently. "Yes," he said finally.

"Good. Then I'll see you tonight, God willing."

He heard the phone being snatched away from her and then the voice returned. "Is everything clear, Michael?"

"Yes, quite. If you harm her, I swear—"

"Now, now, Michael, please don't say anything we shall both regret. Just bring the letter and all will be well, I promise. *Auf wiedersehen.*"

The phone went dead. He handed it back to Karl, who put it away along with his weapon.

"Don't be late," Karl said.

Michael watched him walk away, desiring with every ounce of his being to pounce on the sonofabitch and break his neck. He felt Erika's hand on his arm. She went to embrace him, and he pushed her away. A look of surprise mixed with disappointment flashed across her face, replaced a moment later with one of determination.

"Who was on the phone, Michael. What did he say?"

"I've no idea. But it's someone who knows what we have, what we just received from Jarmann. And whoever the hell it is has kidnapped my mother!" Michael turned and kicked the fire exit door, eliciting a hollow boom. The toe of his shoe left a shallow dent in the metal. He walked to one of the benches and sat down, cradling his head in his hands. "He wants us to meet him on the last ferry from Ostend," he said, continuing. "...or they'll kill her."

"Oh, no.... We can be in Ostend in a few hours. Perhaps we can set a trap?"

"No. No traps. We'll meet them just as they say."

Without another word, he stalked off, leaving Erika to her own thoughts. Which was just as well. Right now, he didn't give a damn what she thought.

32

They reached Ostend by five o'clock that evening, nearly catatonic from exhaustion. Parking in one of the big lots, they reclined the Peugeot's bucket seats and tried to catch up on some sleep. In minutes Erika began snoring softly. For Michael, as bone tired as he felt, the chaos in his mind prevented sleep from overtaking him. Worries about his mother and what might happen at their rendezvous kept his mind chugging along at full tilt. That he would give up the letter he held to save her, there was no doubt whatsoever. And yet, a part of him, a tiny voice in his heart cried out for him to refuse. He understood that part of himself well, the hidden child forever wounded by the loss of his father. It was also the part that wanted to hit back at the men who'd sent him to his death, a blind unquenchable rage. And there was one other thing eating away at his soul: Jarmann's parting words.

"...As far as I know...Friedrich Rainer never had a daughter...."

Erika shifted in her seat, moving closer to him, her scent filling his nostrils.

Who are you, Erika?

He'd asked himself that question a hundred times and none of the answers he'd come up with made any sense. And some of them he'd refused even to contemplate. He found himself growing angry again, yet he couldn't deny that he loved her. And that made the emotional roller coaster ride all-the-more intense.

His eyes grew heavy. Too tired and confused to continue searching for the truth. He welcomed the temporary oblivion of dreamless sleep.

When he awoke, night had fallen and fog had rolled in, thick and white as raw cotton. The streetlights glowed like giant fireflies and the silence was nearly total, save for the punctuation of a fog-horn blatting in the distance. A quick glance at the Peugeot's clock brought him fully awake.

11:40.

Sitting up, he raised the seat back, then shook Erika. She groaned then bolted awake, her eyes wide with sudden terror. "What, what?" she said, breathless.

Michael kept his eyes focused on the ferry, barely discernible through the gloom. "It's almost time. We should be going."

He grabbed for the door and Erika stopped him with a hand on his arm, the warmth of her flesh like a knife in his heart.

"What's the matter, Michael? Ever since we left Bonn, you've been treating me like dirt."

He faced her and saw the pleading in her eyes.

"Nothing's the matter. Let's go."

He climbed out of the car, slammed the door and marched off toward the ferry.

Cursing under her breath, Erika leapt out of the car, leaving the door wide open, and ran after him.

"I deserve better than this!" she said, halting him in his tracks. He whirled, his face twisted in anger.

"*You* deserve better? Piss off! You've lied to me from the very beginning."

"What are you talking about?"

He moved to her, his face inches from hers. "Jarmann told me.... Rainer didn't have a daughter. Never did! So, who the fuck *are* you?"

She began to sob, a flood of tears cascading down her cheeks. For all his anger, he felt a stab of guilt.

"I'm sorry," she cried. "I couldn't tell you...and I wanted to...so much."

She threw herself into his arms and a part of him wanted to return her desperate embrace, to soothe her, to make this nightmare disappear. Instead, he stood there, stock still, his arms at his side. Sensing his reticence, she pulled back and looked up at him.

"I deserve that...I know. I promise you I'll tell you everything. But we haven't time, now. We have to make the ferry. Your mother. I don't want anything to happen to her. Do you believe *that?*"

Strangely enough, he did.

"Yes," he said.

Erika took his hand and they dashed to buy their tickets for the ferry when the Klaxon sounded for final boarding.

They made it aboard only moments before the massive craft pulled away from the dock. They had the lower deck to themselves and the fog, which closed in on them like a giant shroud. The foghorn howled, sounding closer. With a quick turn of his head, Michael surveyed their surroundings, then nodded toward a set of stairs.

"The aft deck is above us. I want you to head for the bridge and tell the captain what's happening. He'll be able to radio ahead."

"I want to stay with you," she said, anxiety creeping into her voice.

"No. I don't know if I should even trust you. But I love you. I must be bloody daft.... Will you do what I ask?"

"Yes."

"You're a love. Now, give me the letter."

She handed him the letter, and Michael kissed her, a quick peck on the forehead. A moment later she disappeared up the stairwell. Michael realized that he was taking a big risk, perhaps a fatal one. If she betrayed him, he would not only lose the letter, but his mother, and his own life, as well. But what other choice did he have?

None.

He waited five minutes then climbed the stairs to the main deck. It appeared to be as deserted as the lower deck. He wondered, for a fleeting horror-filled moment, if perhaps they'd gotten on the wrong ferry. And then a soft feminine voice called from out of the gloom.

"Michael? Have you got the letter?"

He took a step forward, then stopped, unsure from where the voice originated. "Mother? Are you all right?"

"I'm fine, dear."

Four figures loomed out of the fog. He recognized his mother, her face looking haggard and strained. She was flanked by two elderly men, one with a wounded hand and the other holding a silenced pistol. A third man brought up the rear. This one was considerably younger, and had a wary, watchful look about him. He also carried a silenced pistol.

The older man with the gun spoke up. "At last, we meet face to face."

Michael recognized the voice as belonging to the man on the phone. "Will you tell me who you are?"

"But of course, please forgive my lack of manners." He clicked his heels and bowed slightly from the waist. To Michael the old-world gesture would have been comic had the situation been other than it was. "I am Comrade General Werner Mueller, Director of what you call Stasi."

"Why not tell him who you *really* are, *Gruppenführer?*" the wounded man said.

A dark cloud passed over Mueller's face, replaced immediately by an ironic smile. "And this outspoken gentleman is none other than Comrade Pavel Hedeon, head of KGB-Britain." Mueller nodded toward Lillian. "This elegant lady...you already know."

"Let's just cut to it, shall we? You want this letter, why?" Michael asked.

Mueller chuckled. "My, my, such fortitude. Perhaps I have underestimated you, Herr Thorley. I should think my motives would be obvious. This letter will destroy the Bolsheviks. It may not happen immediately, but alliances will fall, and so then the Motherland. Germany will reunite, and our cause will be resurrected."

"Nazi swine! Tell him the truth!" Hedeon screamed.

"The truth? Yes, let us do that. But first, the letter...."

Michael clutched the letter to his chest involuntarily, prompting Mueller to place the gun to Lillian's head.

"The letter. Or I shall kill her.... Then again, perhaps you will not mind if I end the life of a Russian agent."

"What!"

Like so many times in the past few days, Michael felt the world he knew shifting beneath his feet. He turned to his mother and saw the despair in her eyes. His heart sank.

"I'm so sorry, Michael.... For everything."

Michael crumpled the letter in his hands, his knuckles turning white.

"Her real name is Svetlana Dubrova. She married your father as a cover. Her mission was to remain in place until needed. She's lived a lie for over forty years, Michael.... And, so have you.... Now, give me the letter, and I will let her live."

❋ ❋ ❋

Feliks Danya watched the unfolding tableau from the rear deck of the lounge one level above the aft deck. He could feel the situation spinning out of control, which meant it would have to be dealt with drastically. Coughing into his fist, he turned to the man next to him, a tall, stolid Georgian named Tadiz, and nodded. Tadiz acknowledged the signal with a nod of his own, then bent down to an open Haliburton case and began assembling the Dragunov sniper rifle.

❋ ❋ ❋

Michael's eyes blazed with anger. "What did you mean by saying that I've lived a lie, too?"

Mueller grinned and turned to Hedeon. "Why don't you tell him, Pavel? You want the truth revealed so much, tell him yourself...." He grabbed the other man roughly by the hair. "Tell him!"

The look in Hedeon's eyes could only be called murderous, as if any moment he might throw caution to the wind and wrap his bearlike hands around the German's neck and squeeze the life out of him. He turned to Michael, his expression softening.

"You were never to know, Michael. It was supposed to remain a secret between your mother and I...."

It all came clear to Michael in an instant.

"No! It's a lie," he screamed, "a goddamned lie!"

He turned to Lillian, who regarded him with an expression he could only describe as triumphant.

"It *is* a lie, Michael," she said, her eyes shining with affection. "I loved your father, but I also loved Pavel. Telling him that you were his son was the only way I could stay in Britain once the war had ended.... You've only to look in the mirror to see the truth, dear... something Pavel was always too blind to see."

Hedeon's face darkened with anger.

"Harlot!" he shouted, moving to strike her.

Franz grabbed his arm and twisted it up behind his back, eliciting a shriek of agony from the older man.

Michael ignored the scuffle, his attention riveted on Mueller.

"What about the girl, Mueller? Both you and I know she's not Rainer's daughter.... Who the hell is she?"

"You are right about that, my boy," he said, laughing. "She is not Rainer's daughter.... She is mine. Mallory?"

Erika walked out from the shadows behind her father, joining him. Michael stared daggers at her. To her credit, she met his hateful glare with a level gaze of her own.

Mueller gave her an affectionate pat, which she shrugged off. He ignored it. "Please go to Michael and take the letter from him, my dear."

❋ ❋ ❋

Danya sensed his moment approaching and tapped Tadiz, who pulled back the bolt and let it slide back, seating a round into the chamber of the automatic rifle. Kneeling, the Georgian brought the rifle up to his cheek and gazed through the scope. Michael's head bobbed in the crosshairs, then he shifted it over to Werner Mueller.

His fingers tightened on the trigger.

And he waited....

❋ ❋ ❋

Erika moved forward as if her feet were weighed down with lead. Michael watched her, his mind warring with itself. He *wanted* to hate her for lying to him, for leading him on by the nose, and most of all... for stealing his heart. Yet he realized he *couldn't* hate her, and that made it all the worse.

She halted a few feet in front of him, her eyes brimming. "I'm sorry, Michael, I would have told you. I didn't mean for it to come to this."

She extended her hand, reaching for the envelope. Michael hesitated a moment, then looked to his mother, who nodded almost imperceptibly.

To hell with it. It's not bloody worth it.

Michael went to place the envelope into Erika's outstretched hand. Instead of taking it, she grasped his hand, her cool flesh a galvanic shock against his own. His breath caught in his throat when he met her gaze. Her eyes spoke the true depth of her love for him; her mouth silently formed the words. He nodded and let the envelope go, watching as Erika turned to face her father, a look of defiance on her face.

When she didn't move, Mueller brought the barrel of his pistol up and aimed it at his daughter's chest. "Your mother was a sentimentalist, too. It was one of the reasons I left her. Bring me the letter, Mallory. Remember where your loyalties lie."

"Give it to him, Erika, please," Michael said, his grip tightening on her shoulders.

"No, I won't be his little puppet anymore."

Mueller cocked the hammer of his pistol. It sounded like the crack of a whip.

❈ ❈ ❈

Tadiz held his breath, his finger hovering over the trigger.

Now! Get the son of a whore, now!

Smiling, he pulled the trigger.

❈ ❈ ❈

The shot sounded like a cannon's roar, mixing with Erika's scream as a high-powered bullet ripped through her upper chest, propelling her into Michael's arms. Grappling with her leaden form, he lowered her to the deck. She gazed up at him with a pleading look that sent fear knifing into his heart.

The envelope spun off across the deck, coming to rest near the railing. One good gust of wind would consign it to a watery oblivion.

"NO!" Mueller screamed.

With a suddenness of a jungle cat, Hedeon made his move, bringing his ham-like fist smashing down onto Mueller's arm. The German cried out and let go of the gun, which clattered to the deck. Fumbling with his own gun, Franz attempted to intervene and was rewarded by another shot ringing out of the darkness. The bullet tore off half of his head.

Hedeon used the moment to go for the pistol, beating Mueller to it by mere inches. Snatching it up, he placed the barrel against Mueller's stomach and pulled the trigger.

"Father!" Erika tried to stand up.

Mueller groaned and collapsed, bright arterial blood pumping from his wound. Hedeon drew himself to his full height, a look of triumph spreading across his face. Behind him, Michael saw two men standing in the shadows, one of them clutching a rifle in his hands.

"It looks as if the tables have turned, my boy," Hedeon said. He then turned to Lillian, who stood rooted to the deck, a look of horror on her face. "I have long suspected you, my love," he continued. "And you are right—I refused to see the truth of it...of everything. It is an unfortunate failing we Russians have always had to live with. But you, Ninotchka, have committed the unpardonable sin.... You have betrayed Russia."

A look of sadness crept across the Russian's craggy face when he turned the gun on Lillian. For one breathless moment, it looked as if he might pull the trigger. Instead, he tossed the pistol straight up into the air, caught it by the barrel then offered it to her, grip first. He nodded toward Michael and Erika.

"Take it. Kill them both. Prove that you still love the Motherland."

By way of emphasis, the man with the Dragunov turned its ugly barrel toward her.

Lillian stared back at him; her eyes filled with tears. "Don't make me do this, Pavel," Lillian cried. "If you ever loved me, don't make me do this!"

Hedeon remained silent, the lines of his face set in stone.

With an excruciating effort of will, Lillian took the hateful pistol in her trembling hand, letting the barrel point toward the deck.

"Prove you love your country above all, Ninotchka," Hedeon repeated. "KILL THEM!"

Lillian flinched, and Michael watched while she slowly raised the pistol. At that moment, all he could see was the haunted look in her eyes and that dark black hole at the end of the barrel. But what frightened him more than anything was that her hand had stopped trembling; it was rock steady.

And then, before anyone could react, Lillian whirled and fired toward the man with the rifle, and then the taller one next to him. Both men crumpled to the deck unmoving. She turned the gun on Hedeon, who was stunned into immobility.

"Goodbye, Pavel."

The gun in her hand roared again and Hedeon dropped like a stone, a bullet through his forehead. She moved quickly to the railing, picked up the envelope and went to her son. Bending down, she placed a hand on Erika's neck, then nodded. "It's not too bad, but she needs care. I'll get the captain."

She stood and moved toward the bridge.

"Mother?"

Lillian stopped and turned, a quizzical look on her face.

"Thank you."

The puzzled look turned into a sad smile. "I've a great deal to make up for, dear. More than I can ever hope to in one lifetime, anyway...."

Michael glanced out in the direction of the British coastline. "We'll be landing in a couple of hours. We'd better radio the authorities."

"After all this commotion, I should think we can count on quite a welcoming committee."

"No doubt. But I was thinking of the BBC."

Lillian frowned.

"What on earth for?"

The ghost of a smile played across Michael's lips. "Insurance," he replied.

※   ※   ※

Brady watched from his perch above the lounge as the elderly woman disappeared into the belly of the ship, heading for the bridge. He had to admire the old girl—she was one tough bird. Still, what she had done had changed everything. Now that the Russians were dead, MacKinnon's plans lay in ruins and exposure for the British was imminent.

It was time to play his own hand with MacKinnon.

While the events had unfolded before him on the deck below, a plan had blossomed in his mind, one that would satisfy the Home Secretary and get him off the hook for good. Smiling, he could already feel the old sod beckoning.

I'll not be gone much longer, he thought.

Snapping out of his daydream, he returned his attention to Michael, who sat comforting the wounded German woman. It would be *so* easy. Walk up and pull his Walther and....

He shook his head and left the gun stuck in his shoulder holster. He'd always followed orders without question; maybe it was time to start following his conscience. Maybe then the ghost of the boy's father would stop haunting him. The crooked grin returned.

"It's time we made our peace, Mikey," he said. "High time."

Moving to the starboard side of the ferry, Brady walked toward the bow and an uncertain future.

33

Sir Robert Sandon's blood pressure rose when he caught sight of the knot of official vehicles clogging the dock area immediately surrounding the Ostend-Dover Ferry, their flashing lights making for a colorful mélange. The media were out in force, as well, their reporters and cameras all agog at the spectacle before them.

A flock of ambulances stood by and the attendants were already busy bearing stretchers off the boat, their cargoes covered with white sheets. Sir Robert counted six in all. On the last one, however, he caught sight of the girl, Mueller's daughter, Erika, her face deathly white from blood loss. But she was still alive.

Pity.

At least her father was out of the way. At least that was what the report said.

"Shall we move in, Sir Robert?" the young MI6 agent standing at his side asked, his voice taut with eagerness.

They stood far back from the action, partially hidden by their vehicles. Sir Robert shook his head.

"Not until young Thorley appears. If the bloody vampires from the BBC insist on a show, we'll give them one. I want the whole of Britain to see him hauled away in handcuffs. Is that clear?"

The young agent nodded. The five others with him wore the

same grave expression. There was a sudden rise in the level of sound as the reporters reacted. More lights snapped on and were trained on the ferry's gangway. Thorley and his mother appeared, hesitating in the glare of the spotlights.

Sir Robert turned to his retinue of agents. "Right, let's move!"

As one, the seven men charged across the docks, the agents forming a protective cordon around their boss. They shoved through the phalanx of reporters and camera crew and met Michael and his mother when they reached the bottom of the gangway.

Sir Robert grabbed Michael by the arm, his voice rising to be heard above the crowd. "Michael Thorley? I hereby arrest you in the name of the Queen. You will—"

And then it all went wrong.

The reporters closed in en masse, their microphones thrust into his face. One of them, an over-made-up harpy with bleached hair and blood-red mouth, shouted a question: "Sir Robert? We've just been told of a letter sent by Stalin ordering the massacre of a British regiment during the last war, and that our government has known and condoned it all along. Do you have any comment?"

Ignoring the bitch, he stared at young Thorley and saw the smug smile on his face, the look of triumph—and contempt. He also saw the letter clutched in his right hand.

So bloody close. He'd come so close to keeping the affair quiet, as it was meant to be. Now, it was all going to the devil.

Sir Robert turned to the female reporter, who looked at him with her own expression of smug assurance.

"I have nothing to say," he said.

He turned and pushed his way through his own agents and stalked off toward his waiting Rolls. He reached the car, and climbed inside, blinking back tears of rage. "Bloody hell."

D-NOTICE

A moment later the Rolls' headlights snapped on and the stately car moved off, leaving the media circus far behind.

THE SON:
1989

34

He was out of whiskey again. He'd looked through every room in the house, all thirty of them, and there was nothing. Not a blasted drop. He'd gone through a whole case of the single malt given him four years ago, when he'd still enjoyed the favors and influences of his post. Now, all that was left was some bloody cooking sherry in the pantry, and some dusty memories to go along with the dusty house.

Blast.

The sherry would have to do.

Easing himself off the bed, he ignored the overflowing ashtray, dirty dishes, tangled bedclothes and stumbled out of the room and down the hall to the main staircase.

Reaching the ground floor, Sir Robert Sandon cursed when his bare foot slipped on the polished parquet flooring. Had to fire the bloody housekeeper again. None of these people knew how to wax a floor anymore. Like to break his goddamn neck.

Passing through the foyer, he made his way into the kitchen, noting the previous night's bottle—the last of that heavenly Scotch—still stood on the draining board—dry as an Arabian desert.

Inside the pantry, his nose was assaulted by the various smells: onions, garlic cloves, and a dizzying array of spices. He found the single bottle of sherry on the third shelf nearly hidden by a sack of rotting potatoes and covered by a thin layer of dust. It would be just enough to last him until the off-license store opened. That is, if they would still take his bloody checks.

He left the pantry with the bottle cradled in his arms and headed for the library. Bright afternoon light streamed through the tall leaded-glass window and, growling with anger, Sir Robert snapped the shutters closed, plunging the room into a pleasant gloom. That was better, he thought. He'd send that housekeeper packing as soon as she came in on Monday, that is if she hadn't quit. The ungrateful wench!

He grabbed the letter opener and used it to peel back the black foil around the cap, then twisted it off and poured the pale brown liquid into a dusty glass that sat on the stained blotter atop his desk. Nearly filling it, he picked it up in his trembling hand and took a long gulp, grimacing as the full flavor of the cheap wine muscled its way down his ravaged throat, leaving a burning trail behind. Coughing, he refilled it and drank again, finally feeling his nerves steady and his vision clear.

That was when he saw the man seated in the brocaded wingback chair staring at him from the shadows near the empty bookshelves. That was when his guts turned to jelly.

It was him.

He could tell by the Western boots, the cold eyes, and the cruel, arrogant smile.

"Well, well, Sir Robert, me boyo, we meet again," Corwin Brady said, the smile widening. "And it's been far too long, I might add, far too long...."

❋   ❋   ❋

A fire blazed in the grate, keeping the temperature inside Woodhaven to a toasty seventy-eight degrees, enough to keep out the November chill in the air. Michael watched the flames dance and listened while

Lillian puttered in the kitchen readying their supper. He checked his watch for the umpteenth time.

What was keeping them?

Restless, he picked up the telly's remote and snapped it on, flipping the channels until he came to the BBC news. As always, Gordon Honeycombe was reading, his jowly face the epitome of trust and assurance. Chroma-keyed behind him played scenes of Germans celebrating wildly, their faces drunk with freedom and cheap liquor.

"...In an ironic twist of fate, coinciding with the anniversaries of Adolf Hitler's 'Beer Hall Putsch,' and the infamous 'Night of Broken Glass,' a hated symbol of Communist rule has finally met its demise.... The Berlin Wall has fallen..."

The shot behind Honeycombe cut to a scene showing a large section of the wall tumbling to earth, both East and West Germans rejoicing, their ecstatic voices rising to a frenzied pitch.

"...Crowds have been gathering for days in anticipation of this momentous event. And with typical Teutonic precision, the first monolithic slice of that reviled edifice came down at precisely noon Berlin time, heralding the long-awaited end of the Cold War." Honeycombe paused, looking down at his script. "Now, with the Soviet Union itself looming ever closer to final collapse, and with its satellite nations clamoring ceaselessly for democratic reform, it is only fitting that the beleaguered peoples of the once mighty German Democratic Republic begin the long process of reunification with their brothers and sisters in the west, on what has—until now—been a dark date in German history...."

Behind him, Michael heard the door open.

"We're home!" Erika cried, her arms laden with packages from the grocers. Michael felt a thrill go through him as it did every time he saw her. Her wound from the incident on the ferry five years before had healed with few ill effects, and though her father had perished, she seemed less and less affected by the tragedy.

"Need any help?" Michael called.

Erika smiled, catching sight of her husband. "Just with your son," she said.

And then a tiny towheaded whirlwind burst into the room running straight for him. "Daddy! Daddy! Daddy!"

Michael swept the little boy up into his arms and swung him around. Two-year-old Michael Thorley III laughed and screamed with delight.

"What on earth is going on out here?" Lillian asked, bustling out of the kitchen, carrying a tray piled high with sliced beef. She spotted Michael and her grandson and shook her head in mock dismay. "Michael, you're going to spoil that child."

"And I wouldn't have it any other way, mother," he said, lifting the giggling boy onto his shoulders.

Lillian chuckled and carried the plate of meat over to the dining area. The table was festooned with a lace tablecloth and Lillian's best china and silverware, along with half a dozen covered dishes.

"Dinner's on," she said.

Michael carried his son over to a highchair and belted the boy in, while Erika joined him at the table. She kissed him and looked toward the television. "It's begun."

Michael nodded.

"You'll be able to visit your home again, soon."

"My home is here," she said, a wistful look in her eyes.

"Now, now, now! I'll not be having any long faces," Lillian said, pouring wine into their glasses. She handed one to Michael, then to Erika, and then raised her own. "To the future."

Michael raised his glass and felt Erika grasp his other hand. Yes,

Michael thought, to the future. Now that he'd made peace with the past, the future was just fine with him....

❋　❋　❋

"...In other news, Sir Robert Sandon, former head of MI6 was found dead in his Surrey home, yesterday, an apparent suicide. Home Secretary Roger MacKinnon issued a statement that while he is saddened by the news, he feels that it has little relation to the infamous Stalin Order Scandal of 1984, as some are speculating..."

The chroma-key behind Honeycombe changed to footage of Roger MacKinnon being hounded by reporters.

"...When asked if the order has had any measurable effects on current world events, MacKinnon cut the interview short with a curt, 'No comment...'"

Honeycombe arched his eyebrows, while the Teleprompter caught up with him.

"...In a moment, after a brief word, we shall return with the weather for the coming week and the garden report...."

Other Books by Bill Walker

Titanic 2012

A Note from an Old Acquaintance

Abe Lincoln: Public Enemy No. 1

Abe Lincoln On Acid

STALAG

Starring... John Dillinger

ABOUT THE AUTHOR

Bill Walker is a graphic designer specializing in book and dust jacket design who has worked on projects by Ray Bradbury, Richard Matheson, Dean Koontz and Stephen King. Between his design work and his writing, he spends his spare time reading voraciously and playing very loud guitar, much to the chagrin of his lovely wife and two sons. Bill makes his home in Los Angeles.

www.ingramcontent.com/pod-product-compliance
Lightning Source LLC
Chambersburg PA
CBHW030832110726
47900CB00006B/1860